# A ROGUE TO RUIN

DARCY BURKE

DARCY BURKE PUBLISHING

**A Rogue to Ruin**



ISBN: 9781637260012



Book design: © Darcy Burke.
Book Cover Design © The Midnight Muse.
Cover image © Period Images.
Darcy Burke Font Design © Carrie Divine/Seductive Designs
Editing: Linda Ingmanson.



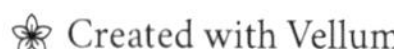
Created with Vellum

# A ROGUE TO RUIN

**The Pretenders**

Set in the world of The Untouchables, indulge in the saga of a trio of siblings who excel at being something they're not. Can a dauntless Bow Street Runner, a devastated viscount, and a disillusioned Society miss unravel their secrets?

**A Rogue to Ruin**

Anne Pemberton was one of the Season's most popular young misses until her betrothed was arrested for extortion at their wedding. Now a social pariah, she can't help but think back to the dashing gentleman she met before the Season started. Though they spent several afternoons exploring East London together, they never disclosed their names. They did, however, share a kiss, and Anne can't forget it—or him.

Former thief Rafe Blackwell is now a respectable gentleman with one goal: to take down the man who murdered his parents. Reunited with Anne, their attraction still blazes strong, and he can't let her get too close, for his heart is forever cold and his mission too desperate. But when Anne seeks to save him—both emotionally and physically—he'll have to embrace the darkness or risk losing the only light he's ever known.

Want to share your love of my books with like-minded readers? Want to hang with me and get inside scoop? Then don't miss my exclusive Facebook groups!

Darcy's Duchesses for historical readers
Burke's Book Lovers for contemporary readers

# PROLOGUE

*Late February 1819*
*London*

Scandal had nothing to do with following the rules and everything to do with getting caught. This was the code by which Anne Pemberton lived and the rationale she used to spend two hours every week tucked into a corner at Hatchard's with a veil over her face while her "chaperone" was elsewhere.

Where that was, Anne never asked, nor did she want to know. She certainly wasn't going to contribute to her godfather's daughter—her godsister?—getting caught.

Anne also didn't care. Not when it allowed her a reprieve from the demands of her parents and an escape into another world. Not the bookstore, but the books themselves. Though she was a fast reader, she wasn't able to finish a story in one sitting. Perhaps she ought to stretch her visits to three hours. Would Deborah mind?

Distracted briefly from the book resting on her

lap and tucked beneath her long veil, Anne refocused her energy. *The Fast of St. Magdalen* was not as enthralling as she'd hoped, which was unfortunate since *The Hungarian Brothers* was one of her most favorite stories.

"Back again, eh?"

The masculine voice invaded Anne's mind and space. She closed the book on her forefinger and turned her head slightly toward whomever had interrupted her.

There were two young men, so she didn't know which had spoken. Both were of average height and girth, dressed in rather average costumes, and in possession of utterly…average features. Though she supposed the one on the right had a rather long nose.

Anne chose to ignore them. Turning her head back, she reopened her book and found her place once more.

One of them coughed. Then they moved. Their legs were now visible beyond her book. Though Anne had taken care to angle her chair somewhat toward the corner, she'd stopped short of sitting actually *in* the corner for fear that would look bizarre and potentially invite notice when she was doing everything in her ability to escape it.

"What are you hiding beneath your veil?" one of them asked.

Anne looked up from the book and scowled at them, though they wouldn't be able to see her expression. "A hideous visage," she snapped. "Now, if you'll be on your way, I prefer my solitude."

"Hideous?" Long-nose glanced askance at his friend. "Sounds intriguing. I think we should have a look."

"And I think you should be on your way." The suggestion, low and deceptively pleasant, came from a third man. His tone was deceptive because the look in his eyes was unmistakably malevolent —even Anne could see it through the gauze of her veil.

She shivered.

Regular-nose pivoted and looked at the new man, who was incredibly tall and impeccably dressed. "Just who are you, her father?"

"Who I am is of no concern to you, and neither is this woman. Move along before I'm forced to help you do so." He took a step toward the younger men.

Whether it was due to his imposing height or his menacing glare or his ominous tone or the nasty scar across his lower lip and chin that marred his otherwise strikingly handsome face, the men abruptly walked away.

Anne exhaled. "Thank you." She eyed him warily. "What do you want?"

"Nothing. It seemed they were bothering you. I only sought to provide assistance."

True relief made her breathe even easier. "I appreciate that. I believed a corner at Hatchard's to be a safe place to avoid interruption."

"Particularly when you've angled yourself away from everyone and you're wearing a veil." The edge of his mouth ticked up, but only briefly. So quickly, in fact, that she wondered if she'd been mistaken. "Would you like me to remain? I won't disturb you."

"Are you offering to be my bodyguard?" Anne turned so she faced him.

"I suppose I am."

"I should decline, but if you have a book to read..." She inclined her head toward the one in his hand. "You're welcome to join me. Is there another chair?" She looked about.

"I'll fetch one." He returned a few moments later, hefting a chair by the back with one hand. Setting it near hers so that he mostly blocked her from the rest of the room, he sat down.

Not only was he tall, but he was muscular in a thoroughly masculine way that differed from most men she'd met. Not that she'd met terribly many as of yet. Her Season was just getting under way.

Through her veil, she made out the aquiline planes of his face, the piercing blue of his eyes, and the lush sweep of his lips. The lower one was bisected by a scar that cut down into his chin. It was pale, indicating the injury had occurred some time ago.

"That must have hurt," she said without thinking. "My apologies. I shouldn't have said that."

He touched his mouth and chin, his gloved finger sweeping down over the scar. "This? Yes. But it happened a lifetime ago."

A lifetime was a very long measure. But she suspected he was quite a bit older than her twenty-two years. He was at least thirty, if not older. Aside from his appearance, he carried a weight and…almost weariness about him that suggested lived experience. Anne possessed none of those things.

He opened his book. Apparently, they were just going to read. And why wouldn't they? That was what she'd come to do, and she'd invited him to join her. Except now that he was here, she was consumed with curiosity and something more visceral. It was as if she couldn't look away from him.

"Are you going to read?" he asked, his deep voice settling into her with a delicious comfort that was akin to burrowing into a warm, soft bed.

"Yes." She tipped her gaze back to her book and tried to find her place. Eventually, she got there; however as she listened to him turn one page and then two, she realized she wasn't reading but just staring at the words.

And stealing covert glances in his direction.

This went on for some time. Anne began to turn pages, but she still wasn't reading them. She wanted to talk to him, but every time she started to, she pressed her lips together.

"You aren't reading, are you?" He didn't look up from his book.

"How could you tell?"

"You just turned three pages in such rapid succession that I must question the speed at which you can read. Especially since prior to that, you were hardly turning pages at all."

Anne smiled beneath her veil. He'd been paying as much attention to her as she was to him. "I'd rather talk to you. Do you come here to read often? Most people come to purchase a book—or books—and leave."

"That is what I typically do, yes," he said rather drily. "You come here to read, however?"

"Every week. Or at least, every week since I arrived in London a month ago."

"You're here for the Season?"

"I am. Are you?"

"I live here. All the time."

"Do you like it? I find London exciting and wonderful—not that I've been allowed to see much of it." She knew she sounded wistful and perhaps disgruntled.

"What would you like to see?"

It seemed a genuine question. Nevertheless, she asked, "You truly want to know?"

"I do."

Anne considered what to reveal and ultimately decided to be honest. If he judged her poorly, so be it. "Covent Garden. I love to watch people, and it sounds like a fascinating place to do so."

He tipped his head to the side, his eyes narrowing slightly. "You are here for the Season and your costume is of high quality, so you must be a Society miss. You're wearing a veil, the reason for which is apparently due to some hideousness. However, if you are here for the Season, I can't imagine there's anything hideous about you."

There was no stopping the blush that rushed to Anne's face, but he couldn't see it anyway.

"Yet you are hiding beneath a veil by yourself—apparently every week—at Hatchard's. Where is your chaperone?"

"I don't need one." She leaned toward him and lowered her voice. "You see, I've a bodyguard instead."

His lips spread slowly into a wide grin. "You've a bit of sauce," he whispered. "I like that."

Anne's breath caught as she stared into his eyes. He looked back at her, but with the veil between them, it wasn't the same. "What about you? You are also finely dressed. Have I netted an earl as my bodyguard?"

His gaze was unwavering as his smile faded. "You have not." There was an edge to his answer that sent a shiver down her spine. "I think perhaps we should remain anonymous—since you are expending such effort to hide your identity."

"People frown on Society misses who don't have chaperones and only bodyguards."

"They do. Your effort is commendable. You will be back here next week, then?"

"I shall."

"Wear your simplest gown. We'll go to Covent Garden."

"I only have two hours." Anne didn't want to

explain further. She liked the idea of anonymity almost as much as she liked the idea of him taking her to Covent Garden. A forbidden excitement embraced her.

"It will be a swift tour, then," he said. "But I promise it will be enjoyable."

Of that, Anne had no doubt.

*One week later…*

After meeting at Hatchard's, Lord Bodyguard—which was the name Anne had given the gentleman—escorted her into his cabriolet and drove them to Covent Garden. Rather, near to Covent Garden, since they left the vehicle in the charge of Lord Bodyguard's tiger while they made their way to the square.

"I think I was right to call you Lord Bodyguard," Anne said as she took his arm.

He turned his head, his brows elevating in surprise. "*Lord* Bodyguard?"

She arched a shoulder. "You seem wealthy."

"Not all nobles are wealthy," he said with a slight laugh. "And not all wealthy men are noble."

"You're also imposing." And intelligent and witty.

"Not all nobles are imposing." The disdain in his tone spoke volumes. "I told you I wasn't an earl."

She waved her hand before he could respond. "I don't care. You're firmly Lord Bodyguard in my mind."

He flashed a brief smile. "Then I shall be Lord Bodyguard."

"What do you call me?"

"I don't."

Anne felt a prick of disappointment.

"What *should* I call you?" he asked as they walked into the square.

Her attention was instantly drawn to the people bustling about, the booths and wagons selling produce, food, and goods, the façade of St. Paul's Church. They were utterly quiet as he squired her around the square. She took in every sight and sound, but by the time they reached St. Paul's, she was beyond weary of her veil.

Pushing the gauze up, she flipped it back over her the brim of her hat and exhaled. "Much better."

"Much."

Anne turned her head to see him staring at her, his gaze shining with appreciation. She couldn't look away. His eyes, a brilliant blue, were the most unusual she'd ever beheld. There was a bright orange mark in the right one, as if there was a fire burning within him that couldn't be contained.

"Miss Dazzling," he said softly, answering the question he'd posed several minutes before.

*Dazzling.* She'd been called beautiful, charming, graceful, but never dazzling.

"I think I'd better be Missus. For appearances' sake."

He smiled. "To be clear, I won't be calling you that out loud."

Just in his mind, as she called him Lord Bodyguard in hers. She tightened her hold on his arm. "What shall we do?"

"Finish exploring the square, and then I'm taking you for oysters."

Anne had heard from her older sister that some

men ate oysters daily to support their reputation as lotharios. She looked at him askance as they continued their circuit. "Why oysters?"

"Because that's what the restaurant is known for. Have you had them?"

"I have not. I must admit they look rather disgusting."

He paused and turned to look at her. "Do you trust me?"

She pressed her fingertips into his sleeve. "I do."

~

*Two weeks later...*

"What manner of sea delicacy do you have in store for me today?" Anne asked as they walked along bustling Paternoster Row near St. Paul's Cathedral. Booksellers and publishers lined the street. "I do hope it's better than last week's caviar,"

Lord Bodyguard sent her a warm, teasing smile. "You liked the oysters on our first excursion."

She squeezed his arm. "I did, but the caviar in Cheapside last week was not to my taste." She pulled a face. The rest of the afternoon had been wonderful. Cheapside was a bustling area with all manner of shops and so many people. Anne could have gleefully gone there again this week.

Before she'd met Lord Bodyguard, she'd looked forward to her quiet reading time at Hatchard's. But the time she spent with him was far more thrilling. This wasn't just the highlight of her week. Recalling their afternoons together and anticipating their next adventure had come to consume almost every one of her thoughts.

With each meeting, they revealed more of themselves, but not too much. While she still didn't know his name, she knew he loved books and was building a library in his new house, did not like to ride, which had shocked her, and that oysters were among his favorite things to eat. She'd been surprised to find she didn't hate them, but that was perchance because of how much fun she'd had with him. Learning to suck the oyster out of the shell had taken effort and patience, and the process had come with a great deal of laughter, as well as a thrilling sense of awareness. Just recalling the way Lord Bodyguard had watched her, his lids heavy and his eyes dark, made her shiver.

Another gentleman waved at Lord Bodyguard from one of the publishing houses they passed. They'd already stopped to speak with two booksellers.

"You spend a good portion of time on this street," she remarked. "Your love of books is perhaps greater than you let on."

At odds with his strong, confident personality, he gave her a sheepish look that she found incredibly endearing. "Guilty. I have endeavored to become familiar with as many booksellers and publishers as possible."

"For your library?"

He nodded. "I will have new literary works before anyone else in London."

"My goodness, that's exciting, isn't it? Is your goal driven by your love of books or the desire to be first?"

He let out a sharp laugh. "You've a keen skill of observation. How did you realize I'm competitive?"

She shrugged. "I didn't. But now I'm very curious."

"I've had to work very hard to achieve my place in this world," he said softly.

Before she could ask why that was, he gestured toward the Chapter Coffee House. "Shall we stop in for a coffee?"

"I've never been to a coffee house. How can I refuse?" She pulled on his arm, drawing him to stop. The pavement was only wide enough for two people to walk abreast, and another gentleman walked toward them.

Lord Bodyguard edged closer to her to give the man more room. Consequently, they stood chest to chest. She looked up into his captivating gaze, and her breath caught.

His other hand gently clasped her hip, holding her as the man moved past them. Lord Bodyguard did not immediately back away, nor did she want him to. Indeed, she could have stood like that all afternoon. It was as if the world had been shuttered out, leaving the two of them alone in this riveting proximity.

"Thank you," she said softly. "For taking me places I could only imagine."

"It's my pleasure." He took his hand from her hip, but then clasped her fingers and brought them to his lips. His eyes never left hers as he pressed a kiss to the back of her glove.

Anne shivered. Not with cold or dread, but with something she'd never felt before—desire. She'd never been kissed, and she wanted Lord Bodyguard to be the first.

They continued to the coffee house, moving more closely together than they had before. He escorted her inside, where they found a table in the back corner. He always sought to keep them away from the center of attention, which she appreciated. It was almost impossible that anyone in this area would recognize her, especially since she was new to town, but it was wise to be careful.

"This is also an inn," he said as he settled her into a chair before taking the one next to her. He looked toward the door, while she was angled toward the wall, which kept her face averted from the main part of the common room. "Writers from out of town stay here when they come to London."

"You know Paternoster Row *very* well."

"I admit I love it. The last day of the month is Magazine Day. That's when periodicals go on sale, and it draws quite a crowd. For someone who likes to watch people, you'd enjoy it."

"Then I will make a point of returning at the end of the month. Too bad it's not a Thursday afternoon."

"I could still bring you. Or meet you here. Actually, if you come, you should dress like a man. Then you'd blend right in. There are far more men on this street than women, so you tend to stand out."

The idea excited Anne. But where would she get a set of men's clothing? "Could I pass for a gentleman?"

He eyed her carefully, his gaze moving down over her. He tipped his head to see around the corner of the table. "It would take some effort, but given your petite size, you could probably pass for a boy. If you bound your, ah, chest." His gaze jerked to hers, his eyes widening slightly. He abruptly stood. "I'll fetch coffee."

Anne watched him as he went to the counter. He was always superbly dressed, from his tall ebony hat to his crisp white cravat to the molded fit of his dark brown pantaloons tucked into his black Wellington boots. His blue wool coat was expertly tailored, hugging the muscles of his shoulders and arms. Seeing him never failed to make her heart skip or her breath catch. Even now, just watching him, she felt a rush of excitement, of anticipation.

He returned with two cups of coffee and set them on the table. Retaking his chair, he offered her a slight smile. "I must apologize for my comment before."

Anne tried to think of what he'd said—her brain had become quite transfixed on him. "Oh, about my chest?" She glanced down at herself, then looked at him and realized he'd followed her gaze.

He snapped his attention from her to the coffee. "I asked for a weak brew for your first taste. Coffee can be quite strong."

She found his awkwardness sweet. "You didn't have to apologize."

"I shouldn't have said something so…intimate." One of his blond brows arched into a sharp peak. "Perhaps we've become too familiar."

"I don't think so." She put her hand on his arm. He looked down at where she touched him, then into her eyes. The moment stretched until she finally said, "Now, show me how to drink coffee."

Withdrawing her hand from his arm, she tamped down the desire that was swirling within her once more. She reached for her cup.

"Do you really need me to show you?" he asked wryly.

"I suppose not." Lifting the vessel, she put her lips to the edge and carefully sampled the dark brew. An intense bitterness snapped across her tongue. She set the cup down rather hard, nearly sloshing coffee over the rim. It was a bit of a struggle to swallow it down. She ran her tongue along the roof of her mouth and backs of her teeth. "That's weak?"

He lifted her cup and sniffed. "Yes." Handing her his cup, he said, "Smell this and tell me what you think."

She inhaled and immediately turned her head to cough and sputter. "Fine, mine's weak."

Suppressing a grin, he sipped his coffee before returning his cup to the table. "It's somewhat of an acquired taste."

She wouldn't have cared if he'd given her dirt in a cup. Nothing could detract from their time together. "I want to come to Magazine Day," she said. "I'll make the necessary plans for a man's costume and a reason to go out." She'd have to ask her chaperone—her godfather's daughter—if they could move their appointment that week from Thursday to Wednesday.

"You're certain?"

"Absolutely."

The orange mark in his eye seemed to glow brighter as he stared at her. His gaze suddenly shifted over her shoulder. His jaw tightened, and an almost imperceptible shadow fell over his features.

He abruptly stood. "Come." Moving behind her chair, he helped her rise.

"What about our coffee?"

"I know you don't really want it," he whispered next to her ear, eliciting another shiver along her spine.

He slid his arm around her waist and guided her toward the back of the common room. They moved through a doorway into a narrow corridor. He stepped in front of her and took her hand.

A prick of alarm shot through her. "Where are we going?"

He looked back over his shoulder and past her. "Someone I don't want to see came into the shop. We'll leave through the back." He continued forward, passing closed doors on either side.

"You seem to know where you're going," she said.

"I'm good at pretending."

His words made her stop. She tugged on his hand. "Is that what we've been doing?"

He pivoted, and she moved with him until her back was against the wall. With more than a foot of height advantage, he towered over her. "What would we have been pretending? I am not a lord. I made that clear from the start."

He'd made it clear he wasn't an *earl,* but she wouldn't quibble. Now that he was so close to her and the space was dim and small, she knew what she'd said was foolish. The time she spent with him was the most real she could be. He didn't expect her to be a perfect young miss or to conquer Society and be the success her older sister wasn't.

"I don't pretend with you," she said softly. She also didn't tell him the complete truth, such as her name, and neither did he totally reveal himself to her. "You see who I am. Don't you?"

"Yes." His answer thrummed in her chest.

"And I see you."

"No." The word came hard and fast. "You see what I want you to see." He put his palm on the wall above her head and to her left as he pressed his body against hers. He tipped his head down and looked into her eyes. "What do you see?"

Anne lifted her hand and touched his cheek. She glided her fingers down to his jaw. "I see a man. A man who makes me feel important and valued. A man I want."

A soft but guttural sound lodged in his throat. "You can't know what that means."

"Can't I?" She slipped her hand between his collar and his neck and moved it back to his nape. Pulling him toward her, she stood on her toes and touched her lips to his.

What on earth was she doing? This was utter madness. It was one thing to traipse all over East London in a stranger's company, but to kiss him?

Only, he wasn't a stranger. She might not know his name, but she knew him—his character, at least.

And now she was kissing him.

He clasped her waist and pulled his lips from hers but didn't retreat. "Brazen," he whispered against her mouth. "Beautiful."

She looked up into his eyes. "Kiss me. Please?"

"I should decline, but fortunately for you, my judgment is questionable." He slid his hand between her and the wall, flattening his palm against the small of her back. Holding her fast, he pressed against her as his other hand cupped the side of her neck, his thumb stroking along her jaw. "Ready?" At her nod, he added, "Remember, I am not who you think me to be."

His mouth crushed over hers, his hands pressing into her, capturing her for the onslaught of his lips and tongue. For that's what it was—a tumult of desire and desperation that echoed her own. She had no idea what he was doing as his tongue slid into her mouth, but she wanted every part of it.

Sensation soared and spiraled, igniting little fires of need throughout her body. But it was the lush beauty of his kiss that captivated her. He tasted of that bitter coffee but there was something else, a masculine flavor and swagger that threatened to sweep her away if the sudden wobbliness of her legs meant anything.

His tongue swept against hers, exploring and teasing, provoking her to respond. She met him with a gentle thrust, and it must have been right because his thumb pressed into her cheek just in front of her ear.

His body was big and solid against her, making her feel both small and secure in his embrace. She never wanted to leave it. Or him.

The kiss gentled, slowing until he pulled back. But he didn't move away. "That was unwise."

She opened her eyes and smiled up at him. "That was heavenly. Please do it again."

The edges of his mouth curved up. "What am I going to do with you?" he murmured.

"Anything you like." She trailed her fingertips along the underside of his jaw toward his throat.

"Brazen *temptress*." He abruptly let her go and clasped her hand, leading her to a door. Once they were outside in a narrow alleyway, he wound around the row of buildings and back onto Paternoster Row. "Time to return to Hatchard's."

Anne sighed. "Pity."

They walked in silence for a moment. Anne worked to organize her jumbled thoughts—and tamp down the persistent desire she felt toward him. "Would it be bad if we told each other who we are?"

"Yes." He didn't pause or even slow. "I meant what I said before—I am not the man you think me to be. If you hope I can court you, know that I cannot. Ever. I should not have kissed you."

Anne hadn't realized until that moment that she had been hoping for something. Perhaps not courtship, but if not that, what? Was she hoping he would tup her in the back corridor of a coffee shop? The idea sent a shameful heat blazing through her. "Then what are we doing together?"

"I don't know."

They went silent again, and it wasn't until he steered her toward his parked cabriolet that she finally stopped, tugging on his arm to do the same.

She looked up at him and put her palm against his chest. "I don't know what we're doing, but it's the thing I look forward to the most. I like you." *I love you.* Yes, that was what she wanted to say, but wouldn't. "I like our adventures. I don't want them to stop."

He stared past her, his pupils narrowing and the orange in his right eye becoming larger. "I don't either." His gaze moved to hers. "But there will come a time when this—us—must."

*Us.*

How she loved that tiny word.

"Then I suppose we'll have to make the most of every moment." She stood on her toes and brushed her lips against his. "When we get to the cabriolet, I'm going to kiss you again because I can. Prepare yourself."

He chuckled low in his chest, his eyes glittering. "I'm learning that I'm not sure I can ever adequately prepare myself for you."

Pleasure flushed through her. "I'll take that as a compliment."

"I meant it at as such." He put his hand over hers, which was still against his chest. "Be warned that I plan to kiss you back."

Anne couldn't wait.

~

*One week later...*

She was late.

More than a half hour.

Rafe Blackwell stood across the street from Hatchard's, just outside the Burlington Arcade, which had opened only a few days prior. His cabriolet was parked nearby, his tiger in command of the vehicle so they could quickly be on their way to Aldersgate Street.

She was *never* late.

Had something terrible prevented her from coming? Perhaps she was ill or hurt. The thought sent a shaft of stark panic piercing straight through him. And that scared him. Four years ago, he'd promised himself that he would never, ever open himself up to such heartache again.

Yet here he was, waiting for a slip of a woman who made his heart race in a way he'd never expected. Not after what he'd endured—what he'd found and lost.

After another quarter hour, he accepted that she wasn't coming. Muttering a curse, he walked into the arcade. London's elite mingled amongst the expensive shops. He wandered into a jeweler and browsed the display cases, stopping when his gaze fell on a cameo carved from oyster shell. He instantly thought of Mrs. Dazzling, because the woman's curls rioted about her shoulders. Mrs. Dazzling's hair didn't quite do that, but one or more of her blonde locks often went astray, despite her best attempts to keep them tamed beneath her hat.

And of course the oyster shell reminded him of her. Would he ever eat another oyster without thinking of their time together?

Without indulging much thought, he sought the

attention of an employee. "I'd like to purchase that brooch."

"Aphrodite?" the middle-aged man asked.

Rafe nearly smiled. Of course it was Aphrodite. He'd always been drawn to depictions of the goddess, though he couldn't exactly say why. "Yes."

The man withdrew it from the case with a smile. "What a lovely gift. I'll wrap it up for you."

Rafe asked the price and paid the man. It wasn't a gift. In fact, he didn't even know why he was buying it.

*Because you can.*

Perhaps that was it. He was a man of considerable means now. To be able to walk into this new arcade, built specifically for Society's most prestigious, and not be regarded as an interloper was an achievement.

Nevertheless, he wasn't satisfied. Perhaps he never would be.

The attendant returned with the brooch wrapped in a box. Rafe tucked it into his coat and left the shop.

Frustration and disappointment warred within him as he made his way back to Piccadilly. He couldn't help but look toward Hatchard's, as if he'd see her waiting for him outside. She wasn't. The depth of his emotions was unsettling. He'd been amusing himself with her, or so he'd thought.

Hell, he'd let his guard down spectacularly. He almost *never* did that, with two distinct exceptions: his sister and Eliza. And both of them were gone from his life, proof positive that he should never let people close.

There were reasons he held himself apart. Self-protection. Unworthiness. Keeping others safe. He was a risk that shouldn't be taken.

He was broken.

It was good she hadn't come. Good for him, but even better for her.

That the discontent he typically carried was now magnified troubled him, but the sensation would fade. She'd been a welcome distraction, and now it was time to let her go. It should be simple. He'd become a master of letting things—people—go. A sharp, quick press on his chest told him otherwise.

Perhaps she'd been more than a distraction.

# CHAPTER 1

*June 1819*
*Mayfair*

The library was nearly complete.

Rafe Blackwell, or Raphael Bowles as he was now known, surveyed the massive room, which was the second largest in his grand new house on Upper Brook Street. Only the ballroom was bigger. He could probably fit the single-room flat he'd lived in with his sister and their "uncle" when they'd been children in East London into the ballroom at least eight times over.

Two footmen carried in boxes of books and set them on a long, rectangular table, which was covered with a cloth to protect the surface. Such consideration was once odd to Rafe. Until four years ago, he'd never owned a table worth covering. Before that, he hadn't owned all that many tables.

And he'd never owned this many books. He thanked the footmen, and they departed. Rafe went to one of the boxes and looked inside. So many books.

He immediately thought of Mrs. Dazzling—books always brought her to mind. Not just because he'd met her at Hatchard's, but because the last time he'd seen her had been that day in Paternoster Row.

He'd considered finding her. It wouldn't be difficult as she was out this Season.

He didn't want to.

That wasn't precisely true. It was *best* if he didn't.

Besides, he expected she was married by now, or would be before the Season ended. She was far too intelligent, charming, and beautiful to last long on Society's Marriage Mart. How he would have hated to participate in such a show.

He couldn't help wondering if he might have. If his life had gone differently. His parents had died in a fire when he was five. He knew very little about them other than that they'd taught him to read, his father had given him a pony, and they'd loved him. The pony suggested some measure of wealth, but Rafe had never known the truth. Their nurse—his and his younger sister's—had rescued them from the fire and delivered them to her brother, who'd taken them to London. When Rafe had asked "Uncle" Edgar where he was from, the man always shrugged and said it didn't matter. What mattered was where he was going.

*Always look forward.*

Rafe had done just that, for it had been far preferable to living in the present, which had often been a horrible existence of hunger, shame, and desperation. Used by Edgar to steal and swindle, Rafe had grown up on the streets of East London, as far away from pony rides and loving parents as one could get.

But now that he'd arrived at his destination, the

posh elegance and security of Mayfair, Rafe was consumed with looking back. Because nearly a week ago, he'd remembered something that could finally illuminate his origins. On the day his younger sister was married, she'd received a coral necklace as a gift. That necklace reminded them of one their mother had worn.

Seeing the necklace on Selina had loosened a memory stuck in the recesses of Rafe's mind. He distinctly recalled sitting in his mother's lap, touching that necklace and looking at a folly nearby. They'd been picnicking on the edge of a lake in the shadow of the folly. Hell, he hadn't even known what a folly was until Beatrix had explained.

Beatrix, whom Selina had met at boarding school after Rafe had sent her there at the age of eleven to protect her from the ever-increasing dangers of their life in East London, had given Selina the necklace. As the bastard daughter of a duke, Beatrix had enjoyed a luxurious childhood until her mother, the duke's mistress, had died. As a child, she'd visited an estate with a folly and so had been able to describe it—a fake temple or other sort of building situated on an estate as a decoration or entertainment. Apparently, some folly owners actually *paid* hermits to live in them. Rafe would never understand the bloody rich.

"Sir?" Rafe's butler, a smooth, silver-haired man of around fifty with a wealth of experience and outstanding references, stood just inside the library.

"Yes?"

"Lady Rockbourne and Mrs. Sheffield are here to see you. They are in the blue room."

Beatrix and Selina.

"Thank you, Glover." Rafe had arranged for guests

to always meet him in the large sitting room that looked out to the garden. It was an elegantly decorated space with just the right amount of intimidating opulence and welcoming warmth. Or so he hoped.

Rafe moved past the butler and made his way to the blue room. Beatrix perched on a settee in the center seating area while Selina paced near the massive fireplace edged in gilt and surmounted by a wide mirror in a Baroque style.

That his sister was wearing a path over his new Aubusson carpet gave him a moment's concern—not for the carpet, but for whatever was driving her nervous movements. "Good afternoon," he said. "I'm surprised to see you both—newlyweds that you are." Selina had married the Honorable Harry Sheffield, a Bow Street constable and second son of an earl, a week earlier, and Beatrix had wed the Viscount Rockbourne just three days ago.

Selina stopped pacing and faced him, her hands clasped in front of her. "We have news. Rather, Beatrix has news."

Beatrix blinked, her pale lashes sweeping over her hazel eyes. "Yesterday I went to Tom's cousin's for a visit. We picked up a pair of kittens for Regan." Tom was her new husband and Regan was her four-year-old stepdaughter. "While we were at Sutton Park, we had a picnic near a lake."

The air in Rafe's lungs escaped in a rush. He said nothing but went to stand near a high-backed chair. Resting his hand on the top, he dug his fingertips into the velvet back.

"I spied a folly across the lake," Beatrix said, and Rafe knew what she was going to say next.

He said it for her. "It was *the* folly."

Beatrix nodded. "Complete with the dolphin and Aphrodite in the center." Just as Rafe had remembered. He'd drawn what he recalled and shown the rendering to both of them.

Rafe squeeze the chair. He couldn't believe she'd found it. "You're certain?"

"Quite. Especially given the proximity to the lake."

"It's at Sutton Park?" Rafe had no idea where that was.

"No, the neighboring estate, Ivy Grove. It's owned by the Earl of Stone."

The Earl of Stone. Who the hell was that? Rafe hadn't yet made the connections he wanted to amongst the highest members of Society. He was well on his way, however, since his sister was now married to the son of the Earl of Aylesbury and his pretend sister was now a viscountess.

The two of them also belonged to a women's philanthropic organization called the Spitfire Society, whose membership boasted duchesses, marchionesses, countesses, and more. Women of influence and prestige.

How in the bloody hell had they found their way here?

Through hard work and persistence. Since meeting at the boarding school more than fifteen years ago, Selina and Beatrix had formed a bond as close as sisters. In fact, they told everyone they *were* sisters, and as a result, Rafe, who had been introduced as Selina's brother, now had a fake half sister. He had no quarrel with the lie, particularly since Beatrix had been family to Selina when she'd needed it most. When Rafe had sent her to the school and abandoned her. He hadn't meant to not see her for nearly two decades, but when he thought of her returning to the life he'd saved her from, he'd stopped writing while continuing to pay for her education. He hadn't seen her again until a few weeks ago.

While he knew it had been the right thing to do, he suffered a deep, piercing anguish that would haunt him the rest of his life. Because while he'd protected Selina from the dangers of East London, she'd had to forge a path for herself and for Beatrix. As two women alone in the world, they'd done whatever they must in order to survive, including swindling and theft. He felt guilty about that too—if Selina's background hadn't been that of a thief and a swindler, perhaps she would have found another way.

He supposed she had, finally. Through love. She and Sheffield were quite thoroughly and wonderfully in love, and Rafe couldn't have been more grateful. The same was true of Beatrix and Rockbourne.

Hopefully, for them it would last.

"Do you know Stone?" Selina asked. "You're clearly lost in thought."

Indeed he was. "No. I'm trying to think if I know of anyone who knows him." In his most recent life, Rafe had been a moneylender called the Vicar. In that role, he'd met some men who moved in Society, most notably the Viscount Colton.

Rafe hadn't ever encountered Stone or heard his name, but perhaps Colton could help him. As it happened, the man owed him a favor that Rafe had yet to claim.

"Tom's cousin, the Countess of Sutton, does," Beatrix said. "Because they're neighbors. I'm certain we could all go to Sutton Park."

He appreciated that, but it wasn't enough. "I want to go to Ivy Grove."

Selina walked toward him, stopping a couple of

feet away, her mouth set in determination. "I do too."

Of course she did. She remembered almost nothing of their parents—just that coral necklace, which he noted she was wearing again. She'd worn it every time he'd seen her since receiving it from Beatrix.

It couldn't be their mother's actual necklace. But they had no way of knowing since Beatrix had purchased it from a receiver shop that Rafe had only recently sold as he'd worked to divest himself of the businesses he'd owned as the Vicar. Rafe had gone back to ask, but they'd only said it had come from Petticoat Lane. Since that was the center of stolen goods in London, the necklace could have come from anywhere.

"Then it seems at the very least, we must be introduced to Stone." Rafe planned to visit Colton as soon as they left. "I'll take care of that."

"How?" Selina asked, her blue eyes narrowing slightly.

"Trust me."

Selina snorted, and Rafe smiled. He'd given her no reason to trust him and was trying to make amends. However, he knew how hard it was for her to trust anyone beyond Beatrix. Letting her guard down with her new husband had been almost too much for her. Luckily, she'd managed to open herself to him, and for that Rafe was both relieved and delighted. No one deserved happiness more than she.

He took his hand from the back of the chair and stepped around it toward his sister. "Lina, you *can* trust me in this. I promise I will keep you involved every step of the way."

"They were my parents too," she said softly.

"I know."

"Do you really think we're going to find out who they were? Who *we* are?"

*That* he didn't know. But he hoped. "I'm going to do everything in my power to make that happen."

Anger flared in Selina's eyes. "Why didn't Edgar tell us more before he died?"

Their "Uncle" Edgar had expired from excessive drink when Rafe was thirteen and Selina was ten. He'd sold them to Samuel Partridge, a criminal who controlled an army of young thieves among other enterprises, such as flash-houses and receiver shops, two years prior but had stayed nearby and kept in occasional contact.

"Because he didn't care about anyone but himself, and it didn't serve his purposes to reveal any more than he did." Which was almost nothing. He had said *one* thing that had clung to a part of Rafe's mind and resurfaced from time to time.

Thinking, Rafe moved toward the window and looked out at the walled garden. With its manicured shrubbery and colorful flowers, it looked like a miniature park, complete with a path, statuary, and a few benches. It was about as far removed from the memories currently clouding his brain as one could imagine.

Rafe turned from the window to face Selina and Beatrix. "The last time I saw Edgar was the day before he died." The man had been a yellowed, shrunken version of himself. "He asked to be buried at the Croydon Parish Church. That didn't make sense to me, and I didn't care to honor any of his wishes, so I ignored him."

The purpose of Rafe's visit had been to gloat about his recent promotion in Partridge's organization. He'd wanted Edgar to know how much better off he and Selina were without him. At thirteen, Rafe had been full of arrogance and bluster. He'd long ago lost the bluster, but some would say he was still arrogant. He preferred confident.

Beatrix rose from the settee. She was petite—a good six inches shorter than Selina's five feet nine. "We drove through Croydon on our way to Sutton Park. Which means it's also on the way to Ivy Grove."

What the hell did that signify?

Selina smoothed her hand down the side of her face. "Why would Edgar want to be buried in a town we never visited—or at least don't remember visiting—which happens to be near a place you recall from our childhood?"

"I don't know, but I'm going to find out." Rafe's mind was already working. He wanted to meet Stone, and he wanted to visit this parish church in Croydon. The latter was probably pointless, but Rafe would investigate every clue.

Selina's gaze crackled with resolve. "I'm going to Croydon with you."

"I don't think I could stop you," he said wryly. "Nor do I want to."

"Good. Let me know when you arrange to meet Stone. And make it soon."

"It will be." Rafe would make it a priority. *The* priority. He looked to Beatrix. "Thank you."

"For what? Having the luck to picnic near that folly?" She waved her hand. "Perhaps this was the way it was supposed to happen."

Fate? Rafe didn't believe in such things. Yet, it was some sort of providence. Perhaps it was simply time that the puzzle of his life—and Selina's—came together. He'd lost hope that their past would ever be revealed.

"I don't know if I believe that," Selina said. "But I'm glad you were there—and that you were observant." She tossed Beatrix a knowing smile that provoked a flash of envy in Rafe. They had a true sisterly bond. He'd abdicated that sibling closeness when he'd left Selina to fend for herself. She said she forgave him, but he wasn't sure he could ever forgive himself.

Perhaps, if he could find the truth about their past, he could start.

~

Setting the book down in her lap, Anne shoved an errant lock of hair into the band tied around her head. A streak of striped fur leapt into the open book but didn't linger, and in her escape sent the tome tumbling to the floor.

Anne exhaled. "It's a good thing I wasn't particularly interested in that." A second blur of tawny, striped fur blazed past her chair, clearly in pursuit of the first one. Given the sizes of them, she guessed the first had been Daffodil, who was the smaller of the two kittens, and the second was her sister, Fern.

Jane, Anne's older sister by four years, strode into Anne's small sitting room. "Where did they go?"

Daffodil streaked by Jane's leg, rustling her gown. Fern followed, leaping back over the threshold in a merry chase.

"Sorry." Jane gave Anne an apologetic smile. "Did they disturb you?"

"Never. They're kittens. I'm only sorry they've gone so quickly."

"They'll be back. Unless they get tired, in which case they will look for Anthony." Jane's husband was their favorite thing to sleep on.

"True." Anne set the book on the table beside her chair.

"Do you mind if I sit for a minute?" Jane asked.

"Not at all." Anne gestured toward the other chair angled near hers in front of the small hearth.

Jane sat and smoothed her hands over her bottle-green gown. Her blonde hair was perfectly dressed, every strand in place, unlike Anne's, which seemed to live apart from the rest of her body, possessing a mind and desire of its own.

"The Season is nearly over," Jane said.

It wasn't a question, but Anne could guess what Jane wanted to know. Anne had chosen to come live with her and Anthony after they'd wed a few weeks ago. Their parents had retreated to the country following Anne's scandalously aborted wedding. Had it already been nearly four weeks since that disastrous day?

No, not disastrous. Marrying Gilbert Chamberlain would have been the true disaster. Instead, she'd only suffered the humiliation of her groom being arrested at their wedding.

Honestly, she hadn't been humiliated by that part, even if Society thought she should be. Far more horrifying was that she'd allowed herself to become betrothed to someone like him. Worse than that, to someone she hadn't loved.

"The furor over the wedding has died down… somewhat," Jane said with what sounded like fake optimism.

"Somewhat but not entirely."

"It will." Jane said this with confidence.

"By next Season, perhaps."

"Are you saying you prefer to continue to decline invitations?" Jane asked.

Miraculously, Anne still received some. But that was due to Jane's founding membership in the

Spitfire Society and the powerful friends she'd made because of it.

Anne frowned. "I don't know."

"You know I'll support whatever you want to do. I can well understand wanting to completely withdraw and thumb your nose at Society."

Of course she could, because Jane had done it herself a couple of months ago. After five years on the Marriage Mart, she'd had enough. Much to their parents' horror, she'd declared herself a spinster and moved into a house in Cavendish Square owned by her friend Phoebe, who was now the Marchioness of Ripley.

Jane had waited to claim her independence until after Anne had become betrothed to Gilbert so as not to impact Anne's reputation. Anne had felt sorry for Jane at the time, but in retrospect, she envied her.

Because of Jane's failure on the Marriage Mart, their parents had put all their hopes on Anne to make a good match. The pressure and expectation had been almost too much to bear. Which was how she'd found herself betrothed to a man she didn't love. She hated to be grateful that he'd turned out to be an extortionist, but she couldn't deny how she felt. Not just because she'd escaped marriage to him, but because she was still free.

Free to choose another path, if it even existed. She thought of Lord Bodyguard often and wished she could see him again. He no longer went to Hatchard's on Thursdays. She knew because she'd started going again two weeks ago. And she planned to continue to keep their appointment, even though it was far too late.

"Ripley is hosting a grand ball to celebrate the end of the Season at Brixton Park in a few weeks. Do you want to attend with us?"

Anne shrugged. She hadn't ever encountered Lord Bodyguard at any of the Society events she'd attended since March and had no reason to think he'd be there. He was perhaps the only thing that could entice her to reenter Society, even for one ball.

"Well, you have time to decide," Jane said with a small smile. "After that, Anthony and I will be going to Oaklands." His country seat. "You're welcome to accompany us, of course. Or you can stay here, and we can have Mrs. Hammond act as your chaperone." Mrs. Hammond was an old family friend who had occasionally performed chaperoning duties along with Anne's godfather's daughter, Deborah, Lady Burnhope.

"I noticed you didn't suggest I go home," Anne said drily.

Jane choked on a laugh. "I would never."

"Good, because I won't." Anne plucked at a loose thread on the arm of her upholstered chair. "Do I really need a chaperone? Perhaps I'd like to declare myself a spinster. Or a spitfire."

"I should find no quarrel with that, but you're far younger than I was when I made that decision." Jane paused to send her a meaningful look. "Once you do, you can't go back."

"Given the debacle of my wedding, I'm not sure it matters."

"People don't blame you. Chamberlain is being transported, for heaven's sake."

Anne had been delighted when she'd heard that. He'd extorted several people, including Anthony, threatening to expose their most dearly held secrets—truths that would ruin and destroy them. In Anthony's case, he'd gone public with his in order to bring Gilbert down, to save Anne from marrying him. She could never thank him enough.

"Good riddance," Anne muttered. She abruptly stood. "I'm going out to the garden."

Jane also rose. "You know I'll do anything you need? You have only to ask."

"I do." Anne gave her a reassuring smile. "Thank you for inviting me to stay with you."

"Not stay with us, *live* with us. You don't ever have to leave."

Perhaps not, but Anne didn't want to be the spinster sister who had no life of her own. Which meant she had to *find* a life of her own.

Anne left the sitting room and descended to the first floor. From there, she continued down the grand staircase to the ground floor. As she reached the staircase hall, she glimpsed a figure standing in the entry hall. At first, she thought it was Tabor, the butler, given the blond hair, but something about the man's form made her stop.

Pivoting, she crept toward the entry hall in curiosity as the man turned to face her.

A gasp sprang from her lips, and her eyes widened. "Lord Bodyguard," she breathed.

One of his blond brows arched as her shock was reflected back at her in his cobalt gaze. "Mrs. Dazzling."

The sight of him made her chest constrict. He was almost unbearably handsome in a green coat and buff breeches, his pristine white cravat nestled beneath the strong, familiar line of his jaw.

"How did you find me?" She sounded quite breathless.

"I didn't. Not on purpose anyway. I am here to see Lord Colton. He is your…?"

"Brother-in-law."

His jaw actually dropped, or so she thought. It happened so quickly that she doubted what she'd seen.

"So you don't know who I am?" she asked.

"I do now."

"Then you are in a better position than I since I shall still have to call you Lord Bodyguard."

"Mr. Bowles?" Tabor came into the hall behind Anne.

*Mr. Bowles.* Anne searched her brain for the name and came up wanting. Why was he here to see Anthony? She had so many questions, and none of them would be answered. Frustration churned in her gut.

"I do hope I'll see you again, Mr. Bowles," she said softly as he came toward her.

His gaze found hers with a dark intensity that infused her with heat. "The pleasure will be mine."

Anne watched as he followed Tabor toward Anthony's study. She longed to spy on them, but there was simply no way to do so. Overwhelmed with nervous energy, she stalked to the morning room and out to the garden. The day was bright and warm, but she had no appreciation for any of the flowers or birds or anything else. Her mind was wholly owned by Mr. Bowles and the fact that he was *here*.

Who was he to Anthony? And what had he meant when he'd said he knew who she was now? Something about the way he'd uttered the words had made her heart beat a tick faster.

Did he simply know her name, or was he also aware of her engagement and aborted wedding? She stalked around the path of the garden, growing angry again that Gilbert had turned out to be such a horrid person and that his behavior had unfairly blemished *her*.

Coming back to the start of her circuit, she stopped and stared at the door to the morning room. She wanted to go inside and barge into Anthony's study. Once there, she'd drag Mr. Bowles… where? She didn't care. She just wanted answers. She wanted to reclaim the connection they'd shared, because she'd felt so awfully alone.

And perhaps she wanted another kiss. Or ten.

Hell. It seemed she may not have fallen out of love with him after all.

# CHAPTER 2

Rafe's body thrummed with anticipation. He needed to focus on why he'd come to see Colton. Instead, he was consumed with thoughts of Mrs. Dazzling—no, Miss Anne Bloody Pemberton. He knew precisely who she was. Just as he'd known her betrothed. Never would Rafe have imagined the poor woman whose wedding had been interrupted by the arrest of her groom was his Mrs. Dazzling.

His?

"I shouldn't be surprised to see you," Colton said, standing near the hearth, his elbow resting on the dark wood mantel. "And yet I am. I wondered if you would ever come calling." He gestured to the pair of chairs situated in front of the cold, dark fireplace. There was no need for additional warmth on this fine summer day.

Rafe took one of the chairs, high-backed, dark blue velvet with arms. Colton sat in the other.

The viscount looked far more relaxed than Rafe had ever seen him. His blue eyes held a warmth that hadn't been there before his marriage to Miss Jane Pemberton.

Mrs. Dazzling's bloody sister. Rafe still couldn't believe it was her.

"Congratulations on your marriage," Rafe said.

"Thank you." Colton's tone was wry. "I presume you've come to claim the favor I owe you."

"Yes. Rather than a list of people I'd like to meet, there is just one man—the Earl of Stone."

Colton pressed his lips together and flattened his back against the chair. "I don't know him very well. I am, however, acquainted with his son, the Viscount Sandon. He's just recently returned from his family's estate in Ireland."

"I need to meet Stone. Preferably at his house south of London."

Colton's dark brows arched briefly. "Ivy Grove?" He tipped his head to the side. "You want me to obtain an invitation for you to Ivy Grove to meet Lord Stone. Do you realize how difficult that is?"

"I do." He didn't, actually, but he could imagine. "Can you manage it?"

Stroking his jaw, Colton let out a breath. "Stone likes to entertain. He's quite proud of that estate. I can try to put a word in Sandon's ear—suggest his father should host something to welcome him home from Ireland."

"You're making this sound not that hard at all."

A dark laugh bolted from the viscount. "My suggestion could go absolutely nowhere. It's nearly the end of the Season. It may very well be too late."

"I appreciate you trying. You'll keep me apprised?"

Colton nodded. "I'll hunt him down at Brooks's later." He eyed Rafe, his gaze sweeping over him from boot to brow. "Will you be seeking entry to one of the clubs?"

Rafe had considered it. He was only concerned with establishing business connections. He'd recently invested in a publishing venture and was about to embark on a property scheme. He planned to build housing for the labor class. Good housing that people deserved instead of the hovels that many lived in. "Perhaps. Are you offering to recommend me?"

"That would be a second favor."

"Or something you would do for a friend."

Colton leaned forward, a spark lighting his gaze. "You think we're friends after all that's gone on between us?"

"I loaned you money, and you paid me back." A current of energy ran through Rafe. He rested his right elbow on the arm of the chair. "I thought we'd resolved the issue of your parents. I never wanted them—or you—to be killed."

Colton had borrowed the funds to settle debts and had continued to gamble. He'd also continued to lose, and he hadn't repaid his loan in the timeframe they'd agreed upon.

At the time, Rafe had certain employees whose responsibility was to collect outstanding debts such as Colton's. In this instance, the employee had taken it upon himself to do more than apply pressure to the debtor. He'd killed Colton's parents on the way to their country estate. Colton was supposed to have been the one on the road that day, and Rafe's employee was to remind him—in plain terms—of his financial obligations. Instead, he'd committed murder.

"Perhaps it was resolved for you," Colton said quietly. "For me, it will never be."

"I do understand." Rafe turned his head toward the hearth. "I lost my parents when I was very young." As soon as the words left his mouth, he wanted to take them back. He didn't reveal things about himself.

So why had he now? He looked back to Colton. Was Rafe truly looking for a friend?

No. He was simply...raw. He was close to finding out who his parents were, and he bloody well needed Colton.

"I'm sorry for your loss," Colton said.

Inhaling, Rafe returned to the matter they'd been discussing. "I don't need you to recommend me to a club. Just the invitation to Ivy Grove, please."

"Just that," Colton said sardonically. "You seem to be doing well for yourself. I'm sorry we weren't able to attend the ball for your sister."

"No need to apologize. It was, I suppose, quite a crush." Rafe winced inwardly—he sounded like a pompous ass. No, he sounded like a Society gentleman.

"The Vicar is in the past, then?" Colton asked, provoking a twitch between Rafe's shoulder blades.

"Completely. I have no desire to resurrect him."

Rafe wanted to ask if Colton's wife knew, and if so, whether she would tell her sister, but that would invite too many questions. Not that it mattered if Anne—hell, he was already first-naming her—rather, *Miss Pemberton* knew who he was. It wasn't as if they had a future together.

Rising, Rafe straightened his waistcoat. "Thank you for your time and assistance."

"I'm only helping you because I owe you for finding the man who was extorting me." Colton stood. "Without your assistance, Chamberlain would not have been arrested."

Colton had come to Rafe thinking the Vicar was the one extorting him. The note the viscount had received had threatened to expose his gambling debts and the fact that those debts had led to the deaths of his parents. Colton had naturally believed it was Rafe since he knew about the debts and, as the Vicar, was engaged in enterprises that pushed the boundaries of legality. But while Rafe had lent money at illegally high rates, owned receiver shops, and had once been the right hand of one of the most powerful criminals in East London, he never engaged in extortion.

Rafe had conducted his own investigation and found Chamberlain, a man of questionable morals who delivered gentlemen in need of loans to the Vicar, responsible. After informing Colton, the viscount had done what was necessary—exposing his transgressions—to ensure Bow Street arrested Chamberlain.

And in so doing, he'd saved Anne from marrying the blackguard. A wave of anger rushed over Rafe. He knew Chamberlain to be driven by avarice and vanity. When Rafe thought of Anne married to him, he felt an irrational need to go to Newgate and beat the man to a pulp before they transported him across the world.

"Chamberlain is a scoundrel," Rafe said coldly. "You did everyone a great service by ensuring he was arrested, especially your sister-in-law."

Colton's brow pleated. "You heard about that?"

"*Everyone* heard about that."

"I suppose so. While I'm glad Anne wasn't trapped into marriage with him, she hasn't had an easy time of it. Her reputation is still stained, I'm afraid."

Rafe hated hearing that. "None of what happened was her fault."

"I know." Colton's gaze was pained.

Rafe could see the man carried guilt about that too. "Surely things will get better." Or not—Rafe had no notion how Society worked. The more he learned, which wasn't much, the less he understood.

"I hope so. The Season is almost over, and perhaps by next year, people will have forgotten, or at least decide to be kind where Anne is concerned." Colton sent him a curious stare. "I appreciate your…concern about her."

*Fuck.* Rafe didn't want to draw attention to that of all things. "I was merely being polite. I look forward to hearing from you about Stone."

Colton nodded, and Rafe took his leave.

Anticipation curled along his nerves as he made his way to the entry hall. His breath caught and held. But she wasn't there.

Good. He shouldn't see her again.

Yet, now that he knew who she was and where she lived, would he stay away?

He had to.

The butler opened the door, and Rafe walked outside into the bright afternoon. He turned in the direction of Grosvenor Square, which he would cut through on the way to his house on Upper Brook Street. Dammit, she was far too close.

When he reached the corner of Davies Street, a familiar form in a veil stepped into his path. Far too close indeed.

"Miss Pemberton," he said, liking the feel of her name on his tongue. Anne would taste even better.

"Mr. Bowles. Shall we take a walk around the square?"

He glanced about. "Do you never have a chaperone?"

"I almost always have a chaperone. Except when I have a bodyguard, if you recall."

Rafe couldn't help the smile that stole over his mouth. "Still saucy," he murmured. "We can't walk around the square and you"—he stopped himself from saying bloody—sometimes the transition from his old life to his new took great effort—"well know it."

She exhaled. "I suppose not." Wrapping her hand around his elbow, she pulled him down Davies Street and into the narrow mews. They stood near the corner of a stable.

Out of view of the street, she removed her hand from his arm and faced him. "Why are you visiting my brother-in-law?"

He wished he could see her face better. He could barely make out the sweep of her jaw and the graceful slope of her nose. Her hazel eyes and delightfully dimpled cheeks were completely obscured.

"I had business to attend."

She put a hand on her hip. "That's all you're going to say? After three months?"

"What does my paying a call on your brother-in-law have to do with the last time we saw each other? I should be interrogating you as to why you failed to keep our appointment to go to Aldersgate Street."

She tipped her head down and turned it to the side. "I wasn't able to meet you."

"Was it because of the kissing?" He shouldn't have brought that up, but damn him if he wasn't remembering the press of her lips and every stroke of her tongue. "I shouldn't have mentioned that. Nor should I have done it in the first place."

Flipping the veil up over her hat, she gave him a wry look. "You speak as if you were the only person responsible. I was a very willing participant." Her gaze softened. "I have never forgotten you."

Seeing her face jolted him back to their wonderful afternoons, provoking an ache. "Not even when you were betrothed?" He hadn't meant to cause her pain, but to point out that she'd clearly moved on. At the flash of distress in her eyes, he hastened to add, "You did what you must. And you *should* forget me." Just as he should forget her.

"Is that what you did?"

"Yes," he lied.

She notched her chin up. "I don't believe you. You wouldn't ask why I didn't meet you nor would you mention my betrothal if you'd forgotten about me, if you didn't care."

*Bollocks.* He didn't want to be cruel, but it seemed he must. "I *don't* care. You were a passing fancy."

She sucked in a sharp breath. "I did *try* to forget you. And yes, I became betrothed because that was expected of me. I felt terrible that I wasn't able to meet you anymore—we were foolish not to share our names. I would have sent word."

"It wasn't foolish at all. I have no regrets." That wasn't entirely true. He should not have kissed her. Hell, he shouldn't have done any of it. But she'd captivated him from the moment they'd met. He'd been hungry for something, a connection, perhaps.

"Well, I do," she said softly, sadness dimming the green parts of her hazel eyes. "I enjoyed our friendship and would have liked for it to continue."

He heard the hope in her voice and sought to squash it. "We were not friends nor will we be. I took advantage of you, and you were smart to put an end to it."

"That wasn't *my* choice. My chaperone was no longer able to escort me to Hatchard's, and I couldn't go alone." She narrowed her eyes at him. "I don't understand why you're being cruel. You can deny we were friends or that we shared a connection"—at her use of that word, he twitched—"but you won't convince me. I was there." She took a step toward him, bringing them closer than they ought to be.

Even so, he didn't move.

"Why can't you at least admit we were friends? Are you angry with me for not meeting you?" She tentatively placed her hand on his chest. "I was devastated when I wasn't able to. I would have given anything to know who you were so I could find you."

He considered telling her that he could have easily found her but chose not to. But in the end, he didn't *want* to hurt her. "We were…friends. That was in the past, however."

Her gaze held his as her hand pressed firmly against him. "It doesn't have to be."

What the hell was she proposing? Rafe took her hand and pushed it down to her side. "Yes it does. I'm not engaging in an affair with you."

Her eyes widened, and he realized he'd misunderstood. She wanted…courtship? That was even worse. She pressed her lips together and twisted her mouth as she glanced away. "You think less of me now, just like everyone else."

Rafe clasped her chin and forced her to look at him. "No. I could never think less of you."

A glimmer of hope threaded through her features. "I wasn't asking for an affair—just what I said: friendship. It would be nice to have someone who doesn't look at me with pity or judgment. You mentioned my betrothal, so you must know what happened."

"I do," he said tightly, still considering whether he should go to Newgate and thrash Chamberlain.

His resolve faltered. She only wanted what he'd offered, that he would never think less of her. He released her. "Anne, I can't be your friend. But I will be a staunch supporter, and if you ever need help, you now know where to find me."

"You called me Anne." The hint of a smile lifted the corner of her lush, utterly kissable mouth. "That's what friends do. So I'm afraid you can't stop what's already happened. We're friends."

Rafe nearly laughed. He wanted to. God, this slip of a woman who had to be ten years younger than him had neatly inserted himself into his mind —into his life—in a way no one else had.

Perhaps not *no one* else. And look how that had ended. That Anne had somehow entered the same realm Eliza had once inhabited was both shocking and horrifying.

"I don't deserve to be your friend, Miss Pemberton, and the sooner you accept that, the happier you'll be." He turned from her and caught the whisper of her answer on the summer breeze.

"*You* made me happy."

Rafe stalked from the mews and didn't look back.

~

Anne hadn't slept well last night. Now that she knew who Lord Bodyguard was, it took a great deal of effort not to pay him a call. Or invite him to Aldersgate Street. Or kiss him.

He was exactly as she recalled—tall, golden-haired, incomparably handsome even with that scar slashing his chin and lip. Perhaps because of it. He exuded a raw masculinity that no other man she'd met in London possessed.

And he wanted nothing to do with her.

Unless she needed help. Then she could call on

him. Perhaps she ought to find some trouble. What could she do that would require his help?

Magazine Day was in a week. She still wanted to attend, and surely he wouldn't want her to go alone... Pfft. That didn't qualify as needing assistance.

"Why are you scowling?" Jane strolled into the morning room where Anne was drinking a cup of coffee. And fixating on Mr. Bowles. What was his first name? She wanted to know, particularly since he knew hers—and had used it.

"My coffee is cold."

"And that provokes a scowl?" Jane chuckled. "I thought we might go out later."

"Where?" Anne asked skeptically. Jane had redoubled her efforts to get Anne out of the house, but what was the point when half of Society treated her like a pariah and the other half shook their heads at her in pity?

"Anywhere. The park? Bond Street? Hatchard's? I know how much you like it there."

"Pardon me." Purcell, Anthony's butler, stepped into the morning room. He inclined his salt-and-pepper head slightly. "Lord Stone is here."

Anne wasn't sure if she felt pleased or bothered. She loved her godfather, but he'd become quite interested in meddling with her life since her parents had left town following Gilbert's arrest, sending countless letters asking after her welfare and how he might provide assistance.

"We'll meet him in the drawing room," Jane said. When Purcell left, Jane narrowed her eyes at Anne. "I thought you liked your godfather."

"I do. Very much." In some ways, she liked him more than her actual father. And while he *was* being meddlesome, he at least did so in a way that was less autocratic and awful than their father.

Jane smoothed the turned-up lace trim on the sleeve of her gown. "At least you have someone who cares for your welfare."

Anne felt instantly contrite. Because of a false rumor started about Jane five years ago, she'd never been successful on the Marriage Mart. And their parents, particularly their father, hadn't let her forget it.

She shot Jane an apologetic look. "I'm sorry you no longer have godparents." They'd died several years ago, and there was no point mentioning their parents. They'd all but disowned Jane when she'd declared her spinsterhood, despite the fact that she'd since wed a viscount. Never mind she was also quite deliriously happy.

"Come, let us meet the earl." Jane preceded Anne from the morning room, and Anne dutifully followed her upstairs to the drawing room.

As they entered the large chamber that overlooked Grosvenor Street below, Stone turned from the windows, a broad smile lighting his blue eyes. His light brown hair formed a widow's peak, which perhaps contributed to the length of his face, along with the cleft in his chin. He was rather tall and still boasted a fit form, despite being in his early fifties.

"My dear Anne," he said, looking to Anne before glancing at Jane. "Lady Colton."

"It's a pleasure to welcome you, Lord Stone." Jane gestured toward the seating arrangement near the windows. "Shall we sit?"

Anne went to her godfather and pressed a kiss to his cheek as he embraced her fondly. "How lovely of you to visit."

"Since you keep declining my invitations to dinner and have not invited me to visit, I decided to take matters into my own hands." He sat in a chair after Anne and Jane occupied a small settee.

A tremor of unease wended its way through Anne. She hoped he just meant coming to see her but feared it was more than that. "I'm so glad you did."

"Did you know Sandon is back in town?" the earl asked.

"Yes, Jane mentioned he was at a picnic last week." Anne hadn't wanted to accompany her.

"Ah, yes, of course." He smiled at Jane, then pursed her lips at Anne. "I take it you weren't there? But of course not. You haven't gone anywhere. You mustn't become a hermit, my dear. It only exacerbates the situation."

And *that* certainly made her feel better. "The Season is almost over. I don't think it matters if I go out. Next year will be here soon enough." Maybe by then, the thought of going to a Society event wouldn't make her stomach churn.

"Good afternoon," Anthony said as he entered the drawing room. He stalked straight toward them and nodded toward the earl. "Lord Stone, welcome." Anthony sat in another chair angled near the settee.

"Afternoon, Colton. I was just telling your sister-in-law that it's past time she reenter Society. I'd like to host a dinner—nothing too large or overdone. It will be the perfect thing to show everyone that she is still the celebrated young woman who captivated everyone this Season."

Not everyone. At least not permanently. Why wasn't Bowles interested in continuing their friendship? Anne told herself to pay attention and stop thinking about him.

Jane looked to her husband. "I don't know if

you recall—or if I ever told you, actually—but Lord Stone is Anne's godfather."

"I don't think I knew that." Anthony cocked his head to the side. "A dinner would be nice, but it's summer now, and the Season is almost over. An event at Ivy Grove would be enchanting."

Why was he encouraging this? Anne narrowed her eyes at her brother-in-law.

He failed to notice. "Perhaps a picnic or a soiree—as you said, nothing overly large."

Stone nodded. "Capital idea. We'll celebrate Sandon's return to London." He cast a grin toward Anne. "And reintroduce Anne in the meantime. This is a wonderful plan!"

No, it wasn't. It was terrible. Anne stared pleadingly at Jane, who pressed her lips together in a brief frown and shot a glance at Anthony, who again seemed not to notice.

"I wonder if I might suggest someone for the guest list," Anthony said. "I've recently made the acquaintance of Mr. Bowles, a fascinating gentleman new to London."

Anne sat up straighter. Perhaps it wouldn't be terrible after all.

"Oh, yes," Jane said, prompting Anne to look over at her again. Now *she* was helping? And why? What did she know about Bowles? Anne felt a moment's panic.

"Mr. Bowles has two sisters with whom I've become acquainted, Lady Rockbourne and Mrs. Sheffield."

Anne blinked. They were members of the Spitfire Society, the club Jane had formed with her friends Phoebe and Arabella, which had become a philanthropic association with well over a dozen members now. And they were his *sisters*? He'd been so close all this time.

"I'll write their names for your list," Jane offered. She rose and went to a writing desk in the corner.

Lord Stone smiled after her. "Yes, a picnic. This will be splendid. I'll send the invitations immediately so we can have the event as soon as possible—Friday, I think."

"So soon?" Anne asked. As much as she wanted a chance to see Bowles, that was awfully fast to plan and execute an event.

The earl waved his hand. "Bah. Plenty of time, and people will adjust their plans to come. I haven't entertained at Ivy Grove this Season." He smiled confidently. Perhaps even overly so. He'd always been a touch arrogant. Anne accepted that as part of who he was.

"We'll look forward to it," Anthony said with a smile.

Anne was torn between wanting to throw something at Anthony's head and thanking him for inviting Mr. Bowles. She could do neither, of course.

Jane returned and handed Anne's godfather a folded piece of parchment. "Here you are. Thank you for inviting them. I don't know if Lord and Lady Rockbourne will come, but it's kind of you to include them."

"Ah yes, an…odd situation." Stone rose as he tucked the paper into his coat pocket. "They will be quite welcome if they decide to come. Best to put all of that Chamberlain family nonsense behind us."

Nonsense? They were a loathsome pair of siblings. Gilbert was about to be transported for extortion, and his sister, the former Lady Rockbourne, had orchestrated the vile rumor about Jane five years ago in order to steer Rockbourne to court her instead of Jane. It had worked, and Miss Dorothea Chamberlain had become the Viscountess Rockbourne. She'd died just a few weeks ago after falling from their balcony. The viscount, father to their young child, had remarried quickly. That *was* perhaps odd, but the new Lady Rockbourne—their friend Beatrix—was lovely.

She was also Lord Bodyguard's sister.

Anne still couldn't believe how their circles intersected, and yet they hadn't met. What if they had done so weeks ago, before she'd met Gilbert Chamberlain? It didn't bear thinking about.

Anne, Jane, and Anthony also stood. Stone took Anne's hand and gave it a squeeze. "I'm so glad to have you back in Society. All the unpleasantness is behind you now. Who knows, perhaps on Friday you'll meet the man who will truly become your husband." He waggled his brows at Anne.

Bloody hell, he wanted her to engage in courtship again? She clenched her jaw and smiled tightly. "Who knows?"

He laughed as he let her hand go. Bidding them good afternoon, he took his leave.

"I'm sorry, Anne," Jane said. "I know you don't want to go, let alone have the earl try to matchmake." She glowered at Anthony. "Why did you do that?"

"Do what?" His dark brows drew together. "You're the one who's been telling me Anne should get out."

Jane darted a glance toward Anne but answered Anthony. "For a stroll in the park or to go shopping, not to a picnic."

"But you tried to get her to go to the picnic last week." Anthony shook his head and muttered, "I do not understand women."

"I'm standing right here," Anne said. "While I

would have preferred that hadn't happened the way it did, there's nothing to be done now." Not when Bowles was going to be there. Assuming he accepted the invitation. Oh, he had to! There was a Spitfire Society meeting tomorrow at the Spitfire house in Cavendish Square, which was now occupied by Mr. Bowles's sister, Selina. Beatrix would likely be there too, and Anne could encourage them, along with their brother, to come to Ivy Grove.

If that came to pass, if Lord Bodyguard would be there, well, Anne would attend with glee.

Anthony gazed at her sincerely. "I apologize, Anne. I was only trying to help."

"As was I," Jane said.

"I know, and I appreciate you both so much. Please don't argue on my account. I rely on your mutual affection—it reminds me there is happiness to be had."

Anthony moved to Jane and slipped his arm around her waist. "Indeed there is, even when you think there isn't. I would know."

Yes, he would. After his parents were murdered last year, he never thought he'd be happy again or that he deserved to be. Jane had nursed him back to health, both emotionally and physically after he'd shown up on her doorstep battered almost beyond recognition. If he could find love, surely Anne would too.

Except, she was fairly certain finding it wouldn't be her problem. Whether it would be reciprocated was a separate issue entirely.

## CHAPTER 3

After being announced by his sister's butler, Rafe walked into the garden room of her new residence in Cavendish Square. The addition of several chairs crowded the room. "Are you expecting an army?" Rafe asked.

Selina adjusted the position of a chair near the doors that led out to the garden. There was typically a table there, but it had apparently been moved out of the room. "Just the Spitfire Society. While our numbers are growing, we are nowhere near an army. Not everyone will be here today, anyway, including Beatrix." She stopped abruptly and stared at him. "You're here because of the invitation." She didn't have to specify which invitation.

"You received it earlier?"

She nodded. "A picnic at Ivy Grove *tomorrow*. How did you manage it? And so quickly?"

Rafe lifted a shoulder. "Someone owed me a favor."

Selina's brow puckered. Frowning, she moved around the chair. "No one disreputable, I hope. We're supposed to have left that life behind."

There was an earnestness and a hopefulness to her tone that nearly made Rafe smile. They'd both been through so much, together as children and then later after he sent her to school and they were apart for an unforgiveable nineteen years.

"Have I told you how glad I am you finally returned to London?" he asked.

She crossed her arms over her chest. "Have I told you how angry I was that I thought you didn't care?"

"Yes. And you don't need to stop. I deserve every cross word you utter, even if I truly was trying to keep you safe." He gave her a wry look. "You've more than demonstrated your ability to take care of yourself."

"Yes, well, I learned from the very best." She inclined her head. "Now, you didn't reassure me as to this person who owed you a favor. Is this someone from your past life?"

"Yes—and no." Rafe swiped the underside of his fingers along his jaw. "Lord Colton owed the Vicar a favor."

Selina muttered a curse. "Were you mixed up in that extortion business with him and Thomas's former brother-in-law?" She referred to their new brother-in-law's—Rockbourne's—deceased wife's brother, Gilbert Chamberlain. The blackguard Anne nearly married.

"Not in the extortion, no. I would never involve myself in such a vile endeavor." He exhaled. "But as the Vicar, I cultivated a relationship with Chamberlain a few years ago. He possessed a certain lack of morality that suited my needs as I sought to gain wealthier, better-positioned clients."

"God, that sounds awful. And yet I understand why that was helpful to your cause." She pressed her lips together.

"The cause to lift ourselves out of the gutter," he said quietly.

They'd both done things they regretted, things that had been necessary to survive or to propel them to where they were now. Seeing Selina happy and in love, and, most of all, secure and safe, made everything worthwhile.

"Yes. I do understand. Completely." Her gaze, tinged with a faint sadness, told him she did.

"Chamberlain was well placed in Society, particularly with gentlemen who needed financial assistance."

"Which the Vicar—you—could provide in the form of high-interest loans."

"That is how I made Lord Colton's acquaintance. Later, at Colton's request, I discovered Chamberlain was the one extorting him. In exchange for my help, Colton owed me a favor. I asked if he could arrange an introduction to Stone, preferably at Ivy Grove. He'd indicated it would be difficult, but clearly he had no trouble whatsoever."

Selina's lips curled into a half smile. "*Clearly.*"

"I had no idea it would happen this quickly, but it's most fortuitous." Rafe was beyond anxious to explore the folly and see if more memories rose to the surface.

"So Colton knows you were the Vicar. Isn't that dangerous?"

"No more dangerous than your husband, a Bow Street Runner, knowing."

"Harry won't ever say anything, even if you two haven't become friends. I do hope that will change," she added.

Rafe doubted the possibility. Sheffield had spent years hunting the Vicar for a crime Rafe hadn't actually committed. Once Sheffield had learned that—and caught the man who'd burned down a flash-house, killing several people inside—he'd let go of his need for vengeance. Still, they hadn't formed a friendship despite the fact that they were now related by marriage.

"I wouldn't worry about Colton. It wouldn't benefit him to say anything. He wants to put his past behind him as much as I do." The viscount wouldn't want to remind people that he'd been buried in gambling debt and had borrowed money that he hadn't initially been able to repay. Or that his failure had led to the murder of his parents.

Selina uncrossed her arms and dropped them to her sides. "How will you manage to speak to Lord Stone in the midst of a picnic?"

"I'm sure there will be an opportunity." If not, he would make one.

"And what will you say? Will you ask if he recognizes you as a visitor to his estate nearly thirty years ago when you were a child?" Squinting one eye at him, she stepped closer, her gaze fixing on his right eye. "You do have the orange spot, and that has been there your entire life. I suppose it's not impossible he may recognize that one defining mark."

"I haven't decided what to say. Perhaps you'll be the one to say something. You'd prefer to be with me when I speak with him, yes?"

She inclined her head. "I would, thank you."

"This is our shared past, Lina. You may not remember any of it, but they were your parents too."

"I wish I remembered something more than a coral necklace." Her hand went to the coral flower pendant she wore that was so very similar to the one that had belonged to their mother.

"Perhaps Ivy Grove will spark a memory for you," Rafe suggested.

She laughed lightly. "I was two and a half years old when the fire took our parents. It's a wonder I recall the necklace at all." She grew serious again. "What about the church in Croydon?"

"I thought perhaps we might stop tomorrow on our way to Ivy Grove."

She hesitated. "Harry will be with me."

Rafe understood what she wasn't saying. "I'd rather it was just you and me. I'm not asking you to keep secrets from him, just that we go alone."

"Thank you. We'll go another day? Soon?"

"Yes." Rafe smiled at her. "Sheffield is a lucky man."

She shook her head. "I'm the lucky one. I hope you will be too—someday."

"I don't need to fall in love to feel fortunate." He didn't need to fall in love at all. Not again.

Anne flashed through his mind like a lightning bolt. He was momentarily blind. Until he blinked.

"Mrs. Sheffield, your first guests have arrived."

Rafe blinked again. "I'll be going." Pivoting, he froze as Anne walked into the room with her sister; at least Rafe was certain it must be her sister, Lady Colton.

Anne's expression flickered with surprise, and Rafe hoped Selina didn't catch it. Except his sister was deuced observant. Such was the learned skill of a successful pickpocket.

"Good afternoon, Lady Colton, Miss Pemberton," Selina said warmly. "Allow me to present my brother, Mr. Raphael Bowles."

Raphael was the name he'd taken to make "Rafe" sound more sophisticated. When he was eight, he'd met a man named Bowles who'd owned a posh gaming hell. Expensively dressed and well-spoken, he'd impressed the hell out of Rafe.

"Good afternoon," Lady Colton said. She was a couple of inches taller than Anne, and her eyes were darker, a true brown with none of the green that made Anne's hazel. Their blonde hair was also slightly different somehow, not in color, but in liveliness, which made absolutely no sense when it came to describing hair. Nevertheless, the word completely embodied Anne's curls, which often escaped their assigned style to graze her forehead, cheek, or neck. All places he wanted to kiss.

*Hell.*

"It's a pleasure to meet you, Mr. Bowles," Anne said, nodding demurely, though he was certain there was nothing demure about her.

Rafe bowed. It was one of the few things he remembered that his father had taught him. "The pleasure is mine. I beg you to excuse me. I've no desire to disrupt your meeting." He smiled before moving past them.

First, however, he caught the intense look in Anne's eyes and the slight parting of her lips. She wanted to say something more, but he wasn't going to give her the chance.

Only, Anne was quite persistent. "Will we see you at the picnic at Ivy Grove tomorrow?"

Rafe looked back at her and her sister. Of course they would be there. If Colton had prompted the event, it made sense they would be invited too. "Yes, I'm looking forward to it."

Anne's mouth lifted into a provocative smile. "I am too."

Leaving before Anne said or did anything else that would stir Selina's curiosity, Rafe stalked from the house. He needed to think about the picnic, about what he would say to Stone.

Except Anne would be at the picnic too. And damn him if that didn't make the event all the more enticing.

~

As Anthony helped Anne from the coach at Ivy Grove, she looked up at the gray sky. "I fear it may rain." She hoped the picnic wouldn't be canceled. Or that Mr. Bowles—Raphael?—hadn't decided not to come.

Anthony frowned as he cast his gaze toward the heavens. "It looks that way. Let us hope your godfather has a contingency." He offered his arm to Jane, and a footman gestured toward the path that would lead them to the picnic.

Anne walked on her sister's other side. She'd been to Ivy Grove on several occasions and hadn't been surprised when a groom had directed the coach toward the lake. It was the perfect place for a picnic. The path rounded a copse of trees, and the Aphrodite temple came into view. As far as follies went, it was an extraordinary example. It was, perhaps strangely, her godfather's favorite thing about the estate. Apparently his father had built it.

Round with a domed roof, the temple boasted nine columns around the perimeter. In the center of the building stood a grand statue of the goddess holding a dove while roses bloomed at her feet. Around the base of the temple were dolphins and other, smaller, sea creatures and shells.

"Do you remember coming here when we were children?" Anne asked Jane.

"I do." Jane nodded. "I remember wanting to fish and not being allowed because Papa said it wasn't appropriate for girls."

"I'll take you fishing, my love," Anthony offered with a smile. "When it's not about to rain."

Several other guests were gathered near the lake where blankets were spread upon the grass. Anne immediately spied Lord Bodyguard, for he was taller than everyone else. She resisted the urge to walk straight toward him.

"Where's Lord Stone?" Jane asked.

Anne scanned those gathered once more. "I don't see him."

"Lady Colton, Miss Pemberton."

Arriving just behind them was Stone's son, Lorcan Mallory, the Viscount Sandon.

"Whyever are you addressing us so formally?" Anne asked with a laugh. "You've known us forever."

"Yes, but Jane is now a viscountess." Sandon bowed to Jane and then to Anne. When he rose, he grinned at them both. "Forgive my father. He's dithering about whether to move the picnic inside." He glanced at the sky where a particularly dark cloud was heading straight for them. "I think he must, but he doesn't always listen to me."

"Perhaps we'll be fortunate and the rain will stay away," Anne said.

Sandon's gaze strayed to where footmen were pouring wine. "I beg your pardon, but I must attend to picnic management. Father wants to hold off on the wine for a few more minutes until those darker clouds pass."

Deciding she'd waited an acceptable amount of time before approaching Lord Bodyguard, Anne looked to where he stood with his sister and her husband. "Let's go and speak with Selina."

Jane nodded, and the trio made their way to Selina, her husband, and Mr. Bowles. Selina greeted them warmly, as did her husband, Mr. Sheffield. Mr. Bowles bowed, and Anne decided he was rather good at it.

Anne positioned herself next to Lord Bodyguard. "Did you see the temple?"

"I did." He looked toward the folly, which stood several yards away. "It's rather hard to miss."

"Come, I'll show you my favorite part."

His brows rose. "You've been here before?"

"Many times." She clasped his arm and led him to the folly. "The Goddess of Love." She looked at him askance but he gave no reaction. "She came from the sea, so the base of the temple is decorated with creatures from the ocean. I love the dolphins, but there is one in particular..." She guided him around to the back of the temple. "Here. This one looks as though it's smiling."

Lord Bodyguard stepped close to the dolphin, whose snout was pointed toward the sky as if it were cresting the surface of the nonexistent water. He touched the stone, his gaze fixed on the animal. "Extraordinary," he breathed.

"Have you ever seen a real dolphin?" she asked. "I have not."

"I've never even been to the sea." He stroked the dolphin's snout. "At least, not that I remember," he added softly.

"You should rectify that. I love the ocean. Something about the sound and smell is incredibly peaceful and refreshing."

"Perhaps I will." He turned his head then looked at her. "We're not in view of anyone else. Isn't that scandalous?"

She arched a shoulder. "Probably." She almost said she was already scandalized, but she didn't want to talk about her aborted wedding with anyone, especially Lord Bodyguard. "So your name is Raphael?"

He took his hand from the dolphin. "Rafe."

"Rafe. It suits you."

A smile teased his mouth. "How fortunate after thirty-two years."

"So that's how much older you are than me."

"How much older is that?"

"Ten years. It seems like a great deal of time, and yet I know several young ladies who married men older than you this Season."

His gaze held hers. "You aren't marrying me, Miss Pemberton."

"You called me Anne before," she whispered. "You can do that when we're alone."

"We should never be alone."

"But we have been."

He glanced toward the picnic area, which they couldn't see. "That was ill-advised." He frowned at her. "I thought I was plain with you the other day—we aren't friends."

"And I explained—plainly—that we are. Stop fighting it."

"I fail to see how we can be friends. Or why. It's not as if I can take you to Magazine Day. Then I *would* have to marry you."

She flashed a smile at him. "Would that be so bad?"

He laughed, and she recalled how the scar on his chin would flatten when he smiled broadly or laughed. She also remembered how the slight ridge in the bottom of the center of his lip felt against her.

"*Please* stop flirting with me, Anne. We can't go back to…before."

"Were we flirting before?" She simply couldn't stop herself. Being with him made her feel so light, so wonderful, better than she had in months.

A fat raindrop landed on his sleeve near her hand.

Rafe looked up, squinting. "Here it comes." He took her hand as several drops began to fall, and together, they raced to a narrow doorway tucked into the side of the stairs that led up to the statue and the main covered area.

He opened the door and pulled her inside before they were completely drenched.

She looked up at him in surprise. "How did you know this was here?"

"I just..." His brow creased, and confusion shadowed his eyes. "I saw the door."

"I was never allowed to come in here." She looked around at the small, dark space but couldn't gauge the size or depth.

"Your hair came loose." He tucked a damp lock behind her ear beneath her hat.

"It's always doing that," she murmured, instinctively lifting her hand and connecting with his. She didn't pull away.

He didn't either. "I remember."

They stared at each other as the rain cascaded outside the door. Someone could come—likely *would* come as they sought to escape the squall. Even so, Anne couldn't move away.

She edged closer to him.

"Anne," he breathed, her name a warning and yet somehow an invitation too.

"Anne!"

Startled, she stepped back as her godfather leapt into the chamber beneath the stairs. "Godfather, you're all wet."

"Quite." He brushed at his sodden sleeves. "I had just returned to the picnic to say we should move inside. Too late, I'm afraid." He looked toward Rafe. "You must be Mr. Bowles."

Anne looked between them. They hadn't yet met?

"I am," Rafe said. "You must be Lord Stone. Thank you for your kind invitation today."

"I'm pleased to welcome you to Ivy Grove. I see

you found the secret room in the folly. Clever of you. Or did my goddaughter bring you here when the rain started?"

"Your goddaughter?" Rafe looked toward Anne, but she couldn't see his face very well now that they weren't standing so close together. Between the darkness of the room and the brim of his hat, she couldn't see his eyes at all.

"Miss Pemberton is my goddaughter," the earl said.

Rafe nodded slowly—that she could see. "That's why you've been here many times."

"Yes, since I was a child," Anne said.

"Since before you can remember." The earl laughed. "Oh look, the rain is slowing down. When it stops, we'll make a run for the house. Well, not a run." He chuckled.

"Should we take the coaches?" Rafe suggested.

"That would be faster—and drier if the heavens decide to weep again. Capital idea, Bowles!" The earl looked to Anne with a grin. "I've just the coach in mind for us, my dear. Sir Algernon has an elegant new vehicle."

Oh no. Her godfather really did want to play matchmaker. Anne wanted no part of that. She silently prayed the rain would continue.

Alas, it did not. A moment later, the air grew silent and the day brightened.

"Wonderful!" The earl stepped outside and looked up. "Come, let us hurry. I saw most of the guests gathered inside the temple around the statue. We'll just go up and tell them all the plan—rush to the coaches and we'll picnic in the ballroom!" He said this with such gaiety, it seemed to have been his plan all along rather than a contingency.

Anne wanted to tell him to go ahead and she

would accompany Mr. Bowles to the coaches, but Rafe was already moving outside.

"I'll see you at the house," he said, inclining his head first toward Anne, then the earl before taking himself off.

She clenched her jaw in disappointment as she took her godfather's arm and went with him into the temple. There, he directed everyone to the coaches and promised blankets and towels when they arrived at the house.

"Ah, there's Sir Algernon." He began to steer her toward the knight, who was perhaps *fifteen* years her senior—suddenly, Rafe seemed quite young.

She tried to dig the heels of her half-boots into the stone. Having already bowed to the wishes of her parents—with disastrous results—Anne resisted doing so again. She wanted to make her own choices, dammit. "I am not ready for courtship. It's too soon."

"Oh, come now. It's not at all too soon. You've wallowed long enough, and you must show Society that you are made of the strongest stuff, that you are above the nonsense that went on."

If he referred to the shameful scandal of her former betrothed and his criminal behavior as "nonsense" one more time, Anne feared what she might do. For now, she pursed her lips, which he either didn't notice or ignored.

"Will you at least meet him?" the earl asked with a bit of a plaintive tone. At least he was asking and not demanding as her father would have done. "This entire event is to support *you*."

"Here I thought it was also to celebrate Sandon's homecoming," she said drily. "I've already met Sir Algernon. But to appease you, I will accompany you to speak with him."

"And ride to the house with him," the earl said with a smile.

"Alone? I think not." It was one thing to spend time alone with Rafe—which she would eagerly do—but she had no desire to risk what remained of her reputation with Sir Algernon. Actually, that wasn't the issue. Her reputation was quite spoiled due to Gilbert. She simply didn't want to be alone with Sir Algernon.

"Oh, here you are, Anne." Jane touched Anne's shoulder from behind.

Anne wanted to hug her with relief. "Yes." She gave Jane a pleading look and darted her eyes toward her godfather.

A befuddled shadow swept across Jane's brow, but then she gave an infinitesimal nod. "Shall we go to the house before it rains again?"

"Indeed." Anne gave the earl an apologetic smile and accompanied her sister and Anthony to the coach. "Thank you," she said as soon as they were out of Stone's earshot.

"Where were you during the downpour?" Jane asked. "I couldn't find you in the temple. I was worried."

"There is a room beneath one of the staircases. I took shelter there."

"With Mr. Bowles?" Jane asked.

"And my godfather." Eventually. She didn't want to discuss what had really happened—that she'd briefly been alone with Rafe—at least not in front of Anthony.

"Well, I'm glad you were able to stay mostly dry. Anthony and I wondered if we should just return to London. We both got a bit damp."

Anne wasn't ready to leave. She'd barely spent any time with Rafe, and she hadn't yet convinced him they should continue their friendship. They'd been able to sneak away together for four blissful afternoons. Surely they could do so again, particularly when the Season ended. “Can we please stay?”

Jane looked to Anthony who shrugged and said, “I have no preference.”

“Then we’ll stay,” Jane said. “But let’s get to the house before we’re drenched once more.”

Anne smiled, eager to find Rafe and convince him they really could be friends.

# CHAPTER 4

The coaches arrived en masse in the drive, and guests hurried inside as another dark cloud approached. Except Rafe. He hung back, his gaze fixed on the façade. Crafted of light stone with a tall, imposing Palladian entry, the house loomed large, making his skin prick with awareness.

He was one of the last to move inside, having lost sight of his sister and Harry. Not that he minded. Seeing the folly had provoked a feeling of familiarity that was even more intense here. He supposed that made sense because he would have certainly visited the house since he'd been to the folly.

It was more than that, however. He *knew* this house. When he walked inside, the entry hall would be round, and if he walked straight through it, he'd find himself in a grand hall with a staircase climbing the left side up to a gallery divided by arches from the space looking down at the hall below.

Taking a shallow breath, he walked up the steps to the open door and moved inside. His movements felt stilted and uncertain, as if he wasn't entirely in command of himself.

*Get hold of yourself.*

But then he froze. The entry hall was precisely as he'd imagined it.

*Of course it is, you dolt. You've been here before.*

Why, then, was he reacting in this manner? It was almost as if he were moving in a dream.

Without thought, he strode through the entry hall and into the staircase hall. Again, he'd gotten every detail just right. His gaze lifted and fixed on the gallery above. He knew what he'd find up there…

"Rafe?"

He heard his name but didn't turn.

Selina's hand touched his arm. "Rafe?"

"I remember this, Lina. Before I walked into the house, I could describe the entry hall, this staircase. Up there is a gallery with portraits." He started toward the stairs, stopping at the first step and turning his head to look at her. "Are you coming?"

She hurried to follow him. "What does this mean?"

"I'm not sure. But I think we did more than visit Ivy Grove."

Selina halted when they reached the top, and he looked back at her. She'd gone a bit pale.

He reached for her hand and gave her a reassuring nod. Together, they walked through one of the archways that separated the gallery from the area overlooking the hall below. At one end there was a chaise, and at the other, a pair of chairs. "Those chairs aren't right," he said. "There wasn't anything there before."

"How are you remembering this?" Selina whispered.

He couldn't answer. Squeezing her hand, he led

her toward the chairs, then abruptly stopped in front of the portrait he'd been looking for.

A gasp from Selina seemed to take in all the air around them. "Who is that?" She looked from the portrait to Rafe and back again. "He looks just like you."

"That's because he's our grandfather. We lived here, Lina. I'm certain of it."

"We lived *here*?" She looked around, the color still gone from her face.

He felt her shake, her body wilt. Releasing her hand, he clasped his arm about her waist and held her steady against him. "Our nursery was on the second floor. We could see the folly from the window." He hadn't remembered any of this before today, but being here, seeing the house, had brought a flood of memories back.

"But this house isn't new, and our house burned down. Didn't it?"

"May I help you?" a feminine voice asked pleasantly.

Rafe and Selina turned in unison. From her garb, the woman was a servant. Her mostly silver hair was pulled back severely from her round face and tucked beneath a cap. Her dark eyes settled on them with curiosity. "May I escort you downstairs to the ballroom?" Her mouth turned down, and she stepped toward them. She looked from Rafe to the portrait, her eyes widening, before returning her attention to Rafe.

"It can't be," she breathed, moving even closer, and stared up into his face. "You are the mirror image, but—" She blinked then squinted slightly. "Your eye…the orange spot…"

Rafe leaned toward her slightly, widening his eyes. "In my right eye, yes."

"Dear Lord." The woman went completely white before crumpling to the floor.

"Bloody hell," Rafe muttered.

"The chaise," Selina said, gesturing to the other end of the gallery.

Rafe bent down and swept the woman into his arms, bearing her to the chaise, where he carefully laid her atop the cushions. "She recognized me."

"I think so." Selina sounded as breathless as Rafe felt.

The woman's eyes fluttered open. She blinked at Selina before looking at Rafe. Lifting her hand to her mouth, she shook her head. Tears gathered in her eyes and spilled down her cheeks.

A cascade of emotions rioted through Rafe, but none so strong as the desperate need to *know*. "Why are you crying?"

"It's you—it has to be."

"Who am I?" He glanced toward Selina. "Who are *we*?"

The woman's tear-filled gaze moved to Selina. "And you must be wee Selina."

Selina's throat worked. "You know my name," she croaked. Rafe wanted to reach for her, but he was unable to move. He could barely think.

The woman sat up and swung her feet to the floor. She wiped the backs of her hands over her cheeks. "Yes, I was a new housemaid when you lived here as children." Deep furrows marred her brow. "You were looking at your grandfather's portrait."

If they had, in fact, lived here and that portrait was their grandfather… Rafe tried to take a breath and couldn't. "Who were our parents? We don't remember. They were lost to us in a fire, but this house clearly did not burn down twenty-seven years ago."

"No, the fire was at your family seat—Stonehaven in Staffordshire. We thought you had died. How are you not dead along with your poor parents?"

Rafe wished those bloody chairs weren't so far away. He feared he was about to collapse too.

"Rafe?" Selina pressed herself to his side and put her arm around his waist. She wiped her hand over her brow. "Who are you?" she asked the woman.

"I'm Mrs. Gentry, the housekeeper here." She rose, her gaze warm and kind. "You poor dears, this is a shock to you, I can see. What can I do for you?" She turned her gaze to Rafe. "My lord?"

*My lord.*

His knees felt weak. Selina seemed to know it as her hold on him tightened.

"Our father was the earl?" he managed to ask.

Mrs. Gentry nodded. "Yes. He was Lord Stone's older brother." She shook her head. "My apologies —*you* are Lord Stone. Oh my goodness, what will your uncle say?"

His uncle. His *real* uncle.

Rafe swiped his hand over his face. Good God, he was a fucking *earl*. Absurdly, he thought of all the people he'd known over the long years of his childhood, when he'd commanded a small army of thieves and later when he'd overseen a dozen receiver shops from Saffron Hill to Petticoat Lane. Or those who had known him as the Vicar.

Selina pivoted with him and pushed him down on the chaise. He pulled her down with him, needing her at his side.

"Would you like a drink?" Mrs. Gentry asked. "Perhaps some port?"

"No. Maybe." Rafe shook his head. He couldn't *think*. And he bloody well needed to. He directed an intense stare at the housekeeper, uncaring if he frightened her with his fierce need to understand. "You're certain I'm—" What the hell was his name even? "Stone's heir?"

The housekeeper shook her head.

"You aren't certain?" Selina asked tentatively, her brow creasing.

"I am. I beg your pardon, this is a shock for me as well. You are not, however, Stone's heir. You were, but now you are Lord Stone. Raphael Jerome Mallory is your name—Jerome was your father—I have always included you in my prayers. But you were addressed as Lord Sandon, of course. Your father called you Sandy, but your mother called you Rafe."

Sandy. The name roused something in him. A horrible sound erupted from his chest—part gasp and part sob. He clapped his hand over his mouth and looked away.

When he'd reined in his emotion, he turned his head back to housekeeper. "Tell us about the fire."

"There you are." Harry Sheffield, Selina's husband, took that inopportune moment to interrupt as he walked into the gallery. "I've been looking all over for—" He stopped abruptly. "What's wrong?"

"Oh, Harry." Selina let out a sound similar to the one Rafe had made.

Sheffield rushed forward and crouched down before her. "What is it, my love?"

Selina threw her arms around his neck and began to cry. Rafe stared at her, feeling as overwhelmed as she looked but also somehow frozen.

Sheffield's gaze met Rafe's over Selina's shoulder. "What the hell is going on?"

"We've had a bit of a shock." That was all he could say?

"Come, we must go downstairs and find Lord

Stone." The housekeeper frowned. "Er, Mr. Mallory."

Selina pulled back from Sheffield and wiped at her eyes before looking to Rafe. "Should we?"

"You must," the housekeeper insisted. "He'll want to know you aren't really dead."

"I require an explanation," Sheffield said. As a constable, he was always on a quest for answers.

Selina touched the side of her husband's head. "You know our parents died in a fire. Mrs. Gentry"—she nodded toward the housekeeper—"recognized Rafe—the orange mark in his eye. She knows who our parents were—the Earl and Countess of Stone." Her voice broke on the last word. Rafe put his hand on her shoulder.

Sheffield's eyes widened, and he gaped at Rafe. "You'll need proof to claim that."

"I'm the proof," Mrs. Gentry said, sounding a bit cross. "And I'm certain the other members of the household who were here when they were children will agree he is Lord Stone. Furthermore, there are bound to be several people at Stonehaven who can do the same."

"Stonehaven?" Sheffield asked.

"The Stone family seat." *My* family seat, Rafe thought. He was a goddamned *earl*. And he had no idea when—or if—that would sink into his brain.

Sheffield narrowed his eyes at Mrs. Gentry. "You're certain it's him?"

"She is," Rafe answered tersely. "Just as I'm certain that I've been here before—that we lived here. I knew what the house looked like before I came inside, and I took Selina directly to a portrait of our grandfather."

"Harry, he knew it was him," Selina said softly. "Then Mrs. Gentry came, and she said so too."

Rafe lightly squeezed Selina's shoulder, then released her. "Yes, let us go downstairs. The ballroom, you say? It's in the corner, I'm not sure which one, and it has doors on two walls that open outside. There's a reflection pool."

Mrs. Gentry grinned. "Yes. That's right."

Rafe stood, his legs finally feeling steady and his heart beating at a slightly slower pace. Sheffield rose and offered Selina assistance. She took his hand and pressed herself tight against his side. Rafe was glad she had him. This was more than a shock; this was unbelievable. An unending barrage of questions assaulted him.

"Follow me, my lord," Mrs. Gentry said. "Unless you remember the way."

"I'm not sure I do," Rafe admitted.

The housekeeper nodded before turning and walking from the gallery.

Sheffield looked at Rafe, his eyes glazed with disbelief. "You're the Earl of Stone?"

Rafe took the most substantial breath he had since walking into the house. "Apparently so."

~

After completing a circuit of the ballroom, Anne had to accept that Rafe wasn't there. Had he left? The day suddenly became far less interesting.

"Ho there, Miss Pemberton. Terrible storm, what?" Sir Alergnon asked as he intercepted her next circuit.

Only a few inches taller than her, with thick brown hair and kind eyes, Sir Algernon Betts-Hinsworth was unabashedly on the Marriage Mart. He'd expressed his interest in Anne before she'd accepted Gilbert's proposal. In hindsight, Anne had chosen very poorly—all because Gilbert had kissed moderately well. After kissing Rafe—and thoroughly enjoying it—that had seemed an important attribute. And since it had seemed Rafe was lost to her, she'd searched for a replacement.

He was not, however, lost to her any longer.

She summoned a smile for Sir Algernon. He was a pleasant sort, even if Anne had no interest in kissing him.

"Yes, it was rather sudden and the rain fierce," she said, remarking on the squall that had sent them all to the folly.

"An indoor picnic is exciting, though, isn't it?"

Exciting wasn't the word Anne would use. "It's better than no picnic."

"Just so, just so."

The footmen had laid blankets around the ballroom and were beginning to set up the food. Outside, the sky had darkened further, and the second storm that had threatened when they'd come inside now unleashed itself upon the earth. Water sluiced down the ballroom windows, and wind shook the trees.

"I'm quite delighted to be inside," Sir Algernon remarked. "I daresay the trip back to London will take twice as long as the journey here."

While he spoke, Anne scanned the ballroom, then stared at the main entrance. The arrival of two people made her breath catch until she recognized them—her godfather's daughter, Deborah, and her husband, Lord Burnhope.

Anne seized on the opportunity to excuse herself. "Pardon me, Sir Algernon. I wish to welcome Lady Burnhope." She gave him a warm smile before hastening across the ballroom.

By the time Anne arrived at Deborah's side, her husband had already gone. "I thought perhaps you weren't coming," Anne said.

"Just late." Deborah patted a slender hand against the back of her elegantly styled brown hair. She always looked as though she'd stepped from the pages of *La Belle Assemblée*. "We were caught in that horrendous storm, and that delayed us further."

Lord Stone came toward them, his brows drawn as he surveyed his daughter. "Deborah, you are quite tardy. As usual." His lips pressed together in disapproval.

"My apologies, Papa. Burnhope had business that held us up, and the weather was uncooperative."

"Writing another treatise on beetles, was he?" the earl asked with a touch of sarcasm. "Well, you are here at last. We've moved the picnic indoors. It would have been nice to have your help when the arrangements needed to be adjusted."

Anne shifted uncomfortably. She'd been present for too many occasions when her godfather had needled his daughter, and Deborah typically pricked his ire in return. It was a contentious relationship. Once, Lord Stone had told Anne he wished she'd been his daughter instead. He'd promptly apologized, but Anne had never forgotten.

Deborah's eyes hardened, but her mouth curved into a smile. "How can I help now that I'm here?"

"I believe it's all been handled. Just supervise Anne, if you will. You're good at that." Stone winked at Anne before going to speak with some of his guests.

"You're good at that," Deborah mocked. She dashed the back of her hand over her brow. "My apologies. Do you actually require supervision?"

The irony was that Deborah *wasn't* good at that. She'd been a terrible chaperone back when she'd allowed Anne to sit by herself at Hatchard's for two hours every Thursday. She'd also been disappointed when Anne's mother had put an end to those excursions so that Anne could focus on her Season. Anne had never asked what Deborah had been doing during those afternoons, but she'd long suspected the time had been spent conducting a romantic liaison.

"No, but your company is most welcome," Anne said. "I was trapped speaking with Sir Algernon." She sent a guilty glance toward him and was glad to see he was now occupied with a group of other guests.

Deborah followed her gaze. "He is on Papa's short list of potential husbands for you."

"He has a *list*?" Anne let out a soft groan.

"Yes, sorry." Deborah let out a light chuckle as she looked down at Anne from her well-above-average height. "He's absolutely committed to seeing you wed with the utmost haste. He was hoping for the end of the Season, but since that is nigh, I expect he'll be disappointed. Unless you marry someone by special license." She laughed again.

Anne couldn't imagine that happening. Not when the only person who came to mind when she considered marriage was Rafe. And *that* wasn't happening, with a special license or otherwise.

"I take it you are not interested in satisfying Papa's expectations?"

"Not at all." Anne gave Deborah a sardonic stare. "Do you blame me after what I went through with Gilbert?"

"Heavens, no. Why you chose him is still a mystery to me."

Anne wasn't about to tell her about the kissing. Besides, it was more than that. She'd chosen someone she could like but not love, which she hadn't realized until after the wedding had been canceled. That she'd somehow found Gilbert likeable was a testament to his skill at cultivating relationships that would benefit him.

"It hardly signifies since nothing came of it," Anne said, eager to dispose of the topic. "In any case, I've no desire to rush into marriage any time soon. As you said, it's nearly the end of the Season anyway."

Deborah eyed her with curiosity. "I suppose I understand, but remember, it's every young lady's responsibility to marry and marry well. And, goodness, it's not as if the road to success is always straight and simple as mine was. Look at your sister. Five years on the shelf and now a viscountess. Though, hopefully, you won't have to wait so long." Her brow creased, and she tapped her fingertip against her chin. "Alas, you are the victim of a scandal, just as she was."

Anger roiled in Anne. She wasn't a victim. At least, she didn't want to be.

"It's good that Papa is helping you," Deborah continued. "Your reputation was not as damaged as your sister's, but it was still wounded. Papa's support will fix things. And it does help that your sister married a viscount, even if he is a wastrel."

Anne gently elbowed Deborah in the arm. "You do realize she's still my sister, and I love her very much? And that I currently reside with her and the wastrel, whom I also happen to love as a brother?"

Deborah laughed gaily. "Yes! I didn't mean to insult, but facts are facts, dear. You are always welcome to come live with me."

Anne would never. She didn't dislike Deborah, but she didn't necessarily like her either. It was a complicated relationship, as many were in families. And Anne considered Deborah, Lorcan, and her godfather family. In particular, Anne didn't like the way Deborah treated her husband. Lord Burnhope was a quiet sort who enjoyed entomology. He was about as different from his fashion-loving, pompous wife as one could be.

"I'm quite happy residing with my sister and brother-in-law." Anne worked to keep her voice even.

Deborah's gaze strayed to Jane and Anthony, who stood together near one of the doors leading outside. "They seem well-suited." Was there an edge of envy in her tone?

"Yes," Anne agreed. "To wed for love is very lucky, isn't it?"

"Only if it's to the right person. Marrying well is paramount. If there's love in the bargain, then yes, that's fortunate indeed."

How cold. And yet that's precisely what Anne had been raised to believe. Until she'd met Rafe, she hadn't thought too deeply about whether she'd fall in love. The hope had been there, certainly, if not the expectation. Then she'd met him, and her world had shifted.

Until it had tipped her right back to where she was supposed to be. Only to toss her into uncharted waters.

Anne looked seriously at Deborah. "Did you fall in love with Burnhope?"

Waving her hand, Deborah laughed lightly. "Don't be silly, Anne. Ladies don't discuss such things."

"But you said—" Anne had been about to say that she'd commented on Jane and Anthony; however, the arrival of Rafe in the ballroom stole the words right out of Anne's mouth as well as the air from her lungs.

He entered in the company of his sister and Mr. Sheffield and…the housekeeper?

"Who is that blond gentleman?" Deborah asked with keen interest.

Anne stiffened but didn't answer her. She was too focused on the fact that Rafe looked a bit pale. As did his sister.

Deborah's sharp inhalation drew Anne's attention. "And who is the woman with him?" She narrowed her eyes and started walking toward them—they were on a direct path to Lord Stone.

"That's Mrs. Sheffield," Anne answered as she walked quickly to keep up with Deborah's longer stride. "The blond gentleman is her brother, Mr. Bowles."

"Her brother?" Deborah scowled as she continued toward them.

Lord Stone extricated himself from the group he was with and greeted Rafe and the others with a furrowed brow, his gaze settling on the housekeeper. Her presence with them was…odd.

Deborah inserted herself into the group, taking a position beside her father. Anne moved to his other side, her attention entirely on Rafe and his impassive expression. He glanced toward her, his nostrils flaring slightly, before he fixed his gaze on Lord Stone.

The earl pivoted briefly toward Deborah. "Allow me to present my daughter, Lady Burnhope. Deborah, I believe you know Mr. Sheffield. This is his wife, Mrs. Selina Sheffield, and her brother, Mr. Raphael Bowles."

Selina's eyes narrowed and her jaw clenched as she regarded Deborah, who had an almost identical expression.

Deborah spoke, offering an icy smile. "What a *pleasure* to see you again, Selina."

The color that had been missing from Selina's face returned. It was clear—at least to Anne—that they knew each other. And the relationship wasn't friendly.

"I beg your pardon," the earl said, "are you already acquainted?"

"Yes," Deborah said, but was drowned out by the housekeeper.

"I'm sorry to interrupt, my lord," Mrs. Gentry said, wincing and sending an apologetic look toward Rafe. Apologetic? Why? Anne was thoroughly confused. But it was more than that. A chill raced down the back of her neck.

Mrs. Gentry faced her employer with determination. "I've—*we've*—a matter of grave importance to discuss with you. Might we remove to a more private location?"

A look of stark annoyance flitted across Deborah's face. She pursed her lips and glared at the housekeeper, who seemed to shrink. Anne wished she was standing near Deborah so she could elbow her again.

"Yes," Deborah said, surprising Anne by agreeing with Mrs. Gentry. "We should excuse ourselves. I have so many questions for Selina. My apologies, *Mrs. Sheffield*." The look she gave Selina could have stripped the wallpaper from the ballroom. And Selina's answering stare would have sent puppies running in terror.

"I can't just leave my own picnic," the earl said crossly. "Regardless of whatever drama is trying to unfold here." He cast an irritated look toward Deborah. "We were about to eat."

"Let them eat while we adjourn to the library. I doubt this will take long." Deborah's malicious smile returned.

Anne had never seen her behave quite like this.

It wasn't just frightening; it was horrifying.

Lord Stone shook his head. "This must wait."

"I'm your nephew," Rafe blurted. It was as if the air in the room thinned, and everyone in the small circle stopped breathing.

Anne watched the color drain from her godfather's face. She felt a similar shock. Rafe was his nephew? How was that possible? Her godfather didn't have any living siblings, and the children of the only one who'd survived to adulthood were also dead.

"My *what?*" The earl's shock echoed inside Anne.

"They are your brother's children," Mrs. Gentry said urgently. "Raphael and Selina. Surely you can see it. Just look at his eye."

Rafe widened his eyes, and it was impossible to miss that definitive orange spot. "Uncle, it seems I am the rightful Earl of Stone."

# CHAPTER 5

The earl—no, not the earl, but Mallory or Uncle, hell, Rafe didn't know what to call him—led them to the library. Stepping over the threshold, a rush of familiarity swept over him. He'd spent time here. With his father. A tide of emotion nearly engulfed him.

"Are you all right?" Anne had managed to find her way to his side and whispered the question. Her gaze was soft with concern.

"No." He saw no reason to lie. At least not to her. Damn if that wasn't as complicated as this entire bloody day.

He looked past her at the rows of books, his gaze traveling along the shelves.

"This is familiar to you," she said.

He nodded before moving, as if drawn by a magnet, to the corner. Without thinking, he reached up and pulled on a thick, dark blue book. The entire shelf sprang open. He grinned, then brought his hand to his mouth. Beyond the door was a small secret room.

Turning, he looked at his sister. "Do you remember this, Lina?" She shook her head—of course she didn't. She'd been far too young. He hated that she recalled none of this, that she'd been robbed of even a fraction of her childhood. Rafe at least had that much.

He surveyed the rest of the occupants of the room. Everyone stared at him except Harry, who was, rightly, focused on his wife. Anne's gaze was full of wonder, while Mrs. Gentry's contained joy. Mallory and his daughter stared at him in shock.

His daughter had known Selina. How? More importantly, what could she expose? *Fuck.*

He and Selina needed to make sure their stories aligned. They both wanted to bury the past twenty-seven years, but now, doing so was critical. If Rafe was to be an earl, he couldn't very well be known as a criminal moneylender or a thief. And his sister couldn't be exposed as a swindler, especially since her husband was a bloody constable.

"But you remembered it, my lord," Mrs. Gentry said, addressing him as he supposed was right, even if it sounded utterly wrong to his ears. He saw his uncle flinch.

Rafe took a moment to study the man. He'd seemed oddly familiar when they'd met earlier, but Rafe had attributed the feeling to being at the folly. He was shorter than Rafe, with light brown hair that formed a widow's peak on his forehead. His eyes were the same blue as his own, but without the orange mark.

That mark.

He'd cursed its oddity over the years, but now it identified him indisputably as Raphael Mallory, the Earl of bloody Stone.

"How did you know that was there?" Lady Burnhope asked with a dubious glower.

Rafe shrugged. "I just did. Just as I knew how to find the gallery and the portrait of my grandfather. *Our* grandfather," he amended.

Lady Burnhope's disgruntled gaze darted to Selina. Rafe didn't like the woman's animosity one bit. She was going to cause trouble.

"I don't understand how this is possible," Mallory said, wiping his hand back and forth across his brow. "Jerome's children died in that fire. We buried them."

Mrs. Gentry stepped toward him, her expression pleading. "You can't deny they are those children. Just look at them. If the mark in his eye isn't enough, you can surely see how closely he resembles your father in that portrait upstairs. And their names are Rafe and Selina. That is too much of a coincidence. What's more, he knows so much about Ivy Grove, as he demonstrated with the bookcase."

"You must accept it," Sheffield said. He'd put his arm around Selina, who looked so stiff that Rafe feared she might break. He looked to Mrs. Gentry. "Presumably, there are others here at Ivy Grove or at Stonehaven who will testify in support of Mr. Bowles's claim to the earldom."

"But he doesn't have to claim it. By law, he is dead." The words left Mallory's mouth in a rush. He looked at Rafe. "Do you even want to be the earl? You wouldn't know how."

Rafe wanted to tell the man he could learn to do anything he put his mind to, but now wasn't the time for arrogance.

Sheffield regarded Mallory with thinly veiled contempt. "Your brother's children are *alive*. Surely that should be a cause for celebration."

Mallory scrubbed his hand over his face before weaving unsteadily to a chair. Dropping onto the seat, he dipped his chin. "Of course. This is just a shock. I can't… I can't fully comprehend that after all this time, they're here." He looked to Rafe, then to Selina. "Your father would be so happy to know you lived. How on earth did you manage to survive?" He paused to take a breath. "Do you remember the fire?"

Selina shook her head, but Rafe answered, "I remember smoke, and I remember being carried away." That was all he wanted to say at the moment. He had too many other questions. And now he was not only desperate to visit that church in Croydon, but he fervently hoped there would be something to learn there.

"Who carried you?" Lady Burnhope—good Lord, his *cousin*—asked. She crossed her arms tightly across her chest, surveying Rafe and Selina as if they were frauds. Which they were. Or had been. Or…not.

Fuck, he didn't know who he was. He couldn't imagine Selina was faring much better. A look toward her confirmed his belief—she was pressed snug against her husband's side, her face drawn, and her gaze icy. He followed the direction and saw that she glared at Lady Burnhope.

"Our nurse," Rafe answered tersely. He stood on Selina's other side and edged closer to her. "What is troubling to me is why our nurse would take us away, change our surname, and not tell anyone she saved us." God, had that woman, whom he barely remembered, even been their nurse? Yes. That much he knew. He remembered the young woman with her nearly black hair and the small brown spot on her cheek. "She used to sing to Selina."

"Lavender Blue," Selina whispered.

Rafe turned his head to stare at her. "Yes." Selina had barely spoken until she was probably four, but she'd sung. "That was your favorite song."

A tear tracked down Selina's cheek. She hastily

brushed it away, her expression stoic even as Rafe saw the emotion quivering beneath.

"It sounds as though the nurse stole you away," Mrs. Gentry said, her expression stricken, then softening. "What happened after she took you? You've certainly ended up quite well." There was a note of pride in her voice that almost made him smile.

"Yes, they did," Lady Burnhope said dubiously. "I always wondered how a girl who said she was from East London could possibly afford to attend Mrs. Goodwin's Ladies' Seminary."

Rafe moved closer to Selina and brushed his hand against the small of her back. That's how this shrew—their bloody cousin—knew her. And Selina had told her she was from East London?

"If you'll excuse us," Sheffield said, coming to the rescue. "This has been most overwhelming. There will be time to share stories and sort out the particulars. With the parliamentary session drawing to a close, my brother-in-law will wish to submit the necessary information to the Prince Regent and the attorney general so that the Committee for Privileges may recognize him as the Earl of Stone with due haste."

Rafe had no idea how any of this worked.

"They'll ask him to prove his birth," Mallory said.

"The evidence will include his memory of living here and of being rescued from the fire. Mrs. Gentry and other employees here and at Stonehaven will give testimony as to his identity. You'll agree the orange mark in his eye is singular proof." Sheffield's commanding tone made Rafe grateful for the man's authority. The constable pierced Mallory with a probing stare. "Do you doubt he is your nephew and she is your niece?"

Mallory hesitated only a brief moment before shaking his head. "I do not."

"I understand this is a shock," Sheffield continued more gently. "Why don't you join us for dinner in Cavendish Square on Monday evening? We'll continue this discussion and make plans for a transition after everyone's had a chance to process this revelation."

"We'll be there," Mallory said, sounding defeated.

Sheffield inclined his head before escorting Selina from the room.

Rafe looked to Mallory. "Uncle." He bowed his head and, turning, allowed his gaze to linger on Anne. She stood somewhat near her godfather—it suddenly permeated Rafe's mind that this woman he couldn't forget was tied to his family—her features taut but her eyes bright and earnest as she stared at him.

Tearing his attention from her, he thanked Mrs. Gentry and followed his sister and brother-in-law out.

The three of them said nothing until they were situated in Rafe's coach. As soon as the vehicle started moving along the drive, Selina turned her body toward the window and looked out into the rain. "My God. This was our house."

"*Is* our house," Rafe corrected.

"*Your* house," Sheffield said softly. He took Selina's hand as she settled back against the squab.

"I can't believe that awful Deborah Mallory is our cousin." She made a face of disgust. "I can't believe any of it, but that part is truly dreadful. Beatrix will be horrified."

"You told Deborah you were from East London?" Rafe asked.

Selina lifted a shoulder. "She was nasty to

Beatrix because she was a bastard. Deborah took every opportunity to flaunt her superiority and wealth. I think it bothered her immensely that Beatrix's father was a duke while hers was only an earl." A giggle jumped from her lips, surprising Rafe—and Sheffield, whose eyes widened briefly. "And her father *isn't* actually an earl." She looked at Rafe in wonder. "*You* are. *Lord Stone.*" She laughed again, a purely joyous sound.

Sheffield turned to his wife. "And *you* are Lady Selina."

"Oh, Deborah will *hate* that." Selina's eyes sparkled with glee.

Sheffield wiped his hand over his face, smiling. "This is an incredible turn of events." He sobered as he regarded his wife. "Are you truly all right?"

"I will be." She briefly rested her head against his shoulder as she looked across the coach at Rafe. "Are you?"

*No.* He still couldn't believe it, and yet his mind was also leaping forward. "What's a bloody Committee for Privileges? It sounds incredibly pompous." Rafe was glad his sister had married a constable who had previously been a barrister.

"It's one of the many committees in the House of Lords. They'll vote on the evidence we present. First, however, we will submit this information to the Prince Regent. After that, the attorney general will need to recognize your claim. The claim will then go to the committee, which will vote."

"So he needs the support of the Prince Regent, the attorney general, and the members of the committee?" Selina asked, her features creasing with worry.

"Yes." Sheffield gave her an encouraging smile. "Don't be concerned, my love. I know the attorney general personally, and my father happens to sit on the Committee for Privileges."

Rafe snorted. "Does it even matter if I'm really who I claim to be?"

Sheffield's brows descended low over his eyes. "Of course it does. However, knowing people in the right places is always an advantage. Surely it was like that in your experience too?" Sheffield was well aware of how Rafe and Selina had grown up.

And he was right—Rafe's experience had been the same. He was afforded all manner of courtesy and deference from the moment he'd become one of Samuel Partridge's favorites. When Rafe had risen in the ranks, his relationships had expanded, and he'd become as respected—and feared—as the man he worked for.

"Your point is taken." Rafe exchanged a look with Selina. She understood it too.

"I truly wouldn't be concerned. This will be a matter of form. There is a wealth of evidence," Sheffield said with certainty. "I will dispatch someone to Stonehaven to interview the retainers." He fixed his tawny gaze on Rafe. "That orange mark in your eye is a fortunate thing."

"I didn't used to think so."

Selina sent him a sympathetic glance. "When we were young, our uncle—who wasn't our uncle —would tell people Rafe was touched by lunacy. Edgar would then ask for donations to pay for a doctor, and he'd provoke Rafe to act out in a frightening manner. Some would take pity and give us money."

"Others ran away." Rafe hadn't thought of that shame in a long time. The things Edgar had made them do were abominable. "Why did he do that?" Rafe whispered. "Did he not know who we were?"

"Why did our nurse take us away and change our names?" Selina's anguish echoed his own.

Sheffield pressed a kiss to Selina's hand. "I'm so sorry, my darling. And for you, ah, Stone?" His look of sympathy was tinged with confusion. "That is your name now."

Something passed between them. Sheffield had despised the Vicar, and now he was offering to help him. Rafe knew it was because of Selina, that if not for her, Sheffield likely wouldn't give a damn. Or so he thought. Now, he wasn't so certain. "I suppose it is. I shouldn't ask it of you, but will you do me a kindness and just call me Rafe? At least when we're alone."

Surprise flickered in the other man's eyes. "I hope you'll call me Harry."

A warm smile spread over Selina's lips. "Whatever happened today, *this* is the very best thing. My two favorite men have reached an accord. This is truly beginning to feel like a family." Her voice caught, and she jerked her head toward the window once more.

The coach was silent for several minutes as they traveled through the light rain. Rafe suffered a tumult of emotions as he tried to plan what would come next. "Will our uncle just give everything over to us?"

Harry nodded. "He'll have to—what's entailed, anyway."

"I have no idea what that is," Rafe said.

"I'll find out."

Selina put her other hand atop their joined ones. "Thank you for guiding us. I don't know what we would do without you."

Rafe didn't either. And he hated that feeling. He'd relied on no one but himself for years now, and he didn't miss the sensation of depending upon others. "He was upset that we're alive."

"Of course he was," Harry said. "He's going to lose nearly everything—his title, his land, his position. If something is unentailed, perhaps you'd consider not contesting its ownership."

"Perhaps," Selina said before Rafe could. She exchanged a dark look with him that said what he was thinking: trust no one. That had long been their creed. It would also be difficult to just give something away. Rafe, was inclined to keep everything he could, and he imagined Selina felt the same.

Rafe focused his mind on what he excelled at: the strategy. "We need a story about our past. We'll say Edgar raised us in London—we needn't be specific about where—and you went to Mrs. Goodwin's. After that, you—" He scowled, cutting himself off. "This is going to be a problem for Beatrix. We can no longer claim her as our sister, which means we have to admit we lied."

Selina massaged her temple. "Beatrix won't care about her reputation. She will likely suggest we say we were protecting her because she is illegitimate."

"What about Ramsgate?" While Beatrix's father, the Duke of Ramsgate, had privately acknowledged her, he'd been clear that he would not do so publicly.

"What about him? Beatrix won't say who her father is. Let Society obsess about who he might be." Selina's tone carried equal amounts disdain and sarcasm.

Rafe frowned. "I'm sorry she'll have to endure that."

Selina put her hand in her lap. "She won't mind. She has what she always wanted—a family." She exchanged a look with Harry and smiled softly.

"You should invite her and Rockbourne to the dinner on Monday," Harry said. "A viscount in your family doesn't hurt."

"Harry, would you mind if we stopped at their house so I can tell her what happened?" Selina asked. "I have no idea if the news will get out, but I want her to hear this from me. She'll be astonished."

Rafe understood that emotion too well. The shock still hadn't worn off. Perhaps it never would.

He was a bloody *earl*.

"I doubt Mallory or Lady Burnhope will disclose what's happened," Harry said. "I suppose the housekeeper will tell the other employees, and it's possible the news could spread that way. I'd say you should be prepared for anything." He looked to Rafe. "If you don't mind, I'd like to tell my father and brother right away so they can also lend their support. You will need all the well-placed friends you can get."

Rafe's mind spun. "Thank you."

"Rafe, what will you say about your past?" Selina asked quietly. "You've been rather vague."

He had to be. Raphael Bowles hadn't existed until this spring. Before that, Rafe had been a criminal, an orphan of London's East End. Thanks to his father teaching him to read at a very young age and his ensuing love of books, he was educated. Books, of course, were exceptionally dear, so he hadn't been able to purchase them. Instead, he'd stolen them from Paternoster Row until a bookshop owner had caught him one day. Rather than send Rafe to prison, Mr. Fletcher had taken pity and allowed him to read the books in his establishment as if it were a library. Dear Mr. Fletcher had died some eight years ago, and now Rafe owned that bookshop.

Harry's brow creased. "You will be scrutinized. Just as you will become one of the most eligible bachelors in London."

*Bloody hell.* Rafe did *not* want that. "Thank God the Season is almost over. Won't everyone be leaving town soon?"

"Next month, but that may as well be a year from now," Harry said. "Say you were educated by private tutors and that you inherited money from the man who raised you."

"Won't they ask who that was?" Selina asked.

Harry shrugged. "Probably, but Rafe can simply say he died a long time ago. Keep things uncomplicated, and be charming. Society will be utterly *enthralled* by your resurrection. You're handsome and wealthy, and everyone will want you to succeed."

Rafe managed to nod even as he felt completely overwhelmed. Now that he finally knew the truth of who he was, he would have to pretend as he never had before. "I am going to find out who that man really was—the man who took us from our nurse and brought us to London. None of this makes a damn bit of sense. Why would Selina and I be declared dead?"

Harry cocked his head. "Speaking as an investigator, I would ask who would benefit from your deaths."

"Our uncle." Rafe and Selina spoke almost simultaneously, their eyes meeting.

"He would have set the fire at Stonehaven?" Selina asked disbelievingly.

"And killed our parents." Ice coated Rafe from the inside out. If he found that to be true, nothing would be able to protect Mallory from his wrath.

"We don't know that for certain," Harry said cautiously. "Yet." He exchanged a look with Rafe that said he would find out.

Rafe couldn't quite believe this man who had hunted him for years was now his ally. Apparently, today was a day of improbable surprises. Not the least of which was the fact that Anne Pemberton was now firmly in his orbit.

And, though he might like to deny his strong attraction to her, *that* was the best part.

~

What was Rafe doing today? Or thinking? Was he sad? Angry? Scared? No, never scared.

These were the questions crowding Anne's mind on Saturday, along with *how can I see him today?* She would see him Monday at the dinner Mr. Sheffield had proposed, but that was too far away. She wanted to talk to him, to understand how he was feeling. It had to be a shock.

Of course it was. He'd had no idea until yesterday that he was an earl.

Anne had relayed the entire astonishing tale to her sister and Anthony during their ride back to London after the picnic. How her godfather had managed to pretend as though nothing had happened, that his life wasn't about to dramatically change, was a mystery to her. But then he'd always been good at being charming. In fact, he'd even hid the truth from Sandon, rather Lorcan, until after the guests had left. Or so Anne believed—that had been her godfather's plan after Rafe, his sister, and Mr. Sheffield had left.

Because Deborah had convinced him not to cancel the picnic. He'd wanted to, saying he would blame the weather and suggest they would all want to return to London posthaste. Deborah had pointed out that they would soon be in the midst of a scandal, so why invite speculation or scrutiny by ending the picnic early?

Anne didn't think it was a scandal, and she *really* thought she knew scandals. Still, it would be *news*. Everyone would be talking about the long-lost Earl of Stone.

And that was why she had to see him. He was going to need all the friends he could get, and she wanted to make sure he knew he could count on her.

But would he? So far, he'd rebuffed her overtures. Sort of. He said one thing, but his eyes and behavior said something else. She'd been certain they were going to kiss beneath the temple yesterday. Until her blasted godfather had shown up. Now, *that* had been a scandal—at least to her.

Jane came into the morning room carrying Fern. Daffodil followed behind them, her tiny kitten legs moving quickly to keep up. "You're still here," she said to Anne as she set Fern down in front of the door that led out to the garden. She opened the door, and both kittens dashed outside. "There you go." Jane left the door cracked open. It was a warm, calm summer morning, quite at odds with yesterday's storms.

"Yes, I'm still here. I wanted a second cup of coffee, and I was reading the paper." Anne rose from the table.

"You needn't leave." Jane frowned slightly. "Is something the matter? You've been awfully quiet since we returned from Ivy Grove yesterday."

"Have I?" Anne asked innocently.

Jane rolled her eyes and moved to the table, taking a chair across from Anne's. "Sit. And don't treat me like I don't know you better than anyone. What's going on in your head?"

Exhaling, Anne sat back down. Was there any

reason not to tell her sister about Rafe? She rather wanted to… "Do you remember when I told you I was in love a few months ago?"

"Yes, quite clearly. Then you were soon betrothed to Chamberlain, and it was evident to me he was not the object of your initial affection. Was I correct?"

Anne nodded. She looked at the tablecloth and laid her hand atop it, her palm against the soft, ivory cotton. "I lost contact with him, but we have recently become reacquainted."

Jane's jaw dropped. "It's Bowles. Er, Stone. Isn't it?"

Withdrawing her hand to her lap, Anne looked straight at her sister. "Yes."

"I have several questions." Jane tried not to look aghast and rather failed. "How did you meet him? And when? Why did you lose contact? Why didn't you say anything?"

"I didn't say anything because all of it is scandalous. Back when I first arrived in London, I used to go out with Deborah every Thursday."

"I remember."

"We didn't actually spend our time together," Anne said slowly. "I went to Hatchard's, and she went…well, I don't exactly know where she went. She just left me alone for two blissful hours."

Jane gaped at her again. "She was supposed to be chaperoning you!"

"I know. But she had something she preferred to do, and I wanted a reprieve from Mother and Father and expectation."

Jane winced. "I'm sorry. That was my fault. If I'd been more successful, they would not have put so much pressure on you."

"That wasn't your fault at all. Chamberlain—that idiot I betrothed myself to—and his horrible sister, God rest her soul, are to blame. They ruined your reputation five years ago. How could you have done anything differently?"

"I don't know," Jane said. "That's the worst of it. I didn't do anything *wrong*."

"Precisely. That's why I decided that actually *doing* something wrong didn't matter. You just have to avoid getting caught. So I wore a veil and sat in a corner and read books at Hatchard's. For two weeks, until Lord Bodyguard showed up." Anne thought of that day often, and it never failed to make her smile. What might have happened if Rafe hadn't arrived? Would those two men have left her alone? She would never know.

*"Lord Bodyguard?"*

"Rafe. Mr. Bowles. Lord Stone."

"I gathered that. But why are you calling him Lord Bodyguard?"

"Because he stepped in to protect me from a pair of odious men."

"Good heavens, Anne, you should not have been alone."

"I was in a bookstore, not walking around Covent Garden by myself. Though I did go there with Rafe. And to Cheapside and other places. After that first meeting, he offered to take me around London to places I would not be allowed to go."

Jane simply stared at her, saying nothing. So Anne continued.

"Those were the best afternoons of my life."

"You *did* fall in love with him," Jane said.

"I did. He does not know that, however. I was not able to continue meeting him." Even if she had, Anne wasn't certain she would have told him that next week. They hadn't even known each other's names. "If you recall, Mother made me stop my weekly outings with Deborah. The Season was becoming too busy. Or so she said."

"If you were in love with him, why did you accept Chamberlain's proposal? Why didn't Bowles, hell, Stone, court you?"

"He wasn't in Society then. I didn't meet him again until he came to see Anthony last week."

"But surely you could have contacted him." Jane shook her head. "Or not. I realize how difficult it was to live with Mother and Father. They would not have allowed you to send a letter to a man you hadn't officially met."

"That's true, but since I'd found a way to escape them for two hours each week, surely you realize I could have sent a letter somehow." She smiled at Jane, who laughed softly.

"Fair enough. You are quite capable. Why didn't you, then?"

"Thank you. Because I didn't know his real name. We agreed to keep our identities secret. I didn't know him, and he didn't know me. So when I failed to meet him, that was the end of it."

Jane's eyes rounded briefly. "How sad. And yet romantic at the same time."

Anne laughed. "I'm glad you think so. I was devastated."

"Then you went on to become betrothed to a man you surely didn't love." Jane laid her hand against her cheek. "Oh, Anne, I am so sorry. And so relieved that your wedding didn't happen."

"No more than I am," Anne said soberly. "Thankfully, that is in the past, and for the first time in weeks, I am looking forward to the future."

"With Stone?"

"I hope so, but I don't know if he reciprocates my feelings. Right now, I can't even get him to admit we're friends." She waved her hand. "That isn't important, however. We *are* friends, and he needs them. I'm worried about him. Yesterday was a shock, and I'm desperate to know how he's faring."

"You'll see him on Monday."

"Along with everyone else. I want to see him *alone*." Anne put her hand back on the table and lightly drummed her fingertips atop the cloth.

"We'll pay a call on behalf of the Spitfire Society," Jane declared, straightening her spine against the back of the chair. "This afternoon."

Anne stared at her sister. "We will?"

"Yes. And I will give you some time alone with him, if he's amenable."

"He will be." Anne had no reason to believe he wouldn't. He hadn't given her the cut direct or anything. She smiled at Jane. "Thank you."

Jane reached across the table, and Anne met her fingertips with her own. "I would do anything to ensure your happiness, even if it includes bending Society's stupid rules. After all, I am not exactly a role model."

Anne laughed. "You *are* the very best sister, however."

"Well, that much is true." Jane winked. "Go don your most fetching walking dress."

Anne was already out of her chair. She could hardly wait to see him.

# CHAPTER 6

Rafe sat brooding in his study, which was just off the library. He stared through the open doorway at the shelves of books and was immediately comforted.

Harry had just left, and while it had been a good visit—Harry's father and brother were ready to stand in support of Rafe becoming the Earl of Stone—it had also left him emotionally raw. Or more raw than he was already after yesterday's revelations.

Lord Aylesbury, Harry's father, had actually known Rafe's father. They'd been friends. And now that Rafe knew who his parents were, there would be more people like him. Rafe hadn't considered all the people in Society who would come forward to tell him and Selina that they'd known their parents. To have that connection… Rafe had to work to swallow past the lump in his throat.

Glover appeared in the doorway. "Sir, you have visitors." Rafe hadn't yet told him he was an earl. How did one announce that? "Lady Colton and Miss Pemberton."

Rafe shot to his feet. Anne was here? "Bring them to the library, please."

Glover inclined his head and departed.

Perhaps Anne could help him determine what to say to his employees. All of it felt so damned awkward—even having employees in the first place. But this was the life he'd aspired to have, to make his father, who would never know, proud. Had he somehow known his father was an earl? Was there something inside him that had driven him to Mayfair, to this life?

He went into the library and smoothed his hand over his hair and down the front of his coat. A moment later, Anne walked in along with her sister. Rafe barely saw Lady Colton as his gaze feasted on Anne. Dressed in a smart, moss-green walking costume, she was the epitome of grace and beauty. And her hair was even completely contained. That part was perhaps a trifle disappointing. He liked when her curls escaped.

They both curtsied. "My lord," Anne said.

A sharp inhalation of breath drew Rafe to look toward Glover, who stood just inside the doorway. He stared at Rafe in question.

"Ah, I'll explain later," Rafe said to the butler. "Thank you."

Glover bowed his head and left. Rafe looked to his guests. "I'm afraid I haven't yet told anyone about my sudden ascension to the peerage."

Anne's brow furrowed. "You didn't suddenly ascend. You're simply newly aware."

"No, he's quite right," Lady Colton said. "He isn't currently the earl. He will be. Next week, probably." She smiled at him. "Please forgive our intrusion. We came to discuss Spitfire business with you, as one of our primary supporters."

Yes, he'd pledged a great deal of money to their endeavors, particularly because Selina was so heavily involved. She planned to start an orphanage that would ensure stable futures for the children who landed there, and it would be located in East London. Rafe could think of nothing more noble to do with the wealth he'd accumulated.

However, he doubted very much that the Spitfire Society was the purpose for their visit. "I see. How may I be of service?"

Anne came toward him. "That's just a poppycock excuse." He nearly laughed at her explanation. "I wanted to see you, and Jane was kind enough to offer to bring me."

"If you wish to talk privately, I'd be delighted to peruse your library." Lady Colton smiled at them, then promptly turned her back as she studied the bookshelves.

Rafe looked at Anne in question, and at her slight nod, he gestured for her to precede him to his study. When they arrived, she turned and walked past him to shut the door.

"Scandalous," he murmured.

"Only if we're caught, and we won't be."

"But your sister is in the library."

"My sister brought me here." Anne arched a pale brow at him. "And my sister nursed her husband back to health after he collapsed on her doorstep beat to ribbons. They were alone in her house for a week. She is not going to blink at my being alone with you behind a closed door. In fact, she is in support of it. She knows, as do I, that you need me."

Rafe stifled a smile. "Do I?" He went to the sideboard where he kept wine and his favorite gin. "Would you care for a drink? So long as wc'rc not being scandalous."

"No, thank you. But please help yourself."

He poured himself a small glass of gin. Taking a sip, he went to the seating area situated in the center of the room. "Shall we sit?"

She went to the settee and perched on the edge, seeming as if she might not stay there. He considered whether he should join her there, but decided it would be more prudent if he took a chair. Distance between them was probably best.

Except she frowned as he moved toward the chair. "Will you sit with me?" she asked.

He should have anticipated that she would voice her desires. She had never been shy about doing so. He admired that about her.

Rafe sat on the settee against one of the high ends, bringing his knee up onto the cushion as he faced her. She scooted back, situating herself more squarely on the settee.

She pivoted toward him. "I wanted to hug you when I arrived."

He was disappointed she didn't. "You think I need comfort?"

"Don't you? Yesterday has forever changed you."

"Has it?"

Her eyes narrowed. "You are answering me with a great many questions today."

He was. "My apologies. I am at sixes and sevens."

She exhaled as she untied her bonnet and set it on the arm of the settee behind her. "Understandably so. I've been concerned."

"Why?" He sipped his gin, enthralled by her care and, frankly, thrilled for the distraction.

She frowned at him. "You just said you were at sixes and sevens."

"I am…overwhelmed. As evidenced by the fact that I haven't even told my employees what happened. I suppose it doesn't feel real to me yet." And it had nothing to do with the title—that was inconsequential compared to what was truly important, that he'd found his parents. He tossed back the rest of his gin, appreciating the heat along his tongue and throat. "What happened yesterday after we left?"

"The picnic continued, even though my godfather wanted to call it off. Deborah convinced him to allow the event to proceed. They didn't inform Lorcan of what happened until after everyone had left. Did you meet Lorcan?" she asked.

Rafe shook his head. "How did he react?"

"He was surprisingly calm. His initial concern was that he would no longer have access to the estate in Ireland. He really loves it there."

"I own an estate in Ireland?" Rafe shook his head. Harry was still working on accumulating a full accounting of the assets that should rightfully belong to Rafe. Perhaps the Irish property belonged to his uncle. Except if his cousin was now worried he wouldn't have access, that seemed unlikely.

"You own many things," Anne said.

"Your godfather was very upset."

She blinked. "Of course. Wouldn't you be?"

"I am upset to learn I was stolen from my home and denied my birthright." His voice had risen. When he thought of the hardship he and Selina had faced and survived, he wanted to rage.

Anne sucked in a breath. She scooted forward on the cushion, her eyes full of sympathy. "I'm sorry."

Rafe stood and took his empty glass to the sideboard. He set it down and looked at the painting in front of him. It was of some nameless subject. He realized he likely now owned countless portraits of his family members. Was there one of his parents, or had it burned in the fire? He was desperate to find one.

He turned to face Anne. "What did Lady Burnhope say?" Rafe was particularly interested in what his cousin would do. She despised Selina and would most certainly be displeased that her foe from school was now her cousin. Selina was utterly disgusted.

"She ranted about the unfairness of it, which wasn't helpful." Anne made a face. "Deborah can be difficult to like."

According to Selina, she was *completely* unlikeable. "You know her well?"

"Very. She was my chaperone when we were meeting at Hatchard's."

Rafe let out a sharp laugh. "She was terrible."

Anne grinned. "Thankfully. Else, we would not have met."

Rafe supposed he should be grateful, then, for meeting Anne and sharing those afternoons was the most wonderful thing in his recent memory.

"Still, she *can* be horrendous. She thought you should let her father keep the title." Anne rolled her eyes.

"Does she have *any* redeeming qualities?"

"She can be helpful. She's gone to great lengths to be supportive after my wedding that didn't happen."

"As she should," Rafe muttered. The thought of Anne marrying that scoundrel still ate at him. Or maybe it was the idea that he'd almost lost her. For a woman he was trying not to be friends with, she'd come to mean a great deal to him. "I doubt she will be so supportive of me, however."

"Probably not." Anne clasped her hands in her lap, and Rafe could suddenly feel them on him—as she stroked his jaw or rested her palm against his chest. "But there will be plenty who will, including me and Jane and Anthony. I will be at the dinner on Monday at your sister's house."

He blinked in surprise. "You will?"

"My godfather asked me to come. I hope you don't mind."

"Not at all." In fact, he was glad to have someone else present who supported him.

Did she, though? The man who was about to lose everything—or nearly everything—was her godfather. How close was their relationship? "Do you think he should keep the title?" he asked. She'd rolled her eyes, but what did that mean?

"I don't think it's that simple. You are the rightful earl. It's a terrible situation for everyone." She smiled sadly. "You've been denied your very identity for nearly thirty years, and my godfather has spent that same amount of time living a life that didn't really belong to him."

She didn't *not* support him. But she clearly sympathized with her godfather too.

He would do well to remember that. "We've changed the location of the dinner. I'll be hosting it here." Selina hadn't wanted Deborah in her house, and Rafe didn't blame her. "Harry is sending word to your godfather this afternoon."

"Mr. Sheffield is a good friend to you. I'm glad."

Yes, he was, and Rafe was still struggling to accept that. "Apparently, his father was a friend of my father's." He abruptly clenched his teeth together and pushed away the emotion that always seemed to be thundering just beneath the surface.

Anne rose and came to him, her brow creased. "I'm so sorry, Rafe," she whispered. "This has to be so difficult. But isn't there joy too? In knowing who you are?"

She was so close. He could wrap his arms around her and pull her against him, bury himself in her scent and softness, comfort himself in her care and tenderness. It was almost painful not to.

Oh, she was much more than a friend. That was absolutely terrifying.

"Joy? I don't know." That wasn't an emotion he often felt. The happiest he'd been in the past four years was when he'd reunited with Selina. But even that had been eclipsed by the fact that he'd kept her away from him for far too long. "Perhaps I'm afraid of that," he said quietly, his voice rasping.

He was also afraid of being the center of attention, of disappointing his parents, of not being the man he should be. How could he be, given how he was raised? How he'd spent almost the entirety of his life? As a criminal and a fraud. Yes, he could play the role of earl—he was so good at pretending. But this wasn't a sham. This was real. This was who he was supposed to be.

What if he failed?

"Oh, Rafe." She moved closer and put her palms against his cheeks. Her brow puckered, and she quickly stripped her gloves away, heedlessly dropping them to the floor. Her bare hands touched his face, and he lost himself in her gaze. "You deserve to feel happy."

He didn't believe that, not after the things he'd done. "You don't know me," he whispered.

"I'm trying to. I *want* to. How can I help? I want to be your friend—like Harry."

Rafe smiled at that. "Please, *not* like Harry."

She laughed softly and, standing on her toes, twined her arms around his neck, as if it were the most natural thing in the world. Rafe lightly clasped her waist. That wasn't natural. What felt natural would be to hold her tightly to him. He didn't do that.

"You're going to be very popular as soon as everyone hears about your claim."

He winced. "I'm afraid of that most of all."

"Are you?"

"I value my privacy." He resisted the urge to move his hands to her back. "Besides, if I'm the center of attention, you can't very well call on me anymore—even in the company of your sister on the pretense of asking about my charitable donations."

She grinned. "Probably not. I'll just have to find a way to avoid notice. I'm good at not getting caught. Speaking of that, if you postpone submitting your claim until Thursday, we can still go to Magazine Day on Wednesday. I've procured a man's costume as you directed."

"Have you now?" His hands slowly crept around her waist despite his best intentions. She was far too close, and he simply couldn't resist. "I must admit I would appreciate just a few more days of anonymity." Besides, Harry had dispatched a clerk to Stonehaven, and they planned to wait for the man's report before moving forward. He would not return before Magazine Day. "How will you get away?"

She lifted a shoulder as she toyed with his shirt collar. "I'll say I'm taking a nap. You can pick me up in the Grosvenor Street mews."

"You've thought this through."

"I have." She gave him a shrewd stare. "I like to plan."

"I do admire a strategic mind." He admired everything about her, from her intelligence to her passion for trying and seeing new things. She seemed rather fearless, he realized, and that was incredibly intoxicating. "Are you afraid of anything?" he asked.

"Being alone." She snapped her lips together in a slight frown. "I didn't realize I was going to say that. In fact, I didn't know I felt that way until this moment."

"I can't imagine you need to worry about that." He splayed his palms against her lower back. "Won't your sister suspect what you're about? Since she brought you here today."

"Perhaps." She tipped her head from side to side. "Probably. I'm not much for taking naps, I'm afraid. It doesn't matter—she won't begrudge me, and she certainly won't tell anyone."

He laughed. "You have a good sister."

Anne beamed up at him. "So do you. I like Selina very much."

He did have a good sister. That morning, they'd traveled to the Croydon Parish Church and spoken to the vicar. He'd hadn't known their "uncle," Edgar Blackwell, but when Rafe had described their nurse, he'd said it sounded like one of his former parishioners—a Pauline Blaylock. Dark-haired with a beautiful voice, she'd left home to take a position as a nurse decades before. Her family had been proud that she'd gone to work for an earl.

Unfortunately, the Blaylock family had all died or moved far away from Croydon, with the exception of one person: Pauline's younger sister. She was married to an innkeeper in Redhill. They hadn't had time to travel farther south to visit her at the Golden Eagle today, but they would soon.

"What time should I be ready on Wednesday?" Anne asked.

Her question jolted him from his recollection of his trip to Croydon. "Ah, ten?"

"So early. For Society, but not for me. I'll be ready." She gave him a coy look and slipped her fingers into the hair at his nape. This was very similar to when she'd kissed him at the Chapter Coffee House. When he'd been swept away by his overwhelming attraction to her. It would be far too easy to allow that again...

He forced himself to take his hands from her and step back. "Are you certain this is wise?"

Her brow furrowed with disappointment. "Going to Magazine Day? I owe you an excursion since I missed our last one."

She was clever. He'd give her that. And it wasn't as if she was manipulating him. He knew precisely what he was doing, that agreeing to take her, hell, seeing her here and now, invited intimacy. At least the physical kind. He wasn't capable of anything else. She needed to know that.

He took her hand and guided her back to the settee, sitting them both down so they faced each other. "Anne, you need to understand something. You've said—repeatedly—that you wish to be my friend. I gratefully accept your friendship. However, I can't accept more, and it seems you...would like more."

She narrowed her eyes briefly and swallowed. "Because I kissed you and nearly did so again just now?"

"Yes."

"Would that be so bad?"

"For you? Yes. You are not the sort of woman I should be kissing."

"What does that mean?" She sounded a bit angry, and her eyes blazed.

"It means a woman like you deserves a man who will kiss you and then marry you. I am not that man, nor will I ever be."

Her gaze calmed, and she regarded him with curiosity. "Why not?"

"Because I was married before, and I don't wish to be again."

She blinked as a slight tremor raced through her. He could see it in the flutter of her throat and the gentle twitch of her shoulders.

"What happened?" she asked.

Rafe worked to keep the specific memories at bay. He never indulged them. To do so was madness and despair. "She died. I loved her very much." More than life. And she'd been carrying their child. The loss of the family he'd so desperately wanted was a hole inside him that would never heal. Vengeance hadn't soothed his pain; nothing would.

Anne's eyes rounded. "Oh." She glanced away. "That's why there's a darkness inside you."

Christ, she *did* see him. "Yes."

Her gaze turned fierce, and she took his hand between both of hers in her lap. "I am your friend, and perhaps I'll be more. Perhaps not. I have no illusions—not after Gilbert Chamberlain. If I learned anything from that experience, it's that I deserve happiness and I won't settle for anything less than what I want."

Utterly fearless. He shouldn't take her to Magazine Day, but nothing could stop him. Not even the stark reality that he didn't deserve to breathe the same air she did. If she knew how he was connected to Chamberlain, she'd realize just how awful he was.

He put his other hand over hers and leaned toward her. "Understand me, Anne—there is more than a darkness. I am *not* the man you think I am, nor the man you want me to be. I am not a knight or a hero who will make you happy forever. If you can accept that, we will go to Magazine Day to make up our lost afternoon. And then we will part as friends. Do you agree?" He held her gaze and stroked his thumb along her wrist.

She nodded. Then he did the unthinkable. He brought his hands up to her face and held her while he put his mouth on hers. She clasped the lapels of his coat, pulling the garment as her lips met his.

The kiss was fast but deep. It wasn't a promise but a regret. A desperate yearning that would never be fulfilled.

Rafe groaned low in his throat and released her. "Go."

She set her hat atop her head and coughed. "My gloves."

He stood and retrieved them from the floor. Handing them to her, he was careful to barely touch her hand. "I'll see you Wednesday."

She nodded, then left.

One stolen afternoon. Before his life irrevocably changed.

~

Ludlow Mallory's coach stopped in front of Rafe's magnificent house on Upper Brook Street. The groom opened the door and helped Deborah alight, then Anne. Her godfather and his son, Lorcan, followed. The four of them stood on the pavement and looked at the grandest façade on the street.

"This is his house?" Anne's godfather asked incredulously. "How wealthy is he?"

"I would say quite," Deborah said with a slight frown.

"He doesn't need to be an earl," Anne's godfather continued. "Nor does he need all my property and assets."

"Nevertheless, he's entitled to them," Lorcan said with resignation. "Including my beloved Kilmaar."

Anne gave him a sympathetic smile. "Perhaps he'll allow you to keep something. You certainly aren't going to be destitute." At least she hoped not. She had no idea how their finances would be once they lost the properties and whatever assets rightfully belonged to Rafe. "I can't see how your cousin would let that happen."

"Do you know him?" her godfather asked sharply. Anne swallowed.

Deborah exhaled. "She's just being optimistic. Which is admirable." She gave Anne a warm smile. "Of course, my life will not be changed."

The former earl gave his daughter a sour look. "Precisely. Optimism is easy for you. And Anne."

"You mean selfishness," Lorcan said, darting a disappointed glance at his sister before apologizing to Anne. "I didn't mean you. Your optimism is appreciated."

Anne hated how defeated Lorcan and his father sounded. She could understand how they must feel. This was such a shock.

Taking a breath and summoning the optimism they seemed to need, she squared her shoulders. "Let's not stand here and gawk." She started up the steps to the door, which opened as she reached the top.

The butler, Glover if she recalled from her visit the other day, admitted them with a nod. After they were all in the entry hall, a footman took Anne's and Deborah's shawls, and a second footman took over the butler's position at the door.

"This way, if you please." Glover led them to the right into an elegant room decorated in reds and golds. There were a few chairs and a settee, but it appeared to be an anteroom. The occupants, which included Rafe, his sisters, and their husbands all stood.

Sisters.

It occurred to Anne that her godfather didn't have two nieces. At least not that he was aware of. Was Beatrix a…by-blow? Why hadn't she thought to ask Rafe about this the other day?

Anne gave her a warm smile, which Beatrix returned. Then her gaze shifted toward Deborah and went instantly cold.

"Good evening," Rafe said. "Thank you for coming tonight and for being flexible with changing the location. It seemed I should host."

"Your house is most impressive," Deborah said. "Is that why you wanted to host? So we could see it?"

"No, that's not why," Selina said icily. "I didn't want to have you in my house."

Deborah's nose twitched, and she flashed a small, malicious smile. "We're just going to be openly hostile?"

Selina shrugged. "Beatrix and I discussed it, and it seemed the most acceptable course. For us, anyway." She exchanged a mildly amused look with Beatrix, and Anne couldn't help but admire their solidarity and sisterhood. She and Jane would do the same in the face of a common enemy.

"Well, if that's the case, then allow me to ask why Beatrix is even here." Deborah glowered at them.

"She's Lady Rockbourne," Beatrix's husband corrected in a clipped tone.

"Of course, I'd forgotten given the hastiness of

your marriage." Deborah clucked her tongue as she regarded Beatrix. "Why are you here? You aren't actually their sister. I suppose you could be my uncle's by-blow, but your father is purportedly a duke."

"Indeed he is," Beatrix said smoothly. She didn't seem the slightest bit agitated by Deborah's needling. Needling? No, her behavior was far worse than that. Anne wasn't sure she would be able to keep from berating her for this.

Beatrix waved her hand. "It hardly signifies. I am quite happy with how things have happened, and I can't say I care if anyone knows I'm a duke's bastard." She turned to her husband, who was gazing at her adoringly. "Do you mind, dear?"

"Not at all." He put his arm around her waist and held her close to his side.

Glover appeared again and announced that dinner would be served. He opened the doors to the adjoining dining room. Before Rafe could approach Anne to escort her in—and she wasn't sure he would have, but would tell herself that he planned to—Lorcan came to her side and offered his arm.

In the dining room, Rafe sat at the head while Selina and Beatrix sat on either side of him. Their husbands sat next to them while Deborah was seated beside Lord Rockbourne, much to her dismay. But then Anne doubted there was anywhere she could sit at the table that wouldn't have been displeasing to her. Her father took the chair next to her, while Anne sat next to Mr. Sheffield with Lorcan on her other side.

A dark red claret was poured, and the first course of dishes set upon the table. The room was completely silent, but a thick tension clogged the air.

"This house is spectacular," Anne's godfather said, looking around the room with its ivory, red, and gold décor. A magnificent mirror surmounted the hearth, reflecting the hundreds of candles flickering in the chandeliers and in the sconces on the walls. There were also several large, stunning portraits, including one by Joshua Reynolds. "You appear to be a man of great means." He picked up his wineglass, settling his gaze on their host over the rim.

"Thank you." Rafe's voice was even, his eyes cool. "I'm new to Mayfair and this house. I've enjoyed the decorating of it." He said nothing to address her godfather's last comment. What could he say? Anne realized she was also curious as to how he'd made his fortune.

"I should say," Deborah remarked as she held her wineglass aloft. "The paintings in this room alone would be the envy of anyone who appreciates art. One can only wonder what the rest of the house looks like." It was clear to Anne that she wanted to see it for herself.

"Yes, I imagine one can," Beatrix said with an overly sweet smile. "I can tell you the art in the gallery is even more impressive. And the library... well, I am not sure you will find its equal in Mayfair."

Deborah's eyes narrowed as she sipped her wine. No, sip wasn't right—she took a very long drink, draining nearly half the glass. She glanced toward the footman to refill it.

After several moments during which the tension seemed to increase, Rafe set his soup spoon down and addressed the table. His blue eyes glimmered in the candlelight, and his hair seemed to shine like gold. "It is my hope that we can find a way to be a family." He glanced toward Selina. "My sister and I have only had each other—until Selina was fortunate enough to meet Beatrix—and the prospect of family is something we never imagined. To find our uncle…" He looked to Anne's godfather. "To be reunited with our father's brother is beyond comprehension. I know this must be a terrible shock for you, as it is for us. But in the end, it will hopefully be a good thing."

The former earl stared at him. "That depends. Do you plan to leave us destitute?"

Sheffield coughed. "That is not Mr. Mallory's intent." Rafe was Mr. Mallory now? She supposed he was and that her godfather *was* still the earl. At least until the Committee for Privileges voted. "He does, however, intend to be the earl as that is his birthright. All entailed estates will, of course, be his. The only properties that are not entailed are your house here in London and Kilmaar in Ireland. The former was purchased by you, so that will remain yours. That you used money that is almost certainly the rightful asset of Mr. Mallory is not something he wishes to contest." Sheffield transferred his attention to Lorcan. "Furthermore, he would like to gift Kilmaar to you."

Lorcan's mouth dropped open, and he clanged his spoon down against his bowl. He stared at Rafe. "You don't want it?"

"*You* do. It's been made clear to me that it's important to you. I can't imagine I'll have occasion to visit Ireland regularly. I would like to see it once, however. Perhaps you'll accommodate me." He smiled at Lorcan, and Anne knew in that moment that she definitely *hadn't* fallen out of love with him.

"You will be welcome any time. Forever." Lorcan glanced toward his father before continuing. "You didn't have to be generous. I keep trying to imagine how I would feel in your position. You must be so angry."

It took Rafe a moment to reply. During that time, he exchanged a meaningful look with Selina. "Yes. It's not that I am upset about being denied my birthright. I am, of course, but it's more than that. I am deeply troubled by losing my parents and being stolen away. I would like to know why."

"So would I," Selina said. "My life would have been different—it *should* have been." She turned a frigid stare on Deborah. "Just think if I had been the daughter of an earl at Mrs. Goodwin's. Imagine us growing up as cousins and how differently you would have treated me."

Deborah had the grace to look down at her soup. She reached for her wine again and took another substantial drink.

Anne wondered if Deborah would apologize. Not tonight, but perhaps someday. Anne hoped so and planned to talk to her about it.

"Lorcan, I appreciate you trying to understand how we feel," Selina said. "That means a great deal to me. And to Rafe, I'm sure."

"It does," Rafe agreed. "I am going to need all the help I can get. I was not raised in this environment."

"You can count on my support." Lorcan lifted his glass in a silent toast.

Sheffield set his glass down after sipping his wine and fixed his attention on the current earl. "Can we also rely on you to provide guidance to Mr. Mallory as he assumes his rightful role? In the absence of his father to teach him, that will fall to you. If he and his sister hadn't been kidnapped—and I think we must characterize what happened to them in this way, for there is no other apparent explanation—you would have been the one to act as steward to Rafe while he grew up as the earl."

Anne held her breath. The godfather she loved would certainly agree. He'd always been kind and supportive. But this was a horrible situation.

Finally, her godfather nodded. "I will help him." He looked at Rafe. "I miss your father."

Rafe's features tensed, and his jaw clenched. "Selina doesn't even remember him."

Anne frowned. Her godfather was trying. But she also knew Rafe was trying too. There was just so much pain and loss. Was there too much for everyone to move forward and leave the past behind? She thought of her own family and whether Jane would ever reconcile with their parents. They'd believed the nasty rumor about Jane five years ago, and after she'd declared her spinsterhood, they'd completely turned their backs on her and encouraged Anne to do the same. Now, Anne had turned her back on them, and she honestly didn't know when she would forgive them.

No, it wasn't that. She *could* forgive them; she just didn't know if she wanted a relationship with them.

Oh, families were *complicated*. Perhaps she'd tell Rafe he was better off without one.

Except that wasn't for her to decide. Not for him.

The first course was removed, and everyone was quiet while the next course was laid.

"When do you plan to present your claim?" Lorcan asked as he served turbot onto his plate.

"As soon as we have all the evidence accumulated," Sheffield answered. "I've dispatched a clerk to Stonehaven to interview the servants. Another clerk will travel to Ivy Grove to take Mrs. Gentry's testimony, along with anyone else who was in service when Mr. Mallory and my wife were children."

Lorcan picked up his wineglass. "So the news will likely not become public this week?"

"I doubt the claim will be ready, but I am not willing to commit to a date," Sheffield said mildly.

Anne looked toward Rafe, and their gazes locked in silent communication. Nothing would happen until after their Magazine Day excursion. But that was perhaps the last time she would see him as Mr. Bowles, rather, Mr. Mallory. As soon as his claim was sent to the Prince Regent and the attorney general, the information would leak into the ton, and Society would be overcome with the news. Everyone would want to meet Rafe. And when the women saw him, they'd want to marry him. Or have their daughters marry him.

Anne didn't like that one bit. Not when she wanted him for herself.

But that didn't matter if he didn't want her in return. Hopefully, on Wednesday she would find out.

"Even a week from now is very soon," Deborah said.

Sheffield gave her a patient smile. "There's no reason to wait." His eyes narrowed slightly. "It's not as if this affects you at all."

Lorcan sent his sister a smug look. Deborah scowled into her wineglass.

"I wonder if you might tell us about our father," Selina asked her uncle. "And our mother."

Anne watched expectantly as her godfather finished chewing. "Jerome probably should have been the second son. He would have done well as a vicar or teaching at Oxford. He liked books."

Rafe smiled at his plate, and Anne felt a burst of warmth. How wonderful that must feel for him.

"And horses," her godfather continued. "He wanted to start a stud at Stonehaven and was in the process of enlarging the stables when the house burned."

Darkness swept away the light in Rafe's features at the mention of the fire. Anne rushed to keep the topic on something pleasant. She looked to her godfather with a smile. "I remember you telling me that you and he used to race when you were young."

"We did. I was the better horseman, but that didn't stop Jerome from constantly challenging me." He flicked a glance toward Selina. "Your mother had an excellent seat. She was always in the lead on the hunt."

"How did they meet?" Selina asked softly.

Anne's godfather shrugged. "During the Season, as one does. I don't recall the specifics."

"As you can imagine, we have many questions," Rafe said. "We hope to find our nurse. If you have any suggestions that might help us, we would be grateful."

"I doubt I would even recall her name," the earl said.

Lorcan gestured with his fork. "You should speak to the retainers at Stonehaven. Perhaps someone there remembers her."

Anne's godfather had lifted his wineglass, but it slipped from his fingers and splashed across his plate and onto his lap. The glass rolled to the floor. He muttered something as a footman rushed to pick up the glass and provide assistance with a cloth.

Rising from his chair, her godfather took the cloth and swiped at his front from belly to thigh. "I'm afraid I must leave. This is a terrible mess."

"I'm sure we can send for something for you to wear," Rafe said calmly. "You needn't rush off."

As the earl kept dabbing at his clothes, Anne realized his hands were shaking. She stood and rounded the table. "We'll go if you need to. It's all right," she said soothingly.

His blue eyes met hers, and she saw the anguish in their depths. Oh dear, this was far more difficult than she'd imagined. He nodded, and Anne turned her head to look first at Lorcan and then Deborah. Then her gaze found Rafe's, and she tried to silently communicate how sorry she was about all this.

"I'm trying," her godfather whispered. "I just… This is all that I am."

She nodded as his children joined them. Deborah put her arm through his. "Come, Papa."

Lorcan turned to Rafe, who'd risen from his chair. "My apologies. We will do this again. It will get…easier."

"I hope so." Rafe moved toward them. "I'll see you out."

Lorcan and Deborah escorted their father, flanking him as they left the dining room. Rafe nodded toward a footman, who left through another doorway. Turning his head, Rafe glanced at his sisters and their husbands before joining Anne. Together, they walked into the antechamber.

"I'm so sorry." Anne kept her voice low and resisted the urge to take his arm. "My godfather is really struggling."

"We all are," Rafe said.

"I know. I just wish this wasn't so painful for everyone."

"How can it be anything else?" His voice was flat, and she wasn't sure what he was feeling. Was he angry, frustrated, something else? Probably all of it at once.

"It will get better." She gave him a tremulous smile and grazed her fingertips against his.

His fingers clasped hers. She looked up at him as they entered the entry hall and breathed, "Wednesday."

With a nod, he let her go. She took her shawl from a footman and sent a last, lingering look at Rafe. His stare was dark and intense, making her shiver, and not with cold.

When they were in the coach, Deborah smoothed her hands over her lap. "Thank you for spilling your wine, Papa. I don't think I could have endured much longer."

Anne had *endured* quite enough. "Deborah, can't you see how awful this is for everyone?"

Her eyes widened, then narrowed to slits. "Of course I can. But I am trying to support my father. He doesn't deserve to be displaced."

The earl, who sat beside Deborah on the forward-facing seat, patted her arm. "Thank you, dear."

"No one *deserves* any of this. Imagine how you would feel if you'd been kidnapped as a child and denied the life you were meant to lead."

"Anne is right." The earl exhaled as he leaned back against the squab. "This is a terrible situation, but there is nothing to do but get through it. I should have stayed at dinner. I just...couldn't." He looked out the window.

"It's all right, Father," Lorcan said.

"That's easy for you to say," Deborah sniped. "You get to keep Kilmaar."

Lorcan stiffened beside Anne. "And Father gets to keep his house in St. James Square. It will be an adjustment, but from what I can tell, our cousin is going to be very generous when it's well within his rights not to be."

The coach drew to a stop in front of Anthony and Jane's house, and Anne was never more glad for such a short trip. She breathed with relief as she stepped down from the coach.

What a disaster. She only hoped things would improve from here. They had to, didn't they?

# CHAPTER 7

Rafe climbed into his cabriolet and set out from the Upper Brook Street mews. As he surveyed the world around him, he wondered how things would be different when the news of his true identity became known.

He drove through Grosvenor Square and turned down Davies Street. At Mount Street, he steered left toward the Grosvenor Mews and immediately caught sight of a young man dressed in dark clothing near the entrance. No, not a young man, but a young woman in a disguise. Would she have fooled him if he hadn't known to look for her? He would never know.

Smiling, he came to a stop as she bounded toward him. She stopped at the cabriolet and pursed her lips.

"Do you need help?" he asked.

"No. This is just new." She hoisted herself up into the seat and grinned at him. "I think I could get used to it. I feel so light. So free."

Rafe chuckled. "But you look so fetching in a gown." He suspected her backside was even more attractive in this costume, but the tails of her coat thankfully prevented his temptation to look.

"Why, thank you," she said with a nod as he drove them toward Bond Street and then Piccadilly when they would head east. "Perhaps I could commission a more feminine version of this costume."

"How would that look?"

"I don't know a thing about clothing design, but probably ruffles." She made a face. "I don't love ruffles. Perhaps it's just the fabric or color. Something like this in a light blue silk? On second thought, I've met gentlemen who wear such things." She sighed. "I suppose I'm doomed to gowns."

He considered suggesting that she might be most comfortable not wearing anything at all, but that would drive their conversation into a realm best left unoccupied. Especially today when they were alone. Again.

"Your sister really didn't mind you coming out with me today?"

"She understood that I was going to find a way. She also knows we will be far from Mayfair. And she thought my costume did a good job of disguising that I am a woman. Do you agree?"

"I don't think I can answer that objectively. I know you're a woman. I can't forget you're a woman. Not even for a moment." Hell, he'd walked right into that forbidden realm after all.

He stole a glance in her direction and saw that she looked rather pleased. He stifled a smile.

"I was sorry about how the dinner went on Monday, especially Deborah's behavior. How were Selina and Beatrix afterward?"

Rafe didn't want to talk about the dinner or his uncle or anything to do with the massive disruption that was about to take over his life. He did, however, appreciate her concern. "They are fine.

My cousin is unpleasant. To clarify, I mean Deborah. I think I might actually like Lorcan."

"He was thrilled about Kilmaar. You are incredibly kind."

"What need have I for an estate in Ireland?" He'd wondered what it had meant to his father, if anything. He had a hundred questions—a thousand or more, really—about his father. The hope he'd had that his uncle might answer them was thin. The man was in turmoil, and while Rafe couldn't blame him, he didn't know if they'd ever be able to have a normal family relationship. Was that what Rafe wanted, some sort of surrogate father?

"Still, it was a lovely gesture, and it will help with the healing, I think."

With *their* healing. How would it help with Rafe's? He wanted information, *needed* it so he could find out why he and his sister had been kidnapped. This was not where he wanted to spend his thoughts today. "Do you mind if we not talk about my uncle or cousins or the earldom? Today, I want to simply be Rafe Bowles."

"Yes, of course!" She touched his arm. "My apologies. I want that too. In fact, you should be Lord Bodyguard while I am Mrs. Dazzling."

"Mrs. Dazzling in a men's costume."

She laughed. "Just so. Why did you and your sister have different surnames? She was Blackwell before she married Sheffield, wasn't she?"

"I was Blackwell too," he said carefully. This was flirting with the topic he wanted to avoid as well as the subject he couldn't reveal under any circumstances—his criminal behavior. "When I moved to Mayfair, I took a different name. Bowles just sounded more elegant." How awful that sounded to his ears. He might as well declare the fact that he was a fraud. But was he, if he was actually an earl?

"Where did you live before? I know it was London."

Much too close to things he didn't want to disclose. If Anne ever learned what he'd been, what he'd *done*... She'd never look at him the same way again. And he rather loved the way she looked at him. As if he were her knight or, more accurately, her Lord Bodyguard.

"Since that was before I was Rafe Bowles, I can't discuss that today," he said with what he hoped was a careless charm.

"You did say that. I'm afraid I am overcome with curiosity about you. I want to know *everything*."

He realized she was still touching his arm. That, coupled with her enthusiasm about him, was a heady combination. If he wasn't careful, he was going to get lost in that forbidden realm with her. And he couldn't. Not even for a kiss.

Did he really think they would get through this day without kissing?

Rafe usually tried to be unflinchingly honest with himself. Perhaps with her, he was indulging in a bit of delusion. That was beyond dangerous.

She settled back against the seat. "Tell me about Magazine Day."

"People come in droves to buy magazines at a discount since it is the end of the month and new periodicals will be available tomorrow."

"I shall rely upon you to steer me to the best ones."

"Are you going to buy some?" he asked. "I though you just wanted to watch people."

"I haven't decided. It's amusing that you thought I wanted to come to watch people when I really wanted to do this in order to spend time with you."

From the corner of his eye, he could tell she was looking at him. "I don't think I've ever met a more straightforward woman."

"I shall take that as a compliment."

"I meant it as one." He couldn't help smiling as he drove down the Haymarket toward Charing Cross.

"What food or drink will you be foisting on me today?" she asked.

"Foisting? I didn't *make* you try oysters or caviar or coffee."

"No, you did not. I love that you introduced them to me. Perhaps we'll find an oyster cart."

"Not in Paternoster Row, but I know of one we can visit later." He looked at her askance. "You truly like oysters?"

She nodded. "Not caviar, though. Sorry."

He chuckled. "We'll see what else we can sample today. You are a *very* curious person, Mrs. Dazzling, and we should feed that curiosity."

As before, Rafe parked the cabriolet off Paternoster Row and left it in the care of his tiger, a boy of twelve he'd rescued from Petticoat Lane several years before. Anne had sat in the vehicle a moment before jumping down.

She let out a sheepish laugh. "I forgot I'm supposed to be a man."

"I did too. I nearly offered you my arm." He was disappointed they had no reason to touch. "Be sure and stay close to me. It will be crowded."

At her nod, they walked to Paternoster Row. "My goodness, this is very busy!" Her gaze scanned the throng of people and the vehicles clogging the street.

They moved much more slowly than their last

visit, stopping to peruse magazines and navigating the crowd. As they reached the front of a bookseller's shop, a child darted from the establishment followed by the shopkeeper, who yelled, "Stop! Thief!"

Rafe moved without thinking, slipping between people and heading the child off before he could get away through the thick crowd. He grabbed the child by the coat. His hat fell off, and dark strands of hair tumbled free past his shoulders. He tried to pull himself out of the coat in order to escape, but Rafe knew that trick well. Sweeping his arm around the child, Rafe scooped him—her?—up and carried him back toward the bookshop.

Hell, Anne. Rafe looked over the heads of those around him and sighted her immediately. She'd made her way toward him but hadn't quite gotten there. Her eyes widened as she saw he carried the child.

Rafe inclined his head toward the bookshop, and Anne nodded in response. Damn. He didn't really want her to witness this, but he couldn't leave her alone outside, even if she was disguised as a man.

"Put me down!" Definitely a girl. She kicked at Rafe's legs and hit him in the back.

"Don't run. And don't steal from me." He set her down but didn't release her. "Agreed?"

She wasn't as much of a child as he'd thought, just small. He estimated she was maybe fifteen.

She glared at him, her dark eyes spitting fire, and dropped the book she was clutching to the floor. "I didn't really want it anyway."

"Yes, you did, and I'm going to let you take it, but only after you tell me why you want it and what you plan to do with it."

The fire in her eyes sputtered, and her lips

parted. She snapped them closed and turned her head toward the shopkeeper. John, a tall, thin man in his late fifties with an austere face, stood to Rafe's left and just behind him. Despite his forbidding appearance, he was one of the kindest people Rafe knew.

The girl looked back to Rafe. "I like to read."

"Good. Don't stop. Where do you live?"

She raised her chin and glowered at him. That was the only answer he was going to get, and he understood why. If someone knew where she lived, they could attack her. It was the same reason she dressed herself to look like a boy. This is how Selina would have been forced to live if Rafe hadn't sent her away to school.

"Do you have work?" Rafe asked.

She hesitated but shook her head. He also understood what that meant—she stole to survive.

"But the book was for you, not to sell for money?"

She nodded, then shot a glance toward Anne, who'd entered the shop and stood a few feet away, effectively blocking the door.

Rafe let go of the girl. "You're going to come here every morning except Sunday and sweep the shop. You'll also do whatever tasks Mr. Entwhistle directs you to do." He looked at John, who didn't reflect even a glimmer of surprise. Rafe then fixed an expectant stare on her. "Agreed?"

"What's wrong with your eye?" she asked, staring at the orange spot.

"It's how I find children like you. You need to stop stealing. You're going to get caught."

She looked away, pressing her lips together. She knew he was right. He could smell the fear beneath her bravado.

Rafe knew how to win her over completely. "If

you need a room, you can have one upstairs." John lived over the shop, but on the uppermost floor, there were a handful of rooms where other young people—mostly boys—had stayed for a time. Rafe had helped all of them find employment.

Rafe picked up the book she'd taken. It was a collection of Greek mythology stories. "Do you like Greek history and culture?"

She shrugged.

"After you read it, tell Mr. Entwhistle what you think." He handed her the book. "Do we have a deal?"

"You're just giving me the book?" She stared at him dubiously.

"I trust you'll be back—for the job, if not the room. I hope you'll take both."

She clutched the book to her chest and stared at him a moment longer before turning and nearly colliding with Anne. "You're a woman."

Anne's gaze met Rafe's briefly before she smiled at the girl. "Yes. What's your name? Seems like your future employer should know it."

"I haven't decided if I'm taking the job."

"Oh, you must. I can highly recommend his character," Anne said, flicking a glance toward Rafe that made his breath catch. "You won't regret it, I promise. I'm Anne, by the way."

"I'm Annie," she said shyly. While Rafe couldn't see her face, he could hear her tone, and he detected the slight curl of her shoulders.

Anne laughed softly. "Then we were destined to meet. You must take this offer of employment and lodging."

"Are you his wife?" she asked, prompting Rafe to freeze.

"Er, no." Anne's gaze found his again, but only briefly. "Just a friend."

"All right, I'll take the job. Will you come back to visit?" Annie asked.

"Definitely. I'll bring you something cheerful for your room upstairs. If you don't mind."

Annie shook her head. "I don't."

"It's settled, then." Anne looked toward the book in Annie's arms. "I will also read that book so we may discuss it. Would you like that?"

"I would. Thank you." Annie turned her head to look at Rafe. "Thank you too."

"See you in the morning," John called with a wave. "Unless you come back later. I'll have the room ready if you do."

Annie nodded before departing the shop far more sedately than when she'd run out the first time.

Anne came toward Rafe, her eyes softening and her lips curling into a lovely smile. "You are much more than a bodyguard. You *are* a hero, despite what you think. You own this shop?"

"I do. You were wonderful with her."

"She needs kindness as much as anyone. I was merely taking your lead." She looked past him at John. "Is he always like this?"

Rafe pivoted so he could see them both.

John gave her a small smile. "Yes."

"How wonderful," she murmured. "I should have realized you owned a shop here, given how much you like the street. And books. How long have you owned this shop?"

Once again, they were venturing too close to things he didn't want to share. Except, he almost wanted to. "Several years."

"Earls don't typically own shops." She clapped her hand over her mouth. "Sorry, I didn't mean to bring that up."

Rafe shot a look toward John, whose brow

creased with confusion. He'd have to explain everything to the shopkeeper. There were *so* many people he needed to explain this to.

Turning back toward Anne, Rafe gestured toward the door. "Shall we go across the street to the coffee house?"

"Yes, but first I need a copy of that book." She went to John. "Would you mind directing me to where I can find it?"

John moved to a display with a stack of books and plucked one from the table. "Nearly our last copy. It's been very popular."

"Annie made a good choice, then." Anne took the book and then reached into her pocket, presumably for money to make the purchase.

"Consider it a gift." Rafe ignored the elevated eyebrows of the shopkeeper.

"Thank you." She didn't turn away from John. Instead, she asked him a question. "You've known Mr. Bowles for some time?"

The confusion he'd displayed when she'd mentioned earls flashed across his features. John coughed. "Yes, Mr. *Bowles*."

Rafe pressed his lips together. "Come, Mrs. D." He clasped her elbow gently.

Anne waved at John and bid him goodbye before they left the shop. "Should I not have called you Mr. Bowles? You have too many identities."

A laugh caught in his throat. He coughed instead. "Yes."

"Hopefully, you will tell me all of them someday." She gave him a warm smile as he guided her carefully across the street between the slow-moving vehicles.

Rafe would never do that—not all of them. He wanted to regain the lighthearted air they'd enjoyed before Annie had tried to steal from his shop.

"Can Lord Bodyguard be the only one that counts? At least, as far as you're concerned."

She looked up at him as they approached the door to the coffee shop. "It will always be."

A tremor rippled through him, and he hated that he'd told her to dress like a man. He couldn't touch her in any way he wanted to, not even to help her into the shop.

Chapter Coffee House was more crowded than on their last visit. Still, Rafe was able to secure them a table at the back. "Tea?" he asked.

Anne took one of the two chairs at the small, round table. "Coffee, please." She gave him a serene look and folded her hands in her lap.

He leaned down and whispered, "You're sitting like a lady. Put one hand on your knee and spread your legs a bit."

She blushed slightly but did as he suggested.

"And stop blushing." The urge to press his lips against the outer edge of her ear or trail his tongue down to her earlobe was nearly overwhelming. He hurriedly took himself to the counter and ordered their coffees.

Belatedly, he realized he should have asked her why she was ordering coffee when she clearly didn't like it. He'd been too distracted.

Shaking himself, he carried their cups back to the table and set them down. He took his seat, noting that her regular color had returned and she was doing her best not to sit like a lady. In fact, her legs were rather far apart, and goddammit if he wasn't distracted all over again.

"Why are you drinking coffee?" he asked, sounding disgruntled because of his unbridled lust. God, was that it? *Yes.* Anne had tied him in knots since practically the moment they'd met. "You don't like it."

"Don't I?" She arched her brow as she gave him a saucy look. Picking up the cup, she took a long sip, then sighed with contentment as she put it down. "I've spent the last three months learning to like it. Now, I'm afraid I can't get through the morning without my cup of coffee."

He stared at her. She'd learned to like it? "Why would you do that?"

"Because it reminded me of you." She took another sip. "Just don't ask me to like caviar, because I don't think I can do that."

The merriment in her eyes was intoxicating. It reminded him of a time before things had felt so heavy upon him. Before he'd lowered his defenses too much. It was a fine balance to feel just the right amount—enough to be thrilled but not so much as to become obsessed. He feared he was already on the edge. Or perhaps even past it. "I won't. The coffee is a delightful surprise."

She looked down at her cup as she ran her fingertip along the rim. She wore gloves, and they were too large for her hands, so he couldn't see her femininity. He could in her face, however. The long sweep of her lashes and the plump curve of her lips declared her womanhood. It wasn't as if he needed to see any of it, for he was all too aware of who she was and the effect she had upon him.

"I know you don't want to talk about your past," she said quietly. "At least not today. But will you tell me how you came to help children such as Annie?" She gave him a tentative look, and he wasn't able to deny the earnest curiosity in her gaze.

He chose his words very particularly. For some reason, he wanted to share things with her. Perhaps because of the way she saw him, the manner in which she didn't make assumptions but truly tried to know him. As if anyone could.

"Selina and I didn't grow up with much," he said slowly. "I've worked very hard to get where I am."

"How?"

That was the part he wouldn't reveal, no matter how good she made him feel or how much he thought he could trust her. Did he? Trust came hard to him, almost as hard as it did for his sister.

"I was fortunate to inherit that bookstore and a small amount of money, which I invested carefully. I will never forget how difficult it was when I was young, however."

"After you were kidnapped from your home." She reached across the table to touch him, but swiftly snatched her hand back. "I suppose I can't really touch you looking the way I do."

"No." At the mention of his kidnapping, he stiffened.

"Well, I think it's lovely that you help children like Annie."

"Will you really visit her?" He sipped his coffee.

"I want to. You don't mind?"

"Not at all."

"Perhaps you'll bring me," she said with a flirtatious smile.

He shook his head. "If you are trying to entice me to continue our acquaintance—"

She leaned forward, her eyes glowing. "Is it working?"

"Yes." The word slipped between his lips before he could stop it. He leaned slightly forward too.

"I have a room upstairs," she said rather breathlessly.

"How on earth…" He couldn't even finish the thought, let alone the question.

"It's under my name, Mr. Dazzle."

Rafe stifled a sharp laugh. "You didn't really use that name."

She lifted a shoulder. "I did. And now I'm going up to that room. If you would care to meet me, it's on the second floor in the back, facing Paul's Alley."

"Your capability is terrifying."

"Is it?" She arched a blonde brow as she rose. "Or is it exciting?" She waggled both brows before going to the back corridor where the stairs were located.

How in the hell had she done this? How did she know where to go? Had she come yesterday and made the arrangements? She was terrifyingly exciting.

And he had no idea what he was going to do about her.

# CHAPTER 8

By the time Anne reached the room upstairs, she was shaking. After she closed the door, she strode into the center of the small room and took a deep breath.

Would he come?

She honestly had no idea. She would give him a quarter hour to decide before going back downstairs in defeat.

In the meantime, she surveyed the room, which she'd visited the day before. The flowers she'd brought were still on the table in front of the window, as was the bottle of madeira and the two glasses. There were two chairs at the table and a short chaise angled near the narrow hearth. The largest piece of furniture was the bed. She'd specifically asked for a room with a wide, comfortable bed. And she'd made sure the linens were of good quality and clean. They were, thankfully, both.

Anne removed her hat and gloves and set them on the nightstand next to one side of the bed. Should she take off her boots? What if he didn't come? Perhaps she should wait.

She checked the timepiece she'd tucked into her coat pocket that morning. Barely five minutes.

Pleased that she'd at least stopped shaking, she went to the window and craned her neck to try to see down the alley to Paternoster Row. She could just make out a sliver of the pavement and street. The crowd had not lessened.

She loved it. There was an energy and boisterousness here that didn't exist in Mayfair. She wondered if Rafe had grown up nearby and hoped he would one day tell her.

He owned a bookshop! And helped children in need. What else didn't she know about him? She hated that there seemed to be so much, but of course there was. He'd lived much more than she had, and that would have been true even if he weren't ten years older. His experience was much different, broader and, from what she'd learned today, harsher.

That was part of the darkness inside him too—along with his wife. A hollow pain spread through her chest when she thought of how much losing her had to have hurt him. He'd said he loved her very much. Perhaps he loved her still. And why wouldn't he? Though she was gone, she was clearly not forgotten.

Anne bent her head to smell the roses on the table. A knock on the door startled her so that she dipped her nose into the petals. "Goodness!" she breathed, putting her hand on the back of one of the chairs to right herself.

He was here. She hurried across the room and stopped short of throwing open the door. "Rafe?" What if it wasn't him?

"Open the door, Anne."

She did so, and he stalked inside. She closed the door behind him.

"You didn't even lock it." He sounded cross. "Does it have a lock?"

"Yes." She set it and faced him. "Better?"

"You should not have been up here without the door locked."

"You're an—" No, he wasn't angry. He was befuddled as he'd been the other day when she'd visited him.

*He is here.*

She kept the smile that threatened at bay. This wasn't victory—not yet. But it was a start. "I should have locked the door. I'm afraid I'm a bit…excited."

He swept his hat off and wiped his hand over his brow. Muttering something, he went to the table and looked at the roses. "This is a very bad idea."

"I like roses." She knew he wasn't talking about the roses. "I brought them yesterday so the room would smell nice."

"You brought them…" He set his hat on the table and spun to face her. "You planned this quite thoroughly." At her nod, he started toward her, moving slowly, like an animal on the prowl.

"A seduction, then?" he asked softly.

A shiver danced along her spine. "I was hoping so, but I'm afraid I'm not well versed in the matter."

"You're not *well* versed. So you are somewhat versed?" He stopped just in front of her. "Anne, are you a virgin?"

Her mouth went dry, and she couldn't speak. So she nodded.

"And you shall remain one."

Disappointment curled through her. "Then why did you come upstairs?"

"Because you gave me no choice. Was I to remain down there hoping you would eventually return? And what if something happened while you were up here?" His eyes glittered dangerously as he moved closer until they nearly touched. "Did you really think I was going to come up here and shag you?"

"I was hoping—"

"Yes, I know that. But hoping and knowing are not the same thing. I've told you repeatedly that I am not someone you should want. I am not a gentleman."

"You are an earl, as it happens."

"I wasn't raised one, and the sooner you realize that and accept I will *never* be the man you want, the better."

She stood on her toes and put her hands on his shoulders. "But you *are* the man I want. Right now. Why do we have to think of anything but this afternoon? We agreed we would spend this afternoon together, to regain the one we'd lost."

His brows arched. "You thought we were going to have sex that afternoon?"

"No, and I was not sure we would today. As I said, I *hoped*." She exhaled. "Will you at least kiss me once more before we go?"

He stared at her, then glanced toward the bed. When he looked back at her, the orange in his right eye seemed brighter than ever. "Why do you want *me*?"

"Because you're kind, considerate, dashing, generous, and completely unlike anyone I've ever known. You treat me like an ordinary woman, not someone who suits your needs or your plans or a prize to be bartered or won." She shook her head. "No, not an ordinary woman, but someone who is special to you. Someone you like and enjoy being with. Am I wrong?"

He breathed an epithet. "No." He dipped his head and claimed her mouth, his lips molding possessively over hers. His arms came around her, pulling her flush against him. The thrill of his kiss and his body pressed to hers crashed through her, quickening her pulse and heating her blood.

She clasped his nape, her fingers digging into his thick hair. His tongue swept into her mouth, and she welcomed him, her body screaming for this and more.

His hands slipped down to her backside, and he lifted her, one hand moving to her right thigh and curling her leg around his waist. She did the same with the other, and he moved, carrying her—toward the bed, if she remembered the room correctly.

What was he doing? He said he didn't want her. No, he hadn't said *that*.

He set her on the bed but didn't move away. His pelvis was still pressed into hers. She could feel the ridge of his sex against hers. Breaking the kiss, he lifted his head as he pushed her coat from her shoulders and set it on the end of the bed.

"I can't give you anything beyond today, and you won't ask me to." He removed his coat and laid it at the head of the bed. "Understood?"

She nodded, her mind and body careening with disbelief and want.

He plucked at the buttons of her waistcoat, opening the garment, and he pulled the cravat from her neck, tossing it aside. Slipping his hand inside her shirt, he slowly traced his fingertips along her collarbone. The movement opened the shirt wider down the front. The V was quite deep, so much so that she'd pinned it closed over her breast. She reached between them and, removing the pin from the fabric, managed to stick it into the coat sitting to her right.

His hand moved down, further separating the lawn of her shirt, opening the V. "You bound your breasts?" His fingers settled lightly against the fabric she'd used to flatten her chest.

"You indicated they might be a problem."

A quick smile flashed across his mouth—so quickly, she might have thought she imagined it, except her body reacted, her insides turning to liquid and her sex fluttering. He lowered his head but didn't kiss her mouth. Instead, his lips moved along her jaw as he pushed the waistcoat off her and tugged the shirt from her pantaloons.

He kissed down her throat, his lips and tongue creating a delicious havoc that made her breathless. But it was the insistent press of him between her legs that made her gasp with want. A desperate need unfurled inside her. Something was just beyond her reach, and she wanted it more than anything.

Then he was gone—not gone, but no longer kissing her. He swept the shirt up over her head. Anne felt a rush of cool air, but she didn't care. She was plenty warm and heating further by the moment.

"How does this come off?" His question was low and full of gravel as his hands skimmed over the fabric crushing her breasts.

She'd tucked the tie underneath the bottom of the fabric and now pulled it free. "Here." She unplucked the knot, and the binding loosened. Working as quickly as her quivering fingers would allow, she unwound the fabric from her torso.

His breath caught when the binding fell from her grasp, exposing her to him completely. For a long moment, he was silent and still. She wondered if he would retreat now, but he cupped her face and kissed her, devouring her mouth in complete and delicious domination. His hand glided down her throat to her chest, his fingers skimming over the slope of her breast. He cupped her, drawing a low moan from her throat. When his fingers closed over her nipple, he triggered an answering pulse in her sex. She pushed against him, seeking that wonderful friction, and he responded, thrusting against her. She cried out into his mouth, still wanting something more.

He pushed her back on the bed, which created distance between them. She whimpered, for she could no longer feel him, hard and wicked, between her legs. Distraction came in the form of his lips trailing down from her mouth to the hollow at the base of her throat to the crest of her breast as he held her.

She thrust her fingers into his hair and clutched his shoulder—an anchor to the sensations that threatened to sweep her away. He kissed her gently, lips and tongue creating a mass of blinding pleasure until he latched onto her nipple and darkness descended completely. She clasped his head hard, holding him to her, vaguely aware that he was also working the buttons of her pantaloons.

A moment later, as he moved his mouth to her other breast, his hand slipped against her sex. He pressed his fingers at the top, and her entire body jolted. She arched off the bed, her hips rising.

His lips were suddenly against her ear as his fingers teased her flesh. "Do you know what's going to happen?" he whispered.

"Not entirely." Her voice sounded completely separate from herself. She didn't recognize it or the wanton she'd become, her hips moving wildly, her hands clutching at him, her body quivering with lust.

"When I touch you here—your clitoris—it feels good, yes?" At her nod, he continued, his voice dark and seductive as he moved his finger over her with deft, increasingly faster strokes. "Good. I'm going to put my finger inside you. It's not my cock, but it's the best I can do for you. And I promise, it will be enough." He licked the outer shell of her ear. "I'm going to fuck you with it, and you're going to come. You're going to let yourself go and feel. Do you understand?"

She whimpered again in response, his words driving her desire to the very edge. She felt as if she might do what he said—come—right then.

Slowly, he slid his finger inside her sheath. "Relax, my sweet," he said softly against her before nipping her earlobe with his teeth.

She sucked in air and clutched his neck before telling herself to do as he bade. Exhaling, she tried to go limp, but there was so much energy racing through her, so much *need*.

He withdrew his finger, then teased her clitoris again. Her arousal climbed, her entire body reeling with desire. He latched onto her neck briefly, suckling her before moving down and doing the same at the top of her breast, but for longer. The sensation was rough but wonderful, and again she arched up, seeking more.

He gave it to her, moving his finger in and out of her. His mouth moved lower still until he reclaimed her nipple, sucking and licking and using his teeth to tug gently on her flesh.

She widened her legs—or tried to, but that brought her pantaloons up. He muttered something, then left her breast. He quickly stripped her boots off, then peeled her pantaloons from her legs.

Then he was quiet, and the air was still.

Anne opened her eyes to see him staring at her sex, his lips parted, his hand against her folds. "What's wrong?" she asked, her voice cracking.

"Nothing is wrong. And maybe that's—" He clenched his jaw. His gaze found hers, and she nearly gasped at the intensity in his eyes. "I don't wish to frighten you."

"You could never." How she wanted him. *Loved* him.

"Don't say that."

She had to strain to hear him. Rising up on her elbow, she reached for him. He pressed his hand against her, teasing her flesh once more.

"Time for you to come for me, Mrs. Dazzling." He cupped the back of her neck and kissed her while his finger, no, fingers, speared into her. "Let yourself go. Don't think. Just feel."

His thumb worked over her clitoris, moving with rapid strokes that drove her body to move. She met his thrusts as he threaded his fingers into her hair, pulling her head back. He kissed her jaw, her throat, the side of her neck, his hand moving over her and into her sex with merciless precision until she sensed what he'd told her.

Sensation rushed through her as she barreled toward something. Her body tightened as pleasure sparked in her core. "Yes," he rasped against her mouth. "*Now.*"

Ecstasy tore through her. She held on to him so she wouldn't spin away into an unforgiving darkness. He guided her through the blissful devastation, his movements slowing.

She collapsed back upon the bed, her chest heaving as she fought to regain her breath. After several moments, she realized he was pulling her pantaloons back up over her. Opening her eyes, she lifted her head to look at him. In profile, his features were drawn, his jaw tight.

"What's wrong?" She sat up and reached for his hand.

"I told you, nothing is wrong."

"You look troubled."

He stopped with her pantaloons and turned his face toward her. "Unlike you, I did not find my release, nor will I." His eyes narrowed slightly. "Don't even try to talk me into that. You've already done enough."

"*I've* done enough?" She found the cloth she'd used to bind her breasts and began to wind it around her torso, despite an almost overwhelming urge to burrow into the covers of the bed and demand he join her.

"I should not have allowed you to talk me into this," he said, fetching her boots and pushing them back onto her feet.

"I have no regrets," she said softly. "And all the gratitude in the world." She tied the binding, though not as tightly as before. Her breasts still tingled from his touch. Her entire body still thrummed. She didn't want it to stop.

He handed her the men's shirt, and she put her hand on his. "Does it really have to just be today?"

"Yes."

"Why?"

He let go of the shirt, taking his hand from beneath hers, and walked away from the bed. "I told you why."

His wife.

Anne pulled the shirt on and found the pin to hold the V closed over her breasts. After tucking the hem into her waistband, she drew on the waistcoat. "I'm not asking you to love me," she said quietly. "I'm only asking to continue what we share. You enjoy being with me, don't you?"

He stood near the table, his back to her. "I do."

But he didn't want to. He felt guilty because of the love he'd borne his wife.

"I'm not asking you to stop loving her either. I would never do that. Nor would I ever wish to take her place."

"You could never." He repeated the words she'd said to him earlier, but they carried an entirely different meaning, one that closed a door rather than opened one.

When her waistcoat was buttoned, she slid off the bed and plucked up the cravat. A small mirror hung near the door. She went to it and tied the cloth around her neck. The knot was far simpler than what she'd done earlier, and frankly terrible, but it was the best she could manage at the moment.

Her hair was an absolute disaster. On its best day, the locks did as they pleased, but today, with the certain thrashing she'd done on the bed, she looked as if a bird had plucked every curl free in an attempt to find the makings for a nest. "You could have just used my hair as the nest," she muttered.

"What did you say?"

She turned from the mirror to see he'd also pivoted and was now looking at her. "I was remarking on the state of my hair. It's a good thing I'm merely trying to hide it under a hat."

Returning to the bed, she found the pins that had been dislodged and set about securing it back atop her head in the most severe style possible.

He came to the bed and picked up his coat, drawing it on with ease. Pity, she liked looking at him in his shirtsleeves. His dark red waistcoat had stretched taught across his shoulder blades, accentuating the muscles beneath. She wanted to see them bare. She wanted to see all of him that way.

Tucking the last pin into her hair, she snagged his hand and held it up to her chest. She looked into his eyes. "Is there no part of you that you can share with me?"

His nostrils flared. "I have shared all that I can."

"I'm not sure I believe you. I would take any part of you. I lo—"

He pressed his hand against her mouth. "Don't. Please."

There was a scent on his fingers. She nodded, and he removed his hand. "Is that how I…smell?"

His eyes darkened, the orange spot smoldering. "I wanted to put my mouth on you and nearly lost that battle. If there was ever going to be a next time, that's what I would do." He leaned forward, whispering, "Then I would kiss you, and you would taste yourself."

Heat shot through her and settled in her sex, renewing her desire. "Well, that's not fair to tease me like that."

"Christ, Anne." He ran his hand through his hair and pivoted so that he was once again in profile. "How the hell am I supposed to keep myself from you when you are so damned tempting?"

Joy bloomed in her chest. "I'd rather you didn't." She moved to stand in front of him. "There is no one else I want. I can be very patient. I tried to move on before, to do what I should instead of what I wanted. I'm not going to do that this time."

He touched her cheek, his lips lifting briefly in a sad smile. "You deserve far better than me. I have nothing to offer you—nothing you truly want. I am trying to be the gentleman you think I am."

"Then I'm right about that at least. Perhaps I'll be right about more." She winked at him and went to fetch her hat. "I suppose we should be getting back to Mayfair." There was no point disguising the disappointment she felt.

He stared at her before going to pick up his

own hat. Setting it atop his crown, he shook his head. "What am I going to do with you?"

"Anything you like. Just name the day and the place, and I will be there. In the meantime, I'll be waiting."

She left the room, knowing he followed her close behind, and hoped that wasn't the last time they would be alone together. If it was, she at least had a memory that would make her smile.

But that wasn't enough. She was going to fight for him. Not because she wanted him more than she'd ever wanted anything, but because she believed he wanted her too.

He just had to see it for himself.

# CHAPTER 9

The following morning, Rafe climbed into his coach and headed to Cavendish Square to pick up his sister. They were traveling to Redhill, to the Golden Eagle, to visit the younger sister of their nurse, Pauline Blaylock.

A nervous energy thrummed through him, but he wasn't entirely certain it was due to hopefully finding their nurse. He couldn't stop thinking of Anne and yesterday afternoon.

Their trip back to Mayfair had been strained—at least for him. Part of it had been his unspent lust, but the rest of it, and perhaps the greater portion, was due to what she'd plainly told him.

And what she'd *tried* to tell him, but he'd stopped her from saying. He couldn't even allow himself to finish her sentence in his head. Eliza had loved him, and look where that had gotten her.

Instead, he thought about Anne's honesty, her unabashed desire, how she made no apologies for being precisely who she was and pursuing what she wanted. He'd been like that once. As a boy, he'd possessed enough ambition for every young thief he'd led. He believed that if he worked hard and sought higher and higher ranks and responsibility, he'd find power and respect.

Years later, he'd found what really mattered and what he was trying so hard to avoid feeling again: love.

In the end, his ambition and his pursuit of happiness had completely destroyed not just his love, but his life. He could never go back to the way he was before, hopeful and…vulnerable. Anne couldn't possibly understand that. Nor would he ask her to.

As he dropped her back at the Grosvenor Mews, she'd reminded him that she would be patient. She'd been earnest but gleeful, in possession of a boundless optimism he wasn't sure he'd ever enjoyed. How could he, given the way he'd been raised?

The coach stopped in front of Selina's house, and the footman ran to the door to let her butler know they'd arrived. A few moments later, Selina walked toward the coach, and the footman held the door as Rafe offered his hand to help her up.

"Thank you." She took the forward-facing seat, which he'd left vacant for her. "I'm glad the weather will be dry today."

Redhill was a four-hour drive each way. The journey could have been made faster if they rode. But he did not and neither did Selina. She, however, was learning, under the tutelage of her husband. He, like Rafe, was the son of an earl, and, unlike Rafe, knew how to bloody well ride a horse.

When Rafe let himself think about all the things he'd lost, specifically the things he'd missed doing with his father, he was nearly overcome with rage and sadness. This was yet another reason he would keep Anne at bay. No one deserved to be with a man as consumed by darkness as he was. And

Anne had seen it, meaning it wasn't just how he saw himself.

"You seem pensive," Selina said from beneath the elegant hat she wore.

Rafe ignored her comment. "You look like such a lady. You also look happy."

"I am. You look pensive," she repeated. "But it seems you aren't going to discuss that with me."

No, he was not. "I suppose I'm just anxious about today. I hope Mrs. Gill is able to direct us to her sister."

"Have you thought about what you would say to her?" Selina asked softly, her lip curling. "Not just asking her what happened, but what her actions did to us, to our lives."

Rafe could hear her anger, could feel it in his chest. "Yes, but mostly I think of what I would say to Edgar. I'm fucking furious I won't have that chance."

"All that time, he said they'd rescued us, that we should be grateful." Selina's jaw tightened as she looked out the window. "He used us." She looked at him across the small space, her blue eyes clear, save a tiny glimmer of pain. "Do you think she knew what he meant to do?"

"We'll hopefully find out. Soon."

"I hope so. If this doesn't lead us to her..." She exhaled and pressed a hand briefly to her cheek. "We'll have to find a way to let it go. It's not as if we can change the past. And now we have a future." She shook her head. "I never imagined what I have found, and now to learn that you are an earl. Someday, I suppose it won't seem like a dream."

"I keep waiting for that, so do let me know when it happens for you."

She laughed. "It's very strange, isn't it? Where we find ourselves."

"Certainly no stranger than where we've been." He settled himself against the squab. "On that note, we have a long journey ahead of us. Amuse me with your exploits as Madame Sybila, the fortune-teller." He arched a brow at her. "You chose a rather obvious name, did you not?" Sybila meant prophetess or seer.

She shrugged, smiling. "It was also relatively close to Selina so that I might hear it and answer more quickly." Taking a deep breath, she launched into the story of how Madame Sybila came to be —after she and Beatrix had met a fortune-teller early in their travels. The trip to Redhill passed quickly and pleasantly, even if there was a tang of bittersweetness as Rafe thought of their lost years.

At least they'd found each other again. Their parents were lost to them forever.

Redhill was a coaching stop on the way to Brighton, so there were several inns in the town. The Golden Eagle was of medium size with a bustling stable yard.

Rafe and Selina left the coach in the capable hands of Rafe's coachman and groom and went into the inn. Built within the last fifty years, the Golden Eagle was newer than some of the others they'd passed and in fine condition. The common room was clean and cheerful, with a bank of windows along the front that invited plenty of light.

A lively serving maid greeted them with a wide smile, her dark curls peeking from beneath her cap. "Stopping in for a bit, or do you need a room?"

"Just stopping in," Rafe said. "We're looking for Mrs. Gill. Would you let her know Lady Selina Sheffield and Lord Stone are here to see her?" He and Selina had discussed how to introduce themselves and ultimately decided they should use their actual titles in the hope that it would persuade her to be completely honest.

The maid's blue eyes flashed with surprise. "Right away, my lord. My lady." She dipped a curtsey to them both before disappearing through a doorway at the back of the common room.

"That sounds so odd," Selina said.

It was as odd as suddenly owning multiple houses across England and being responsible for the livelihoods of everyone employed at them. Rafe had spent a few hours the night before questioning Thomas, Lord Rockbourne, his pretend brother-in-law. As a viscount, he was able to share many things with Rafe about his properties, his army of employees, and serving in the House of Lords. There was an astonishing amount to learn, and Rafe took his new role very seriously.

Selina surveyed the room. "I'm nervous."

"I am too."

A woman emerged from the same doorway where the maid had disappeared. Her dark hair was almost completely covered by a cap, and her features were drawn tight as if she was nervous too.

"Lord Stone?" she asked tentatively, her gaze flicking toward Selina. "Lady Selina?"

"Yes," Selina answered. "You are Mrs. Gill?"

The woman, who was perhaps ten years older than Rafe, nodded. "How can I be of assistance to you?" She clasped her hands in front of her narrow waist.

"I'll get straight to the reason for our visit," Rafe said. "We're looking for your sister, Pauline Blaylock. Do you know where we can find her?"

"It's imperative we speak with her," Selina added.

The flesh around Mrs. Gill's mouth tightened

and paled. “She’s here. She’s quite ill, however. Indeed, she isn’t expected to survive much longer.”

Rafe and Selina exchanged a panicked look. If they’d delayed the trip another day… Thankfully, they hadn’t. “May we speak with her? As my sister said, it’s incredibly important.” Rafe asked.

Mrs. Gill cocked her head to the side. “She worked for the Earl of Stone, but that can’t have been you. That was years ago. I was a child when she left to take the position.”

“She was our nurse,” Selina said, sounding a trifle impatient. “May we see her?” She took a breath and smiled, perhaps realizing she seemed anxious. “She used to sing to me. I don’t recall much from when I was young, but I remember that.”

“Her voice was from the angels,” Mrs. Gill said with a nostalgic smile that quickly faded. “She hasn’t been able to sing for some time now. Come, I’ll take you to her room.”

The innkeeper’s wife led them back through the doorway from whence she’d come. Rafe followed behind Selina, his body thrumming with anticipation.

They moved down a narrow corridor to a room at the end. Mrs. Gill opened the door and invited them inside. A figure formed a small lump in the bedclothes. The smell of sickness permeated the space.

“Polly,” Mrs. Gill called softly as she approached the bed. “You have a pair of guests. I think they may make you smile. Let me help you sit up.” She propped the pillows against the headboard and lifted the figure higher in the bed.

Now visible, Pauline Blaylock looked much older than her probable age, which was likely not yet fifty. Her gray hair was gathered back from her face, but strands clung to her sunken cheeks. Her dark eyes seemed faded, as if she'd stared at the sun too long. She appeared a woman without much time, her pallor grayish and her body withered. If Rafe had come upon her, there would have been no recognition from him.

"Who are they?" Pauline asked her sister, her expression confused.

"This is Lord Stone and Lady Selina Sheffield. They said you were their nurse."

Rafe went rigid. Selina clasped his fingers briefly.

Pauline's eyes widened, and she let out a terrible sound that was part sob and part shriek. "It can't be you."

Swallowing a cruel retort, Rafe moved closer to the bed. Mrs. Gill stepped out of the way. "It is." He bent low so she could see his eye. "You recognize me, don't you?"

"Lord Sandon," she breathed. Then her gaze drifted past him, fixing on Selina. "My precious girl."

"She is not and was never *your* girl," Rafe said coldly. He had absolutely no sympathy for this woman on her deathbed. She'd stolen them from their life.

Pauline looked back to Rafe, her body seeming to shrink beneath his stare. "No. I am glad to see you both looking so well. You are Lord Stone now?"

The serving maid came to the room, interrupting them. Mrs. Gill excused herself, closing the door after she left.

Selina moved to the bed. "Yes, he is Lord Stone. I am Lady Selina Sheffield. My husband is the son of the Earl of Aylesbury."

"As it should be," Pauline said softly as tears

pooled in her eyes. "As it should be. I am glad I am alive to see it. To see you both well."

Rafe chafed at her apparent joy. "We have only recently learned who we truly are. We have spent our lives wondering about our origins as we fought to survive. We have many questions, and you owe it to us to answer them to the best of your ability."

Pauline's dry lips parted. She licked them as she looked toward Selina, perhaps hoping she would be less demanding than Rafe.

"Why did you kidnap us from Stonehaven?" Selina asked. "We know about the fire and that we were presumed dead."

Her pallor went from gray to white. "I didn't kidnap you. Not really." She winced. "It's a terrible, awful tale," she whispered.

Selina took Rafe's hand and squeezed. "Tell us. And don't leave anything out. It seems you are not long for this world and we would have the truth. We can't ask Edgar—our 'uncle'—nor can we ask our parents."

"Was Edgar even your brother?" Rafe asked, impatient to hear the story.

"Oh, yes. He was the eldest of us. He was a footman at Stonehaven. He was sent there after starting at Ivy Grove. That's how I was hired as your nurse." She coughed, and a tear tracked down her lined face. "Water, please?" She inclined her head toward a pitcher and glass on a table at the end of the bed.

Selina went to pour the water. She then helped the frail woman sip a bit.

"Thank you," Pauline said, gasping. "Are you certain you want to hear this? Perhaps it's better to let the past alone, especially since you both appear to have landed on your feet."

"You have no idea what we have endured,"

Selina snapped. She clutched the glass in her hand, and Rafe wondered if she might dump it on the woman's head. "You stole us from our home. I was barely more than a babe. Your brother forced us to steal and lie and swindle. My brother had to save every penny we earned to send me away to school before I was raped and forced into prostitution."

Pauline shrank into the pillows, her eyes wide and filling with tears once more. "I didn't know. At least you went to school."

"Where I was ridiculed for being less than my peers, and when I left to take *respectable* employment, I was raped anyway." The revelation shook Rafe. He put his hand on his sister's lower back, steadying her as much as himself. "And since then, I've had to scrape a living together to keep myself and my sister fed."

"You didn't have a sister," Pauline said, confused as she wiped a tear from her cheek.

Selina swore as she went to slam the glass down on the table. When she returned, she stood close to Rafe, and he put his arm around her gently.

"Never mind our sister," Rafe said. "This isn't a day for our revelations but for yours. Why did you take us away from Stonehaven and give us to Edgar?"

"You won't like it," Pauline said, sniffing. "Your uncle hated your father. He wanted everything your father had, so he took what he could. He paid Edgar to start the fire, and we were to ensure that you"—she looked pointedly at Rafe—"and your father died."

A blinding rage took hold of Rafe. He gripped Selina harder than he should as the world around him went red.

"He didn't die, however," Selina said from

somewhere that sounded quite far away. "But our father did."

"He'd been given laudanum so that he wouldn't be able to escape. Your mother refused to leave him. Her maid told me to take the two of you to safety. But I was supposed to make sure you were trapped." She looked from Rafe to Selina. "I couldn't do it. I couldn't leave you in the fire. So I took you and ran."

"You left our parents to die?" Selina's voice was closer now, but so small. The question pierced Rafe's heart. This woman and her brother had taken everything from them.

"You did this for money?" he asked, his vision clearing while a dull throb started at the back of his head.

"More money than I could ever make in a lifetime as a nurse."

He curled his lip. "Yet you're dying in the back room of your sister's husband's inn."

She turned her gaze to the wall. "I have made many poor choices."

"What did you do after you ran away?" Selina asked.

"I was afraid of your uncle, that he'd catch me. Edgar wanted to take you, so I let him. I knew he was going to London. I went there too, but I didn't stay long. I lost all my money and came here, where I married."

Selina practically growled in frustration. "Your life sounds rather normal."

Rafe repeated everything Pauline had said in his mind. Now, he summarized it out loud. "I want to make sure I understand: my uncle, Ludlow Mallory, arranged to murder my father and me. You know this for a fact?"

Pauline looked him in the eye. "Yes. He asked

Edgar to start the fire and later spoke directly with me and Edgar to discuss the details. He visited Stonehaven about a week before the fire to make the final arrangements."

"And you never once thought to alert our father or the authorities? You had no hesitation about killing a man and his five-year-old son?" Selina's voice was rough with anger and despair.

"I did." Pauline closed her eyes briefly and pushed her head back into the pillow. "But I was young and foolish."

"Greedy," Selina said tightly, crossing her arms over her chest.

"Fortunately for you, there is still time to do something right," Rafe said.

"What's that?" Pauline's lids drooped as she looked up at them.

"You'll provide testimony to a clerk in the event that you don't live long enough to testify at the trial."

She shook her head so hard that she started coughing once more. Rafe glanced at Selina, but she continued to stare malevolently at the woman in the bed.

He went and picked up the glass of water, then waited for her coughing to subside before helping her to take a few sips.

"I can't do that," Pauline croaked.

Selina violently uncrossed her arms, elbowing Rafe in the process. "Why not? You can't be afraid for your life. It's nearly at an end."

"No, but I won't cause trouble for my sister and her husband. They've been good to me. Lord knows I don't deserve it. But *they* don't deserve the taint of being associated with someone like me and what I've done."

Rafe clenched his hands into fists as fury tightened every one of his muscles. "So you'll let a murderer go unpunished. You were party to the deaths of our parents and the servants who also died in that fire. And you allowed my sister and me to be forever changed." Damaged.

"You're a monster," Selina whispered.

Pauline had the gall to raise her chin and give them a clear-eyed stare. "I could have lied to you, but I told you the truth. I will go to my grave with a clearer conscience at least. You can either look backward or you can look to your future. It looks rather wonderful, doesn't it?"

Rafe snorted. "That was precisely the fucking nonsense your brother said as he used us for his own gain and then sold us to a criminal." He turned his head to Selina. "We should have brought your husband."

"Yes. In fact, I'll see if he can come tomorrow. I'm confident there is ample reason for him to arrest her."

"What?" Pauline started coughing once more, more violently than she had yet. Her face turned red.

"My husband is a Bow Street Runner," Selina said with clear satisfaction. "You've admitted your crime to us. Unless you'd care to change your mind about speaking with a clerk who will take your testimony?"

"Water, please," Pauline rasped. When neither Rafe nor Selina moved, she nodded vigorously. "I'll talk to the clerk."

Selina went to pour more water and brought her the glass. She even helped the invalid drink. Pauline continued to cough, and her sister returned.

"Oh, Polly, you've worn yourself out." She

looked toward Rafe and Selina. "I think you must let her rest now. It's time for her medicine."

Rafe pinned Pauline with a dark stare. "The clerk will be here tomorrow. Don't die before then."

Mrs. Gill gasped and drew her hand to her chest as her eyes widened. "What a terrible thing to say."

"Your sister has done far worse," Selina bit out in a clipped tone. She hesitated before looking toward Pauline once more. The anger seemed to drain from her as he shoulders sagged and her features turned sad. "You used to sing *Lavender Blue* to me. All I remember is my mother's coral necklace and that song." Her voice was soft and haunting. It broke what remained of Rafe's heart.

Tears filled Pauline's eyes again. "I loved you. I thought you and your mother would be fine. Your uncle promised me that. I am so sorry for my part in what happened."

Mrs. Gill frowned at her sister. "Polly, what are you talking about?"

Pauline weakly lifted her hand in a feeble wave. "Later. I need to sleep." She seemed to sink deeper into the bedclothes. Her eyes closed.

Rafe gritted his teeth and lightly touched his sister's back to guide her to the door. Selina didn't move, however. "Did that necklace burn in the fire?" she asked.

It took a moment for Pauline to respond, and she didn't open her eyes. "No. You had it. She came to the nursery to make sure you got out of the house. You wanted her, but she needed to go find your father. You reached for her and grabbed the necklace. It came off, and you held on to it as we left the house."

Rafe's heart broke again as he watched the despair carve deep lines into his sister's face. Her back bowed with the weight of her grief.

"I made sure it was with you when Edgar took you."

Was it possible, then, that the necklace Beatrix had given to Selina had belonged to their mother?

"When the clerk comes tomorrow to take your testimony, he's going to bring a necklace. You will tell him if it's the same one. I am not certain it is, but you will know."

Pauline didn't respond.

"I'm sorry, but you must go," Mrs. Gill pleaded.

"You'll keep me apprised of her condition," Rafe said. "Send word to me at Upper Brook Street in London. Tomorrow, a clerk will come to take her testimony about the matter we discussed today. You must admit him, do you understand?"

Mrs. Gill nodded.

Rafe inclined his head, then guided Selina from the room. They walked in silence from the inn and waited to speak until they were seated in the coach on their way back to London.

Selina stared out the window as they drove north through Redfield. "She may die before the clerk arrives."

"She probably will, just to spite us."

"Our uncle is a murderer," she said quietly, her gaze fixed outside the coach.

"Yes. I want to kill him, Lina."

She turned her head toward him then, her blue eyes dark and piercing in their intensity. "No. You are *not* a murderer."

"You know that's not true." He'd told her what he'd done to the man who'd killed his pregnant wife, the man who'd brutally ripped away the best part of Rafe. "When it comes to those I love, I will do anything." His throat burned, threatening to close with emotion. "I worked so hard to protect you, to keep you safe. None of it mattered. I failed. What you said in there—"

She held up her hand. "I was upset. Besides Beatrix, the only other person who knows what happened to me when I was a governess is Harry. And don't ask me who my employer was, because it doesn't matter. That was twelve years ago. I left, and I've never looked back."

Rafe understood wanting to bury the horrors of the past. "I'm so bloody sorry. I never should have left you at that school."

"You did the best you could. Regardless of what happened to me, it was probably better than if I'd stayed in London. You know that to be true."

He did, but learning what had happened after she left the school, when she was supposed to have been embarking on a bright future that he'd made possible, absolutely crushed him. He did his best to hide that fact.

"Back to Mallory," Selina said with a shake of her head and taking a deep breath. "You can't kill him. I would much prefer to see his crimes made public and for him to hang. Harry will help us. There is no one better."

While Rafe understood her need for a public accounting for their uncle's crimes, he didn't share it. He only cared that the man paid with his life. It would be easy enough for Rafe to ask someone from his past to take care of the deed. The counterfeit Earl of Stone could die at the hands of a footpad.

Except Rafe knew firsthand that the man's death would do nothing to ease the pain. He'd ended Samuel Partridge, but it hadn't brought Eliza back, nor had it assuaged the piercing ache of losing her. Only time had made that less difficult to bear.

So Rafe would gladly witness his uncle's public shame and degradation when his crimes were exposed. Then he would watch the vile man's body dangle from a rope.

"We need more evidence," Rafe said flatly. "Even if Pauline survives to tell her tale to the clerk, it will be her testimony—that of a dead woman—against that of our uncle, who has been a respected member of Society his entire life." Rafe wanted to hit something.

Her gaze darkened. "Then we'll get more evidence. Perhaps the clerk Harry sent to Stonehaven will learn something."

"It would be best if we could send word before he returns to London, alerting him of what we've learned. However, that will be difficult given Stonehaven's distance." It was a three-day journey by coach in the most favorable of weather.

Selina returned to looking out the window as they left Redhill behind. Rafe focused his white-hot rage into a cold determination for revenge.

After some time, Selina asked, "What if we could get him to confess?"

Rafe wasn't sure that would be possible. "I don't know him well enough to say. I suppose we could try." Christ, how? If only they knew him better or knew someone who did, who could provoke him...

Anne.

She'd known him her entire life. He looked at her as another daughter, and in fact, might even care for her more than his own daughter. It was perhaps his only redeeming quality.

No, Rafe wouldn't even give him that. In fact, when he thought of Mallory holding affection toward Anne, Rafe grew more furious.

"You're thinking of something," Selina said.

"Yes, but don't ask me what. I don't know if it will work." He couldn't reveal the truth to Anne and risk her telling her godfather. "We need to keep what we learned today to ourselves—and Harry."

"And Beatrix. I don't keep secrets from her."

Rafe exhaled. "Fine. But she and Rockbourne must swear secrecy."

Selina nodded. "They will. You'll be the earl soon. Things will get even easier then."

Perhaps. Rafe put no trust in such things. He trusted his sister and himself.

And he was going to do whatever necessary to make their uncle pay for his crimes. Even if he had to use Anne to do it.

## CHAPTER 10

Two days felt like a lifetime, particularly when Anne had no idea how many more days it would be before she saw Rafe again. She wandered downstairs to the library and ran into Jane, who promptly frowned.

"Why are you looking at me like that?" Anne asked.

Jane's eyes narrowed. "Why do *you* look like that?"

"Like what?" Anne tried to sound light and even lifted her shoulder in the hope of conveying a careless attitude. She was fairly certain she'd failed spectacularly given the deepening concern in Jane's brow.

"As if you've just received the most disappointing news. You haven't, have you?"

What would that even be? Anne tried to think of the most disappointing thing. Not ever seeing Rafe again. And since she currently had no plans to do so, yes, she supposed it was the equivalent of the most disappointing news ever. God, she was a pathetic mess of unrequited love.

"I have not," Anne said, debating whether to

confide in Jane about what had happened between her and Rafe the other day.

The butler came into the library, interrupting anything Anne might have said. "Lady Colton, Mr. Mallory is here to see Miss Pemberton."

"Please show him in," Jane said.

After the butler departed, Jane looked toward Anne, her brows climbing. "He's calling on you?"

Anne's heart pounded, and her belly flipped. "I wasn't expecting him to."

"That explains your demeanor," Jane said with a light smile. "I'll leave you alone, but with the door open, and I'll sit just outside. Not to eavesdrop, but to pretend there's just a bit of propriety happening." She winked at Anne just before Rafe stepped into the room.

Everything faded into the background around him. He looked spectacular, his golden hair combed into a perfect, rakish style, his dark gray costume with burgundy waistcoat fitting his physique impeccably. Anne's throat went dry as she recalled their last encounter, when she'd been stripped nearly bare in his embrace. Her pulse raced as a thrilling heat swept through her.

He bowed his head. "Lady Colton. Miss Pemberton."

"Lord—" Anne stopped herself. "Mr. Mallory." He was not yet Lord Stone. Nevertheless, she'd wondered if he was an earl on the very day they'd met. Perhaps there was something intrinsically noble about him.

The butler left, and Jane stepped toward the door. "Good afternoon, Mr. Mallory. I presume you'd like to speak with my sister. I'll be just outside." She glanced toward Anne before departing the library.

Rafe walked toward her. "Your sister is very accommodating. What does she know?"

"She knows about our…friendship, how I feel about you." She looked up at him, her body swaying, aching for his touch. "I did not tell her any specifics about the other day." Warmth rose in her cheeks to match the heat in her core.

"I came to ask a favor, if I may." He was being very reserved. Was that because the door was open? Or because he truly wasn't going to continue their…whatever it was?

"Shall we sit?" She gestured to the settee to her left.

At his nod, she perched on the edge, angling herself toward him. He also sat somewhat sideways, facing her. Their knees nearly touched. They were so close, but the bare inch felt as though it were a canyon.

Anne couldn't imagine what favor she could grant him. At least not one that matched his current behavior. "I gather this is not a favor of a… personal nature?"

His eyes flickered with heat. "No." Some of the anticipation curling through Anne dissipated. "I would like to get to know my uncle."

This surprised her, but she was pleased. "I think that's wonderful."

"It seems I should. I haven't ever had family beyond my sister, and we've been apart for some time." He looked away from her. "I will never get my father back, but it seems his brother might be the next best thing." He said the last few words slowly, as if he were choosing his words with care.

Anne smiled, glad that he'd come to this decision and that he'd sought her out to help. "This is brilliant. You'd like my assistance?"

He nodded. "I'm not sure how, but he's like a second father to you, isn't he?"

"I suppose he is. In some ways, I like him better than my father, particularly after learning how my father treated Jane." She shook her head, not wishing to revisit that just now. "Now that my father is gone—at least for now—my godfather has taken it upon himself to fulfill a parental role." She chuckled. "Whether I want him to or not."

"And do you want him to?"

While Anne wasn't keen on reentering Society for the purposes of finding a husband—and that was clearly what her godfather wanted her to do—she couldn't deny that it was nice to have him there. She'd always had parents, and now that she didn't, it was strange. Perhaps even a bit...lonely. "I suppose I do. I appreciate that he cares about my welfare and my happiness. Especially after what happened with Gilbert. Except, he thinks I should marry immediately." She twitched her shoulders. "Why do so many people think marriage is the answer to everything?"

"I surely don't know," he said drily. "I would never suggest such a thing."

No, she imagined he wouldn't, particularly given his experience. She pondered how to bring them together. It was a difficult, sensitive situation. First, she should gauge her godfather's current sentiment. He'd been very upset after the dinner on Monday.

"You should spend time together," she said. "Perhaps in a group at first, but then just the two of you." An idea struck her. "Sandon, I mean, Lorcan is lovely. If you wouldn't mind, I could also speak to him. I do believe he feels a slight relief that you've returned. He is far more in love with that Irish estate than fulfilling any duties here, which would be required after his father dies." She shuddered. "How I detest thinking of such things."

"Death comes to us all, Anne," he said quietly. Again, she felt a pang of sorrow. And regret for making the comment knowing what she knew, that death had been a central part of his life.

After a moment, Rafe said, "Lorcan seems... pleasant. The most pleasant of the three of them, anyway. Please, whatever you organize, leave Deborah out if you can?" He gave her a pleading look that made her smile.

"I will do my best. She *can* be unpleasant." Anne frowned. It was more than that. "Hearing that she was cruel to Beatrix and Selina has made me question my relationship with her."

"Good."

The sharp one-word response drew Anne to snap her gaze to his. She glimpsed that darkness in him once more, and a faint shiver tripped across her shoulders.

"I'll try to arrange something soon—a dinner here, if Jane and Anthony are amenable," she suggested. "After that, perhaps you can go riding with Lorcan and my godfather."

"No." The word was as crisp and definitive as the one he'd uttered a moment before. "I don't ride."

She knew he didn't like riding, but hadn't realized that meant he *didn't*. "At all?"

"I never learned. I wasn't raised to be an earl, Anne."

She knew that, of course. But she realized there were still many, many things she didn't know about him. Things she wondered if she'd ever know. "They could teach you."

An abrupt laugh spilled from him, and he shook his head. "Definitely not."

"Why not? You said yourself that your father can't return, so why not look to your uncle to teach you?"

That darkness pulsed from him once more, his eyes narrowing dangerously. "My father gave me a pony and had started to teach me. I don't think I could let my uncle continue the tutelage. That is too…close." He looked away again, his features tense, his body stiff.

Anne touched his leg and scooted slightly toward him so their knees touched. "I'm sorry. I should have realized. I suppose since I think of your uncle as family, I want you to think of him in the same way. Particularly since he *is* your family."

He put his hand on hers. "It's fine. This is not easy. That's why I came to you for help. I don't know where to begin."

She nodded once. "We'll start with a dinner—without Deborah. I'll speak with Lorcan and explain that my goal is to bring you and your uncle together. It's for the good of everyone. Lorcan will see that, and my godfather will too. Eventually. Once he's grown accustomed to how things must change."

"How long will that be, I wonder?" There was a sardonic quality to his tone that prompted her to take his hand between both of hers.

"Have faith," she said. "You have a family, and while families can be incredibly disappointing, they can also be lovely. I am going to hope that yours will be the latter."

"Unlike yours. Your sister notwithstanding," he said. "You have no contact with your parents at all?"

A ripple of discomfort passed through her. "Not at present. I can't yet forgive them for Jane. I will in time. For now, it's good to have distance."

They sat in silence for a moment, his gloved hand between her bare ones. She idly wondered if he would mind if she stripped the offending accessory away.

"Would it be all right if I came to the dinner I arrange for you and my godfather?" she asked.

"I expect you to be there. Please."

She'd thought so, but wanted to be sure. "And will that be the only time I see you?"

His gaze riveted to hers. "It should be."

Between his words, she heard the barest chance for something more. She would seize any opportunity. There was an undercurrent between them now. Where they'd always been at least slightly flirtatious, this was more. There was a depth, a *need,* to their connection.

"I'd like to visit Annie soon," she said.

He arched a brow. "You've neatly arranged that, haven't you? A reason for us to be together."

She prickled at his words. "I didn't arrange it," she said sharply. "I told Annie I would visit, that I would bring her something for her room, and I am a woman of my word."

"Of course you are." His tone softened. "My apologies. I meant it as a joke, and it came out badly." He exhaled and clasped one of her hands. "I'm so often unbalanced with you." He tipped his head to the side and regarded her with a seductive curiosity.

Her insides fluttered with giddiness. "As I am with you."

"Indeed? You seem confident and assured, as if you know exactly what you want."

"I do. I want you. I've made no secret of that. Whether you come with me or not, I will see Annie."

His finger stroked the inside of her wrist. Was he aware of it? "When?"

An insistent desire pulsed from where he touched her wrist. "Monday, I think."

"You can't go alone. I'll take you."

"I wouldn't go alone. I'd take Jane probably." *But I'd rather go with you.*

"Would that be better?" he asked. "Perhaps she doesn't approve of you going out with me a second time. I notice she left the door open today as opposed to when she allowed you to be alone with me at my house with the door closed."

"She'll let me go because she knows I'll go anyway. Shall I dress as a man or a woman?"

There was a slight hiss as he sucked in a breath, his gaze moving over her and eliciting a response just as potent as if he touched her. Anne tingled everywhere, particularly where he teased her wrist. And his finger wasn't even bare.

"A woman, please." The request was low and thick. "Wear your veil. I'll pick you up in the mews again."

She nodded because her voice seemed to have deserted her.

He lifted her arm and pressed his lips to that spot inside her wrist that now burned from his touch. His eyes met hers. "Irresistible."

"Am I?" she breathed.

"We'll see." He set her hand in her lap and stood. "I'll fetch you at one on Monday."

Anne rose, her legs wobbly. "I'll speak with my godfather and let you know what he says."

"Thank you." He bowed his head to her and left.

Trembling, she sank back down onto the settee. She was vaguely aware of voices just outside the library before Jane came in. Anne composed herself, sitting straighter and tucking the usual stray lock of hair behind her ear.

"What did he want?" Jane asked without preamble as she sat next to Anne on the settee.

"You didn't hear?"

Jane rolled her eyes with a smile. "I told you I wouldn't eavesdrop, and I meant it."

"He asked for my help with getting to know his uncle."

"Oh." Jane sounded disappointed. "That's all?"

"Yes and no. I asked if we could return to Paternoster Row so that I may visit a girl I met on our last visit. She works in a bookshop there, and I promised we would discuss the book she was reading. She's an orphan." Anne wanted to share how Rafe had helped her, but it seemed he kept that part of himself private. She should ask him first.

"That's lovely of you. Is he going to take you?" There was a slight hesitation to her question and in her expression.

"Yes, on Monday. I know it isn't wise of me to go out with him again, particularly since I am not going to wear a disguise. I will wear a veil, however."

"Anne, your reputation barely survived the wedding debacle." She winced. "You know I hate saying that."

"I do. But it *was* a debacle." Anne had discovered the truth about her extortionist betrothed. Jane had learned that their parents had believed the salacious rumors about her five years prior. Anthony had bared his transgressions to the world in order to see Gilbert prosecuted. Debacle was perhaps an understatement.

Jane gave her a sad smile. "You can't keep seeing him. I hope you aren't...taking unnecessary risks."

Anne was fairly certain what she meant. "We're

not having sex, if that's what you're referring to." She took a deep breath. "Please don't ask me not to go. I made a promise to Annie, and I can't resist spending one more afternoon with him."

"If only you didn't love him," Jane said softly and with great understanding.

"If only." Anne rubbed her thumb along her wrist where he'd touched her, kissed her.

"What are you going to do to help him with Stone?" Jane shook her head. "Mallory. Oh bother, when will their names be settled?"

"I don't know about the earldom." Anne had been too distracted to ask how things were going on that front. The current earl would almost certainly ask her when she spoke with him, and she would have nothing to say. Which was fine with her. "I will try to solicit Lorcan's help. This transition is very hard for his father. I do hope he and Rafe can find an accord. They're family, after all."

"You know that doesn't necessarily mean anything. Families can be terrible to each other." Jane's bitterness toward their parents, especially their father, had lessened over the past few weeks, but there was a hurt Anne wasn't sure would ever go away.

"In this case, neither my godfather nor Rafe did anything to harm the other so I hope they will be able to move forward. Would you mind hosting a dinner for the three of them? And us of course. I thought it might be best to get together on neutral ground."

"An excellent idea," Jane said. "Just them and Sandon, sorry, Lorcan? Not Deborah?"

"No, Rafe asked if we could exclude her, and I can't say I blame him."

"Me neither." Jane wrinkled her nose. "I've never liked her. Sorry."

"No need to apologize. I am well aware she aggravates most people. She seems to like doing that." In fact, Anne was surprised she'd hadn't yet stirred up trouble for Beatrix or Selina by bringing up their acquaintance at boarding school.

"I'm sure it won't be a problem to host a dinner. I'll speak with Anthony. I assume you'd like to do it sooner rather than later?"

"Yes, please."

Jane nodded. "I won't tell Anthony about your excursion on Monday, just as I didn't tell him about the first time."

"I'm not asking you to lie to him," Anne said. She would never want to come between her sister and her husband.

"I know. But this is your private business, and he would understand that." She took Anne's hand and gave it a squeeze. "Just promise me you'll be careful. Don't let Stone, Mallory, whatever you call him, take anything you aren't willing to give."

Anne would give him anything. He already had her heart.

~

Jane spoke to Anthony straightaway, and he readily agreed to host a dinner for Rafe and his newfound family. Shortly thereafter, Anne and Jane arrived at Anne's godfather's house on Bruton Street just outside Berkeley Square.

His butler admitted them upstairs to the drawing room, and the soon-to-be-former earl joined them after a few minutes. Unfortunately, Lorcan was not at home. Anne had hoped he would be present for this conversation.

Her godfather smiled at them as he entered, but

the usual brightness was missing. There were deep lines etched into his forehead and around his mouth, as if he'd spent the last week frowning since learning his time as the earl would soon come to an end.

"I'll let the two of you speak in private," Jane said.

The earl's brows shot up briefly in surprise. "Thank you. There's a chamber through there." He pointed at a doorway.

Jane inclined her head and shot an encouraging look at Anne before leaving.

Anne sat down in a dark, puce-colored chair with polished wood arms. Her godfather took the identical chair angled nearby.

"Are you well?" Anne asked with concern. "You haven't been far from my thoughts."

"Thank you, my dear." He grimaced. "It's been a trying week."

"I'm certain it has. I was hoping Lorcan would be here too."

"Lorcan?" he asked, sniffing. "He's still Sandon for the time being. Are you not thinking of me as the earl anymore?"

"You have always been and will continue to be my godfather." Anne worried this was going to be even more difficult than she'd anticipated.

"Hmm. Will you think of *him* as the earl? My nephew?"

"When the title is his, yes."

He harrumphed and looked away for a moment. When he returned his gaze to Anne, there was a frigidity that made her flinch. "Should it be? I have considered whether I ought to contest his claim."

Anne stared at him. She had not expected this. "But it's his birthright."

"He wasn't raised to be the earl. We know next to nothing about his character. He may be ill-suited to the rank."

"It's his birthright." She knew she was repeating herself, but it was apparently necessary. "You can't decide if he should be the earl or not."

"That's what the Committee for Privileges must do," he said, flicking a speck from his knee. "They will decide if he's worthy."

Anne had to clench her teeth to stop herself from gaping at her godfather. He couldn't really hope to keep the title from Rafe? His character was wonderful, better than most gentlemen she'd met. How many of them helped orphans who would surely end up on the street?

"Mr. Mallory's character seems quite admirable," she said with a calm she didn't feel. "I can't imagine he wouldn't bring honor and integrity to the title."

Her godfather's eyes narrowed intently. "You speak as if you know him, but you've only met him on two occasions, isn't that right?"

She wasn't going to lie, so she ignored the question. "He lost his parents at a young age and had his identity stripped away. I can't imagine you would contemplate denying him his birthright now."

"It isn't that, my dear." His features relaxed into a mix of sympathy and sadness. "I only want what's best for the earldom. Many, many people rely on me for their livelihood. I have responsibilities in the House of Lords. I wouldn't be doing my duty if I didn't question this man who has come from nowhere."

"He didn't come from *nowhere*."

Her godfather stiffened. "Didn't he? He appeared in Society this year, buying a very expensive house in Mayfair. Where did he come from that he has that kind of money, and why has no one met him before now? It's all very peculiar."

It wasn't peculiar. He'd simply lived in another part of London. Wasn't that what he'd told her? She realized he'd revealed very little beyond telling her about his wife. And he hadn't shared anything about her either.

"I know this is hard for you, but he is the rightful earl. If he hadn't been kidnapped, he would be the earl now. You gained from his loss. That's not his fault, nor should he continue to suffer for it."

"You're quite defensive of him."

"I would be of anyone in his position. Try to imagine having your very identity stolen and hidden." She shook her head, her heart aching anew for Rafe. "It makes me incredibly sad."

"You've a kind heart, Anne," he said softly. "I haven't decided what I will do."

"Will you tell me if you plan to contest?" she asked.

"I will."

How was she supposed to invite him for dinner now? Should she tell Rafe? She wouldn't want him to be shocked if his claim was contested. But if her godfather decided not to contest, she would upset Rafe for nothing and perhaps permanently damage their relationship.

Wasn't her godfather doing that already? How could he be a loving uncle to Rafe if he didn't trust him?

*There is much you don't know about him.*

The voice in the back of her mind was like an irritating fly buzzing about her head. She wanted to brush it away, but it was persistent and, unlike the fly, not without merit.

"My apologies, my dear," he said with a faint smile. "You came here to pay me—and Sandon—a call. What can I do for you?"

Anne weighed whether to continue with her purpose for coming. Perhaps the act of trying to create a bridge between him and Rafe would help him come to accept the inevitable—Rafe was going to be the earl.

"I came to offer my help to you, actually," she said brightly. "I think you and your nephew should get to know each other. You can ask him all the things you're wondering and determine for yourself that he'll be an excellent earl. Jane and Anthony have agreed to host a dinner. I thought"—she caught herself before calling him Lorcan again—"Sandon could join us."

"And Deborah?"

"Ah, I hoped this first time could be just the three of you."

He nodded. "A good instinct." He surprised her by winking.

Anne relaxed slightly. She tried to see this situation from her godfather's point of view. He'd inherited the earldom when he hadn't expected to and done a wonderful job. As far as she knew, his estates were prosperous and he was an esteemed member of the Lords. It made sense that he wanted to make sure it would be in good hands.

"Come to dinner and spend time with Mr. Mallory," she said. "You can teach him to be the earl he needs to be. He doesn't have a father, and you are the closest thing he has."

"As I said, you've a kind heart, and your speech is incredibly moving. It's too bad you can't become a member of Parliament." His tone held a condescending edge that Anne had grown accustomed to in Society but that still grated her nerves.

She gave him a benign smile. "Perhaps someday that will change." She stood. "I'll let you know when the dinner will be. And you'll let me know if you're going to contest his claim?"

He rose. "I will."

"I truly hope you don't. I believe you'll regret it."

He lifted a shoulder. "I haven't yet decided, but I must do what I think is best. That is my duty."

Anne tried not to frown. She said goodbye, then went to fetch Jane. When they were settled in the coach, Anne recounted the meeting.

Jane sat silent, her eyes widening, as Anne detailed what her godfather had said. "Contesting the claim would be a mess. I can't believe he's considering it. It's not as if his nephew's identity is in question. He *is* the child of the former earl."

Anne nodded. "Exactly. I didn't convince him not to do it, but I hope I said enough to give him pause. Perhaps Lorcan can help persuade him."

"Lorcan might support him," Jane said. "He stands to lose the title too."

Anne waved her hand. "He doesn't care so long as he has Kilmaar." It occurred to Anne that if Rafe didn't marry and have children, which it seemed he didn't want to, Lorcan would still inherit.

Jane hesitated before asking, "Will you tell Rafe?"

That question weighed heavily on Anne's mind. "My godfather said he would inform me if he plans to contest Rafe's claim. I'll alert him then. I don't want to poison any chance for a relationship between them."

Jane made a noise in her throat. "Isn't the earl already doing that?"

Anne nodded. "I thought the same thing. But I see the predicament—and pain—they're both in. They have been or will be harmed. In correcting the wrong done to Rafe, my godfather will suffer."

"You are kind to think of them both. I'm not sure I could do the same if it were Anthony."

In truth, Anne held more sympathy for Rafe, and she would be outraged if her godfather went forward with contesting Rafe's claim. At the same time, she heard Rafe telling her he didn't deserve her, that he wasn't the man she thought he was. What was he hiding? And was there some way it would prevent him from living up to his duties as an earl?

She wanted answers. And she didn't want to discuss her trepidation with Jane. Nor did she want to admit that her godfather's concerns were perhaps valid and definitely unsettling.

Because she thought she knew Rafe. She liked him. She enjoyed his company.

She *loved* him.

But could she really if a huge part of his life was unknown to her? Was she a fool?

She hoped not.

# CHAPTER 11

Taking Anne back to Paternoster Row today was a very bad idea.

Rafe knew it the moment he saw her standing in the Grosvenor Mews, her face cloaked with a veil and her body draped in a stunning walking costume trimmed with gold buttons and piping, with a long, dark blue spencer that mostly covered the ivory skirt beneath. After pulling the cabriolet to a stop and helping her inside, he climbed in beside her and caught her vibrant floral and spice scent.

A *very* bad idea.

Nevertheless, he drove through the mews and went east. All the while, he worked hard not to think of her proximity or what had happened the last time they'd made this trip together.

"What is in the package?" he asked, nodding toward the item she carried.

"It's a pillow for Annie's room. I did promise her something. I embroidered some books along the edges."

Rafe was extremely touched by her thoughtfulness. "You're one of the kindest people I've ever met." In fact, he'd met only one other woman who came close, his sister notwithstanding.

"Thank you." Their gazes caught and held, and it seemed the electricity he felt also swirled between them, indicating she felt it too. At length she said, "I wondered if you might tell me how you came to inherit the bookshop."

He knew the more time he spent with her, the more she would want to know about him. He felt the same way about her, except she was rather open about herself, her past, her feelings. Whereas he was purposefully mysterious. For her protection.

*Or for yours?*

Rafe shrugged the thought away. "When I was young, I liked to spend time there. Mr. Fletcher was the owner, and he allowed me to read as if he operated a library." A smile crept over his mouth unbidden. "He was a good man."

"Where did you live?"

"In Cheapside." He shifted uncomfortably because that wasn't true. At least not back then. "Perhaps I'll show you where later, if we have time."

She turned toward him, and though he couldn't see her face clearly through the veil, he could sense her enthusiasm. "Really? That would be wonderful. I'd love to see it."

He returned to what she'd asked originally. "Mr. Fletcher left me his shop when he died, as well as a fund."

"And that's how you started to accumulate your wealth?" She briefly touched his thigh. "I apologize for my curiosity. Knowing you had nothing and elevated yourself to where you are today is astonishing."

He heard the pride in her voice and couldn't help but feel a bit of the emotion himself. But the sensation quickly evaporated because the truth was far more sinister than she thought. He'd already accumulated some of his wealth—the start of it, anyway—before Fletcher died. In fact, Fletcher had left him the shop and a modest sum of money in the hope that Rafe would turn his back on his criminal enterprises entirely.

Rafe had wanted to. But wanting something and having the means, both externally and internally to do it, were completely different things. It wasn't until he'd met Eliza that he'd finally wanted to leave his criminal life behind.

"Your curiosity is understandable," he said evenly. "Mr. Fletcher's generosity was paramount to my success. I was fortunate."

"You deserved that, at least." Her voice was soft but carried a hint of steel. "I spoke to Anthony and to my godfather. When would you like to have the dinner?"

"Soon, I should think."

"Thursday?" she asked.

"That would be fine, thank you. I appreciate your help." Rafe had his own curiosity about how her meeting with his uncle had gone. Had he betrayed anything about what he'd done nearly thirty years ago?

Rafe had gone over and over the conversations they'd had, trying to pick out anything his uncle had said that could incriminate him. There was nothing, of course. Except his anger and disappointment—that had been clear. But that reaction proved nothing. It made sense that a man who'd been an earl for twenty-seven years and would now lose the title and everything that went with it would be upset.

Anne settled back against the seat and in so doing brought herself more closely against him.

Her heat pressed into his thigh and his arm. He should move away, but he did not.

"Are you trying to make yourself irresistible?" He immediately cursed himself for flirting with her. "Never mind. Whether that is your objective or not, it's beyond your control." At least where he was concerned. He hadn't wanted a woman the way he wanted her since Eliza. And if that didn't frighten him, nothing could.

"Are you saying I don't even have to try?" she asked coyly.

He couldn't help but laugh. Then he steered the conversation to their upcoming visit with Annie and whether Anne had already finished the book about Greek mythology.

"Of course. I wouldn't want to disappoint Annie."

He couldn't imagine she would ever disappoint anyone.

When they arrived at the bookshop, Rafe gave the cabriolet over to the tiger, who went to park in Warwick Lane. Rafe guided Anne into the shop where she pulled the veil from her face, flipping it up over her bonnet.

"Oh, I'm taking this thing off," she muttered, removing the hat.

John greeted them warmly.

Anne looked about. "Where is Annie?"

"She'll be here presently," John said.

Annie dashed from the back of the shop, looking much tidier than she had on their first meeting. She sent a cautious glance toward Rafe before settling her attention on Anne with a smile. "Good afternoon."

Anne gave her a broad smile. "Good afternoon, Annie. I'm so pleased to see you again. How have you settled in here?"

"Quite well, thank you."

"Wonderful." Anne held out the wrapped pillow. "I brought you this for your room."

Her eyes lighting, Annie's mouth formed a small O as she accepted the package. "Thank you."

"Go on, open it," Anne encouraged with a smile.

Annie carefully tore the paper away and exposed the small ivory pillow. Colorful embroidered books of varying sizes marched along the edges. "It's so beautiful." She lifted her gaze to Anne's. "I've never owned anything so lovely."

"Well, you do now," Anne said matter-of-factly. "Did you read the book so we may discuss it?"

Annie blinked as if she was having a hard time, and Rafe knew she must. To be the recipient of so much kindness and generosity after what she was used to was almost unbelievable. "I did. I thought we might go to the back of the shop."

Anne looked toward Rafe. "Should Mr. Mallory join us?"

A look of distress creased Annie's features. "Is that your name?"

Rafe exhaled. The child ought to know him as Mr. Bowles, but it was likely she also knew him as Mr. Blackwell if anyone had told her who he used to be. Several of the folks on Paternoster Row had met him as Rafe Blackwell. Indeed, John sometimes had trouble thinking of him as Bowles.

That was the problem with changing your name and not severing ties with everyone who knew you as the previous name. This bookshop was the one constant from when he'd been Blackwell and then Bowles. He'd divested everything as Blackwell over the past few years and replaced them with Mr. Bowles' interests. Now he was on the verge of changing his identity yet again, but he didn't need to hide that he'd been Mr. Bowles. Furthermore, that would be impossible since that was how he'd been introduced to Society.

"I am actually Lord Stone," Rafe said. "Or I shall be, perhaps by the end of the week." He'd explained the revelation to John when he'd stopped by the shop Saturday afternoon.

Annie's eyes rounded. "A lord?" She looked to Anne. "Er, I don't know how to curtsey."

"I can teach you, if you'd like," Anne said. "Come, show me to the back, and we'll have a lesson."

Nodding shyly, Annie clutched the pillow to her chest and led her toward the rear of the shop. Anne cast a look at Rafe over her shoulder, silently asking if he was coming.

"I'll be along shortly," he said before turning to John. "I see she's wearing the clothes I brought on Saturday."

"Indeed. She was most grateful. Please thank your sister."

Selina had gathered the clothing for him and been pleased to do so. Rafe took a step toward the back to join the ladies.

"Ah, you should be aware that there is something…afoot back there," John said, his brows climbing.

"What's that?"

John cracked a smiled. "I won't spoil the specifics. Suffice it to say that all the help you've given is now being directed back at you."

Oh God, what did that mean? And why was John clearly amused by it?

"I see." Except he did not. But he planned to.

Rafe stalked to the back of the shop. There was a storeroom, an office, and a sitting area near the stairs that led up to the apartments upstairs. It was in the latter where he found Anne, along with three boys, two of whom still lived upstairs and one who had moved out nearly a year before. He'd taken lodgings in Cheapside where he'd become a tailor's apprentice. The lad was quite skilled with a needle. Rafe had kept in contact with him and had even commissioned his shop to make some of his clothing for the Season.

"Daniel," Rafe said, extending his hand to the sixteen-year-old with thick russet hair and sizing him up. "You're looking taller. What brings you here today?"

"I, ah, had the afternoon off, sir. Charlie and Bart invited me to come by."

Rafe looked around the room and noted a table and two chairs had been set in the center. The table was adorned with a nice but simple cloth, and a complement of mismatched dishes.

He looked at Anne, who was seated in one of the chairs. "Where's Annie?"

"She went to fetch tea," Anne replied.

The youngest of the boys, Charlie, dashed up the stairs while Bart went to hold the other chair. "Will you sit, sir? We have tea and cakes for you and Mrs. Dazzling."

"Mrs. Dazzling." Rafe blinked at Anne, who lifted a shoulder. "Mr. Entwhistle told you her name?" Rafe asked Bart, a lad of thirteen with dark blond hair and an eye that didn't track normally, always straggling behind the other when his gaze fixed on a subject.

"Yes, sir," Bart said. "Will you sit?" he repeated.

Rafe went and took the chair. "Thank you." He leaned toward Anne. "I thought you were going to discuss the book with Annie."

"I thought so too." Anne lifted a shoulder, looking as bewildered as he felt. "I showed her how to curtsey, but then she insisted I sit."

John's words came back to him—they were trying to help him? How?

Annie came down the stairs bearing a teapot wrapped in a cloth. She set it on the table as Charlie followed her with a plate of biscuits.

"Thank you," Anne said. "This looks lovely. Won't you be joining us?" she asked the children.

They all shook their heads, with Daniel answering, "No. This is for you. In fact, we'll leave you alone now." He looked to the others, and they began to file up the stairs, starting with Charlie.

Anne turned in her chair, looking at Annie. "I thought we were going to discuss the book."

"I, er, I didn't finish it."

"You said you did," Anne said with a slight, confused frown.

Annie gave her a sheepish look. "I forgot." She ran up the stairs, prohibiting further discussion.

Daniel was the last to go, but before he got out of sight, Rafe called out to him. "What are you really doing here? If it's to see me, going upstairs is not the way to do that."

Pink swathed Daniel's cheeks. "I forgot something. I'll be back down shortly." He ran upstairs, leaving Rafe and Anne alone.

"Have you any idea what's going on?" she asked.

"No." He again thought of what John had said. Rafe took in the nicely set table, the biscuits, the tea. Could they be trying to play the role of matchmaker?

"Would you care for tea?" Anne asked, picking up the pot.

"Yes, please."

She poured their tea and then added sugar to hers. "Sugar?" At his nod, she finished his cup.

He picked it up and took a tentative sip to

gauge the warmth. Nicely hot, but perhaps the weakest tea he'd ever tasted.

Anne sampled hers and, judging from the movement of her eyebrows, had come to the same conclusion regarding the strength of the brew. "Well, it's certainly not coffee."

He laughed. "No, it is not." He took another sip before setting his cup down.

Taking a biscuit from the plate, Anne nibbled a corner of the square. Again, she reacted, this time her eyes widened slightly and her lips puckered.

"Oh dear," he murmured, plucking a biscuit to try. He took a small bite and recoiled at the amount of salt. "Perhaps not as sweet as one might expect."

Anne set her biscuit on her saucer and used a napkin to dab her mouth. "Bless them for trying."

"Now I know not to refer any of them for a baking apprenticeship."

Giggling softly, Anne set her napkin on the table. "They went to a great deal of effort. I wonder why."

Rafe had his suspicions but didn't want to share them. He didn't need any help when it came to trying to pair him with Anne. It was taking all his control *not* to couple with her, physically or otherwise.

Anne studied him, a smile curling her lips. "They care for you very much."

"How do you know?"

She'd only been alone with them for a few minutes.

"They were exceptionally kind when I arrived, saying that any friend of yours was a friend of theirs and they were delighted to meet me." Her brow creased. "Now that I think of it, they seemed to put extra emphasis on the word friend."

"Hmmm." That was all Rafe could think to say.

"That *is* how I introduced myself to Annie last week. But this tea for just the two of us is clearly a planned endeavor by the lot of them. You've no idea why?"

Rafe caught a flash of bright blond hair—belonging to Charlie—peeking around the wall of the staircase. "Charlie? Is there something you need?"

There was no response, but neither was there the telltale sound of feet ascending the stairs. Rafe tried again. "Charlie? Come out, please."

A moment later, Charlie crept down the stairs and trudged to the table, guilt etched into his features. "Yes, sir?"

"Why are you spying on us?"

The boy was ten, with a sweet nature. Rafe had brought him to John last fall after Charlie's mother had died.

"They sent me down to see what's going on. Whether you were kissing yet or not." Charlie made a face. "I didn't want to come, but they said I was smallest, so it should be me."

Anne's brows shot up as she darted a look at Rafe. He would have laughed if he didn't, in fact, want to kiss her so badly.

"Is that the point of this endeavor?" Rafe asked. "To get us to kiss?"

"Annie said you'd get married if you kissed."

*Hell.* What if they'd already done more than that?

Anne put her hands in her lap. "And you all think we should get married?"

Charlie nodded vigorously. "Mr. Bowles needs someone to look after him the way he looks after all of us."

Rafe stood. "All right, Charlie. Tell your friends this was very nice, but...Mrs. Dazzling and I are not getting married. Nor are we kissing."

Exhaling loudly, Charlie started to turn toward the stairs. "They won't like it when I tell them."

Rafe went to the boy and touched his shoulder. "I appreciate your efforts very much. Please thank them for me, will you?"

"I will. Annie's still going to be disappointed." As he climbed back up the stairs, Rafe's throat tightened.

"That was very sweet," Anne said softly from just to his left.

He hadn't realized she'd gotten up from the table. "Yes."

"You have quite an extended family."

Rafe blinked in surprise. He'd never thought of them like that. He helped children when he could. Some went on to find their way, and a few, like Daniel, even kept in touch. Others accepted his support for a time, then disappeared. Thankfully, there were fewer of those.

"Selina and I were alone. The man who cared for us, who claimed to be our uncle, wasn't particularly kind." Rafe would have given anything for an adult to take a genuine interest in him, beyond what use he could provide. There'd been one woman—a friend's mother—but she'd struggled at the time, drinking too much gin and with too many children of her own. Still, she'd looked after him and Selina as much as she could. He'd kept in contact with her even after she'd stopped drinking and gotten married, and Selina had rekindled their relationship when she'd returned to London a few months prior.

Anne touched his sleeve, her fingers curling around his arm just below his elbow. "You don't say much about your childhood. I know your sister went to school. Did you?"

"No. I was privately tutored." The lie fell from

his tongue, but he supposed it was perversely true. He just hadn't been tutored in the same things he would have been as the son of an earl.

"How did that man come to care for you? What happened to him?"

Rafe brushed his hand through his hair, effectively dislodging her grasp. "I don't like to discuss it. I don't like questions."

"I know. But I can't seem to stop myself asking them."

Rafe went back to his chair, turning his back to her. "He was responsible for our kidnapping. He brought us to London from Stonehaven. He died a long time ago."

"Why would he take you away?" The anguish in her question was answered by the anger trapped inside him.

"I can't ask him, can I?" Nor did he need to. Edgar had taken two children whom he could use to fatten his own pockets through swindling and thievery.

He exhaled and took a sip of his weak, lukewarm tea, not because he wanted it but because it was something to do. "This was very nice," he whispered, looking at the table and moved by the children's thoughtfulness. "We should at least finish one cup of tea and our biscuits."

"Yes, we should." Anne joined him at the table, and they both sat.

He took a large bite of the biscuit and choked it down with a swig of tea. Anne did something similar, though she took a smaller taste. She also winced slightly as she swallowed.

"What's your favorite kind of biscuit?" he asked.

"I don't think I have one." She tipped her head to the side. "I do love almond."

"I like that too. I'm afraid I'm a glutton for marzipan."

Her eyes glowed with amusement. "Oh yes, I can eat an entire tray at Yuletide."

"I think I'm more partial to cakes than biscuits." He crammed the last of the biscuit into his mouth and swallowed it down with the rest of his tea. "Especially after today." He laughed, and she joined him.

He held out his hand. "Give me your biscuit. I'll finish it."

She hesitated, but only briefly, before depositing the half-eaten biscuit into his palm. "You are a gentleman, regardless of what you say."

Perhaps he was. At least with her. She seemed to bring out the very best in him. This moment, this ordinary situation, had been mostly absent from his life. And wasn't this what he wanted? Christ, he'd become far too maudlin since learning who he really was.

He ate the rest of Anne's biscuit in two bites, then stood and offered her his hand. "Come, I want to take you somewhere."

She put her hand in his and rose. "Shouldn't we thank the children?"

"They're probably listening." He turned his head toward the stairs. "Thank you, Daniel, Bart, Charlie, and Annie."

Anne giggled, her eyes lighting. He grabbed her bonnet and gloves from a small table against the wall, then led her to the back door and outside to a narrow alley that ran between the buildings.

Clutching her hand tightly, he guided her through the alley to where it met Warwick Lane. He located the cabriolet and helped her inside as the tiger held the horse. She set her bonnet on her head and brought down the veil as he settled in next to her.

He drove them out to Paternoster Row, but instead of turning west, he went east toward Cheapside.

"You're not taking me for caviar, are you?"

He laughed. "No. We're not even stopping along Cheapside."

"That's a shame. I thoroughly enjoyed our afternoon here." Her head moved from side to side as they entered the thoroughfare, and though he couldn't see her face, he knew she was delighted.

"This is perhaps my favorite part of London." He hadn't told her that when they'd come before. He'd always kept his guard up, but suddenly, perhaps because of what the children had tried to do, he just didn't want to make the effort.

"Even more that Paternoster Row?"

He chuckled. "It's close. Cheapside wins slightly, only because of its greater size. I imagine how it might have been hundreds of years ago when the streets earned their names—Ironmonger Lane, Bread Street, Milk Street. I wonder what those people who lived here would say if they could see it now."

"They would be amazed. At all of London."

Just before they reached Poultry Street, he steered them to the right onto Bucklersbury Lane. Partway down, he pulled the cabriolet to the side and came to a stop.

"You can see Mansion House quite well from here," she said, gesturing to the end of the street in front of them.

"Yes." Seeing that grand house had been one of the reasons he'd chosen Bucklersbury Lane for his own residence. He looked to the left at the house in front of where they'd stopped. "This is my house."

She lifted her veil and took in the narrow brick façade. "This is where you lived as a child?"

He shook his head. "This is where I lived the past four years. Would you like to come inside?"

"Very much."

He helped her from the vehicle and returned the cabriolet to his tiger's care. Offering her his arm, he guided her up the steps. He inserted a key in the lock, and by the time they walked into the entry hall, Mrs. Watts came hurrying to greet them.

A short, stocky woman, the housekeeper also served as his cook. Her biscuits were never too salty, and she was, in fact, the reason he adored cakes.

"Mr. Bowles," she said with a smile, her gaze flitting to Anne. "I didn't expect to see you today."

He'd stopped in on Saturday when he'd visited the bookshop. "This wasn't a planned visit. Allow me to introduce my friend, Miss Anne Pemberton." He realized he should not have used her real name, but as he'd learned on the way here, it seemed he didn't particularly care about hiding things at the moment.

Mrs. Watts bobbed her head, her white mobcap pinned tightly to her gray curls since it didn't move even slightly. Whereas Anne, after removing her bonnet, nodded, and a slender blonde curl fell against her temple.

"Welcome," Mrs. Watts said. "Can I get you anything?"

"I'm going to give Miss Pemberton a brief tour." He took Anne's bonnet and her gloves and set them on a narrow table beneath a mirror along with his own. "I'll let you know if we require anything."

"Very good." Mrs. Watts turned toward the back

of the house. "I have warm spiced cakes if that interests you," she called before she disappeared.

"That is very tempting," Anne said. "Much more tempting than salty biscuits." She looked around the small entry hall, with its marble tile and solitary painting.

"You'll find this house wanting after my residence in Upper Brook Street."

Her eyes met his. "I don't think I could find anything wanting about you."

Her words heated him, and he let them, relishing the connection between them instead of resisting it. He showed her the dining room and the library, which looked rather sad since most of his books had been moved to Mayfair.

"You outgrew your library," she said. "Is that why you moved?"

"I moved because I wanted to live in the best place."

She looked up at him. "And Mayfair is the best? I'd say the best is wherever you're happiest."

Then that had been the small house he'd lived in with Eliza near Blackfriars. The first place where he'd felt he belonged. "Where have you been happiest?" he asked.

"Right now. Here, with you." She squeezed his arm. "I would ask you the same, but I doubt you'd tell me. Though, perhaps I'm mistaken. You've already revealed more of yourself today than in all the time I've known you. Thank you," she added softly.

"I'll show you the drawing room upstairs." He escorted her from the library and up the staircase that wound back on itself.

Decorated in yellows and golds, the room was warm and inviting, or so Mrs. Watts told him.

"This is beautiful," Anne said, taking her hand

from his arm and walking around the perimeter. "But it looks as though you just furnished it yesterday. Everything seems so new and untouched." She stopped at the marble fireplace with its gilt decoration.

"I rarely spent time in here. Yellow was Eliza's favorite color."

Anne faced him, her shoulders tense. "Eliza was your wife."

"Yes." He walked toward her. "But she never lived here. I bought this house after she died." They'd dreamed of living in such a place. And they'd been so close. He'd started looking at properties in Cheapside just before she'd died.

"Yet you decorated a room for her." Anne's head tipped back slightly as he came to a stop just before her. "You loved her very much."

He drew a stuttering breath. "More than life. She was going to have our child." It was his fault they were gone, victims of the choices *he'd* made. He bit the inside of his lip, trying to make a physical pain overshadow the emotional one.

Anne took his hand and led him from the drawing room back to the staircase hall. "What else is on the first floor?" She'd recognized his anguish and sought to banish it.

"My private rooms. Do I need to show them to you?"

"*Yes.*" She gazed up at him expectantly with perhaps a bit of silly exasperation that made him laugh.

Smiling in spite of the melancholy that had gripped him a few minutes ago, he took her into his sitting room.

"Now, this is *your* room," she said, letting go of his hand and turning in a circle to survey the space.

"Why do you say that?"

"Dark, brooding colors with hints of brightness." She picked up the bright orange pillow on the dark blue chaise. "Like this. It reminds me of your eye."

Laughter did escape him then. "Well, that might have been on purpose. A friend gave me that." A lover who'd come here on occasion but whom he hadn't seen in months.

She waggled her brows. "So I'm not the first friend you've brought to your private rooms."

He advanced on her, pinning her so the chaise hit the backs of her legs. "You're the best one I've brought here."

Her eyes lit with pleasure. "Well, that's lovely." She glanced toward the closed door that led to his bedchamber. "I can guess what lies that way. Are you going to show me that too?"

"I know you want to see it."

"I'd like to do more than *see* it."

He traced his fingertips down her cheek and across her jaw to her chin. "What did you have in mind?"

"I think I'd like to spend some time there. If you're amenable."

The stiffness of his cock and the desire pulsing through him said he was more than amenable. Even while his brain urged caution. "We shouldn't."

"We shouldn't have gone to Paternoster Row today either. I think I've come to know you rather well, Lord Bodyguard, and you don't always adhere to the rules." She put her hands on his chest and, pressing her palms flat, slid them up to his collarbones. "And you know I don't. The key is not getting caught breaking them."

"You are a siren."

"And I'm going to look at your bedchamber." She slipped from between him and the chaise and went to open the door. With a glance over her shoulder, she smiled at him, then went inside.

He had no choice but to follow her into madness.

She stood near the wide bed and crooked her finger at him. Powerless to resist, he went to her.

A few strands of her hair brushed her nape, tempting him. She touched his cheek. "I know you don't want me to say this, but I love you. And I want you to do what you told me before. With your mouth. Then I want to touch you. Please?"

Dear Lord, she was going to completely break him. Except he was already broken.

"If I do that, there will be no going back," he rasped. "Do you understand?" At her nod, he started to unbutton the front of her costume, a long garment that covered her upper half and exposed the blue and ivory of her skirt. "You're going to marry me, Anne."

Her eyes rounded as her hand dropped down to his shoulder where she squeezed him tightly. "What?"

"If I'm going to put my mouth on you and you're going to perchance do the same to me, we will wed. If you accept that, we may continue."

She put her hands on his, stilling his movement. "That doesn't seem a reason to marry."

"It's more than you had with your former betrothed, is it not?"

"It is."

He didn't move despite his body demanding he do so. "I await your decision."

"Yes, I'll marry you."

# CHAPTER 12

Rafe kissed her with a blistering heat as his fingers continued to unbutton her spencer. He moved quickly, with wondrous precision, divesting her of the garment with ease. His tongue lashed against hers, claiming her in a torrent of sensation. It was as if something had been unleashed inside him, that he'd let himself free of whatever bound him.

She wasn't going to be the only one undressed this time. Tugging at his cravat, she pulled the silk loose and tore it from his neck. He drew back slightly, not quite breaking the kiss, as he removed his coat. His lips played with hers and he nipped her flesh before looking down at the laces crossing over her chest. "This isn't a typical garment."

Her underdress had been constructed as a sort of full petticoat and wasn't meant to be worn without the spencer over it. The laces in the bodice kept the garment snug and allowed her to don it without assistance. "It comes loose quite easily." She untied the front, and it fell open, revealing her corset. He pushed the straps of the garment over her shoulders and down her arms. She slipped out of the dress and gave it over to him.

He carefully took the dress and the spencer he'd cast on the bed and draped them over a chair. Perching on the edge, he pulled his boots off and set them aside. "Come here," he said, his eyes glittering with promise.

She went to the chair and stood between his parted legs.

"Your foot, please." He reached down, and she placed her foot in his hand. Scooting back on the chair, he lifted her foot and placed it between his legs on the seat cushion. Her toes grazed him as he unfastened her half boot. When he'd removed the boot, he moved to perform the same task on her other foot, exchanging one for the other.

Except when he finished with that one, he didn't let her go. Instead, he curled his hand around her ankle and pulled her foot around his thigh and set it on the cushion behind him. Though she still wore her corset, petticoat, chemise, and stockings, she felt incredibly, thrillingly exposed in this position.

His hand moved up her leg, pausing behind her bent knee. Shivers of anticipation danced along her flesh, and desire pooled in her sex. With his other hand, he pushed the skirt of her petticoat up, revealing the leg propped on the chair.

"Come closer," he whispered, wrapping his palm around her thigh and sliding it up to her backside. He grasped the side of her clothing that fell against her standing leg. "Hold this side up at your waist."

Unable to take a deep breath, she did as he said, clutching the fabric at her waist. This completely opened her sex to him.

He trailed his hand down her backside, his fingertips gliding along the crease between her cheeks. She inhaled sharply before he moved back up the side of her thigh and brought his hand around to her front. "Beautiful."

He stroked along the edge of her folds, his thumb finding her clitoris. His other hand clasped the hip of her standing leg, urging her closer to him so that she could feel his breath against her.

She moaned softly as he gently massaged her flesh. He swept his finger inside her.

"So wet and ready. I could take you right now. But I want you wetter still." He pumped into her, finding a spot that made her see white as she clenched her eyes closed. "Hold on to me, Anne. But don't let go of your skirt."

She switched the garment to her other hand and used her right to brace herself on his shoulder. His left hand slid from her thigh to her backside as he licked her sex. She was not prepared for the sensations that swept through her or the sudden quiver that overtook her legs. Now she understood why he'd told her to hold on to him.

His cheek brushed her thigh as he kissed and suckled her flesh. The intimacy of it, how very exposed she was, shocked her. But she didn't retreat. If anything, she dug her fingers into his shoulder and arched into him. Perhaps he knew what she wanted. Of course he knew. He thrust his tongue inside her, and she cried out.

His hand moved to cup the back of her thigh, holding her elevated leg in a firm grip as his mouth moved over her, licking and teasing her flesh. Bringing his other hand back over her hip, he slid his finger into her as he sucked at her clitoris. Ecstasy rolled over her, and she felt the rush of an orgasm fast approaching.

Before it came, he gentled his touch, retreating just enough that the pleasure remained but didn't overwhelm her. She wanted the tide to sweep her away and whimpered.

He parted her sex, holding her open for his tongue as he thrust in and out. Her muscles tensed as she babbled incoherently, begging for release.

Still, he didn't let her come. He abruptly stood, gathering her into his arms and taking her to the bed. He set her on the coverlet with a roughness that matched the tumult raging inside her.

Shoving her skirts up, he spread her legs and buried himself between them. He clasped her thighs and set them on his shoulders as his mouth plundered her sex. The pleasure built until she perched on the edge. He stroked her clitoris, and she tumbled into sweet, dark oblivion.

She clutched his head, pulling at his hair as she bounced back up, cresting higher than before, spasms racking her body. There was no time to find the earth before he was gone from her.

Opening her eyes, she saw him unbuttoning his waistcoat. She pushed herself up, eager to see him. But when she reached for him, he wrapped his hand around her nape and pulled her mouth to his. "I told you what I would do." He kissed her, as he said he would, and she tasted herself.

He'd been right. There was no going back after this. She didn't want anyone to see or feel or taste her the way he had. And she didn't want anyone doing the same for him.

She unfastened the two remaining buttons on his waistcoat and pushed the garment open. He dragged his mouth from hers to discard the clothing. She clutched at his shirt, tugging it from his waistband, and narrowed her eyes at him. "You're mine."

His left brow arched, and his expression was so

handsome, so seductive, she nearly whimpered with need again.

"Mine," she repeated, pushing at his shirt.

He ripped the garment over his head and dropped it to the floor.

Anne surveyed the muscled expanse of his chest and abdomen. From the contoured planes of his shoulders to the soft discs of his nipples and lower to the ridges of his ribs and the muscles that rippled down to his waistband. There were scars, like the one on his face, small, pink clues to the life he'd led before. She longed to ask him about them, and she would, but not now. Now, she wanted to see all of him.

She glanced at his breeches. "Are you going to take those off, or should I?"

"Which would you prefer?"

In answer, she unbuttoned his fall. She moved slowly, hopefully teasing him as he'd teased her. No, to do that, she needed to affect him physically. She scooted toward him and kissed the hollow of his throat. A vibration started beneath her mouth and came from him as a soft moan. Encouraged, she licked down and over to his nipple, where she used her lips and tongue the way he'd done with her.

He sucked in a breath and twined his hand in her hair. Surprised it had remained up this long, she felt it give away and tumble around her shoulders.

She kissed her way down to where his breeches gaped open. Slipping her hand into the garment, she found the hard shaft of his sex and marveled at how soft his flesh felt. She tried to push the fabric down over his hips. Thankfully, he added his assistance, freeing his cock completely.

"I can put my mouth on you too?" she asked, recalling what he'd said and more than excited by the prospect.

"If you want to." His voice was a bit higher than normal. "Here." He wrapped his hand around hers and showed her how to stroke him from base to tip and back again. On the third time down, she pointed her finger and swept it along the soft sac beneath.

"You can cup them." He sounded like he was clenching his teeth.

She didn't look up to verify if that was true for she was far too engrossed in her task. With each stroke, he seemed to surge against her. A drop of wetness gathered at the tip. Apparently they could both be wet—she knew he would be later, when he released his seed.

"You can also move faster," he murmured, his voice low and coarse. "If you like. But that will send me to the brink."

"Will it?" She glided her hand around him with more speed then cupped his balls. Pitching her head down, she breathed against his tip. "And my mouth should do the same?"

"Yes." He pressed on her head, urging her forward.

She licked him, a slow, languid glide around the head and down the underside along a thick vein. Curling her hand around the base, she brought her mouth back up then sucked him along her tongue.

He swore violently, his hand tugging her hair. "Go slow. Please. I won't last if you don't."

He hadn't guided her wrong yet, so she did as he asked and swallowed his length with a slow glide before easing back once more. She did this more times than she could count, tasting the salt of him on her tongue.

"Anne, I can come in your mouth or I can shag you. Which do you want? And decide quickly."

She released him and looked up into the strained contours of his face. "Can't I have both?"

"Not today."

"Which do *you* want?" She continued to stroke him with her hand.

Wordlessly, he stripped the rest of his clothes away then did the same for her, nearly tearing her petticoat in the process of wresting it from her body. She helped him with the chemise and had barely cast it away before he picked her up and rotated her on the bed.

He knelt on the mattress and moved between her legs, his gaze sweeping over her body. His lids drooped as his head came down and he claimed her mouth. She arched up from the bed, eager for his touch. He cupped her breast and toyed with her nipple, pinching and tugging as their kisses, hot and wet, grew shorter and more desperate.

Panting, they explored each other, their hands moving eagerly over heated flesh. He swept his fingertips down her side and clasped her hip. She splayed her palms on his back and moved them down until she found the curve of his backside. When his hand moved between her thighs, she held her breath. Her sex, already sensitive, ached for him.

He moved his hips, and his cock was against her, nestled at her sheath. He stroked her clitoris, stirring her desire, before he guided himself into her.

"Breathe, Anne. I'm going to go very slowly."

He did. Even more slowly than she'd done when she'd had him in her mouth. She wanted him inside her completely, but as her flesh stretched to accommodate him, she realized this was for the best.

It didn't hurt, but there was a tenderness. Of course there would be. She'd never done this before. "I'm so glad this is you," she said softly, cupping his nape.

He looked into her eyes. "Thank you. For this gift—for you." He slid completely into her then, or so she thought because she felt incredibly full. Brushing her hair back from her face, he ran his thumb over her forehead. It was such a sweet, caring gesture, and again she was aware of the stark intimacy between them, of knowing and feeling someone in a way she never had before. "Are you all right?"

"Yes. Is this…all?"

He chuckled and gave her a swift kiss. "No. This is just the beginning. Wrap your legs around me."

She did, curling her thighs against his.

"Higher," he said. "Around my waist."

Oh, that was better. She thought she was full before, but he seemed to slide even deeper. "Oh Lord," she breathed.

"Lord *Bodyguard*," he said with a smile just before he began to move.

He withdrew and thrust into her again, still moving incredibly slowly. She felt his body quiver, sensed the power that he kept under a tight rein. Though she'd never experienced this, she knew when he moved more quickly, they would both get where they wanted to be—to the brink as he'd said before when he'd cautioned her against going too fast.

She swept her hand down his back and settled her palm on his backside. "Are you going to speed up?"

"Siren," he breathed. He did go faster, but only incrementally. "We're doing this my way. Next time, you can be in control."

Next time. And there would be a next time because they were getting married.

Joy and pleasure crashed over her at the same time. She closed her eyes and gave herself over to the lead of his body. As he eventually moved faster and faster, the pressure inside her built. Until she quite suddenly plunged completely into ecstasy. Her sex tightened, and she gripped him with her legs and hands lest she lose herself completely.

She just began to rise to the surface when he cried out and drove into her. He kissed her neck and throat as she cast her head back and held him to her. He thrust a few more times, his body shuddering. She swept his hair back from his forehead and kissed his temple.

When his body stilled, he fell to the side, gathering her against his chest and bringing her with him. Stroking his arm, she listened to his breathing even out. He slid from her body and rolled to his back, holding her to his side.

"That was quite lovely," she said, smiling as she put her hand on his chest. "Next time, I get to control things? I can't quite envision how that can happen with you…doing what you do."

"Well, you can tell me exactly what you want and what to do. You've never had a problem with that before."

She laughed and felt his chest rumble gently beneath her hand.

"But I think maybe you'll be on top, riding me."

Pushing herself up on her elbow, she looked down at him. "Like a horse?"

"Somewhat. I can't say because I don't ride."

She tried to envision it, straddling him with his

cock inside her. Her legs would go around his hips. "Do you thrust up in that position?"

"Yes, but I can try not to, if you prefer."

She thought of him moving beneath her and decided she wanted that very much. "I suppose I can't say for certain right now, but the thought of you under me doing what you just did… I can hardly wait, honestly."

He cupped her face and pulled her down for a long, lingering kiss. "You are an astonishing woman, Anne."

"When will the wedding be? I suppose you'll need to write to my father." She made a face.

"You're of age."

She was, but it was the right thing to do. "Yes. We don't need his permission. We must have the banns read, however." She calculated in her head. "We can marry any time after the twenty-fifth." She frowned. "That's so far away."

"It's not as if you won't see me before then."

"But like this?"

"We've been…innovative on plenty of occasions."

She laughed again as a joy she'd never imagined surged through her. "If you become the earl soon, you could just get a special license and we could marry right away. That's what Anthony did when he wed Jane. They didn't even get married in a church."

He curled a lock of her hair around his fingers. "Is that what you'd like?"

"I like whatever allows me to be with you. And a special license means we wouldn't have to be apart at all."

"Then I shall get a special license as soon as I may."

What if her godfather contested his claim? Uneasiness settled through her. She shivered.

"Are you cold?" he asked, pulling her more tightly against him.

"Yes. I should get dressed." And cleaned up.

"I suppose we must. You need to get home. We've been gone too long."

She should tell him that her godfather had doubts about him. Except she'd learned so much about him today, seen the goodness and generosity inside him. She'd convince her godfather that Rafe would bring honor and integrity to the earldom.

He kissed her forehead before sitting up and swinging his legs off the side of the bed. Anne touched his back. "You'll be a wonderful earl."

He looked at her over his shoulder. "You're biased."

"Because I know you, and I'm right."

His lips parted as if he was going to respond, but he didn't. Turning his head straight, he left the bed and went to a dresser.

A moment later, he returned with a cloth and gave it to her before gathering their clothing.

Yes, she knew him—the man who owned a bookshop and a house in Cheapside. The man who'd adored his wife and lost her and his unborn child. Her heart ached and longed for this man.

Even so, she couldn't dismiss the persistent feeling that there was more of him that he kept concealed beneath the surface. The part of him that couldn't love her—or that he wouldn't allow to. Yet.

She pushed her apprehension away. There would be time to discover all his secrets.

A lifetime.

~

On the return drive to Mayfair, Rafe wondered if he'd made a mistake. Not about the sex or even about marrying her, but about the reasons for it.

Rather, one reason.

Marrying her would give him access to her godfather, and hopefully to evidence that would prove he'd killed his brother and plotted to kill Rafe. It wouldn't be enough to simply reclaim his stolen title, Rafe needed to see his murdering uncle strung up for his crimes.

He glanced over at Anne as he drove into the Grosvenor mews. Her face was hidden by the veil, but he didn't need to see her features to feel the visceral attraction that had only intensified since he taken her to his bed.

At the very least, he should tell her about her godfather, and he would. Soon. He wouldn't regret asking her to marry him. The matter with Mallory wasn't the primary reason behind it, not that it mattered. It was done. They would be wed, and Rafe would ensure her godfather was punished appropriately.

He pulled the cabriolet to a stop and got out to help her descend from the vehicle. Squeezing her hand, he leaned his head down next to hers. "Don't come to my interview with Colton." He was going to drive around to her brother-in-law's house to speak with him about the marriage. "I know you're tempted."

She exhaled. "You know me too well. Though it will pain me, I will refrain from interrupting. I will send you a note about dinner with my godfather as soon as I confirm Thursday evening."

He straightened. "I promise I won't make you

wait long until I pay a call. Perhaps tomorrow we can walk in the park?"

"That would be lovely. Every moment until then will seem an eternity."

He laughed before kissing her hand. "Read some romantic poetry."

She tugged on him until he bent his head once more. "I will imagine you beneath me tonight. That will be far more titillating."

"Siren," he hissed, wishing he could kiss her. Soon.

He released her hand and climbed back into the cabriolet, where he watched her disappear into one of the stables. Exhaling, he adjusted his seat to ease the pull of his breeches on his erection.

"Siren," he repeated as he left the mews and drove onto Grosvenor Street. In front of Colton's house, he stopped the vehicle and gave it over to the tiger. "Thank you, Tim. I won't be long."

The butler admitted him to the entry hall and kept him waiting only a moment before taking him to Colton's office. The viscount was just moving toward the center of the room as Rafe entered.

"Thank you, Purcell," Colton said, his gaze moving past Rafe.

Rafe heard the door close behind him. "You might want a glass of brandy."

Colton snorted. "That's a hell of a greeting. I rarely partake anymore, and never at this time of day." He frowned. "Why would I need a drink?"

"Let's sit." Rafe went to the chair he'd occupied on his last visit while Colton perched in his, looking expectant. Or perhaps just outright apprehensive.

"You have the look of the Vicar about you," Colton said slowly.

*Bloody hell.* "What does that mean?"

Colton shrugged. "I can't say exactly, just an aura of foreboding. What villainy are you about?"

"I'm not a villain." He'd left his hat and gloves in the hall and now ran his hand over his chin, his fingertips sliding along the smooth ripple of his scar. Distractedly, he wondered what Anne had thought of the knife scars on his torso. She had to have noticed. Her attention had been complete and intense.

"Bowles? Rather, Mallory? Or should I just call you Stone?" He shook his head. "You've more names than the Bible."

"Perhaps you should call me Rafe." He realized that wasn't how it was done among the peerage. Men such as Colton would call him Stone. "Because we're to be brothers-in-law. I've come to tell you that Anne and I are going to be married."

Colton shot to his feet, his face turning a mottled shade of red. "The hell you are. Get out."

"Please sit," Rafe said calmly. "I know what you must be thinking—"

"Do *not* presume to know me or my mind. How in God's name do you even know her well enough to marry her? This is unconscionable." He paced to the sideboard, where he eyed the brandy before stalking back toward Rafe. "You were right about that bloody drink."

"Yet you didn't pour one."

"No, and I won't. I buried myself in any bottle I could find after my parents were murdered. Which was *your* fault." He held up his hand before Rafe could speak. "Indirectly, but if you hadn't sent your man to intimidate me into repaying your loan, they would still be here."

"You know how deeply I regret what happened to your parents." Now that Rafe knew he'd lost his own parents as the result of someone else's evil deed, he felt worse. "You're right," he whispered. "That was my fault. You have every reason to despise me. I would."

Colton stared at him. He gripped the back of his chair, his jaw and throat working. "I don't know what you're about, but I'm not letting you near Anne. She's already been hurt enough by that blackguard Chamberlain. God, you have your hands in that too."

"No, I didn't. I had no idea Chamberlain was courting her. I never would have allowed it."

"You wouldn't have allowed it? Just who the hell do you think you are?" His eyes widened. "How long have you known Jane's sister?"

"A few months," he answered tightly. "We met by chance, and I thought that was the end of it. Then I met her again here."

"Here? At my house?" Colton picked up the back of the chair and slammed it down.

"I would have met her anyway. Her godfather is my uncle."

"The only reason you know that is because of *me*." Colton sat back down and rested his elbow on his knee so he could drop his forehead into his hand. "If I'd never gambled, I wouldn't have gone to you for money. My parents wouldn't be dead. My sister-in-law wouldn't want to marry a criminal." He peered through his fingers at Rafe. "She does want to marry you?"

"Yes." Rafe coughed. "And might I point out that she may not even be your sister-in-law if not for me."

"Oh, bloody fucking hell!" Colton dropped his hand from his head and straightened. "It doesn't matter how we got here, only that you leave. You can't marry her. You must understand that, don't you? Think of who you are."

"*Were.*" Rafe stiffened his spine and used his iciest Vicar voice. "I'm the Earl of Stone."

"Not yet you aren't. I wouldn't be surprised if you'd manipulated that situation somehow, perhaps assumed the identity of a dead boy."

In a jolt of fury, Rafe leapt from the chair and pinned Colton to his. He curled his hand around the viscount's neck. "Don't ever say that. *I* am that boy. Like you, I should be dead and my parents are gone, mur—" Rafe released him and turned away, stalking away to the edge of the room. He fought to catch his breath and calm his racing heart. His vision tunneled, and he clenched his hands into fists.

"Were you going to say they were murdered?" Anthony asked softly.

Rafe wasn't going to disclose anything, not to this man who held him in such contempt. And perhaps rightfully so. "It doesn't matter. They are long dead." He slowly turned, twitching his shoulders and flexing his hands. "I am going to marry Anne, and I am not going to hurt her. There is no one I care more for in this world, except my sister. I expect you understand that too." Like him, Colton had a younger sister.

"I do. Sarah married a cad like you. Well, not like *you*, but a cad just the same."

"I thought she married your best friend."

Colton waved his hand. "Wait until your sister wants to marry your best friend. Only that won't ever happen since your sister is already wed." He blew out a breath. "Does Anne know who you were?"

As far as Colton was concerned, Rafe had been the Vicar, a man who lent money at a higher-than-legal rate. He had no idea of Rafe's life before he'd reinvented himself as a moneylender in Blackfriars.

"No." Rafe had never planned to tell her either, but that had been prior to becoming betrothed. Fuck, this was a tangle.

"You must." Colton stood and gave Rafe a stony stare. "You worked closely with Chamberlain, and while I know you weren't party to his extortion, you used him to gain new borrowers—men from his circle that you would not have had access to."

Rafe wiped his hand down his face and swallowed a frustrated groan. He hadn't considered Chamberlain before he'd proposed. Hell, he hadn't considered much of anything. He just knew that she loved him, wanted him, and he wanted her too. She was also potentially the key to gaining what he needed to take down his uncle.

A goddamned tangle indeed.

"I'll tell her." Rafe met Colton's gaze. "You won't say a word."

"Do it soon, and tell me when it's done. I'll speak to her before the final banns are read. I won't let her get to her wedding day again only to realize the man she plans to marry isn't who she thought."

Put like that, Rafe was no better than Chamberlain. In fact, he was worse. As far as he knew, Chamberlain hadn't used her for anything like Rafe was planning to do.

No, he *wasn't* using her. He cared for her. That their betrothal would benefit him in his quest was simply an added benefit.

"I will protect her," Colton said firmly. "Family is of the utmost importance to me, and she is my family. And in the absence of her father, I take full responsibility to ensure her well-being."

"You're a good brother-in-law," Rafe said quietly. He exhaled and glanced up at the ceiling. "I became the Vicar to better myself. I'd stopped charging that higher interest rate a few months after you repaid your debt. And I stopped intimidating people who weren't on time with their payments." He looked at Colton and felt a bone-deep regret. "I am so sorry about your parents."

It was a long moment before the viscount responded, and when he did, his voice was low and harsh. "Thank you. I hope you love her. It can save you, you know. It saved me. Without Jane, I don't know what would have happened to me."

Rafe didn't love Anne, though. He wouldn't.

"With her, you can find the strength to look forward instead of back," Colton continued. "I imagine that must be hard for you right now after learning who you are."

"Yes." He swallowed, trying to keep his throat from constricting. "My entire life was stolen from me. Please don't come between me and Anne." In that moment, he knew why he'd asked her to marry him. She'd been the only tether he wanted to hold on to since Eliza and, before that, Selina. People like her didn't come along very often, and when they did, you clasped them tightly and you never let them go.

Colton nodded solemnly. "I'll give you time."

"I am going to write to her father," Rafe said. "Not for his permission, but because I should. I should, shouldn't I?"

"Yes." Colton's lip curled. "He's an ass. I hope he doesn't return to London for the wedding. I'd just as soon not see him after what he put Jane through."

"Perhaps I'll tell him the wedding will be in August. You and Lady Colton will be gone by then, yes?"

Colton actually smiled. "Yes. Perhaps you won't be the world's worst brother-in-law after all."

"I will try not to be." Rafe meant it. He'd never

been part of a family, and now he had Selina's husband's large extended family, Selina's pretend sister Beatrix and her new husband and their daughter, and soon he'd have Anne and her sister and the man standing before him. He supposed he also had to include his blood family. No, he'd never call his uncle family. *Never.*

"Thank you for not calling me out," Rafe said wryly. "That is what you lords do, isn't it?"

"*We* lords, and yes, sometimes." His eyes narrowed slightly. "And don't provoke me. I'm still not in favor of this. If Anne gives me any indication she's not happy, I'll put a stop to everything."

"Understood. But you won't have to. If Anne is unhappy, I'll let her go." Somehow, in the span of an afternoon, that thought had become almost unbearable.

Rafe left a few minutes later, and by the time he arrived in Grosvenor Square a short while after that, he was more than ready for a glass of brandy. He stalked into the house as Tim took the cabriolet to the mews.

Glover intercepted him as he walked through the entry hall. "My lord, Lady Selina and Mr. Sheffield are here to see you. They are in the library." The butler had taken to addressing Rafe as "my lord" and Selina as "lady" since learning of his title. Glover did not care that he wasn't yet officially the earl. Rafe appreciated the small act of solidarity.

"Thank you." Rafe made his way to the library, intent on at least the brandy.

When he entered, Harry stood from the settee where he sat with Selina. Both looked…anxious.

"This must be important, since you're here waiting for me." Rafe realized he didn't have liquor in the library and bitterly resented the oversight. "Should I go into my office to fetch brandy? Gin?"

"The clerk returned from Stonehaven." Harry's statement sounded ominous.

Rafe's interest and attention were wholly piqued. He strode to a chair near the settee and sat down, eager for the report. "And?"

"He spoke to everyone. There are perhaps a half dozen retainers who were there at the time of the fire, most of them grooms or gardeners. One member of the household, the housekeeper, is still there. At the time of the fire, she was eleven years old. Her father was the steward. He died trying to save your parents."

Rafe clutched the arms of the chair, his heart twisting.

"Rafe." Selina's voice was soft and soothing.

He looked at his sister and saw his anguish mirrored in her gaze. Nodding slightly, he exhaled and loosened his grip on the chair. "She remembered the fire?"

"Yes," Harry answered. "Quite distinctly, as it was a traumatic event for her. She said the bodies of the children—of you and Selina—were not recovered. That will bolster your claim significantly."

Rafe didn't give a damn about the claim. At least not compared to what really mattered: punishing his uncle. "Was the clerk able to gather any evidence against our uncle?"

Harry grimaced. "Not specifically. However, one of the grooms recalled that a footman disappeared shortly after the fire. He remembered him because they'd been friends."

"How is that evidence?" Rafe asked. "It doesn't seem unusual that someone would leave following such an event, particularly since his job was presumably no longer needed. A footman requires a house for employment."

"While that would be true, the groom said it was peculiar because the footman's sister was your nurse, and she did not disappear. She testified that the children died, that she'd been unable to save them. She also said the only reason she was alive was because her brother had rescued her."

"*Fucking hell.*" Rafe shot out of the chair and paced to the other side of the room, his thoughts crashing into anger and frustration. He vaguely thought that he hadn't cursed so much in one day since moving to Mayfair. But today deserved every epithet he produced.

"Edgar took us away, and Pauline stayed to cover their crime," Selina spat.

Rafe spun around at the vitriol in her voice. She sounded the way he felt. "It's good that Edgar is dead and Pauline is soon to be."

Selina pressed her lips together. "She already is. The clerk Harry sent to take her testimony returned a little while ago."

Harry frowned while bitter disappointment glittered in his gaze. "I deeply regret I wasn't able to find someone to go until today. I should have gone myself on Friday."

"Don't," Selina said. "You were busy with other matters."

Rafe stared at a line of books on one of the shelves in front of him. If he didn't love them so much, he would throw every single one to the ground. He wiped his hand back over his forehead and ruffled his hair in frustration.

"Now what?" He stalked back to them and sat down again. "How do we ensure Mallory is prosecuted? He fucking killed our parents."

Harry looked at him with grim determination.

"I'm still working on that. I won't lie—it doesn't look easy right now. But I've never let that stop me."

"Harry will find the proof we need," Selina said with far more conviction that Rafe possessed.

"Good, you be optimistic for us both." He felt as if the tenuous hold he had on this new life, this life he'd worked so hard to achieve, was slipping fast. Had he really become engaged just today? "I should mention that I'm marrying Anne Pemberton."

Selina sat straighter and blinked at him. "Truly?"

"I proposed to her today, and she accepted. The banns will be read Sunday. We will wed the last week of July."

"Congratulations," Harry said with a hint of caution. "Are you happy?"

"What?" Rafe stared at him, unseeing, for a moment. "Yes. Of course."

"It's very sudden, isn't it?" Selina asked.

"I've known her for months, so no. It's nowhere near as *sudden* as you and Harry getting married after a few short weeks of acquaintance." He looked at Harry. "I would like to be the earl before we are wed. Is that possible?"

"Entirely. I started drafting the claim last week, and now that I have the information from Stonehaven, I will finish it with due haste."

"Excellent." Rafe slumped back against the chair.

Glover stepped into the library. "My lord, Lord and Lady Rockbourne are here."

Rafe waved his hand toward himself. "Show them in, please."

The butler left and a moment later, Beatrix and her husband entered. They wore matching expressions of apprehension.

"What's wrong?" Selina asked, starting to rise.

Beatrix, who truly looked as if she could be related to Selina and to Rafe, in spite of her diminutive stature, waved her back down. "Here." She handed a newspaper to Selina and sat down on the other side of her on the settee.

Thomas, Beatrix's husband, stood nearby. "Rafe," he said with a nod before giving Harry just the physical acknowledgment.

"Rafe, this says you are the resurrected Earl of Stone." Selina looked up at him and handed him the paper. "Near the top."

He took it from her and perused the article under the words, LOST EARL OF STONE IS ALIVE? It detailed that he and Selina were the presumed dead children of the former earl. "How did this find its way to a newspaper?"

Harry stood. "I will ask them directly."

Selina briefly took his hand. "Thank you." She turned her head to Beatrix. "People are going to start questioning who you are. I'm so sorry."

Beatrix shrugged, appearing untroubled. "I am prepared for the onslaught of judgment and dismay when we inform them I am illegitimate and only pretended to be your sister to avoid being ostracized. I am also ready for the confusion and distress when some of them wonder how to treat me since I am a viscountess." She grinned at them, and Rafe couldn't help but respect and admire her blithe attitude.

Selina relaxed slightly. "The Beatrix I met at school over fifteen years ago would not have been so secure." She smiled at her. "I'm so proud of you."

"Thank you. I get all of my courage from you, dear sister. No one can stop me from thinking of you that way."

"Nor me," Selina said fiercely.

"I do wonder what my father will say." Beatrix looked to Thomas. "I suppose I should warn him."

Thomas frowned. "He doesn't deserve that."

"Probably not," Beatrix said gaily. "What about you, Selina? Are you ready for the difference in the way people will treat you now?" She glanced toward Rafe. "And you?"

Selina exchanged a look with Rafe and shrugged. "I suppose." She exhaled. "I knew it was coming. I just wanted another day or two."

Harry faced Rafe. "I'm going to submit your claim to the Prince Regent and the attorney general tomorrow morning. However, before I finish it, I'm going to the newspaper to find out how they learned this information." He bent and kissed Selina's brow. "I'll see you at home later."

"We'll drop her at Cavendish Square," Beatrix offered.

Harry thanked them and left.

Rafe rose. "If you'll excuse me, this has been a thoroughly eventful day."

Selina also stood, as did Beatrix with her. "Rafe became betrothed today. Goodness, that will be in the newspaper soon too." She looked at him. "When do you plan to announce it?"

"How the hell should I know?" He scrubbed his hand through his hair again. "Am I supposed to make an announcement, or will Anne?"

"Anne Pemberton?" Beatrix asked in surprise. At Selina's affirmative response, she added, "Excellent choice. I like her very much. Though, I'm surprised she agreed to marry someone so soon after her other wedding." She made a face of disgust before her expression transformed into a warm smile directed at Rafe. "You must have completely won her over. Congratulations, Rafe. I hope you'll be very happy."

Thomas cleared his throat. "I would say that Miss Pemberton's family should make the announcement. You may wish to discuss the particulars with Lady Colton."

Rafe didn't want to discuss anything anymore today. He tugged gently at his cravat, but didn't untie the knot. "Now, if you'll excuse me, I'm in need of a brandy. Then I've apparently a betrothal to announce."

Selina came toward him and touched his arm. "I'm so glad for you." She searched his gaze, as if trying to read if he truly was happy. "Please let me know if I can help."

"I'm sure you can." He kissed her cheek and departed the library.

If all went according to plan, he would be an earl and a husband before the month was out. And hopefully his uncle would be on his way to the noose.

# CHAPTER 13

Anne stifled a yawn as the coach drove through Berkley Square.

"You're tired today," Jane noted from beside her.

"I slept rather fitfully."

"Because of the betrothal?" Jane had been thrilled for Anne, if surprised that Rafe had actually proposed since there had been no official courtship. She'd noted that people would find that of interest. Anne had said she planned to tell people that they'd met at Ivy Grove and their courtship had been swift.

"And the story in the paper." Anne had wanted to see Rafe after reading the article identifying him as the presumed dead heir to the Earl of Stone. But she'd settled for sending him a note saying she was thinking of him. She'd yet to receive a response, which had probably also contributed to her sleeplessness.

"I am curious to find out your godfather's reaction to that newspaper story," Jane said as the coach turned onto Bruton Street and came to a stop in front of the current Earl of Stone's residence.

Anne imagined he wasn't pleased. However, he

couldn't avoid the inevitable. Rafe *would* be declared the earl. "We will discover it shortly," she said to her sister as the coachman opened the door.

A few minutes later, they sat in the drawing room awaiting Anne's godfather's arrival. This time, Jane would remain with her for the entire visit.

Her godfather hurried into the room, his features taut with distress. "Ah, Anne, and Lady Colton." A weak smile stretched his lips. "I'm afraid you've caught me on my way out."

"I see," Anne said pleasantly, afraid that he was, in fact, very upset about the newspaper article. "I came to share some news."

"Oh?" He stood a moment longer before taking a seat, though he was clearly ready to leave as soon as Anne said what she came to say.

She hesitated, wanting to ask him about his agitation first, but ultimately revealed her news. "Yesterday, I became betrothed to your nephew."

Anne didn't think it was possible for the earl to sit any farther forward on the edge of the chair, but he did. His eyes rounded and his jaw dropped. "What? How?" he sputtered.

"After we met at Ivy Grove, we found we had much in common. He has called on me a few times," she fibbed, "and we decided we suit. I expected you would be happy since you were so intent on reintroducing me to the Marriage Mart. Furthermore, I am actually marrying into your family. Isn't it wonderful?"

He blinked several times. "Yes, of course. I'm just surprised. You didn't mention he was courting you when you visited the other day."

The skepticism in his tone was slightly annoying. "Things happened rather quickly. I really can't tell if you're pleased or not. Is this because you're planning to contest Rafe's claim to the title?"

"I still haven't decided. But I must do so very soon because his claim was presented today. I expect you already know that."

She didn't, and that disappointed her. "I want you to know what a good person Rafe is. There is much you don't know about him."

"Then please inform me," he said, settling back in the chair and trying to appear serene despite the tic in his jaw.

Hesitating, Anne glanced at her sister. Should she reveal what she knew of Rafe? The things he kept private and only very recently exposed to her? "He just is."

"Unless you can point to something that proves what you say, I'm afraid I'll need to reserve judgment."

Frustrated by her godfather's behavior and driven by the need to defend the man she loved, Anne turned her back on caution and hoped Rafe would understand. "He owns a bookshop on Paternoster Row and has for some time. He's made wise investments and built a considerable fortune. He helps orphans find employment and provides them housing if they need it. He is liked and respected in Cheapside." She recalled all the people who knew him from when they'd visited Paternoster Row and Cheapside during their stolen afternoons. Every one of them—and there were many—had greeted him warmly.

"So that's where he lived before?" her godfather asked. "Cheapside?"

"Yes." She thought of his house there and how his wife hadn't lived at that residence. It bothered her that she didn't know where he'd lived before then, but she was still learning all there was to know about him, just as he was about her.

Her godfather tipped his head to the side. "Will he continue in trade, I wonder?"

"Does it matter?" Jane asked, saying what Anne was thinking.

"I suppose not." He pursed his lips and stared at Anne a moment. "I care so very deeply for you, my dear. Are you certain you wish to wed yourself to this unknown man? There will be some who will never accept him, even if he is declared the earl."

"Then those people will be the lesser for it," she said coolly, irritated that this man who'd been a second father to her wasn't being more supportive.

"I beg your pardon, my lord," the butler interrupted from the doorway. "Lady Burnhope is here."

Deborah swept into the drawing room, the hem of her gown brushing the butler's legs as she moved by him. She blinked in surprise at Anne and Jane. "You're Papa's guests?"

"Yes, dear," the earl answered. "But I am just leaving. I must be off to Westminster." He rose.

Deborah clucked her tongue. "Because of this business with Bowles."

"His name is Mallory, and you know it." Anne exchanged a look with Jane. "We know you're behind the newspaper article about Rafe's identity."

Eyes rounding, Deborah lifted a shoulder. "I don't know how you can claim that. I certainly didn't inform the newspaper."

"Not directly." Anne glowered at her. Harry had learned that someone from Deborah's household had supplied the rumor. "Can't you just mind your own business?"

Deborah blinked in affront. "This *is* my business. My father's business anyway, and that makes it mine. My goodness, we don't know a thing about Bowles. Should he even be the earl?"

Anne began to see how her godfather might have been encouraged in his doubts about Rafe. Had Deborah urged him to contest the claim?

"I just learned he is from Cheapside," the earl put in.

Deborah's fair brows arched as she glanced toward her father. "How mundane."

Anne rose, her legs quivering with anger, and Jane stood beside her. "You should know that I became betrothed to him yesterday."

"Did you?" Deborah sniffed. "Well, he is incredibly attractive, so I'll congratulate you for that." She looked to her father. "Meeting in the Lords?"

"Your cousin has submitted his claim for the title to the Prince Regent."

Deborah's brow puckered. "When will the committee meet to decide?"

"Not until the attorney general refers the matter. That could happen quickly. Or not. It depends on Prinny." He brushed his hands over his front. "Now, if you'll excuse me, I must be on my way." He went to Anne and took her hand, giving her a half smile. "I just want you to be happy and secure, my dear. I feel it is my duty, especially in your father's absence, to ensure your well-being. Please pardon me if I'm being overbearing or dubious. You are very dear to me, and while your betrothed is my blood, I feel as though I have a primary commitment to you given our shared past." He squeezed her hand before nodding at Jane and leaving.

Anne didn't doubt his sincerity or his concern for her. Still, she wished he could get past his own feelings of loss and disappointment with regard to the earldom. Or at least *try* to understand how this was for Rafe.

"This is very hard for him," Deborah said softly, surprising Anne with the caring tenor of her voice.

Jane rounded her eyes briefly at Anne while Deborah stared after her father. "I imagine it is," Jane said a bit sourly. "Anne was merely hoping he might be a bit more enthused about her happy news."

Deborah turned her attention back to them, her blue eyes sharp. "Can you really expect that, though? My cousin has come out of nowhere and completely upended Papa's life. He will lose everything—his name, his standing, his assets…*everything*."

"He won't lose you," Anne said. "Or me. Or Lorcan."

Deborah pursed her lips. "That is not the same, and if you can't see that, you are incredibly naïve."

Jane rose to Anne's defense. "No, she isn't. Anne is trying to focus on what's truly important—people and family."

"I suppose that is important to the both of you, what with your parents all but turning their backs on you."

Anne blew out an exasperated breath. "Good Lord, Deborah, sometimes you can be so thoughtless."

"I prefer to think I'm realistic." She smiled benignly, seeming untroubled by Anne's assessment. "I'm only asking you to think of Papa. You must do as you must. Marry my cousin or don't marry him. Just don't be surprised if Papa can't be happy about it."

Jane touched Anne's arm. "We should go. We've arrangements to make."

"When is the wedding?" Deborah asked before they could make their way from the drawing room.

"The twenty-sixth." Anne pulled the date out of her head simply because it was after the twenty-fifth. She hoped that day would be amenable to Rafe. If not, they could move it, but she preferred not to now that she'd told Deborah.

"Lovely. I'll look forward to it."

Anne and Jane left, remaining quiet until they were seated in the coach.

"I suppose you must invite her," Jane said, gritting her teeth. "But how I wish you didn't have to. I never liked her, and I admit I couldn't see how you could."

"She didn't always show her less appealing side to me. I think she knew how much her father cared for me and sought to ensure we were close." Or somewhat close anyway. "She was a good chaperone at least."

"She was *not*." Jane laughed. "I suppose it depends on how you define good. She was helpful to you but a complete failure in her duties."

"Yes. But without her failure, I would not have met Rafe, so for that I must be grateful."

"Speaking of Rafe," Jane said. "What you said about him is true?"

"Yes."

"He and his sister both support orphans, which makes sense given their own history." But it was more than that. He specifically helped children who had no one and were at the mercy of their environment. "He built everything he has on the kindness of one man, the owner of the bookshop Rafe now owns. It's astonishing, really."

"Mmm, yes," Jane said softly.

Anne wondered if Rafe truly would come to walk in the park today. Since he hadn't confirmed, she wasn't sure if she ought to expect him or not. It might be that he was busy. With her godfather rushing to Westminster, things might be happening quickly regarding the earldom.

"Was I too quick to judge my godfather?" Anne mused aloud. "Deborah, for all her faults, did make a valid point about how he must be feeling."

Jane patted her hand briefly. "You are too kind. But yes, I thought the same thing. It's scary how often we do that." She flashed a smile. "He is likely in a turmoil and now one of the people closest to him—you—is aligning herself with the man he perceives as the architect of his destruction."

"That's not at all hyperbolic," Anne said drily.

"Not at all." Jane flashed a grin. "I actually think that may be how this seems to him. As Deborah said, from his perspective, he's losing everything."

"I am trying to see his side, truly. I suppose a part of me is clinging to him as my godfather since, well, our parents…" She couldn't seem to find the words to say what their parents were.

"I can understand that. I would probably do the same. In fact, perhaps I would hold on even more tightly since I think you at least have the chance for reconciliation with our parents."

Anne shook her head. "There is no chance for me. Not unless they apologize to you."

"You are the kindest, most loyal person. I hope your betrothed knows how lucky he is."

Did he? Anne certainly felt as though she was fortunate. She just hoped she could keep both her godfather and her husband. Even so, she would choose Rafe if she had to. "I hope my godfather will be able to come to terms with Rafe being the earl. I would hate for them to be at odds forever."

"It is going to take time, I think," Jane said. "The question is how much."

"However long it takes, the earldom will be Rafe's. Of that I'm certain."

~

Rafe walked from his house on Upper Brook Street through Grosvenor Square to Colton's house on Grosvenor Street near Bond Street, arriving at half past four. Since his claim had been submitted that morning, he'd received a flurry of invitations for the final events of the Season.

Wasn't that what he'd wanted when he'd moved to Mayfair?

The butler admitted him into the foyer. "I'll inform Lord Colton you're here," he said.

"And Miss Pemberton, if you would. Thank you."

The butler passed Anne as she came into the entry hall, her steps light and her face breaking into a wide smile. "Finally!"

He couldn't help but grin at her reaction to his arrival. He hadn't realized how much he'd been looking forward to seeing her until that moment.

She didn't stop coming toward him until she was close enough to touch his chest. "Did you come to walk in the park?"

"Among other things. Would it be all right if we spoke for a few minutes? In private?"

"Yes." She led him into the library and closed the door behind them.

"Will we be disturbed?" he asked from the center of the room, where he turned to face her.

"Hopefully not, since I closed the door."

"Well, I'll be brief." Which was too bad, because now that he was alone with her, he only wanted to take her in his arms and kiss her.

Maybe lay her down on the settee and lift her skirts…

He reached into his coat and pulled out the small box he'd brought for her. She stopped before him, her gaze falling on the object in his hand. "This is for you," he said.

She inhaled sharply before a smile teased her lips. "A betrothal ring?"

"No. Sorry to disappoint you. I haven't had time to purchase one. Plus, I'd like to know what you want."

"Whatever you choose." She looked up at him. "And you could never disappoint me."

Except he would. As soon as he told her the truth about his past, who he'd been and the things he'd done. But perhaps she would understand?

He hated the thought of telling her and not because of his feelings. She didn't deserve the inevitable disappointment.

Still, he had to tell her, or Colton would. Rafe would have to do so before Sunday when their betrothal was made public by the reading of the banns. That way she could decide not to marry him if she so chose. His gut clenched at the thought of losing her. He realized if not for Colton, he would likely not tell her at all.

He would at least delay telling her. These days of living with joy for the first time since Eliza's death were too heady to ruin. He'd do it on Friday. Or Saturday.

She took the box from him and opened the lid. The cameo he'd purchased at the Burlington Arcade nestled on a bed of ivory velvet. Her gaze lifted to his. "It's beautiful. But if you didn't have time to buy a betrothal ring, how did you have time to get this?"

"I bought it the day you didn't meet me at

Hatchard's. When you didn't come, I went into the Burlington Arcade across the street—it had just opened. I saw this and it reminded me of you, both the profile and the fact that it's oyster shell. It's actually Aphrodite."

"Like the folly," she whispered, tracing the goddess's head with her fingertip, her lips parted. When her eyes met his once more, she blinked away a tear. "Thank you. I'm so sorry *I* disappointed you that day." She sniffed. "It's the loveliest gift I've ever received. I can't believe you bought it after I left you waiting. I'm so sorry. I wish we'd told each other our names. I would have sent you a message." She edged closer to him. "I never would have let you go."

Rafe cupped her face and lowered his head. She met his kiss with such a sweet and wild abandon that he moaned softly, deep in his throat. He clasped her lower back and slid his tongue along hers. She put one hand on the back of his neck, her fingers moving between his collar and flesh.

Afraid he wouldn't be able to stop kissing her, touching her, he lifted his head. "I'm glad you like it."

"I don't like it. I love it. Here." She handed him the box while she pinned the brooch onto the bodice of her pale blue gown. "How does it look?"

"Perfect. Like you." He'd never seen anyone lovelier.

Never?

He felt a pang of sorrow as he thought of Eliza. He hated that he was replacing her. No, Anne was not a replacement. She couldn't be, no matter how much he grew to care for her.

A rap on the door drew Anne to turn her head. When she looked back at Rafe, she frowned slightly, then exhaled. "I suppose our private time is over."

"So it seems. One more thing. Selina has invited us, along with Beatrix and her husband and your sister and Colton, for dinner at Cavendish Square tomorrow night."

"Lovely! I wondered if I was going to manage seeing you tomorrow." With a delighted grin, she took the box from him and went to open the door.

Her sister and Colton stood outside, the latter glowering at Rafe as if he wanted to run him through with a sword. Rafe decided to look at Lady Colton instead. Her gaze was on Anne's dress. "Did you just get that?"

Anne touched the cameo. "Yes. It's a betrothal gift. Isn't it spectacular?"

"Quite," Jane said with a grin. "It looks a little like you."

"That's what Rafe thought." She glanced back at him, her smile bright. "Is everyone ready to walk to the park?"

"Yes. I brought your hat and gloves," Lady Colton said.

Ten minutes later, they were on their way toward the park. Rafe and Anne led the way with Colton and his wife following behind. "I hope you don't mind, but Phoebe and Ripley are going to meet us," Lady Colton called.

Anne looked back over her shoulder. "I don't mind at all." She looked toward Rafe as they walked into Grosvenor Square. "Do you know Ripley?"

"Yes, we've met. I'm looking forward to his ball on Saturday. I've long wanted to see Brixton Park, the maze in particular." He darted a look at Anne, noting that she smiled mischievously when he mentioned the maze. "Will you be there?"

"I will now." She gave him a look of seductive promise that made him wish it was Saturday night. "I've been mostly avoiding Society events, but now that we're betrothed, I don't have to fear being bothered by gentlemen looking for a wife." She squeezed his arm gently. "And you don't have to worry about anyone looking to snare you in the parson's trap now that everyone will know you're about to become an earl."

He found it fascinating, and galling, that without the title, he was somehow less attractive, particularly because he was in trade, a fact he hadn't tried to hide. People already knew he owned a pleasure garden in Clerkenwell—he'd met Selina's sister-in-law there before she and Harry had wed. But did he want them to know he also owned a bookshop and, as of very recently, a publishing venture? He had many investments, but presumably other peers did too. "I think I need to go to earl school," he murmured.

"What's that?" Anne asked, leaning closer. "Did you say earl school?"

"I did."

She laughed softly. "Hopefully, my godfather will handle that. You can start on Thursday evening."

Rafe's good mood faltered. He would no sooner take advice or direction from his uncle than he would from the lord of hell.

A few minutes later, they entered the park through the Grosvenor Gate. The afternoon was bright and warm, and the park was positively teeming with Society's finest. Rafe began to doubt the wisdom of coming here today of all days. The day he'd submitted his claim to the earldom of Stone.

Just inside, they met the Marquess and Marchioness of Ripley. He was a dark-haired, easy-going gentleman with a somewhat rakish reputation. Until he'd fallen completely and unabashedly in love with his wife, one of the founding members of the Spitfire Society. Like Anne's sister, Phoebe had also come close to marrying. But in her situation, she'd left her groom at the altar. Anne had told him it was because she couldn't bring herself to marry him.

"Afternoon, Mallory," Ripley said. "Or should I say Stone?" He grinned good-naturedly. "I'm sure you've quite a story to share. The Lords was abuzz today with the news—and with speculation."

"There's not much to tell," Rafe said blandly. "My sister and I were kidnapped and only recently learned our true identities."

Ripley cracked a half smile. "I don't believe that for a moment, but I won't bother you for the details. Know that I'm happy to hear them if you ever want to share, but it isn't important. Are you ready to take on the duties of the earldom?"

"Ripley sits on the Committee for Privileges," Colton said.

*Shit.* Rafe hadn't known that. He should have asked Harry for a list so he could be informed. Not that he cared about making an impression. He hated being caught unaware.

"Yes," Rafe said, answering the marquess's question. "I am eager to reclaim my birthright." As if it could wipe away the past twenty-seven years. Nothing ever could.

Ripley assessed him with a sympathetic stare. "I can only imagine how that must feel. I'm just glad you've discovered who you are, who you're meant to be."

Rafe sensed the man's words were genuine. "Thank you."

"Shall we walk?" Lady Ripley asked with a smile.

"Yes," Anne answered, clutching Rafe's arm more tightly as they set out toward Cumberland Gate. They took up the rear as Ripley and his wife talked with Anne's sister and Colton.

People standing off the path covertly watched them as they walked by. Some of them whispered. "Everyone is staring," Anne murmured.

"I expected that."

"And they don't even know we're betrothed—that would have been enough. Does it bother you?"

"Not particularly." He could ignore it. As a lieutenant to Samuel Partridge in London's East End, Rafe had been a sort of neighborhood royalty. People had watched him as he walked past or treated him with deference. Women tried to catch his eye, and men worked to earn his respect and favor.

"Good afternoon!" Lady Satterfield greeted them from next to the path. "Miss Pemberton, how lovely to see you out."

"Allow me to introduce Mr. Mallory," Anne said. "Rafe, this is Lady Satterfield. She is a member of the Spitfire Society."

Rafe bowed his head. Selina had mentioned the countess, indicating she was a kind and generous person. She was also very well respected in Society, and her stepson was the much-revered Duke of Kendal. Rafe wondered if he was also on the Committee for Privileges. From what he understood, the duke was a powerful figure in the Lords.

Thc countess, who was perhaps in her late fifties, smiled warmly at him. "You're soon to bc declared the Earl of Stone, I hear. I'm very pleased to make your acquaintance. I knew your parents. They were absolutely wonderful people."

She stood with two other women, who stared at him with excited interest. Lady Satterfield introduced them as Lady Exeby and Mrs. Childers.

Rafe ignored them in favor of hearing more about his parents. "I'm always pleased to meet someone who knew them. I barely remember them."

Lady Satterfield's eyes creased with sympathy. "I've met your sister on several occasions. Your mother would be so proud of her commitment to charitable works."

"Which sister is that?" Mrs. Childers asked.

"Lady Selina Sheffield," Lady Satterfield replied.

"Lady Rockbourne isn't really his sister," Lady Exeby muttered while trying to smile.

"Yes, Rafe is shortly to become the Earl of Stone, and I will be his countess," Anne said with more volume than was necessary. Enough volume that people nearby turned their heads.

Rafe stared at her, his heart pounding. Now their betrothal was public. She couldn't withdraw without causing a scandal. A sense of relief flashed through him along with a jolt of self-derision. She no longer had the choice she deserved when she learned the truth about him. And damn him, it seemed he'd unconsciously wanted that. He was a selfish, coldhearted blackguard, and he was afraid of losing her.

Lady Satterfield's eyes lit with joy. "You're betrothed?"

Anne gave his arm another squeeze. "Yes."

"How wonderful. I'm so happy for you both."

Lady Exeby and Mrs. Childers' eyes rounded briefly. "*Such* happy news," one of them said. Rafe couldn't remember who was whom.

"A shame you didn't give anyone else a chance

on the Marriage Mart," the other added with a laugh.

"I didn't need to. Miss Pemberton is everything I could want in a countess. If you'll excuse us, we will continue on." He inclined his head before escorting Anne away, his pulse uneven.

"I'm sorry," she murmured. "I blurted that out after Lady Exeby mentioned Beatrix. And I told my godfather earlier."

Rafe tensed more than he already was, his neck and shoulder blades tightening. "What did he say?"

"He wasn't pleased, but he was more fixated on your claim. He was on his way to Westminster."

"To do what?" Rafe wondered if his uncle was urging members of the committee to reject his claim.

"He didn't say specifically."

Rafe noted she kept her gaze trained forward, and her body had stiffened as they discussed her godfather. Had something happened? "You don't have to keep anything from me," he said softly. "I imagine my uncle is angry and perhaps even wishes I had never been found."

She turned her head swiftly, her gaze hot. "Don't say that! Yes, he is upset, but he's trying to accept this shocking change to his life. Just as you are doing."

Her defense of him rankled, but what did Rafe expect? The man was a part of her life, as close as family.

They walked in silence for a moment before Anne asked, "Where will we go after the wedding? Or do you prefer to stay in London?"

He wanted to ask why she'd changed the subject but decided the park was not the place to have a conversation about his murdering uncle. "I honestly hadn't thought that far ahead."

The staring seemed to grow worse as they reached the intersection with another path. The Ripleys and Coltons turned to the left, but Rafe was sorely tempted to continue to the Cumberland Gate and leave the park entirely.

"You slowed down," Anne observed. "Shall we stop?"

"Don't we need to keep up with your chaperones?"

"Probably, but the park is very crowded. It's not as if you can compromise me here." She lowered her voice. "As if you hadn't already."

Her sensual tone drove a stake of longing straight through him. He struggled to focus on anything other than taking her in his arms. "I think I'd like to visit Stonehaven after we are wed."

Her face softened. "Yes, of course. I imagine you'd want to see your family's ancestral home."

He suddenly realized his parents were buried there—Harry's clerk had made the discovery. While he wanted to see their graves, he was anxious. Would it be too painful to see the house? Could he ever spend time there? "I want Selina to come too," he murmured, his mind caught in the past. He wasn't sure what was more troubling to him at the moment—the pain of that loss or the pain of potentially losing Anne.

"Certainly. Let's catch up to Jane and the others and tell them we want to return home."

He blinked away the fog in his brain. "We don't have to."

She gave him an encouraging smile and quickened her pace toward her sister, pulling him along. They were speaking with another couple to the side of the path.

"Here they are," Jane said with a smile. "Arabella, you know my sister Anne. This is her betrothed, Mr. Raphael Mallory, soon to be the Earl of Stone. May I present the Duke and Duchess of Halstead?"

Anne glanced up at him. "Arabella was a founding member of the Spitfire Society and is a dear friend of Jane and Phoebe's. She and her husband have been in the country the past several weeks—the duke unexpectedly inherited his title. Perhaps he has advice for you on suddenly becoming a peer."

Halstead, dark-haired and dark-eyed, with an easy smile, inclined his head toward Rafe. "I'd be happy to share a brandy—or ten—and tell you all about it. I understand you're about to become an earl." His gaze turned sympathetic. "The situation is entirely different, however," he added softly. "My condolences."

He'd apparently heard the entire story. Rafe appreciated the man's sentiment. "Thank you."

Jane sidled closer to Anne and Rafe as Anthony began speaking with the others. "It seems the entire park is talking about Rafe's claim. Do you want to continue, or would you rather return home?"

"Home," Anne answered quickly.

Nodding, Jane suggested they could all return to Grosvenor Street for refreshment if they were so inclined.

As they left the park through the closest gate, Rafe felt a surge of relief. It wasn't that he didn't want to face the gossip. He didn't particularly care. But he was bound to meet more people who'd known his parents, and after thinking of their graves, he wasn't ready for that. Not today. Not on top of grappling with what he was going to say to Anne. And when.

"Will you mind if I don't stay?" he asked Anne.

"Of course not. I mean, I'll miss you, but I understand. Truly." She stroked his forearm with her free hand. "That just gives me more time to look forward to tomorrow. And all the days after that."

He longed to kiss her, to thank her for her unwavering support and love. Things he didn't deserve.

# CHAPTER 14

Jane was already in the drawing room when Anne walked in on Thursday evening. Anthony hadn't yet returned from Westminster. Rafe, as well as her godfather and Lorcan, would arrive shortly. She was nervous about having them all together, but hopefully Lorcan's presence would ensure his father and Rafe got along. She'd tried to speak with Lorcan about whether his father meant to contest Rafe's claim, but hadn't been able to.

"Your ring is so beautiful," Jane said, taking Anne's left hand and holding it up so the diamond and emeralds sparkled in the light of the chandelier.

Rafe had given her the betrothal ring the night before at his sister's house. It had been a wonderful evening of warmth and laughter. Of family. Despite that, there'd been something off about Rafe, as if the darkness she sometimes sensed inside him had been more present. Unfortunately, she hadn't had an opportunity to speak with him about it. They'd only been alone a scant few minutes at the start of the evening when he'd given her the ring before his sisters had excitedly burst in to congratulate them.

Anthony strode into the room, making his way directly to Jane and placing a kiss on her cheek. He looked a bit harried. "My apologies for nearly being late."

Jane took his head. "Is everything all right?"

"Depends on what that means, I suppose. It's all right for me. And for you, probably. For Anne's betrothed?" He sent a sympathetic glance toward Anne.

Anxiety pushed at Anne's chest. "What happened?"

"It's expected that the attorney general will refer Mallory's claim to the Committee for Privileges tomorrow."

"That's what's supposed to happen," Anne said, wondering why Anthony thought this was bad for Rafe.

Unfortunately, Purcell entered at that moment and announced the arrival of Anne's godfather and cousin.

"Good evening, my dear," her godfather said with a smile as he came toward her. Taking her hand, he settled his gaze on her ring. "My but that is...large."

"It's spectacular," Lorcan said with a grin. "Congratulations, Anne."

"Thank you."

Before Anne could assess her godfather's mood, Purcell announced Rafe's arrival.

Her gaze went to Rafe, and she instantly felt calmer. His features were so familiar to her now. So beloved.

His eyes crinkled at the corners as he looked at her, but he didn't quite smile. After greeting Anthony, he moved to Anne's side.

"Good evening, Uncle," he said evenly before looking to Lorcan. "Sandon."

"That won't be my name much longer. Address me as Lorcan, if you please."

"And you must call me Rafe, regardless of my title. We are cousins, after all." Rafe extended his hand.

Lorcan shook his hand. "Yes, we are."

Anne watched her godfather's expression tighten and hoped it wasn't a harbinger for another aborted dinner like the last one. She gave him a bright smile and then put her arm through Rafe's. "I'm so pleased to have you all here for a family dinner, for that's what this is. Whatever happens, I hope this is the first of many times we share together."

She felt Rafe stiffen when she'd said, "whatever happens." Perhaps she should have worded that differently. Of course he would be the earl. She realized she was trying to lessen her godfather's pain, and that wasn't really her place. He was a grown man, and he simply had to accept that his nephew was alive and well and rightfully the Earl of Stone.

Purcell informed them that dinner was ready. They made their way downstairs to the dining room behind Anthony and Jane.

Anne clutched Rafe's arm tightly. "All right?" she murmured.

"So far," he answered quietly.

"It will be fine. Good, even. You'll see." She really hoped it would be.

They took their places at the table in the breakfast room since they were a smaller gathering, with Anthony and Jane at either end, Anne and Rafe on one side, and her godfather and Lorcan on the other.

Anne exchanged a look of hopeful determination with Lorcan, who was directly across from her. While she hadn't been able to speak with him in person, she'd sent him a note asking for his help to facilitate the nascent relationship between Rafe and Lorcan's father.

As the first course was served, Anne sent up another silent prayer that this dinner would go better than the last.

Anne's godfather took a drink of wine and set his glass back down before addressing the table. His gaze settled on Rafe, who sat across from him. "There's no point avoiding the issue that is likely occupying everyone's thoughts. It sounds as though the attorney general will refer your claim to the Committee for Privileges tomorrow. The entire matter could very well be decided by early next week."

"That is my understanding, yes," Rafe said, his tone as measured as it had been in the drawing room. Something, however, simmered beneath his calm surface. Anne felt it more here than she had upstairs. Her hope for a pleasant evening began to dim.

Anne looked between the two men and noted the frigidity in each of their gazes. Something wasn't right. Why would Rafe ask to get to know his uncle better, to forge a relationship, and then look at him like this?

And her godfather… Had he decided to contest Rafe's claim? Anne's stomach twisted into a knot. She should have told Rafe and now regretted not doing so. Placing her spoon on the table as her desire to eat fled, she clasped her hands in her lap.

The current earl—Ludlow—stared at Rafe with a palpable arrogance. "I expect you think this matter will be settled quickly and in your favor. I wouldn't be so certain if I were you. My contest to your claim is even now being delivered to the Prince Regent and the attorney general."

Rafe set his spoon down and barely rested his palms, flat, on the table on the outside of his place setting. Anne could see the tension in his fingers and the tendons of his wrists.

"Why are you contesting my claim? You don't argue that I'm not, in fact, your nephew, and as such, the rightful heir."

"That is true, but in this instance, one must determine who is best to hold the title. I *do* argue that is not you." He picked up his wine, and the air in the room was as thick as cold butter. "You seem surprised, which in turn surprises me. I would have thought my goddaughter would have told you I was considering this action."

Rafe's head turned toward her slowly. His features were impassive, but in his eyes, there was the barest flash of hurt.

Anne reached for him, her fingers lightly grazing his thigh beneath the table. His leg twitched, and she snatched her hand away. He was angry with her. Disappointed.

As he should be.

She'd hoped, foolishly, that her godfather would come to accept Rafe and the fact that he would be the earl. It seemed her godfather was not the man she thought.

Lorcan's brow creased as he looked at his father. "Why would you contest Rafe's claim? You've no idea what sort of earl he will be. Furthermore, it doesn't matter what you think, because the title is *his*."

"As I've said to many people, including you and Anne, on many occasions, it is up to me to see to the welfare of all the people at my estates. They depend upon the earl—me—to provide them with their livelihood. I also have responsibilities to our government, to the people of our kingdom. Knowing what I have learned about my nephew has led me to believe he cannot carry out these duties. Nor should he."

What was he talking about? What had he learned? "I told you what a good man he is," Anne blurted, glaring at her godfather. "How he helps people."

Ludlow looked at her with a mix of condescension and sympathy. "That is what you said, yes. However, that is not who he really is. Did you know your betrothed has gone by many names?"

She knew he'd been Blackwell and then Bowles. Lifting her chin, she gave her godfather a cold stare. "Yes."

"Did you know he was a man called the Vicar?"

Anthony abruptly stood. "Enough. Stone, I think you should go."

Jane also rose, her eyes round. "*He's* the Vicar?" She looked toward Rafe in disbelief, then frowned at her husband.

Anne looked around the table in confusion before fixing on Rafe beside her. "Who is the Vicar?"

"I am," Rafe said softly, his gaze trained across the table on his uncle. "You've done some investigating, I see."

"Yes, and my response to your claim details all of it: that you are a criminal moneylender known as the Vicar, that you led gangs of thieves and owned many receiver shops with which to fence the items the children who worked for you stole—"

"*Stop.*" Rafe cut him off, his voice icy and sharp.

Anne tried to process what her godfather had said. Rafe was a criminal?

Jane stepped out from her chair, staring at her

husband. "I can't believe you let my sister become betrothed to him!"

"He said he'd tell her everything, and I was stupid enough to believe him." Anthony glared at Rafe.

Rafe turned in his chair toward Anne, his face still devoid of almost all emotion except a simmering rage. "I should have told you all this, and I'd planned to. I just..." He glowered toward his uncle, his lip curling and his hands clenching into fists. In that moment, he appeared a criminal, like a man who could hurt someone without much effort or concern.

Ludlow's eyes glittered across the table. "Don't forget to tell her how you worked closely with her former betrothed, how Chamberlain delivered gentlemen in need of loans to the Vicar's doorstep and how you took advantage of their desperation."

Now Anne stood, unable to remain still another moment. But her legs shook, and she had to clasp the back of the chair for support. "You knew Gilbert?"

"Yes."

"Did you know I was marrying him?" She put her hand over her mouth as bile rose in her throat. "Would you have let me?"

Rafe bolted out of his chair and took a step toward her. "Never. I've thought of killing him for bringing you shame." His jaw clenched.

"You'd kill him..." She shook her head, her vision swimming. Lowering her hand, she fought to take a breath. "You deny none of this."

He shook his head as a glimmer of sadness, and perhaps regret, flickered in his eyes. "No. I was a thief. I worked for one of the most powerful criminal bosses in East London. As the Vicar, I lent money at illegally high rates, including to your brother-in-law, to whom Chamberlain introduced me."

Anne couldn't believe how wrong she'd been about this man. "You told me you'd disappoint me, that I couldn't know who you really are." She wrapped her arms around her middle as if she could stop the pain slashing through her. "But I didn't listen." She'd been such a fool.

"I'm glad you didn't."

She opened her mouth, but only a sob came out. Her hand itched to slap him, to physically hurt him the way he was hurting her. "You're a blackguard," she breathed before running from the dining room. She didn't stop until she reached her sitting room on the second floor.

A moment later, Jane came inside, her face drawn. "Anne? Oh, Anne." She rushed forward and put her arms around Anne, stroking her back.

Anne remained stiff and unyielding, the emotions she'd withheld when she'd run from the room locked up tightly inside her. "Two broken betrothals. Is that a record?"

Jane released her. "I don't know. Is that what you want?"

"How can I marry him? Won't he be arrested for his crimes?" Her anguish threatened to break free. She brought her hand to her mouth and bit her knuckle. Moving away from Jane, she worked to settle the hysteria bubbling inside her. "Two broken betrothals to two criminals. One thing is for certain, I think I've proven to be a bigger failure than you. Because, of course, you weren't a failure at all, but a victim of someone else's malfeasance. I, on the other hand, have attracted the worst sorts of gentlemen and not only encouraged them, but *chose* them." Anne laughed without a trace of humor.

Jane started to move forward, but Anne shook her head, stopping her. "What can I do?"

"Nothing. If Mother and Father will have me, and I doubt they will, I'll go to them. If not, perhaps I can find a position at a school or as a paid companion."

"Anne. You don't have to leave. You can stay here always. Come to Oakhaven with us. You and I can leave right away, if you want."

Anne didn't know what she wanted. At least not right now. Well, that wasn't entirely true. She knew one thing. "Would you mind just leaving me alone?"

Jane hesitated, but ultimately nodded. "I'll check on you later."

Anne didn't respond, nor did she move until Jane left the room, closing the door behind her. Then her only movement was to wipe away the tear that fell down her cheek.

~

The need to follow Anne from the dining room nearly overwhelmed Rafe. But he didn't move. Instead, he pivoted and fixed his rage on the reason for all of it: his uncle.

Mallory stood from the table, taking time to finish his glass of wine as he did so. "I suppose I should go," he said to Colton.

Colton gritted his teeth. "That would be best."

Turning to his son, Mallory set his wineglass down. "I'll wait for you in the coach if you need a minute." He moved around Lorcan and departed the dining room.

Rafe wasn't going to let him go so easily.

Stalking after his uncle, Rafe caught up with

him in the entry hall. "You won't win," he called after the man's back.

Mallory slowly turned. "This isn't a game, my boy. This is life. Unfortunately, you were dealt a bad hand—a pity, truly. But I can't in good conscience allow you to take this title. It wouldn't be right or prudent."

Rafe glowered at the footman, who retreated from the hall, before advancing on his uncle. "You dare speak to me of righteousness or prudence or conscience? You killed my parents." His voice nearly broke, and his hands twitched with the need to curl themselves around the older man's neck. "You tried to kill me too, and would have, if not for the *conscience* of my nurse."

Mallory stared at him expectantly, one of his brows arching pompously. "Can you prove any of that?"

Rafe barely held himself in check. "I will."

"I don't think so." Mallory clucked his tongue with disdain. "Because I didn't do any of it."

The smugness in his gaze told Rafe the opposite. It also told Rafe that his uncle wanted him to know, that he reveled in it. It *was* a game to him.

"He was your brother," Rafe whispered. "Your blood. As am I. As is Selina. She didn't deserve the life she's been forced to lead."

"I'm quite proud of how my niece has turned out. Her husband is the son of an earl." Mallory's imperious gaze swept over Rafe. "You've done incredibly well for yourself. That should be enough. Let it be enough."

"Father, leave him be." Lorcan came from behind, carrying his and Mallory's hats and gloves, and paused near Rafe. "I'm sorry. I didn't know he was going to contest."

Anne had known. And she hadn't told him.

Lorcan and his father left. Rafe stared at the closed door, his body thrumming with barely leashed rage. The sound of another person in the hall drew him to turn his head. Colton stood a few feet away, hands on his hips.

"You should go too." Colton sounded nearly as defeated as Rafe felt. No, not defeated. Rafe would fight his uncle with every breath he had. He wanted to fight *for* Anne with the same.

Was she better off without him? Probably. Hadn't he been telling her that since practically the moment they'd met?

Colton blew out a breath and dropped his hands to his sides. "I told you to tell her the truth. Now she's going to be humiliated again with another broken betrothal."

Rafe swallowed as Colton moved toward the doorway to the staircase hall. "You assume she's going to end it."

"What choice have you given her? The exposure of your past will take what everyone has already been talking about—your resurrection and betrothal to Anne—and twist it into an utter spectacle. After everything Anne's been through, you can't expect her to endure that again."

It was a vicious blow to his gut so that Rafe nearly doubled over. He *should* have told her. Better yet, he never should have become involved with her at all. "I would still marry her," he said softly, his soul aching.

She likely didn't want him, and he'd have to accept that. Unlike his uncle, he would.

Colton pressed his lips together. "That will be up to her."

"Will you tell her I'm sorry? And if she's willing to hear me out, I will tell her anything and everything she wants to know."

"I'll try, but I may be persona non grata tonight with Anne and my wife." Colton grimaced. "Anne may not want to see you again. Who you were is pretty damning." He rubbed his hand across his forehead. "However, I know something about redemption, and about finding someone who can not only forgive you your sins but help you forgive yourself." His eyes met Rafe's. "I'll do what I can, but expect the worst."

"I always do."

The footman had returned to give Rafe his hat and gloves. Taking the accessories, Rafe departed the house, setting off toward Upper Brook Street the same way he'd arrived: on foot.

The evening was warm, perfect for trouble. In his youth, he would have spent a night like this thieving and fighting, earning one of the myriad nicks from his opponent's knife as they fought bare-chested amidst the cheers of their comrades, the light of the moon, and the scent of cheap gin.

He crammed his hat on his head and shoved his gloves into his pocket. Perhaps he should go looking for such trouble tonight. It would be a simple thing to return to one of the neighborhoods where he'd been a prince, where men and women had flocked to his side, eager for his approval and leadership. He could get any one of them to end his uncle's existence. Rafe wouldn't even have to do it himself.

Killing was one crime he'd avoided at all costs. Except for the singular occasion when there had been no other option. When vengeance had been wholly necessary. Even now, four years later, he felt no regret.

Still, he wouldn't do it again. Unless he was driven by another's violence. Not to him, but to those he cared about. Selina. Anne.

Hadn't that violence already happened? Mallory had murdered his parents. He deserved the same fate as the man who'd killed Eliza.

A righteous anger welled within him. He abruptly pivoted and stalked back the way he'd come, passing Colton's house and ignoring the pull he felt toward Anne. Onward he kept until he reached Bond Street.

Perhaps he wasn't really meant to be the earl. Perhaps he wasn't worthy.

Hailing a hack, he directed the driver to the only place he'd ever belonged. In the rookeries of East London, no one found him lacking.

There, he could be anything he wanted. He'd just do it alone.

# CHAPTER 15

"You ride as if you were born on a horse," the Viscount Northwood, Harry's older-by-five-minutes twin brother, said as they walked their mounts from Green Park. "And this is only our second lesson. It's nauseating, if you must know."

"Thank you?" Rafe allowed himself to smile.

When Harry had suggested his brother teach him to ride, Rafe had bristled at first. But then he'd surrendered to sense. He *should* ride a bloody horse. Not just because he was going to be an earl, but because his father had wanted him to. His father had loved horses and planned to breed them at Stonehaven. Rafe was perhaps a ways off from doing that, but when he let himself look to the future—hopefully someday soon—he wanted to pursue his father's plans.

"Are you ready to tell me what happened at the dinner last night?" North, what nearly everyone called him, looked at him askance as they rode through Berkeley Square.

Rafe hoped he looked accomplished enough on the horse so as not to draw notice. At least, no more than he was already receiving by currently being the most notorious man in London. He tugged his hat lower over his brow.

Rafe had told North about the dinner on Wednesday before their first lesson. When they'd set out earlier, North had inquired about it, but Rafe had avoided the question.

"Not particularly, but you'll learn soon enough. My uncle is contesting my claim. He's using my past as an orphan in East London who had to steal to survive as proof that I'm not up to the task."

"Filthy whoreson." North gave his head a shake. "I'm sorry to hear it. I'm sure you'll prevail. No one is questioning your identity. The title is yours."

"It will be."

A short time later, they rode into the Mount Street mews. North kept his horse at his father's stable, and Rafe was borrowing the earl's horse until he went to Tattersall's to purchase his own.

As he dismounted, Rafe winced due to a sharp pain on the right side of his chest. He'd found the knife fight he'd been looking for last night.

As they handed their horses over to a pair of grooms, North's father, the Earl of Aylesbury, arrived in his coach. Stepping down from the vehicle, he blinked in surprise at Rafe. "Afternoon, Mallory. I was just thinking about you." His brow was deeply furrowed. Whatever his thoughts, they hadn't been good.

"You're just from Westminster?" North asked.

Aylesbury nodded. He eyed Rafe warily.

"I know you sit on the Committee for Privileges," Rafe said. "Don't worry, I don't plan to ask you about my claim or my uncle's counter claim. Did you receive that today?"

"A short while ago. The attorney general delivered it rather quickly since we were already taking up discussion of your claim." Aylesbury was taller than average, with a somewhat youthful appearance despite being in his later fifties. His brown hair was partially gray, making it appear light, while his eyes were a dark coffee brown. He stepped to the side so the grooms could take care of the vehicle and horses, gesturing for North and Rafe to accompany him.

"I don't feel as if I'm speaking out of turn to tell you there are some who are alarmed by the revelations in your uncle's counter claim. They plan to ask you to answer questions before the committee." He grimaced. "Is any of it true?"

"I haven't read it, so I can't say for certain. I believe he accuses me of having been a criminal?"

"Yes. A thief, a fence, and an illegal moneylender."

Rafe held his head high and kept his spine stiff. "All of that is true."

"Hell," the earl breathed, looking to the side. When he returned his attention to Rafe, his gaze had darkened. "Then your uncle may very well retain the title."

The injustice of it, given what Mallory had already gotten away with, made Rafe clench his hands into fists. "He murdered my parents. That fire was his doing. He wanted the earldom and was willing to kill my father—and me—to do it. My nurse decided she couldn't let me die, so she and her brother kidnapped me and my sister."

As he spoke, the earl's and North's eyes widened.

"Does Harry know this?" North asked.

"Yes. He's been investigating the crimes. Unfortunately, we have not been able to find proof of my uncle's involvement." A horrible, scratchy heat climbed Rafe's back and settled at his nape, making him perspire.

Aylesbury scrutinized him. "How do you know he was to blame? Don't think I'm doubting you. If Harry is helping you, I trust you are right."

"Selina and I spoke to our nurse recently. She was quite ill and has since expired, so she is unable to provide testimony."

North put his hands on his hips, his tawny eyes narrowing with frustration. "Well, that's bloody inconvenient."

"She spoke specifically about my uncle's plan to have the fire kill my father and me so he could inherit the earldom. He didn't want my mother or Selina to die, apparently." When he thought of his mother trying to save his father and dying in the process, he wanted to rage at anyone who could support Mallory's position.

Aylesbury stared past Rafe and let out a low sound. "That...makes sense." He looked at Rafe and hesitated.

Rafe's skin pricked with foreboding. "What?"

"I knew your father very well. I liked him immensely. When I think about how my son married his daughter, I'm a bit overcome." He cleared his throat, and his brow furrowed. "There was a rumor that your uncle had also fallen in love with your mother during her first Season. But she chose your father."

The heat on Rafe's neck and spine intensified. He recalled what their nurse had said about their uncle, that he'd wanted everything his brother had. Did that include his wife?

Rafe struggled to breathe. "You're saying my uncle was jealous." He tried to fight through the thoughts assaulting his brain. "What was he planning? Wasn't he married to my aunt when my parents died?"

"Yes, she didn't become ill until ten years ago or so."

"Christ, was he going to kill her too so he could have my mother?" Nausea swirled in Rafe's gut.

"I doubt he would admit it even if that were true," Aylesbury said with disgust. "We should inform the committee of all this information."

North crossed his arms over his chest. "Without evidence?"

"I think we must. I don't doubt the veracity of any of it. Why would Mallory lie?" The earl looked to Rafe. "You wouldn't, would you?"

"I've freely admitted my criminal past. That should answer your question."

Aylesbury exhaled. "Indeed it does."

"Can we assume you had a reason for that behavior?" North asked. "You were kidnapped, were you not?"

"We were. Our nurse's brother was a footman at Stonehaven. My uncle enlisted him to start the fire. The nurse was to save Selina but leave me to die. She took us both and gave us to her brother. She was afraid because she hadn't followed my uncle's instructions. Her brother brought us to London, where he used us to steal and swindle. After a few years, he sold us to a man who ran a number of gangs."

Both men stared at him, their expressions full of first shock and then sympathy.

"I am not proud of my past but I *am* proud I survived it," Rafe said. "I did what I had to do with what was available to me."

Aylesbury clenched his jaw. "Harry will find the proof you need."

"He's running out of time," North said, earning an angry glare from his father.

"Well, you have my vote." Aylesbury clapped

Rafe's upper arm. "You're part of the family, and we won't turn our backs on you."

"Thank you." It was all Rafe could think to say. He was incredibly humbled by this man's acceptance. It gave him hope that there was perhaps a small chance Anne would forgive him.

As he walked toward Upper Brook Street, his thoughts turned completely to her. He'd barely slept last night, wondering if she'd been able to find her rest.

Would she give him the chance to apologize? To explain?

He didn't know how long he could wait to find out. It seemed the more time passed, the less likely he would be able to win her back.

*Be patient.*

He wanted to scream the word no, that he was done being patient. If he waited for Harry to find proof of Mallory's crimes, justice might never be done. And if he waited for Anne to summon him, he might lose her forever.

Rafe wasn't going to let either of those things happen.

~

Moonlight spilled through the opening in the drapes in Anne's room. Lying on her side, she forced herself to close her eyes and try to sleep. Though why she expected this time would be any different from her other attempts over the past two hours was a mystery.

*Because you're a bloody optimist.*

And because she couldn't stop thinking of Rafe. Of how much she loved him. Of how she missed him. Of how hurt she'd felt.

She'd thought of little else all day, choosing to

remain in her bedchamber and sitting room in order to brood by herself. Jane had visited a couple of times, but Anne hadn't felt like talking.

Except she *did* feel like talking—just not to her sister. Anne wanted to say *many* things...to Rafe. She'd held the conversation several times in her head.

*Stop. Sleep.*

She closed her eyes more tightly and willed her body to relax. This shouldn't be difficult. She was exhausted.

Clearing her mind, she focused on the weight of her limbs, the softness of the bed, the scent of lavender from her pillow. Yes, this was better. She was so tired...

The sudden press of a hand over her mouth and the weight of a large, warm body against her back filled her with a desperate panic. She tried to breathe but couldn't. Terror streaked through her veins as her eyes flew open.

"Shh. It's me." Rafe's voice was soft and deep beside her ear, sending a shiver of longing down her spine. Her fear receded and was instantly replaced with an equally strong emotion—lust.

"Will you be quiet, or do I have to tie something around your mouth so you'll listen to me? Nod if you'll be quiet."

She nodded, and he eased her to her back. Keeping his hand against her mouth, he threw his leg over her and straddled her thighs. She bit the inside of her lip to keep from moaning. She was an absolute wanton. After he'd lied to her, she wanted him more than ever.

He slid his hand down her neck and kept his palm pressed against the base of her throat. He wasn't wearing gloves, so his flesh was bare against hers above the edge of her night rail.

Anne gulped air, her chest moving rapidly as her lungs filled and emptied. She stared up at him, her eyes wide so she could drink in the shadowed planes of his face, only partially illuminated by the moonlight.

"I'm sorry," he murmured, his hand moving down between her breasts over her heart. His pinky finger stretched over her right breast. Her nipple tingled, aching for his touch.

"How did you steal into my room?"

He gave her a lopsided smile that would have made her sigh. But that was before. As aroused as she currently was, as much as she wanted him physically, she was still angry.

"I'm a thief, remember? I'm quite good at stealing into places I shouldn't be, though I haven't done so in quite some time."

"Yes, *I* remember. It seems, however, you forgot to tell me." She kept her hands at her sides, but considered pushing him off her. Except she doubted she'd be able to. "Do you plan to sit on me all night?"

"No, just while I explain."

"I'm still angry with you."

"I can tell. You've every right to be." He pulled his hand from her, and her body rose slightly off the bed, following the appendage as a disappointing cold washed over her. "I'm so sorry, Anne."

"I want to be angry."

"Do you want to rail at me? I would only ask that you not wake the household. Unless you want company. I would prefer to suffer your verbal flaying in private. Or would you rather have an audience?"

"No." Nor did she want to castigate him. "Damn you." She pushed at his chest.

He grabbed her wrists and pinned her arms on either side of her head. "Yes. I am and have been quite damned."

He had. More than anyone should have to endure. Gritting her teeth, she glared up at him. "I still love you."

His breath caught, and his teeth flashed in the moonlight. "Good, because I love you too."

Anne gasped just before he lowered his head and kissed her. His lips commanded hers as he pinned her to the bed. Holding her fast, he plundered her mouth, each lick of his tongue and graze of his teeth igniting a new fire of longing inside her. She arched up, wanting more, and moaned with need.

Tearing his mouth from hers, he kissed along her jaw and down her neck. Hot, frenzied kisses that ravaged her flesh.

"God, I want you in every way," he rasped. He held her wrists as his mouth descended, finding its way to her nipple where he licked and sucked her through the thin lawn of her night rail.

Anne whimpered as she rose off the mattress and pushed herself into him. "*Please.*"

He growled against her and released her hands. Cupping her breast, he pulled at the top of her chemise, making a small tear in the fabric just before he latched onto her.

She cast her head back, squeezing her eyes closed and giving herself over to the mad sensation of his lips and tongue. He plucked her other nipple over and over, drawing louder and louder moans from her throat.

His hand skimmed down her abdomen, and he pushed up the night rail. When his hand slipped between her legs and found her sex, she opened her eyes and pushed at him. "No."

He stopped abruptly, lifting his head. "No?"

"You said I could be on top this time."

His frame gently sagged with relief. "I did."

"You are wearing all your clothes."

"I am." He rolled to his back. "In the interest of expediency, you need only unbutton my fall and remove my cock. That's the only part of me that really matters at the moment."

"That is highly debatable." Anne sat up and went to work removing his boots, dropping first one then the other to the floor. "I like many parts of you. All of them, actually. My only complaint is that I haven't spent nearly enough time exploring them." She pulled his stockings off next.

"I would beg of you that you don't take that time right now. I am, ah, quite desperate." His voice was low and dark, and perhaps even on the edge of breaking.

"Are you?" She straddled his knees and cupped him through his breeches and smallclothes. "Yes, I'd say you are." She flicked one button open while continuing to cradle his shaft through his clothing.

He sucked in a sharp breath, his hands gripping the bedclothes at his sides. "*Anne.* Please."

She released another button as she rubbed her hand along his length. "I think I'm enjoying this. Aren't you?"

"No. Yes." He threw his head back. "*Yes.*"

She quickly popped open the remaining buttons on that side of his fall and slipped her hand inside his breeches. "No smallclothes?"

"I don't always wear them." He sounded strained, as if he were being tortured.

Sliding her hand along the warm ridge of his cock, she moved her other hand lower, cupping his balls through his clothing. "Is this painful, Rafe?"

"In the very best way. Faster. *Please.*"

"You said I get to control things this time. So I think I'll go as fast as I like. I think you deserve a bit of torment, don't you?"

"Yes." He moved his hands to her thighs, his fingers digging into her. His eyes opened and found hers in the near darkness. "Do your will. I am yours."

She unbuttoned the other side and drew the flap down, exposing him. He was so hard, so hot. Heat pulsed in her sex. She suddenly felt as tortured as he looked.

"Tell me what to do," she whispered.

"Take off your gown. Now."

Reluctant to release him, she removed the garment quickly and immediately clasped him again, moving her hand along his length. She realized he wasn't wearing a coat. Just a waistcoat. And a cravat that had to be annoying. Without slowing her strokes, she reached up and pulled the knot free.

He squeezed her thighs. "Straddle my hips."

She moved up and gasped as her sex covered his. His hips rose, and she rolled with him.

He reached between them, putting his hand over hers. "Rise up, just a bit."

Following his command, she lifted slightly, and he positioned himself at her opening. "Slide down and take me," he rasped.

She slowly lowered herself, and he filled her with his flesh. She let go of his cock. He did the same as she came down completely.

This was different from the first time. She felt him in a completely new, deeper way. Sensation rocked through her, coaxing her hips to move.

He gripped her hips tightly. "*Yes.* Like that. Ride me."

*Ride.* She splayed her palms on his chest and adjusted herself until she found the perfect angle. Moaning, she began to move, gradually finding a rhythm that stroked the most wonderful spot inside her. And if she pitched forward just a bit more, he rubbed against her clitoris and…

Anne cried out as pleasure began to build inside her. He moved one hand to her breast, pulling and teasing her nipple. The resulting sensations were overpowering. She began to shake, her body pushing her to move faster, to take him deeper.

He pulled her down and suckled her breast, his hand tangling in the ends of her hair grazing her arm. Falling back, he groaned. "Yes, Anne. Ride. Harder. Faster."

Her muscles began to clench as her release floated just beyond reach. His hand moved between them and stroked her clitoris. It was all she needed to find that elusive rapture.

She cried out as her body split asunder. He clasped her hips and drove up into her relentlessly. She was practically senseless, her body a quivering vessel for his release.

He started to shout but immediately muffled his voice, throwing his arm over his mouth. Anne pitched forward, her limbs limp. He caught her against his chest and cupped the back of her head, his fingers threading through her hair. Digging his fingers into her scalp, he kissed her, claiming her again, as if she had any doubt that he owned her body and soul.

His kiss gentled, his thumb tracing the edge of her ear as he murmured her name over and over into her mouth. She sighed into him and rolled to the bed. "You're still wearing too many clothes."

Pushing herself up on her elbow she unbuttoned his waistcoat. His chest moved slightly faster than normal as his breathing regulated. She opened the waistcoat and pressed her hand beneath the garment against his shirt.

She felt something wet. "What's—" Investigating the dampness, she shot straight up, gasping. "Is that blood?"

He lazily opened his eyes and blinked, lifting his head slightly off the pillow. "That? Oh, yes." His lips spread in a satisfied grin as his lids drifted closed once more. "Last night, I was stabbed."

# CHAPTER 16

Anne leapt out of the bed and lit the candle on the side table. Holding it over him, she stared down at the slowly spreading dark red stain. "Why on earth were you *stabbed*?"

"Knife fight. You should have seen my opponent. He fared much worse."

Blowing out an agitated breath, Anne set the candle down and went to fetch the pitcher of water, basin, and a cloth.

She poured the water into the basin and wet the cloth. "You're going to bleed all over my bed."

"Damn, you're right." He opened his eyes again—finally—and sat up. "It's not that bad." He looked down and winced. "It really isn't, I promise."

"Take off your waistcoat and give me your shirt." She put her hand out as he divested himself of the garments. The waistcoat went onto the floor, and he delivered the shirt into her grasp. "This is probably ruined."

"I'd ruin a thousand of them if it meant I could have tonight. With you."

A flush of heat raced through her as he scooted closer to the edge of the bed. She gently pressed the damp cloth on the cut, dabbing up the blood.

Pulling the cloth back to find a clean area, she pressed down on him again, drawing a soft gasp from his lips.

"Do you need stitches?" she asked.

"No."

"How do you know?"

"*You* asked me. Why would you *think* I'd know?"

She looked at the many scars marking his chest, shoulders, and arms until settling on the scar cutting through his chin and lower lip. "This was not your first knife fight."

"No."

"Why?" She held the cloth against his wound and with her other hand, ran her thumb over a scar on his left shoulder, then another on the front of his upper arm. That one was long, maybe four inches.

"When I was young, it was how we gained respect and exerted our dominance. Proving your strength was critical to survival. Not just for me, but for Selina. Before I sent her away to school."

"*You* sent her away."

He nodded. "She would have been raped and forced into prostitution if I didn't."

Anne swallowed. She couldn't imagine such a life. "How old were you?"

"Fourteen. She was eleven. I'd saved enough by then to pay for her school, and I kept moving up in the ranks. By then, I was running one of Partridge's receiver shops."

"What's that?"

"A place where we fenced stolen goods. The gangs of thieves would steal the items, and I would sell them. I ran several of them by the time I was sixteen. Partridge trusted me. He liked me."

"Who is Partridge?"

Rafe's features hardened. "*Was.* He was the man

who purchased me and Selina from our 'uncle'—the man who kidnapped us from Stonehaven. He was a footman there, and his sister was our nurse."

Anne fought against the tide of emotion welling up within her. Lifting the cloth, she studied the gash. Perhaps two inches wide with neat edges, the damage didn't look great, especially since the bleeding had stopped. "You need a bandage."

She started to turn, but he gripped her upper arm. His eyes were dark and intense, the fiery orange spot burning with promise. "It will be fine. For now." He took the cloth from her fingers and scooted toward the center of the bed before adjusting the pillows and settling back against the headboard. "Sit with me."

Anne climbed onto the bed and sat next to him. She laid her head on his shoulder.

"You are the loveliest nursemaid." He put his arm around her and draped the cloth over his cut.

"Why did you get into a knife fight last night?"

He exhaled, his fingertips stroking her arm. "After the dinner, I found myself going to the only place I truly know, the only place where I belong. Or used to, anyway."

She angled her head so she could see his face. "The men there fight with knives like the children do?"

"Mostly for money, but also for the other reasons I mentioned before. I thought it would make me feel…not better, but more like myself."

"And did it?"

He shook his head.

She traced the scar on his chin, starting at the base and slowly moving up to his lip. "And this was from a fight?"

"A particularly fierce one. I was seventeen. The other lad wanted to kill me."

She tensed, lowering her hand to his chest. "Did you—"

"No, but Partridge had it done. He didn't want anyone to question my authority again. That was the last time I fought, until last night."

"That you managed to survive your childhood is astonishing." Anne's throat tightened. "Not only that, but look at what you've built, what you've become. And I don't mean an earl. Even if you weren't going to be ennobled, you've accomplished so much. You seem destined to be great."

"It never felt like that. Every day was a struggle."

"Even the days with your wife?" she asked softly. When he stiffened in response, she blurted, "I'm sorry, I shouldn't have asked you about her."

He pulled the cloth away from his chest and tossed it to the side of the bed. "I'm glad you did. I won't keep anything from you. Not anymore." He turned, and she lifted her head from his shoulder. "What I wanted more than anything was a family. I lost my parents, I missed my sister. By the time I was twenty, I was smart enough to recognize that Partridge and the other men in his employ were *not* a family. Still, it was the most secure I'd ever been, and at that time, Selina was lost to me. She'd left the boarding school to take a position as a governess." His eyes briefly closed, but not before she saw the flash of pain in their depths.

She didn't want to interrupt, so she waited for him to continue. In the meantime, she skimmed her fingertips across the varied slopes of his muscled chest.

"When I was twenty-five, I fell in love with Eliza. She was the daughter of a cobbler. Dark-haired and so full of vibrancy and laughter, she was everything I dreamed. Her father didn't like me, but she believed he would come around. I wanted to earn his approval, and not just for her, but for me. I craved her family, that sense of belonging that had eluded me my entire life."

His words curled around her heart and made her love for him expand. Emotion cinched her throat, and she flattened her palm against him. Perhaps the heat of his flesh would warm the chill inside her.

"I planned to leave Partridge's employ. To do that, I reinvented myself as the Vicar, a moneylender in Blackfriars."

At the mention of that name, a tremor passed through her. She wanted to ask how he'd become acquainted with Gilbert, but again, she wouldn't interrupt.

"Partridge didn't like that I left." Rafe's jaw clenched. "I was his best officer, you see. He gave me an ultimatum: return to his employment or he'd ruin my life. I thought he meant my new business endeavors. In addition to lending money, I also owned my own receiver shops—and the bookshop in Paternoster Row. And I was making other investments, looking to the future, because by then I had a wife, and soon I would have a child." His voice cracked.

Anne cupped his neck, stroking her thumb along the underside of his jaw. "I'm so sorry." She assumed he was going to tell her that Eliza had died in childbirth.

He took a deep breath and looked into her eyes. "This is where I may lose you—and I won't blame you for it. Every time I told you I wasn't worthy or that you could never know everything about me, this is what I was referring to. It isn't just that I was married or my wife died. Or even that Partridge killed her—and our unborn child."

Rafe's body went completely rigid. Anne held

her breath, desperate for him to continue and yet terrified by what he might say next.

"It's that I killed him in retribution. I stole into one of his flash-houses where he was, and I cut his throat open, just as he'd done to Eliza."

Anne clapped her hand over her mouth lest the sob gathering in her chest escape. After everything he'd endured, to suffer the loss of the family he was building was unimaginable. It was no wonder he held himself apart, that he'd tried to keep her at arm's length.

When she trusted herself to speak, she lowered her hand. "You haven't lost me. And you won't. I still love you. I will always love you."

"Truly?" He brought his hand to the side of her neck. "I can't imagine you loving me when I can't really love myself. When I lost Eliza, I lost myself. I didn't think I could be found."

"Well, *I* found you. And I'm not going to let you go."

He dragged his thumb along her jaw. "Sometimes the depth of my emotion frightens me," he said softly. "It's why I tried so very hard to hold myself from you, despite being pulled quite strongly toward you from the moment we met. Losing Eliza, discovering how I lost my parents... If I lost you—"

She shook her head fiercely, thrilling at his admission of the way he felt about her from the very beginning. "You won't."

He smiled, but there was a sadness in his eyes that pressed on her heart. "I will always be afraid of losing those I love. That's simply what happens to me."

"You haven't lost Selina."

"No, but I nearly did. We were apart for almost twenty years, and that was my fault."

She put her hands on his cheeks, holding him tenderly. "None of this is your fault. How can you even think that?"

"It's amazing what you can get yourself to believe."

"Then believe this: I love you, and you're quite stuck with me." She lifted her left hand from his face. "I have the betrothal ring to prove it."

"I was certain you'd want to cry off," he whispered.

"I was angry." The edge of her mouth lifted in a wry smile. "But I really didn't want to endure a second broken engagement because my betrothed was arrested." She inhaled, the smile fading. "You aren't going to be arrested, are you?"

"I don't think so. At least not according to Harry."

"He would know." Anne caressed his jaw, his collarbones.

He put his hand on her thigh, the warmth of his palm heating her skin. "You had every right to be angry, particularly about Chamberlain. He's a blackguard. I've had to talk myself out of having him thrashed in Newgate."

"You could do that?"

"I know many people," he said darkly.

"How did you meet Gilbert?"

"He came into a gaming hell I owned near Covent Garden."

She gaped at him. "You also owned a gaming hell?"

"Two. I sold them last year." His fingers skimmed along the rise of her hip.

"Is there anything you haven't done?"

One side of his mouth ticked up. "I haven't been an earl."

"Not yet," she said with determination. "You need a bandage. And some rest."

"Are you inviting me to stay?"

She slipped from the bed and picked up her dressing gown from the bench at the foot. "For a while."

"I'll go before it's light."

Tying thc gown closed, she went in search of something to use as a bandage, eventually finding an old petticoat in the bottom drawer of a dresser. She tore a strip of fabric from the hem and hoped it would stretch around his chest. To be sure, she ripped off a second length.

When she returned to the bed, he was under the covers, which were pulled up to his mid-abdomen. Half the rigid muscles were visible, and she licked her lips. He was so very handsome.

"Are you going to stare at me or put the bandage on?"

Exhaling, she busied herself with the task of tying the strips of cloth together and then wrapping them around his chest, taking care to cover his wound. She knotted the ends over his sternum and surveyed her work. "That should be fine, provided you don't exert yourself."

"That's a shame."

"What manner of wife will I be if I don't look out for your welfare?" She removed her dressing gown and lay it back on the bench before sliding into the bedclothes.

Before she could reach his side, he turned and drew her back to his chest. "We will try to sleep, then." He kissed her temple, her cheek, the spot below her ear, his breath tickling her flesh.

Anne sighed, settling back against him and reveling in the warmth of his embrace. This was all she'd ever wanted. No, it was more than that.

This was heaven.

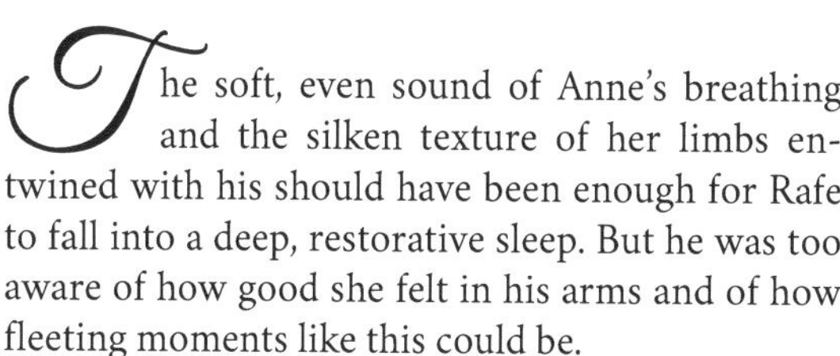

The soft, even sound of Anne's breathing and the silken texture of her limbs entwined with his should have been enough for Rafe to fall into a deep, restorative sleep. But he was too aware of how good she felt in his arms and of how fleeting moments like this could be.

He closed his eyes and buried his face in the fragrant softness of her hair. Nuzzling the back of her neck, he gently cupped her breast.

"It doesn't feel like you're trying to sleep," she whispered.

"Just getting comfortable."

She wiggled her backside against his erection. "Is that what this is?"

He laughed against her neck and kissed her shoulder. "I can't help it if you're irresistible."

"I won't contribute to making you bleed again."

"You don't have to." He trailed his lips across her flesh as he lightly teased her nipple. "You don't really need to move at all."

She arched slightly when he pinched her flesh between his fingers. "Mmm. I don't know if I can stop myself."

"Actually, you will need to move your leg a bit." He reluctantly released her breast and skimmed his palm down her abdomen before bringing it across her hip. "Like this." He gripped her thigh and bent her leg at the knee. "That's better." He traced his fingertips along the back of her thigh and up along the curve of her backside. Dipping the pad of his forefinger into the cleft, he moved down and then forward until he found her wet sheath.

Anne's muscles tensed, and she sucked in a

breath as he pushed inside her. She lifted her leg higher, granting him easier access to her sex.

"Even better," he murmured, kissing her shoulder with lips and tongue before nipping her flesh. He traced her clitoris with firm, circular strokes. Her hips moved, seeking his touch as she moaned softly.

"Please. Rafe."

He speared two fingers into her and pumped several times. "Take me into you," he whispered against her ear, moving faster.

"I want," she panted. "I want all of you. Please."

"If you insist." He snagged her earlobe with his teeth as he gripped his cock and guided himself to her sex. "Arch your back a bit, my love."

She accommodated, and he thrust up inside her, her wet heat welcoming him. He closed his eyes and moved his hand to her thigh, holding her as he rocked slowly in and out of her body.

The muscles of her back tightened against her chest, as did the ones in her leg. He could feel her working toward her orgasm and began to move faster.

He moved his hand back to her breast and thrust up deep into her, drawing a low, gravelly moan from her throat. She cast her head back, exposing her neck, and he latched onto her sweet flesh as he stroked and tugged at her breast. Her hips twitched as her sex clamped around him.

"Come for me, Anne." He pulled on her nipple and swept into her with a persistent rhythm, his own release building as pleasure suffused him.

She cried out, turning her head into the pillow to muffle the sound as her muscles squeezed his cock. He gritted his teeth to keep from shouting as he spent himself inside her.

Several minutes later, after he'd left her body,

she turned and snuggled against his side as he lay on his back, his breathing returning to normal. "That wasn't particularly restful."

"It was the best I could do," he said. "I look forward to showing you just how much I can exert myself in bed."

She cupped his cheek and drew his head toward hers so she could kiss him. "I look forward to that too, among many other things."

"I still can't believe you want to marry me after everything you've learned." He stared into her eyes as if he could look long enough to see that she'd changed her mind.

"You're a good man. You've been a victim of tragic circumstances."

He looked up at the ceiling, a familiar anger simmering inside him. "I don't like being a victim. I've worked hard to take charge and be in control. I hate feeling helpless."

"We all do." She kissed his shoulder and flattened her palm on his chest. "I hated that I felt like I had to marry Gilbert. I wanted you. And I didn't even know who you were. I regretted that anonymity pact we made more than anything."

He heard the scorn in her voice and held her more tightly. "I do too. There are many things I regret. My association with your former betrothed is near the top of the list. Not telling you about him is right there beside it."

"I am not without blame. I should have told you my godfather was thinking of contesting your claim. I love you both, and I wanted so badly for you to forge a relationship. He'd been a second father to me my whole life. I hoped he could be the same for you, especially after we became betrothed."

Rafe tensed at the mention of his uncle. "Do you love him still?"

"I don't know." Her hand pressed down on his chest. "I don't trust him. Nor do I like him."

Despite everything that had gone on between them, the secrets revealed, the wrongs confessed, Rafe hesitated to tell her what he knew he must. "I've been reluctant to share something with you. Something that will forever change your feelings for him."

She came up on her elbow and looked down at him. The blonde curtain of her hair fell on his shoulder and arm, the silken strands tickling his flesh. "This doesn't sound good at all."

"It's not. It is perhaps the worst thing you can imagine." He tried to take a deep breath, but his lungs wouldn't quite cooperate. Instead, his ribs shuddered, and ice coated his veins. "Selina and I visited our nurse a week ago. She was ill, on her deathbed, in fact, but she confirmed that she and her brother, the footman who worked at Stonehaven, were responsible for the fire and for ensuring that my father died. However, they were also supposed to see that I died too."

Anne froze above him, her eyes fixed on his, her lips parted, but no breath escaped her mouth.

Rafe continued, "The nurse couldn't bring herself to murder a child, so she took me and my sister and gave us to her brother. He brought us to London."

"What does my godfather have to do with this?" The question was a bare whisper, a dark fear she didn't want to voice or face, and he couldn't blame her.

He cupped her face, tucking her hair behind her ear. "He paid them to start the fire and ensure my father and I died in it. He wanted my mother to live, but she refused to leave without saving my father. It may be that Mallory wanted her for himself. He'd loved her too, but she chose my father."

Anne breathed, but shallowly. Other than that, she still didn't move.

"Anne? I know this is too much to bear—"

"It's *insane*." She fell back onto the bed, shaking.

Did she not believe him? Rafe steeled himself, for he had no proof beyond the words of the now deceased nurse. He rose up on his hand so he could see her face. "It is true, however," he said quietly.

Silent tears leaked from the corners of her eyes and into her hair. She opened her mouth but didn't speak, instead just gently shaking her head.

"I'm so sorry, Anne." He itched to wipe her tears away, but he still wasn't sure what she was thinking. "Should I go?"

Her gaze snapped to his. "No. Why would you ask that? And don't apologize to me. None of this is your fault—I'll keep saying that until we are quite old and gray. But it also wasn't the whim of fate. My God, your uncle did this?" Her voice diminished as she spoke until the last word was merely a breath.

"He did, and the worst of it is that I have no evidence."

She pushed herself to sit up and he did the same. "What about your nurse?"

He grimaced as his frustration boiled. "She died."

"And her brother is also dead?" At his nod, she narrowed her eyes, her features tightening with determination. "There has to be something."

"Harry is looking. He sent someone to Stonehaven who interviewed everyone who worked on the estate when the fire happened. They recounted details that support the nurse's story—they didn't find my or Selina's bodies, and the nurse and her brother, a footman, disappeared after the fire."

"Well, that *is* something."

He slumped back against the headboard. "It's not enough. Not when Mallory has submitted a counter claim detailing my crimes and unworthiness to hold the title. It's not as if he's lying about that."

"Perhaps not, but he *is* lying. And I'm going to prove it. He trusts me. I'll get him to confess."

Rafe sat up straight and clasped her shoulders. "Absolutely not. He's a dangerous man. If he doesn't personally commit murder, he is not above hiring it to be done."

"He's not going to murder me," she said with a certainty he would never possess. "But maybe he'd murder you. He meant to when you were, God, five?" Her voice broke, and tears filled her eyes once more.

Rafe put his arms around her and drew her against him. "Shhh. That was a lifetime ago. I'm here. I'm alive."

She hugged him back fiercely, squeezing him so that he could barely breathe, and he did not care in the slightest. "And I need you to stay that way." Pulling back, she tucked her wild curls behind her ears. "We need a plan. Tomorrow is the ball at Brixton Park. I can arrange to go with my godfather and—"

He took her hands. "Absolutely not. If you're going to try to get him to confess, you need witnesses. In any case, you will not be alone with him. Ever. Do you understand?"

"I understand. But you can't be there, at least not with me. I have to convince him that I'm ending our betrothal and that I hate you now, that he was right." She made a face. "I will have to work very hard not to toss up my accounts saying that."

"Please, Anne, you don't need to do this. I won't put you in danger."

"We'll plan everything perfectly." She looked away from him, her mind clearly working. "We'll need Harry and Anthony, perhaps Rockbourne too."

"You've already come up with a scheme."

Her lips curled into a smile. "Perhaps. Or at least the beginning of one."

He thrust his hands into her hair and pulled her to him for a long, searing kiss. "I never imagined I would love someone again. I never wanted to."

Her answering smile was bright and wonderful, and it filled all the darkest crevasses in Rafe's heart. "I'm glad you let down your guard and decided to let me in."

"Just promise you won't leave me." He couldn't bear to lose anyone else.

"I promise." She kissed him again, and it was as if he stood in the sun, eyes closed as delicious warmth bathed his soul.

He loved her optimism, her determination, her absolute ferocity to protect and care for those she loved. If anything happened to her as a result of this scheme, there would be nowhere Ludlow Mallory could hide that would keep him safe.

# CHAPTER 17

The summer night was warm and perfect. The moon was up, and the stars were growing brighter by the moment in a nearly dark sky. The scent of roses, honeysuckle, and fresh-cut grass filled the air. The sounds of the ball carried on the faint breeze: laughter, conversation, and the music emanating from the ballroom, though most everyone was outside, either in Brixton Park's famed maze or the surrounding area. It felt like a pleasure garden such as Vauxhall, not a private estate hosting perhaps the last large ball of the Season.

Despite all that, Anne stood near the maze with Jane and Anthony and felt none of the giddy excitement such an evening should herald. Instead, she was a bundle of apprehension as she went over their plan in her mind for the hundredth time and prayed nothing would go wrong.

If things went awry, it certainly wouldn't be because they hadn't thoroughly prepared. Or that they didn't have enough help. In addition to Anne and Rafe, their extended families were also part of the scheme—Jane and Anthony, Selina and Harry, Beatrix and Thomas. Even Harry's brother, North.

"Have you seen him yet?" Jane asked, surveying the crowd. They'd arrived nearly an hour ago and had spent time speaking with the hosts, the Marquess and Marchioness of Ripley, as well as several other friends.

"Rafe or my godfather?" Anne hadn't seen either despite looking desperately for them both. Ludlow, because finding him and luring him inside was the start of the plan. And Rafe because, well, she wanted to see him.

No, she *needed* to. Seeing him would give her all the courage she needed. Not that she was afraid. She was angry. And ready to ensure her godfather paid for his crimes.

"Mallory," Jane answered.

"No, I haven't." She'd assumed Rafe would be easy to spot, given the fact that he towered over most people. A tall, blond gentleman several yards away caught her eye. Anne took a step forward. "Is that Rafe?"

Jane clasped her arm. "You're not supposed to speak with him. In fact, if you come into contact with him, you must give him the cut direct. You've a role to play for your godfather."

"I know." And for that reason, she must not cross Rafe's path, for she really didn't want to give him the cut direct, even if it was only pretend.

Anthony leaned toward them. "Here comes Mallory." No one in their tight circle referred to him as Stone or the earl anymore. He was Ludlow or Mallory or, perhaps most often, *that blackguard*.

A rush of anticipation—and not the good kind—swept through Anne. She straightened her shoulders and hoped he wouldn't be able to see the fury beneath her lies.

Jane gave Anne's hand a quick squeeze before edging closer to Anthony on her other side.

Ludlow smiled as he approached. "Good evening, my dear Anne. Jane. Colton." He inclined his head toward Anthony who greeted him with a clipped "Stone."

Anne worried that he sounded annoyed and hoped it didn't prick her godfather's curiosity. She rushed to distract him. "Godfather! I'm so glad to see you."

"In truth, I'm surprised to see you. You avoided Society after Chamberlain was arrested, and I feared you would go into hiding again given what's come to light about your most recent betrothed." He gave her a sad look that only further exacerbated her ill feelings toward him.

Flexing her hands, she summoned a smile. "I've decided not to let your nephew get the best of me. I'm better off without him, and I want everyone to know it."

"Hear, hear!" Ludlow crowed, beaming with pride.

Anthony looked to Ludlow and then Anne. "Will you excuse us? Jane and I wish to go speak with the Duke and Duchess of Halstead."

"Of course," Anne said, eager for them to leave, for then she could get her godfather into the house where she would get him to confess his crimes while Harry and his brother North listened. She glanced toward the house, where the two brothers stood in the shadows watching for her and Ludlow.

"Have you been into the ballroom?" Anne asked. There was a chamber nearby with refreshments and separate seating areas in which to meet and gather. Adjoining that was a smaller chamber where she could get her godfather alone and leave the door ajar so Harry and North could eavesdrop.

Harry would then come in and arrest Ludlow for the murder of Rafe's parents.

"I haven't yet."

She smiled up at him eagerly. "Would you mind escorting me? I'd love to see it."

Before he could answer, Deborah strode up to them, rather, she wobbled. "Evening Papa, Anne." She frowned at Anne then took her hand. Holding it between her two palms and squeezing, Deborah looked intently into Anne's eyes. "Papa told me about my cousin—that scoundrel. It's good you found out now. Before the wedding. Can you imagine if you had a second betrothed arrested on your wedding day?"

"Deborah!" Ludlow whispered urgently. "Keep your voice down. You aren't helping dear Anne."

"No, I suppose not." She hiccupped, bringing her hand to her mouth and letting Anne go. "My apologies, Anne." Her eyes narrowed at something in the distance. It was evident she'd already had much to drink. "Look at them milling about as if they should be accepted in Society. Disgusting."

"Who?" Ludlow asked, pivoting so he could look in the direction of Deborah's gaze.

"Those pretenders—my cousin, *Selina*." She said the name as if it were a vulgarity. "And her fake sister, the bastard. I suppose I must suffer Selina's presence since she's managed to marry well, but Beatrix is a bastard and should be shunned."

Anne had been momentarily stunned by Deborah's vitriol, but managed to speak through her gritted teeth. "Except she also married well."

"Bah. She took advantage of Rockbourne. He was grieving. She's a liar and a fraud. And a bastard." Her voice rose as she spoke, and heads around them turned in their direction. It was too much to hope that no one had heard what she'd said.

"Deborah!" Anne's godfather repeated, his brows pitching low as his forehead creased.

"Excuse me, I couldn't help but overhear you, Lady Burnhope." The Duke of Ramsgate joined them. Of average height with an above average paunch, the duke was a widower and also the next-door neighbor of Beatrix. Had he come to her defense?

"I wasn't trying to be quiet," Deborah said with a sniff. "Everyone must know there is a fraud in our midst."

"I'm afraid I can't allow you to malign Lady Rockbourne." The duke turned toward where Beatrix was standing with her husband and Selina. "Beatrix, would you come here, please?"

After exchanging looks with her husband and Selina, Beatrix started toward them. Thomas and Selina followed. Though Beatrix was small in stature, she carried herself with an enviable confidence.

"Good evening," Beatrix said cheerily when she arrived. She gave Ramsgate a pleasant smile, which she also bestowed upon Anne and Ludlow. When her focus turned to Deborah, however, her smile faded and her blue eyes frosted.

Ramsgate gestured to Beatrix and spoke loudly and clearly, his gaze pinned to Deborah. "Allow me to present my daughter, *Lady* Rockbourne."

Deborah's milky-blue eyes widened and her jaw dropped. She sputtered but said nothing.

"Didn't I tell you my father was a duke?" Beatrix said quietly so that only those in their small circle, which included Thomas and Selina, could hear.

Ludlow exhaled loudly and took his daughter by the arm. "Excuse us." He gave Anne an apologetic look before steering Deborah toward the house.

*Dammit!* Anne's shoulders bunched as she watched them go. She was supposed to be in Deborah's place!

"Just like Deborah to ruin everything," Beatrix said with a quiet heat.

Selina murmured in agreement before smiling broadly. "But that was brilliant." She turned to Ramsgate. "I don't know what provoked you, but thank you."

"Yes, thank you." Beatrix stared at her father. "I don't know what to say."

"You don't need to say anything." The duke's voice was gruff. "I should have claimed you long ago, at least when you came out this Season. Although, you didn't need my help to marry well." He nodded toward Thomas, who inclined his head in return. "You have my thanks. I am glad to be on good terms with my next-door neighbor again. Perhaps you'd like to come to dinner next week?"

"I would, actually," Thomas said. "And I think Beatrix's half brother would probably like to join us."

"Lovely." Beatrix looked so happy that Anne nearly forgot about her own consternation.

Shaking her head, Anne was about to excuse herself so she could follow Ludlow and Deborah, but she couldn't really do that by herself. Well, she *could*, but she shouldn't. Blast, it was annoying to be unwed!

"Selina, would you mind accompanying me inside to the retiring room?" Anne asked.

"Not at all." Selina gave Beatrix's hand a squeeze and sent her a wide grin before joining Anne and going toward the house. "Deborah does her best to be awful, but we'll find a way to turn this to our advantage."

Anne hoped she was right. "Let's hurry."

They picked up their pace, and as they neared the house, Anne made eye contact with Harry, who nodded in response.

When they reached the door, Selina stopped. "I'll leave you here. Good luck."

"Thank you." Anne went inside to the saloon, a large room with several seating areas. One, in a far corner, was occupied, and Deborah was lying on a chaise in another corner.

Eyes closed, with her hand draped across her forehead as if she'd fainted, Deborah looked pale. Anne had no sympathy for her.

Poking her none too gently, Anne leaned down. "Deborah."

"What?" Deborah's eyes fluttered open, but only barely. "Oh, Anne, it's just you." She closed her eyes once more.

Normally, Anne would ask after her welfare, but she had one objective, and it was imperative she complete her task. She also didn't particularly care to make nice with Deborah and probably never would again. "Where did your father go?"

"That way." Deborah waved her hand in no particular direction.

"Deborah, open your eyes," Anne said sharply. "Where did he go? Show me."

Deborah's lids slowly lifted. She pointed to a doorway to her left. "That way."

Towards the ballroom. Good. Anne exhaled as she went in the direction Deborah indicated. She didn't give Deborah a second thought.

The next chamber was a sitting room with two doorways. The first led to the ballroom. Anne could see couples dancing and hear the music. It was possible he'd gone there, but Anne decided to try the other door.

As she approached, she heard voices.

"Tall, imposing bloke with the nasty scar on 'is chin. Blond, ye said?"

Anne stopped and listened, surprised at the coarse speech here of all places. They had to be talking about Rafe. Tensing, she edged closer to the door, which was open just the tiniest sliver.

"Yes. Why isn't he dead yet?" Ludlow's voice was easy to discern.

Fear sliced through her. She hoped Harry and North would arrive soon.

"We want the money first."

"That was not our arrangement," Ludlow said testily.

"What 'ave we 'ere?"

The door opened suddenly. A hand grabbed Anne by the forearm and yanked her inside. The door snapped shut behind her.

Anne gasped as all heads in the room turned toward her. Besides her godfather, there were six men, all dressed as if they belonged here at a Society ball, but judging from their speech, they clearly did not.

"I was just looking for you," Anne said to her godfather, her heart beating wildly.

"She were listenin'," the man holding her arm said. "I saw 'er through the crack in the door."

Ludlow took a few steps toward her, his gaze wary. "Anne, what did you hear?"

"Nothing." She hoped they couldn't see the fear in her eyes or the throb of her pulse in her throat.

"She's lyin'." The man gripped her arm more tightly. "I can feel her shakin'."

Exhaling, Ludlow wiped his brow. "Anne, dear. You shouldn't have come here."

"We can take care of 'er when we take care of yer nephew."

Anne's breath snagged, and she struggled not to make a sound despite the fear curling around her chest.

Ludlow tossed a glare at the man who'd mentioned Rafe. "Do be quiet." He sighed as he contemplated Anne. "I don't know what you've heard, but it can't be nothing. You do look rather frightened."

Her mind scrambling, she fought to come up with something to say. "Only because you're meeting with men who sound like…ruffians."

"You heard them mention my nephew."

"Yes." Anne tried to remain calm even as her arm began to ache from the brigand's grip and panic clawed at her insides. "But why should I care? I want nothing to do with him. I despise him."

Ludlow smiled. "Of course you do. After tonight, he will never bother you again."

This was not anything they'd planned for. And it suddenly seemed an obvious oversight. The man had killed before to gain the title. Why wouldn't he do it again to keep it?

Because it had seemed he had another plan to get what he wanted, to simply ruin Rafe's chances to be named the earl.

"You plan to kill him?" She spoke loudly, hoping that Harry and North were by now in the next room.

His brow furrowed, and he actually had the gall to look distressed. "I didn't say that, did I?"

"She 'eard what Renny said," the man holding her snapped. "About taking care of 'er as well as yer nephew. And I told ye she were listenin'."

"No one's 'taking care' of my goddaughter. Come, Anne, you can leave with me now."

The man who'd been standing closest to Ludlow pulled a pistol from his coat. "Best to make sure she doesn't talk."

"No!" Ludlow took her hand and pulled her away from the man, bringing relief to Anne's arm. "She'll leave with me."

"I can't just leave," Anne said, flailing for any reason to stay and prevent them from killing Rafe. "My sister will miss me."

"We'll send a footman to tell her." Ludlow nodded at one of the men. He and another left the room via another door. "There, now you can leave with me. I'm going to Ivy Grove. You can spend the night. Lorcan is supposed to come too. He's around here somewhere." He started to pull her toward the door the other men had just left through.

Anne dug her heels into the carpet and pulled her hand from Ludlow's. "No. I can't leave."

"She's goin' to warn 'im," the man with the gun said. "Ye can't trust 'er."

"Of course I can," Ludlow said. "Can't I, dear?"

She took a step backward. "I can't go with you, Godfather, not without speaking to Jane. Let me go and do that. In fact, why don't you come with me?" She started toward the door, but the man who'd pulled her into the room beat her to it. He wasn't very tall, but he was thick and menacing just the same. He bared his teeth, two of which were missing in the front.

"She's goin' to ruin the plan." This came from behind Anne. *Close* behind her.

Before she could fully register the fear rising in her throat, everything went black.

~

Keeping his distance from Anne—and the entire start of the plan—was driving Rafe crazy. He'd arrived at Brixton Park with Selina and Harry, but had separated from them early on. Harry was staying close to the house, along with his brother, watching for when Anne lured her godfather inside.

They'd discussed the plan thoroughly and repeatedly, but that didn't alleviate Rafe's anxiety in the slightest. He still worried something might go wrong, and here he was on the other side of the maze, separated from all of them.

He was also the object of many people's interest, some of whom approached him to brazenly ask about his claim to the earldom. Most, however, looked at him from a distance and spoke amongst themselves. And Rafe didn't give one whit.

A footman came by with a tray of champagne. Rafe took a glass and nearly downed the entire contents in one drink.

He caught sight of Harry, Selina, Beatrix, Thomas, and North stalking toward him and clenched the glass so tightly in his hand that it broke, cutting his thumb. He shook his hand out, dislodging the bits of glass from his flesh.

To a one, their expressions were grim. An icy fear that Rafe had only experienced once before in his life slowed the blood in his veins. "*What?*"

It was Harry who spoke. "Anne's gone. We followed her into the house, but we were waylaid by Deborah. She made quite a scene, and by the time we extricated ourselves, we couldn't find Anne or Mallory."

Rafe ran his shaking hand through his hair. "Let's split up and look for her."

Harry nodded. "We were thinking the same."

"We'll recruit Anthony and Jane too," Thomas said, "And Ripley. I'm sure he'd want to help, and he can rally his servants to the cause. I'll take care of it." He took himself off.

North started to turn. "I'll go to the stables."

"He wouldn't take her into the maze, so I don't think we need to look there," Harry said.

Rafe felt an overpowering sense of helplessness. He couldn't breathe. "Do you think he took her from the estate?"

"It's possible. I'll hunt down his coach." Harry gave Rafe an anguished stare. "I'm sorry."

"We'll stay with Rafe," Selina said, quickly squeezing her husband's hand before he left.

Rafe started around the maze toward the house. "We need to look. Did they search the entire house?"

"I think just the downstairs. They wanted to let us—and you—know what happened before too much time had passed."

How much time? How long had Anne been gone? He stopped suddenly.

"What is it?" Beatrix asked from his left. Selina stood to his right.

"Are we even sure Mallory took her? He wouldn't hurt her, I don't think." Hell, could he really be certain of that? The man had murdered his own flesh and blood. Rafe felt sick.

As Rafe struggled to draw a breath and calm his racing pulse as well as his careening insides, a footman in sharp blue livery walked straight toward him. Good, Ripley had already engaged the retainers. Perhaps they'd found her!

"Mr. Mallory?" the footman asked.

"Yes?"

"I've a message for you from Miss Pemberton. You're to meet her at the folly."

Rafe's heart beat even faster. "Where is that?"

The footman pointed away from the house down a hill. "It's not terribly large, but you can't miss it. Would you like me to take you?"

"No. I need you to find Lord Northwood and Mr. Sheffield or Lord Rockbourne and tell them we've gone to the folly to find Miss Pemberton."

The footman nodded once. "Yes, sir."

Rafe spun about and strode toward the hill.

Selina and Beatrix had to practically run to keep up with him. Hell, why wasn't *he* running? They'd reached the top of the hill, and he broke into a sprint, letting gravity help him along the way.

"Rafe, wait!" Selina called, but he didn't slow.

At the base of the hill, he caught sight of the pale stone of the folly. It was smaller and far less ornate than the one at Ivy Grove. This looked more like the partial ruins of an abbey that Henry the Eighth had destroyed.

"Anne?" he called as he arrived at the folly, his chest heaving.

A dark figure stepped out from behind one of the walls, his hand arcing up. Rafe ducked and drove forward with his shoulder, catching the man in the groin. The brigand collapsed with a grunt, but another took his place, his arm coming down and the blade in his hand glinting in the moonlight. Rafe tumbled to avoid the blow and immediately rolled to his back. The floor of the folly, made of flat rocks pieced together, did not make for a soft landing.

He stood over Rafe and snarled, brandishing the knife as he bent. There was a flurry of activity then, of dark red and turquoise skirts swirling and multiple bodies moving. The man above him groaned and pitched forward. Rafe rolled to the side, narrowly avoiding his falling body.

Jumping to his feet, Rafe whipped his knife from his boot and started toward another villain. Glancing around the folly, he counted four men on their feet with the fifth on the ground. Plus Selina and Beatrix, who were wielding their own knives.

"Come at me!" Rafe yelled, trying to distract the men from his sisters. And yes, Beatrix was his sister in every way that mattered, in a way that blood, such as that which he shared with his uncle, did not.

Two of the men turned their attention to Rafe. One called, "Flank him!"

Rafe was ready for them. He held up his right arm as a shield while wielding the knife in his left. That his left was his dominant hand usually gave him an advantage, as his opponents weren't expecting that.

Holding off one with his arm, he lunged toward the other, aiming his knife for the underside of the man's chin. While the one man's blade sliced through Rafe's sleeve and nicked his flesh, he caught the other's jaw. Unfortunately, he moved fast enough to avoid real damage.

With a low growl, Rafe threw his leg out and tripped the man who'd cut his arm, sending him to the ground.

"Rafe, I have a pistol!" Beatrix shouted.

"Use it!" he called.

The report of the weapon filled the night air as one of the men fell to the stones.

Suddenly, there were more people, and a moment later, the remaining three brigands were on the ground.

Harry stood over them, pistol in hand. "You're

all going to face the magistrate. I work for Bow Street."

One of the men swore.

Rafe moved to stand next to Harry. "Where is Anne?"

The trio stared up at him but said nothing. He bent down and grabbed the one on the left by the front of his coat. "Tell me where she is, or I will cut out your entrails and make you eat them."

The color drained from the villain's face as he looked wildly toward Harry. "Ye can't let 'im do that."

"I don't think I can stop him. After all, he's only trying to prevent you from escaping. Who are you working for?"

"No one," snapped the man in the middle.

Rafe dropped the first man and transferred his attention to the one who'd just spoken. "You just happen to find yourself dressed like Quality in the middle of a ball to which you weren't invited with the intent of luring me away." He put his foot on the man's neck. "Who are you working for?"

"I'd tell him if I were you," Harry said blandly.

Eyes wide, the criminal blurted, "Lord Stone. He took the chit with him."

Rafe pressed his boot down. "Where?"

"Ivy something," the man croaked.

"Ivy Grove," Rafe said as he turned and started from the folly.

"Wait!" Harry called, grabbing him by the arm. "You can't go alone."

"I don't care who comes with me, but I'm going *now*."

Anthony and Jane arrived with their host, Ripley. The latter man frowned as he surveyed the scene in the folly. "Bloody hell," he muttered.

"Ripley, we need horses," Harry said.

The marquess nodded. "Tell the head groom at the stable I said to saddle whatever you need."

Rafe started toward the house. He was only vaguely aware of the stable's location, but he'd find it. He ran, but not at the sprint he'd used to get to the folly.

"This way," Harry said, bumping his arm as he ran by.

Following him, Rafe was heartened to see that not only Harry had come along, but also North and Anthony. They arrived at the stables a few moments later, and Harry took charge, for which Rafe was most grateful. His emotions were a jumbled wreck. He couldn't imagine Mallory would hurt his goddaughter, but he'd already concluded the man was capable of anything.

If he hurt Anne…

Waiting for the horses to be readied was agony. Rafe paced as the three other men stood stoically. When at last the horses were saddled, Rafe asked which was the fastest.

The head groom indicated a tall black one. "This one here."

"Are you certain you wish to ride that horse?" North, of course, was aware firsthand of Rafe's limited skill.

Rafe understood the man's concern. "Yes." Rafe pulled himself onto the beast's back.

"Right behind you," North said, climbing onto another horse.

They left the stable yard at a walk, and it was an interminable several minutes before they navigated past the dozens of vehicles that had made the trip from London. But once they reached the open lane, Rafe kicked the animal into a full gallop and hoped he possessed enough skill to catch his malevolent uncle before it was too late.

# CHAPTER 18

The swaying of the coach turned Anne's stomach as she fought her way to consciousness. Her head throbbed, and it took her a moment to recall what had happened. Actually, she didn't know what had happened at all after one of her godfather's accomplices had hit her.

Opening her eyes the tiniest amount, she saw the dim interior of the coach. She was on the rear-facing seat, lying down, with her feet dangling over the cushion. Her godfather sat on the opposite seat, his head cast back, eyes closed.

They hit a bump, and Anne groaned as pain exploded in her head. She lifted her hand to press against her skull.

"You're awake," Ludlow said. His voice actually held a tinge of concern, and for that Anne wanted to smack him. She wanted to smack him for many things.

"Where are we going?" she croaked.

"Ivy Grove."

Brixton Park and, more importantly, Rafe were behind them. "You're a horrible person," she said, struggling to sit up. Collapsing back against the squab, she breathed heavily as the pain in her head hammered in time with her pulse. "You won't be able to kill Rafe like you did his parents. He's smarter than you. More capable too. You see his background unfavorably, but he is well-equipped to survive people worse than you." She prayed he would be safe. It was one thing to know he was strong and skilled and another to keep faith that he would escape his uncle's machinations whole when his parents had not.

"Think what you must," Ludlow said coolly. "I am still your godfather, whom you have always loved. Nothing has changed."

When he put it like that, she had to fight another wave of nausea. She had loved him. Respected him. In some ways, liked him more than her own father. And he'd always been a murderer. "Everything has changed." She clenched her jaw as they hit another hole in the road. "I see you for who you truly are. I hope you hang."

He blew out a breath. "That is, I pray, unlikely. My men will shortly dispatch my nephew, if they haven't already."

Anne wished she had a weapon. "There are many who are aware of your crimes, including Rafe's brother-in-law, who is, if you recall, a Bow Street constable. You *will* hang."

"There is no proof of anything I've done." He sounded so calm, so utterly assured of himself. "I've been very careful."

"I know you plotted to kill Rafe, and I will give testimony. *That* is evidence."

He frowned at her, his eyes sad in the light from the lantern hanging on one side of the interior. "You don't have to do that. I wish you wouldn't. I don't want you to become a liability."

"You think I'll turn my head the other way and

simply continue on as if I didn't know what you are, what you've *done*?" She blinked. "You're mad."

"You may think so, but I am not. I was driven to do what was best for the earldom, for my dear Alicia."

Anne was fairly certain that had been Rafe's mother's name. "She wasn't *your* dear. She was your sister-in-law."

"Because she chose poorly. My wife was always frail. I knew she wouldn't live into middle age. Alicia and I had a chance to be happy together."

"Except she *chose* to stay with her husband, to die beside him. She chose love," Anne said softly. "Love always wins."

"One can hope," he said with a faint smile. "Sometimes it just needs a little help. I do hope you'll choose wisely, unlike Alicia. Just remember all the happy times we've shared and how much I love you. You've been a far greater daughter to me than Deborah." He wrinkled his nose. "Such an embarrassment tonight."

Now that Anne saw her godfather's true nature, she began to understand perhaps why Deborah was so unpleasant. She might share some of whatever made her father morally deficient, or it might be that she'd suffered as a result of his deficit.

"I feel sorry for Deborah," Anne said, putting her hands on either side of her head and exhaling. "I can only imagine what sort of negativity and malice you've fed into her mind."

"Don't pity her. She'll come out all right, just as I have. Just as I *will*."

"You won't," Anne promised, fixing him with a dark stare. "You won't retain the title, and you will hang." She simply couldn't reiterate that enough. "I will expend every ounce of energy I possess to ensure both come to pass."

His eyes narrowed. "Then you'll give me no choice. That saddens me, dear."

He sat forward in the seat and lifted his arm. Anne braced herself, uncertain what he meant to do. The sound of a gunshot rent the air, and the coach veered to the side. Ludlow fell back, and again Anne wished for a weapon so she could leap upon him and attack him.

Another pistol shot cracked, and this time, the coach careened wildly. For a terrifying moment, Anne feared they were going to topple over as they left the road.

The vehicle slowed, but only slightly. The ground was rough, and they bounced mercilessly. The ache in Anne's head intensified, and she pressed her hands more tightly to her skull as if she could relieve the pain by holding her head more still.

Suddenly, Ludlow lunged from his seat to the door and threw it open. He leapt from the coach, and the door swung wildly.

Anne fell, gasping, from the cushion as the coach hit a large bump. A horseman rode by the open door, and Anne prayed whoever it was could get the coach to stop.

For several agonizing minutes, Anne suffered the punishing bouncing of the coach over the uneven terrain. But the vehicle was slowing, thank God. Finally, it came to a stop. She fell back onto the floor, her head spinning, and closed her eyes.

"Anne!"

Rafe's voice seeped into her aching brain. He scooped her up from the floor and carried her from the coach. The soft night breeze soothed her pain. She opened her eyes, but knew who held her.

He stared down at her, his eyes wide with fear,

his face drawn with lines of distress. "Are you all right?"

She nodded and realized her error. "Ow, that hurts."

"It's all right now, my love." He carried her away from the coach. "You're safe now."

"Where is Ludlow?" She tried to lift her head to look around. "He jumped from the coach."

"I saw that." Rafe turned. "Harry's got him. And North."

Anthony rode up, leading a second horse. He dismounted and strode toward them. "All right, Anne?"

"Yes, just a nasty headache."

"Thank God." Anthony gazed at Rafe with admiration. "That was a hell of a leap."

Anne turned her head to look up at Rafe. "What is he talking about?"

"I had to jump from the horse to the coach. I shot the brigand who was sitting on the coach box. When he fell, he took the coachman with him. Someone had to stop the vehicle."

She couldn't help but smile. Capable didn't begin to describe this man. "How dashing."

Another gunshot sounded, and Anne flinched. "What happened?"

Rafe started toward where Harry and North had been dealing with Ludlow.

"I can walk," Anne said.

"But you aren't going to." Rafe quickened his pace.

"How is she?" Harry asked.

"Fine," Anne answered. "Just a headache. What happened?" She craned her neck to see, but was having difficulty. "Would you please put me down?" she pleaded. "I'll hold on to you, I promise."

Rafe set her down, but held her tight against

him. She gasped at the sight of her godfather sprawled on his back, blood spreading in a thick stain over his chest between the lapels of his coat.

"Anne?" he garbled, his eyes staring straight up at the moonlit sky.

"I have nothing to say to you," she said.

"Lorcan should be the earl, not that pretender," Ludlow managed between gasps.

Rafe moved to stand over him, taking Anne with him. "I am not a pretender," he said softly. "I'm the Earl of Stone."

Blood spilled from Ludlow's mouth as he fought to speak. No sound came out save a long, rasping breath. Then he was still.

"I'm sorry, Anne," Harry said. "He pulled a pistol from his coat. I had to shoot."

"I understand. You did what you had to." She ought to feel sad, but she was angry with herself for standing by this horrendous man, for believing that he was struggling with the loss of the life he'd known. But it was a life he'd stolen from the man beside her.

She was also relieved that Rafe was, indeed, still standing beside her. Turning toward his chest, she reached around him and clasped his right arm. He winced as soon as she touched him.

"Are you all right?" She let go and wished for more light so she could see if he was wounded.

"Just a nick on my arm."

She frowned at him. "What is a nick to you may be a gaping wound to someone else."

"It really is only a scratch. I promise, my love."

For now, she'd take his word for it. "How did you find me?"

"Mallory attacked the wrong people," North said with a shake of his head. "They lured Rafe to the folly at Brixton Park, presumably with the intent of killing him. They didn't realize he'd have his sisters with him, and that they are every bit as skilled with a knife as Lord Stone here." He inclined his head toward Rafe to indicate he meant the true earl.

"Are they all right?" Anne asked, shocked. "Selina and Beatrix, I mean. I don't care about the men who were working for my godfather."

"Yes, they're fine," Harry said. "And most of the men will be able to stand trial."

Anne looked down at her godfather. "He was mad." She clutched Rafe more tightly.

Harry raked his hand through his auburn hair. "I need to find the coachman and that last brigand."

"I'll help," North said, and Anthony joined in.

A coach stopped on the road, which was perhaps a quarter mile distant. "Rafe?"

Anne recognized Selina's voice.

"Here!" Rafe called.

A few minutes later, Selina, Beatrix, and Jane arrived, the latter of whom rushed forward and enveloped Anne in a tight hug. Though her head hurt, Anne embraced her sister with a mix of relief and overwhelming love.

"I'm so glad you're safe," Jane said through tears. Suddenly, Anne was crying too, and the pent-up emotion of the evening spilled from her as she held on to her sister.

It was several minutes before they separated. Jane wiped her face and sucked in a sharp breath as her gaze fell on Ludlow. "Is that…?"

"My godfather, yes," Anne said. "It's a long story that I will gladly tell you later. Suffice to say that I am not sorry he is dead." She suddenly felt exhausted to her very bones. The earth began to tilt. Rafe swept her into his arms before she fell.

She closed her eyes as he carried her to the

coach and placed her inside. She clasped his hand. "You're coming with me, aren't you?"

He pressed a kiss to her wrist before he climbed inside and lifted her onto his lap. "Darling, I am never letting you go."

~

The first rays of dawn speared over the horizon as Rafe stared down at his sleeping betrothed. They'd come back to Brixton Park, where he'd carried Anne upstairs to a room Ripley had prepared for her.

Rafe had no idea how the rest of the party had gone, but assumed London would be abuzz tomorrow with the story of Ludlow Mallory and his band of brigands. He didn't care about any of it, just that Anne was safe and whole.

He wiped his hand over his face and leaned back in the chair beside her bed, closing his eyes. Exhaustion weighted him, but his mind was too busy to sleep. Everything would be simpler now that Mallory was dead. No one would contest his claim to the earldom, at least.

Would it really be simple though?

He couldn't change the fact that everyone knew about his past. He might never be accepted. Hell, perhaps the Committee for Privileges might decide that Lorcan would be the better earl. Rafe wasn't sure he could bring himself to lament the loss of the title if that came to pass. Again, it only mattered that Anne was here with him and that their future lay before them.

"Rafe?"

He opened his eyes and bolted forward. "Yes?"

Anne winced as she blinked at him from the bed. "This is the worst headache I've ever had."

One of Mallory's brigands had hit her pretty damned hard. Rafe wasn't sure which one, and that was for the best since Rafe probably would have done the same to him in return.

He moved to sit beside her on the bed and gently kissed her forehead. "It will be for at least a day or so, I'm afraid."

"You're speaking from experience?"

"I've suffered a blow like that a time or two," he admitted.

She took his hand between hers. "You will never suffer again. Not while I draw breath."

"My fierce avenging angel." He laughed softly.

"I told you that you're mine. I protect what's mine."

"Lucky for me. I'd hate to be in opposition to you." He shuddered, and she laughed.

Lifting her hand to her head, she grimaced. "Ow, don't make me laugh."

"I'll try not to. At least not until you're healed."

"When will you officially become the earl?" she asked.

"I have no idea."

She looked about the room. "Aren't we still at Brixton Park?"

"Yes."

"Then ask Ripley. He's on the Committee for Privileges. He'll tell you."

Rafe chuckled. "It's the middle of the bloody night, Anne."

"After what would have been one of the best balls of the Season and is now legendary given what happened. I guarantee there are plenty of people up and about, and the host is one of them." She pushed on his chest. "Go find out."

"Why is this important right now?"

She stared at him as if he were the one with a

head injury. "Because the sooner you become the earl, the sooner you can get a special license, and the sooner we can be wed."

"Your priorities are astonishing."

"They're perfect, and I know you agree."

She was right. He did. "Fine, I'll go find Ripley. Shall I bribe him?"

She opened her eyes wider with sharp interest. "Do you think that will help?"

His answering laugh was much louder this time. "I'm trying to show that I'm *not* a criminal anymore."

"Oh, yes. That's true." She settled into the pillow, a thoroughly charming and rather satisfied smile curling her lips.

"You look pleased with yourself."

"I am. I've snared the most handsome, the most fascinating, the most *wonderful* man in London. No, the world."

It was hard not to feel flattered and...loved. Rafe swallowed past the lump in his throat. He leaned down and kissed her. "Sleep. You need it."

"I'll try." She turned and snuggled into the bedclothes.

Rafe watched her for another moment before turning toward the door. He contemplated whether he should don his coat and cravat, which he'd removed hours ago, and ultimately decided not to bother.

Before he reached the door, there was a soft rap. He opened it to find Jane standing on the other side of the threshold, her expression gently creased with anxiety. "How is she?" she whispered.

"I'm fine," Anne called from the bed.

Smirking, Rafe shook his head. "She's fine."

"Sounds like it," Jane said wryly. "I bring news

from Ripley. Do you want to hear it?" she asked loudly.

Rafe heard movement from the bed and turned to see Anne struggling to sit up. He rushed to her side to help. "You need to rest," he admonished.

"I *am* resting. I didn't leap out of bed and do a jig, did I?" She looked past him toward Jane, who'd come into the chamber. "What news?"

"It seems the members of the Committee for Privileges who were present tonight, and it was the majority of them, have already decided that Rafe will be the earl."

Anne's face brightened, and her reaction was even more thrilling than the news itself. "Truly?"

Jane nodded. "They will formalize it on Monday." She turned to Rafe and curtsied. "My lord."

As the reality of this change settled over him, Rafe began to understand just how much his life had altered and would continue to do so. He would bear no resemblance to the boy or young man he'd been. A part of him was sad. For all his mistakes and regrets, he couldn't deny who he was.

"What of my past?" he asked softly. "Didn't they care?"

"They did," Jane said slowly. "But, they understood that you were kidnapped, that you did the best you could in the life that was thrust upon you through no fault of your own. They also know of your kindness and generosity to orphans." She touched his shirt sleeve. "That speaks volumes about your true character, Rafe."

"She's right," Anne said, still beaming. "I'm so glad the committee saw that. Oh, this is wonderful. Now you can get the special license." Her brow furrowed. "Do you think you'll be able to get it on Monday, or will you have to wait for Tuesday?"

"Since you need a few days to recover, let us say

at least Tuesday, with a wedding no sooner than Wednesday." She pouted slightly, and he laughed.

"Fine, Wednesday. I suppose I can wait that long."

Rafe didn't want to wait either, but he'd managed thirty-two years without this spectacular woman. He supposed he could manage three whole days.

She narrowed her eyes at him. "But make it early on Wednesday."

He found no quarrel with that. "As early as possible."

Jane grinned. "Where will you have the ceremony?"

Rafe looked to Anne in question. "It's up to you."

"No, I want you to choose. You are embarking on a completely new life. Let us start it wherever you would like."

"I honestly don't care, so long as you're there." He turned to Jane. "We'll have it at my house on Upper Brook Street."

"Excellent. Do let me know how I can help. I'm sure your sisters will also be involved."

"Are they still here?" Rafe asked. He knew Harry had returned to London with the prisoners as well as Ludlow's body.

"Yes. Lord Rockbourne returned home to be there for his daughter in the morning, but Beatrix and Selina wanted to stay in case you needed them."

Rafe was overcome with the support of so many. "Thank you. All of you. Anne and I are so lucky to have family like you."

Jane started to turn, but paused to say, "Don't feel as if you need to come down now. Everyone is taking a rest before breakfast. You should do the same. I won't say where you're sleeping." She pressed her lips together, her eyes twinkling, then turned and went to the door.

"You're the best sister!" Anne called just before Jane closed the door behind her.

Anne scooted over in the bed and held the covers back. "You heard what she said. You need to rest."

"That is all we are doing," he said, removing his waistcoat, then his boots and stockings.

"You can take the rest off," Anne said. "I promise I won't try to seduce you. Besides, I'm still wearing my chemise."

"First, you should know by now that the presence or absence of clothing has no bearing on whether we can shag. Second, there is no *try* when it comes to seduction. You either will or you won't."

Perhaps against his better judgment, he opted for comfort over common sense and removed the rest of his clothing before sliding into the bed beside her. He gathered her gently into his arms, pressing himself to her back.

"Are you saying if I want to seduce you, I can?" she asked breathlessly. "I don't even have to put forth any effort?"

"Oh, I appreciate effort." He nibbled her earlobe. "But you mustn't exert yourself."

She wiggled her bottom against his erection. "Like you didn't the other night?"

He knew where she was going, just as he knew he was going to lose this battle. "You are utterly irresistible," he whispered against her ear as he stroked his hand along her thigh.

"Good. I was counting on just that."

# EPILOGUE

*August 1819*
*Stonehaven, Staffordshire*

After twenty-seven years, there was no indication that there had ever been a fire. The parts of the house that burned, a full two-thirds, had been repaired to seamlessly match the part that had survived. And even though Ludlow had been in charge of the renovation, Rafe didn't hate it. Because it was different—the décor inside—he felt no sense of familiarity, not like he did at Ivy Grove.

That was preferable, he'd decided. He wasn't sure he could bear that sense of having lived here, not along with the sadness he already felt knowing what had happened here.

He'd arrived four days ago with Anne, while Selina and Harry had come two days later. Finally, Beatrix and Thomas, along with their daughter Regan, had arrived yesterday.

"Are you ready?" Beatrix came out onto the terrace that overlooked the back garden where Selina and Rafe were waiting.

"I don't know," Selina whispered, her eyes tense.

"Come. It's time." Rafe offered his arms to both of them, and they left the terrace.

The path to the estate's small church with its cemetery wound up a gentle slope. It was a good half-mile distant atop a hill and obscured from the house by a copse of trees.

Rafe hesitated as they reached the gate. In the center of the cemetery sat a large tomb. The steward had said this was where their parents rested.

"You go," Beatrix said, taking her hand from Rafe's arm. "I'll be here if you need me." She gave them both an encouraging smile.

Exchanging a look with Selina, Rafe took a deep breath and opened the gate. He gestured for her to precede him.

Selina walked sedately to the tomb. Several names were carved on the outside. "How many generations is this?" She put her gloved hand over a few of the names. "Five?"

"Looks like it," he said.

She moved her fingers to the names they wanted to see: Jerome and Alicia. Their parents.

"We're here," she whispered. "Do you think they can see us?"

"I don't know." He knew it was silly, but he hoped they could. He closed his eyes tightly and tried to see them. It was hard. He couldn't really visualize their faces, just vague images of his mother's blonde hair and her coral necklace and his father's warm smile. Why did he remember that but not the color of his eyes?

He'd searched every wall in the house for a portrait of them, but there were none. And the servants, much to their dismay, weren't aware of any. They had been, to a person, kind and wonderful to him and Selina—and to their families.

"Do you think they'd be proud of us?" Selina asked, the doubt in her voice matching the emotion within Rafe.

"I hope so." He took her hand. "We did our best, Lina. We survived. They would be glad for that, I think."

"Yes." She took her hand from the stone and wiped her cheek.

Rafe didn't want to see her tears for fear they would cause his to fall. In the end, they did so anyway, making slow, wet tracks down his face.

Selina sniffed. "I'm glad they have always been together. I would want the same with Harry."

"And I would with Anne." He thought briefly of Eliza, whom he would always love and miss, but whom he'd finally been able to let go.

"I always thought we were so unlucky." Selina squeezed his hand, then pivoted to face him. "But we aren't. We can really look forward now, can't we?"

He turned to her. "I plan to. And I will always be here for you. I'm sorry that wasn't always the case."

"As you said, we survived. That's what matters." She put her arms around his middle and hugged him.

Rafe held her close and whispered, "I love you."

"I love you too."

After a few moments, they separated. Selina turned back to the crypt and pressed a kiss to her fingertips, which she then brushed over their parents' names. "I may not have known you, but I love you too."

Rafe wanted to repeat the sentiment, but he

couldn't. His throat was too tight, his emotions too strong.

Selina put her hand through his arm once more, and they turned back toward the gate. The three of them were quiet as they returned to the house.

Before they reached the terrace, Anne came running outside. "Rafe! Selina! They've found the most extraordinary thing!" Her eyes glowed with joy.

Rafe glanced toward Selina before hurrying inside to the drawing room. His breath immediately caught at the sight before him—a large portrait of a family of four leaned against a chair.

Selina brought her hand to her mouth. "Is that…?"

Harry, who was present, along with Thomas, came toward her and put his arm around her waist. "You and your parents, yes."

A sob slipped from her mouth, and Harry held her close.

Rafe walked slowly to the painting and crouched down. Now, he saw them in his mind—his mother's dazzling smile and his father's bright blue eyes. She sat in a chair holding Selina on her lap while Papa stood to the right, his hand on Rafe's shoulder. Rafe's attention was on the pair of greyhounds at his feet, one spotted and one gray. "This is Fitz and Roy," he said, smiling. He'd completely forgotten about them.

Selina's hand clasped his shoulder just before she knelt down beside him, her face close to the painting. "I can't—" She gasped, her hand going to the coral necklace at her throat. "Is that…? Is it the same?"

It was hard to tell at first glance, but Rafe

studied the necklace in the portrait and then looked at the pendant around his sister's neck. It was an exact match. "It can't be," he breathed. "That's surely impossible."

"It looks the same to me," Beatrix said softly from next to Selina. "Even if it isn't the same necklace, it looks as though it could be. Surely that's some sort of sign. I know you both think Fate is silly, but—"

"I don't. Not anymore." Rafe stood and helped Selina to her feet. How could he think that when so many things had aligned in his favor, things he didn't deserve or that should perhaps never have come to pass? His gaze settled on Anne, the second great love of his life. Yes, he believed in destiny.

"Where did they find this?" Selina asked, wiping new tears from her face as Harry came to her side.

"In a corner of the attic," Anne said cheerfully. "The housekeeper took it upon herself to search every nook after we exhausted our search. She didn't want to say anything in case she found nothing. You should have seen her exuberance."

Rafe went and took Anne's hand. "She should have been here. I must thank her."

Anne grinned. "I know she'll be delighted to see how happy you are."

Selina exhaled as she pressed her hands to her cheeks. "Oh, what a day this is."

"You haven't heard everything." Anne went to a table near the door. "The post arrived and there are letters for you and Beatrix. *From Deborah.*"

"What?" Beatrix and Selina asked in unison, their stares of disbelief first colliding and then moving to Anne.

"Yes," Anne said, delivering the letters to each of them. "She also wrote to me because she thought you might burn them before you read the contents."

Beatrix snorted. "That's the smartest thing Deborah has ever said."

"If you don't want to read them, you don't have to, but they contain apologies. At least that's what she wrote in my letter. Along with an apology to me and to Rafe."

Rafe whistled through his teeth. "Do you think she means them?"

Anne lifted a shoulder. "Does it matter? It's not as if we're going to invite her to dinner."

There was a beat of silence before everyone laughed.

Beatrix marched to the fireplace and tossed the unopened letter onto the cold hearth. Selina joined her and followed suit.

"Aren't you even a little bit curious what she said?" Anne asked. "She was quite obsequious in her letter to me."

Selina and Beatrix exchanged a look, then giggled. "Well, then, perhaps we should read them," Beatrix said. "Later." She bent to retrieve them and set them on the mantel.

As Rafe surveyed the room, he didn't think his heart could be any more full. This was the life he'd always wanted, the life he wasn't sure he would ever have.

Everyone discussed the portrait, and the housekeeper came in so Rafe and Selina were able to thank her. At length, everyone but Rafe and Anne left until they planned to reconvene for dinner.

Anne moved closer to him on the settee and leaned against his chest. "I'm so glad they found the portrait. Your family is so lovely."

"Does it make you sad?" he asked quietly,

thinking of how her mother had come to London for their wedding, but not her father.

She turned her head to glance up at him. "Why? Because my family is not quite so lovely?" She settled back against him. "No, I'm not sad. My mother apologized and made up with Jane. That's all I wanted."

Rafe wrapped his arm around her middle. "And your father?"

"He'll either come around or…he won't. But that's his concern, not mine. I am quite satisfied with my choices." So was Jane with hers. Their mother had felt horrible about the way they'd treated Jane and about the expectations they'd thrust upon Anne. That both her daughters had ended up happily wed was a gift for which she was most grateful. Her joy—and contrition—had been clear.

After several minutes, Anne turned her body so she could look at Rafe, nestling against his side. "You've gone quiet."

"I can't stop staring at the portrait." He and Selina had spent the better part of the last hour studying it intently, as if it could reveal the answers to all their questions. "I want it to talk to me, but I know it can't."

"Really? I think it does." Anne cocked her head. "It tells me your parents adored you—the way your mother is glancing toward you as she holds Selina so close. Your father's grip on your shoulder and his loving smile. I can also hear, quite clearly, how much you loved those dogs."

Rafe couldn't help laughing, and it felt so good. "I'd forgotten about them. Yes, I loved them. I wanted them to sleep with me, but Mama said no. Papa let them anyway—once or twice." He remembered their soft coats.

Anne rested her head on his shoulder. "Would you like a pair of dogs, my lord?"

"I think I would."

"Excellent. When we have a son and daughter of our own, we'll have a portrait painted just like this one."

Rafe put his arm around her and kissed her head as a lock of her hair came free. He would never tire of her optimism and her fierce confidence that she would achieve all she wanted. "I suppose we should exert some effort toward having a son or daughter."

She tipped her head back and arched a brow at him. "I think we exert plenty of effort." Pressing her hand against his chest, she slid it up beneath his cravat. "On second thought, I think we can do better. I'm up to the challenge. Are you?"

He leapt from the settee and swept her into his arms. She let out a happy cry that was part gasp and part giggle.

"Let me show you how *up* I am." He kissed her soundly as she curled her hands around his neck.

She sighed as he carried her from the room. "Do hurry."

He doubled his pace toward the stairs. "As you command, my lady."

Rafe feared his heart would burst with love, and he knew with sudden clarity that for the first time in twenty-seven years, he was safe.

He was home.

Ready for your next Regency passion? Welcome to the **Phoenix Club**, where London's most audacious, disreputable, and intriguing ladies and gentlemen find scandal, redemption, and second chances. **The Phoenix Club series** starts with a prequel short story, **INVITATION**, coming March 2021! The first novel, **IMPROPER**, will be released May 25, 2021!

Thank you so much for reading A ROGUE TO RUIN! It's the third book in The Pretenders series. I hope you enjoyed it! While there are no scheduled releases for upcoming books in The Pretenders series, there are some characters who have politely asked me if they could have stories. I probably can't say no to them, so stay tuned!

Would you like to know when my next book is available and to hear about sales and deals? Sign up for my VIP newsletter at https://www.darcyburke.com/readergroup, follow me on social media:
Facebook: https://facebook.com/DarcyBurkeFans
Twitter at @darcyburke
Instagram at darcyburkeauthor
Pinterest at darcyburkewrite
And follow me on Bookbub to receive updates on pre-orders, new releases, and deals!

**Need more Regency romance? Check out my other historical series:**

**The Untouchables**
Swoon over twelve of Society's most eligible and elusive bachelor peers and the bluestockings, wallflowers, and outcasts who bring them to their knees!

**The Untouchables: The Spitfire Society**
Meet the smart, independent women who've decided they don't need Society's rules, their

families' expectations, or, most importantly, a husband. But just because they don't need a man doesn't mean they might not *want* one…

**The Phoenix Club**

Society's most exclusive invitation...

Welcome to the Phoenix Club, where London's most audacious, disreputable, and intriguing ladies and gentlemen find scandal, redemption, and second chances.

**Wicked Dukes Club**

Six books written by me and my BFF, NYT Bestselling Author Erica Ridley. Meet the unforgettable men of London's most notorious tavern, The Wicked Duke. Seductively handsome, with charm and wit to spare, one night with these rakes and rogues will never be enough...

**Love is All Around**

Heartwarming Regency-set retellings of classic Christmas stories (written after the Regency!) featuring a cozy village, three siblings, and the best gift of all: love.

**Secrets and Scandals**

Six epic stories set in London's glittering ballrooms and England's lush countryside.

**Legendary Rogues**

Five intrepid heroines and adventurous heroes embark on exciting quests across the Georgian Highlands and Regency England and Wales!

If you like contemporary romance, I hope you'll check out my **Ribbon Ridge** series available from

Avon Impulse, and the continuation of Ribbon Ridge in **So Hot**.

I hope you'll consider leaving a review at your favorite online vendor or networking site!

I appreciate my readers so much. Thank you, thank you, *thank you*.

## ALSO BY DARCY BURKE

**Historical Romance**

*The Untouchables: The Pretenders*

A Secret Surrender

A Scandalous Bargain

A Rogue to Ruin

*The Phoenix Club*

Invitation

Improper

Intolerable

*The Untouchables*

The Bachelor Earl

The Forbidden Duke

The Duke of Daring

The Duke of Deception

The Duke of Desire

The Duke of Defiance

The Duke of Danger

The Duke of Ice

The Duke of Ruin

The Duke of Lies

The Duke of Seduction

The Duke of Kisses

The Duke of Distraction

*The Untouchables: The Spitfire Society*

Never Have I Ever with a Duke

A Duke is Never Enough

A Duke Will Never Do

*Love is All Around*

*(A Regency Holiday Trilogy)*

The Red Hot Earl

The Gift of the Marquess

Joy to the Duke

*Wicked Dukes Club*

One Night for Seduction by Erica Ridley

One Night of Surrender by Darcy Burke

One Night of Passion by Erica Ridley

One Night of Scandal by Darcy Burke

One Night to Remember by Erica Ridley

One Night of Temptation by Darcy Burke

*Secrets and Scandals*

Her Wicked Ways

His Wicked Heart

To Seduce a Scoundrel

To Love a Thief (a novella)

Never Love a Scoundrel

Scoundrel Ever After

*Legendary Rogues*

The Legend of a Rogue

Lady of Desire

Romancing the Earl

Lord of Fortune

Captivating the Scoundrel

**Contemporary Romance**

*Ribbon Ridge*

Where the Heart Is (a prequel novella)

Only in My Dreams

Yours to Hold

When Love Happens

The Idea of You

When We Kiss

You're Still the One

*Ribbon Ridge: So Hot*

So Good

So Right

So Wrong

## PRAISE FOR DARCY BURKE

### The Untouchables: The Spitfire Society Series

### NEVER HAVE I EVER WITH A DUKE

"Never have I ever given my heart so fast . . . an enticing addiction that stays on your mind and in your heart long after the story is through."

– *Hopeless Romantic*

'There was such a fabulous build-up to Arabella and Graham's first kiss that when they finally give in to it I wanted to high five somebody.'

– *DragonRose Books Galore Reviews*

### A DUKE IS NEVER ENOUGH

"I loved Phoebe and Marcus! Whether as individuals or together, they are just wonderful on the page. Their banter was delightful, and watching two people who are determined not to start a relationship do exactly that was a whole lot of fun."

– *Becky on Books....and Quilts*

"I love the passion between Marcus and Phoebe and not just the steamy bedroom scenes they had, but the passionate nature of their relationship. Their feelings for each other went far past that of just the physical even if they didn't realize it."

– *DragonRose Books Galore Reviews*

**A DUKE WILL NEVER DO**

"I have wanted to see Anthony's story since we first met him in The Duke of Distraction from the Untouchables series. He just begged to have a warm, loving, and very caring lady to heal his heart and soul, and he certainly found her in Jane."

– *Flippin' Pages Book Reviews*

"How they care for each other, how they heal each other and hurt each other simultaneously is the very heart and soul of this intriguing story."

– *The Reading Café*

THE UNTOUCHABLES SERIES

**THE FORBIDDEN DUKE**

"I LOVED this story!!" 5 Stars

-*Historical Romance Lover*

"This is a wonderful read and I can't wait to see what comes next in this amazing series..." 5 Stars

-*Teatime and Books*

**THE DUKE of DARING**

"You will not be able to put it down once you start. Such a good read."

-*Books Need TLC*

"An unconventional beauty set on life as a spinster

meets the one man who might change her mind, only to find his painful past makes it impossible to love. A wonderfully emotional journey from attraction, to friendship, to a love that conquers all."

-Bronwen Evans, *USA Today* Bestselling Author

**THE DUKE of DECEPTION**

"...an enjoyable, well-paced story ... Ned and Aquilla are an engaging, well-matched couple – strong, caring and compassionate; and ...it's easy to believe that they will continue to be happy together long after the book is ended."

*-All About Romance*

"This is my favorite so far in the series! They had chemistry from the moment they met...their passion leaps off the pages."

*-Sassy Book Lover*

**THE DUKE of DESIRE**

"Masterfully written with great characterization...with a flourish toward characters, secrets, and romance... Must read addition to "The Untouchables" series!"

*-My Book Addiction and More*

"If you are looking for a truly endearing story about two people who take the path least travelled to find the other, with a side of 'YAH THAT'S HOT!' then this book is absolutely for you!"

*-The Reading Café*

**THE DUKE of DEFIANCE**

"This story was so beautifully written, and it hooked me from page one. I couldn't put the book down and just had to read it in one sitting even though it meant reading into the wee hours of the morning."

*-Buried Under Romance*

"I loved the Duke of Defiance! This is the kind of book you hate when it is over and I had to make myself stop reading just so I wouldn't have to leave the fun of Knighton's (aka Bran) and Joanna's story!"

*-Behind Closed Doors Book Review*

**THE DUKE of DANGER**

"The sparks fly between them right from the start... the HEA is certainly very hard-won, and well-deserved."

*-All About Romance*

"Another book hangover by Darcy! Every time I pick a favorite in this series, she tops it. The ending was perfect and made me want more."

*-Sassy Book Lover*

**THE DUKE of ICE**

"Each book gets better and better, and this novel

was no exception. I think this one may be my fave yet! 5 out 5 for this reader!"

*-Front Porch Romance*

"An incredibly emotional story...I dare anyone to stop reading once the second half gets under way because this is intense!"

*-Buried Under Romance*

**THE DUKE of RUIN**

"This is a fast paced novel that held me until the last page."

*-Guilty Pleasures Book Reviews*

" ...everything I could ask for in a historical romance... impossible to stop reading."

*-The Bookish Sisters*

**THE DUKE of LIES**

"THE DUKE OF LIES is a work of genius! The characters are wonderfully complex, engaging; there is much mystery, and so many, many lies from so many people; I couldn't wait to see it all uncovered."

*-Buried Under Romance*

"..the epitome of romantic [with]...a bit of danger/action. The main characters are mature, fierce, passionate, and full of surprises. If you are a hopeless romantic and you love reading stories that'll leave you feeling like you're walking on clouds then you need to read this book or maybe even this entire series."

*-The Bookish Sisters*

**THE DUKE of SEDUCTION**

"There were tears in my eyes for much of the last 10% of this book. So good!"

*-Becky on Books...and Quilts*

"An absolute joy to read... I always recommend Darcy!"

-Brittany and Elizabeth's Book Boutique

**THE DUKE of KISSES**

"Don't miss this magnificent read. It has some comedic fun, heartfelt relationships, heartbreaking moments, and horrifying danger."

*-The Reading Café*

"...my favorite story in the series. Fans of Regency romances will definitely enjoy this book."

*-Two Ends of the Pen*

**THE DUKE of DISTRACTION**

"Count on Burke to break a heart as only she can. This couple will get under the skin before they steal your heart."

*-Hopeless Romantic*

"Darcy Burke never disappoints. Her storytelling is just so magical and filled with passion. You will fall in love with the characters and the world she creates!"

*-Teatime and Books*

## Love is All Around Series

### THE RED HOT EARL

"Ash and Bianca were such absolutely loveable characters who were perfect for one another and so deserving of love... an un-put-downable, sensitive, and beautiful romance with the perfect combination of heart and heat."

*– Love at 1st Read*

"Everyone loves a good underdog story and . . . Burke sets out to inspire the soul with a powerful tale of heartwarming proportions. Words fail me but emotions drown me in the most delightful way."

*– Hopeless Romantic*

### THE GIFT OF THE MARQUESS

"This is a truly heartwarming and emotional story from beginning to end!"

*– Sassy Booklover*

"You could see how much they loved each other

and watching them realizing their dreams was joyful to watch!!"

– *Romance Junkie*

**JOY TO THE DUKE**

"...I had to wonder how this author could possibly redeem and reform Calder. Never fear – his story was wonderfully written and his redemption was heartwarming."

– *Flippin' Pages Book Reviews*

"I think this may be my favorite in this series! We finally find out what turned Calder so cold and the extent of that will surprise you."

– *Sassy Booklover*

**WICKED DUKES CLUB SERIES**

**ONE NIGHT OF SURRENDER**

"Together, Burke and Ridley have crafted a delightful "world" with swoon-worthy men, whip-smart ladies, and the perfect amount of steam for this romance reader."

–*Dream Come Review*

"...Burke makes this wonderfully entertaining tale of fated lovers a great and rocky ride."

–*The Reading Café*

**ONE NIGHT OF SCANDAL**

"… a well-written, engaging romance that kept me on my toes from beginning to end."

–*Keeper Bookshelf*

"Oh lord I read this book in one sitting because I was too invested."

–*Beneath the Covers Blog*

**ONE NIGHT OF TEMPTATION**

"One Night of Temptation is a reminder of why I continue to be a Darcy Burke fan. Burke doesn't write damsels in distress."

– *Hopeless Romantic*

"Darcy has done something I've not seen before and made the hero a rector and she now has me wanting more! Hugh is nothing like you expect him to be and you will love him the minute he winks."

– *Sassy Booklover*

SECRETS & SCANDALS SERIES

**HER WICKED WAYS**

"A bad girl heroine steals both the show and a highwayman's heart in Darcy Burke's deliciously wicked debut."

–Courtney Milan, *NYT* Bestselling Author

"…fast paced, very sexy, with engaging characters."

*–Smexybooks*

**HIS WICKED HEART**

"Intense and intriguing. Cinderella meets *Fight Club* in a historical romance packed with passion, action and secrets."

–Anna Campbell, *Seven Nights in a Rogue's Bed*

"A romance...to make you smile and sigh...a wonderful read!"

*–Rogues Under the Covers*

**TO SEDUCE a SCOUNDREL**

"Darcy Burke pulls no punches with this sexy, romantic page-turner. Sevrin and Philippa's story grabs you from the first scene and doesn't let go. *To Seduce a Scoundrel* is simply delicious!"

–Tessa Dare, *NYT* Bestselling Author

"I was captivated on the first page and didn't let go until this glorious book was finished!"

*–Romancing the Book*

**TO LOVE a THIEF**

"With refreshing circumstances surrounding both the hero and the heroine, a nice little mystery, and a touch of heat, this novella was a perfect way to pass the day."

*–The Romanceaholic*

"A refreshing read with a dash of danger and a little heat. For fans of honorable heroes and fun heroines who know what they want and take it."

*-The Luv NV*

**NEVER LOVE a SCOUNDREL**

"I loved the story of these two misfits thumbing their noses at society and finding love." Five stars.

*–A Lust for Reading*

"A nice mix of intrigue and passion...wonderfully complex characters, with flaws and quirks that will draw you in and steal your heart."

*–BookTrib*

**SCOUNDREL EVER AFTER**

"There is something so delicious about a bad boy, no matter what era he is from, and Ethan was definitely delicious."

*-A Lust for Reading*

"I loved the chemistry between the two main characters...Jagger/Ethan is not what he seems at all and neither is sweet society Miss Audrey. They are believably compatible."

-Confessions of a College Angel

**Legendary Rogues Series**

**LADY of DESIRE**

"A fast-paced mixture of adventure and romance, very much in the mould of *Romancing the Stone* or *Indiana Jones*."

*-All About Romance*

"...gave me such a book hangover! ...addictive...one of the most entertaining stories I've read this year!"

*-Adria's Romance Reviews*

**ROMANCING the EARL**

"Once again Darcy Burke takes an interesting story and...turns it into magic. An exceptionally well-written book."

*-Bodice Rippers, Femme Fatale, and Fantasy*

"...A fast paced story that was exciting and interesting. This is a definite must add to your book lists!"

*-Kilts and Swords*

**LORD of FORTUNE**

"I don't think I know enough superlatives to describe this book! It is wonderfully, magically delicious. It sucked me in from the very first sentence and didn't turn me loose—not even at the end ..."

*-Flippin Pages*

"If you love a deep, passionate romance with a bit of mystery, then this is the book for you!"
-Teatime and Books

**CAPTIVATING the SCOUNDREL**

"I am in absolute awe of this story. Gideon and Daphne stole all of my heart and then some. This book was such a delight to read."

*-Beneath the Covers Blog*

"Darcy knows how to end a series with a bang! Daphne and Gideon are a mix of enemies and allies turned lovers that will have you on the edge of your seat at every turn."

*-Sassy Booklover*

## Contemporary Romance

### Ribbon Ridge Series

A contemporary family saga featuring the Archer family of sextuplets who return to their small Oregon wine country town to confront tragedy and find love...

The "multilayered plot keeps readers invested in the story line, and the explicit sensuality adds to the excitement that will have readers craving the next Ribbon Ridge offering."

*-Library Journal* Starred Review on YOURS TO HOLD

"Darcy Burke writes a uniquely touching and heart-warming series about the love, pain, and joys of family as well as the love that feeds your soul when you meet "the one."

*-The Many Faces of Romance*

I can't tell you how much I love this series. Each book gets better and better.

*-Romancing the Readers*

"Darcy Burke's Ribbon Ridge series is one of my all-time favorites. Fall in love with the Archer family, I know I did."

*-Forever Book Lover*

## Ribbon Ridge: So Hot

### SO GOOD

" ...worth the read with its well-written words, beautiful descriptions, and likeable characters...they are flirty, sexy and a match made in wine heaven."

*-Harlequin Junkie* Top Pick

"I absolutely love the characters in this book and the families. I honestly could not put it down and finished it in a day."

*-Chin Up Mom*

### SO RIGHT

"This is another great story by Darcy Burke. Painting pictures with her words that make you want to sit and stare at them for hours. I love the banter between the characters and the general sense of fun and friendliness."

*-The Ardent Reader*

" ...the romance is emotional; the characters are spirited and passionate... "

*-The Reading Café*

**SO WRONG**

"As usual, Ms. Burke brings you fun characters and witty banter in this sweet hometown series. I loved the dance between Crystal and Jamie as they fought their attraction."

*-The Many Faces of Romance*

"I really love both this series and the Ribbon Ridge series from Darcy Burke. She has this way of taking your heart and ripping it right out of your chest one second and then the next you are laughing at something the characters are doing."

*-Romancing the Readers*

## ABOUT THE AUTHOR

Darcy Burke is the USA Today Bestselling Author of sexy, emotional historical and contemporary romance. Darcy wrote her first book at age 11, a happily ever after about a swan addicted to magic and the female swan who loved him, with exceedingly poor illustrations. Join her Reader Club newsletter for the latest updates from Darcy.

A native Oregonian, Darcy lives on the edge of wine country with her guitar-strumming husband, incredibly talented artist daughter, and imaginative son who will almost certainly out-write her one day (that may be tomorrow). They're a crazy cat family with two Bengal cats, a small, fame-seeking cat named after a fruit, an older rescue Maine Coon with attitude to spare, and a collection of neighbor cats who hang out on the deck and occasionally venture inside. You can find Darcy at a winery, in her comfy writing chair balancing her laptop and a cat or three, folding laundry (which she loves), or binge-watching TV with the family. Her happy places are Disneyland, Labor Day weekend at the Gorge, Denmark, and anywhere in the UK—so long as her family is there too. Visit Darcy online at www.darcyburke.com and follow her on social media.

facebook.com/DarcyBurkeFans
twitter.com/darcyburke
instagram.com/darcyburkeauthor
pinterest.com/darcyburkewrites
goodreads.com/darcyburke
bookbub.com/authors/darcy-burke
amazon.com/author/darcyburke

Printed in Great Britain
by Amazon

59839265R00206